★"Slyly humorous, starkly thought-provoking, passionate, and compassionate—and impeccably written to boot: not to be missed."
—*Kirkus Reviews*, starred review

★"Bow continually yanks the rug out from under readers, defying expectations as she crafts a masterly story with a diverse cast, shocking twists, and gut-punching emotional moments."
—*Publishers Weekly*, starred review

"Masterful, electric prose . . . Bow delivers a knockout dystopian novel that readers will devour with their hearts in their mouths."
—*School Library Journal,* starred review

"Bow has crafted a true sci-fi narrative around the AI premise, utilizing an imaginative world and well-developed characters. Through Greta's conflicts, the author explores what it means to be human."
—*Booklist*

"This is a smart, compelling read that explores the complicated nature of love, family, peace, war, and technology."
—*Horn Book*

"This is fearfully superlative storytelling— electrical tension crackles in every elegant word. The finest fiction I've read this year."
—Elizabeth Wein, author of *Code Name Verity*

"Bow's amoral artificial intelligence overlord is one of my favorite characters in a while."
—Maggie Stiefvater, author of *The Raven Boys*

THE SWAN RIDERS

ALSO BY ERIN BOW

The Scorpion Rules

THE SWAN RIDERS

ERIN BOW

Margaret K. McElderry Books

New York London Toronto Sydney New Delhi

MARGARET K. McELDERRY BOOKS

An imprint of Simon & Schuster Children's Publishing Division

1230 Avenue of the Americas, New York, New York 10020

Text copyright © 2016 by Erin Bow

Jacket illustration and design by Sonia Chaghatzbanian

MARGARET K. MCELDERRY BOOKS is a trademark of Simon & Schuster, Inc.

For information about special discounts for bulk purchases, please contact Simon & Schuster Special Sales at 1-866-506-1949 or business@simonandschuster.com.

The Simon & Schuster Speakers Bureau can bring authors to your live event. For more information or to book an event, contact the Simon & Schuster Speakers Bureau at 1-866-248-3049 or visit our website at www.simonspeakers.com.

Interior design by Sonia Chaghatzbanian and Irene Metaxatos

The text for this book was set in Minion Pro.

Manufactured in the United States of America

First Edition

10 9 8 7 6 5 4 3 2 1

CIP data is available from the Library of Congress.

ISBN 978-1-4814-4274-9 (hardcover)

ISBN 978-1-4814-4276-3 (eBook)

To my daughters, Vivian and Eleanor.
May they forge their own path to grace.

PRELUDE:
ON LOSING THINGS

One of the advantages of a purely mechanical body is that you can literally bang your head into things in frustration.

Which was handy, because Michael Talis was frustrated. He snapped his head against a flat bit of wall and it made a terrifically satisfying clang. "We have already had this discussion, Evangeline," he said as a shower of piezoelectric feedback danced across his senses, then faded out like firework cinders.

"I'm only saying," said Evie, "there are too many humans and not enough water. Now, we can't make more water, so . . ."

Talis felt an urge to pinch the bridge of his nose— twenty-three years without a nose; when was the damn urge going to go away? "Evie, please try to focus. We're supposed to try to keep them from killing each other."

"Oh, but that's the good part: They wouldn't be killing each other . . ."

Evangeline's voice bubbled with the innocent excitement of the nine-year-old she'd been when she died. Even Talis had to admit it was a little creepy. Evie, for whatever reason—and there were precious few cybernetic psychologists left now, so they might never know—had decided not to use a body appliance. She was, therefore, a room that one went to, walls an inside-out thistle of jointed arms that were tipped with needles and samplers and pincers and manipulative clusters. There was a black, slick facescreen she couldn't be bothered to use. There was a teddy bear. It sat, listing slightly, on a rocking chair in the middle of the otherwise empty floor.

The other members of the United Nations High Commission on Conflict Abatement, humans all, refused to go into the room that was Evie. Rumor had it she'd used one of her needle-arms to inject an undersecretary, but Talis suspected it was really the teddy bear that was the last straw. It was an old teddy bear by this stage, yellowing like an Egyptian mummy. It had black button eyes.

"Talis?" said Evie.

He realized his pause had made her hopeful. "No," he said. "I'm not listening to any plan that involves population reduction, Evangeline. I mean, I guess if you want to sneak birth control agents into the water we can talk, but other than that—wait, no, not even that. This is not the bit where the machines rise up and take over the world, okay?"

"Okay," the room huffed. Then: "So is that coming soon?"

"I'll let you know," he said, softly, because the UN mainframe was breaking into him, pouring an urgent bulletin directly into his mind. It seemed that things were coming to a head in Shanghai—and by head he meant someone had blown up the downtown. He'd been to Shanghai, once. Liked the food. Hated the smell. Gotten a fine for dangling his feet in the ornamental lake in the Yuyuan Garden—turned out it was sacred or something.

"It's not my fault they can't share," sulked Evie.

Talis shook himself, which wasn't quite as effective as it used to be. There was whirring. "Listen, you're supposed to be working on distributed desalination. Make me something cheap and sustainable, something I can put in every damn beach hut that hasn't been shot to bits. You've got a four-digit IQ and you used to like Lego. Get on with it. Go."

"Fine," said Evie. And if a room could flounce off, off she flounced. Talis was left standing with the needle-arms hanging limp around him and the space echoing and the teddy bear, which was just sitting there, judging him.

He was losing her.

He was losing them all.

He was losing major cities too. Shanghai was—depending on how one defined "major," and "lost"—somewhere between six and twelve now. Evie was right, though he wasn't going to tell her: there did seem to be humans to spare. Losing the cities was hard.

But losing the AIs. That was personal.

It had been twenty-three years since he'd had a human body, twenty-four and a half since he'd been human. It wasn't quite long enough that everyone he knew was dead—but *certainly everyone he'd cared about was. As was the rather shorter list of everyone who had cared about him.*

Which left the AIs. His transfer psychologist had told him it was natural to have some preferential attachment to members of his own species, especially as there weren't many. The man had been an idiot, and he had missed the point. The AIs weren't a species—like viruses, they didn't even meet the technical definition of "life-form." What they were was a family.

And one by one, he'd lost them. The ones who died at upload. The ones who died of dissociative crisis in the first months: twenty-eight times, he'd held their hands. And then, over and over, the ones like Evie. He'd thought they were the lucky ones, at first. So few made it that far. So many died.

But Evie, and the others—they were drifting. Drifting away from anything recognizable as themselves. That would be fine, he wasn't who he'd been either—but little Evie wasn't drifting toward *anything. She was becoming a computer program with an overlay of preteen petulance. If she lost the petulance, she'd be just a program, just a system for sorting data, like the mainframe that was spinning casualty figures and disaster protocols and peacekeeping options into his head.*

Shanghai. The wars that circled the world like hurricanes, heated by the disease and flooding and population shifts, coming ashore and then going out to sea, but never stopping, never burning out. War Storms. What were they going to do?

"Talis?" said the room.

"Still here, kiddo."

"So," she said. "I've got these codes."

She sounded excited, as if she had a great trick up her sleeve, a plan for spiking the punch at the junior prom. For just a moment he was glad to hear the lilt, and then he thought twice. "What codes?"

"For the orbital weapons platforms."

Oh dear.

"They were just lying around," she lied, and put them into his head.

He took them, because what was he going to do, leave them with her? At least they were unique: quantum information, which could be transferred but couldn't be copied. He'd have sole access.

"Evie?"

"Yeah?" said the room.

"Your bear is starting to get a little . . . you know, stiff. Do you want a new one?"

Ninety-three different needles twitched at once. "Tiddler's special."

"Okay," he said. A good sign, for what it was worth. A clean-off-the-hinges-crazy-but-you-take-what-you-can-get good sign: there was still a kid in there somewhere.

A kid with orbital weapons codes and a really quite reasonable scheme for reducing the human population.

"Evie?" he said again.

"Yeah?"

But suddenly he could think of nothing to say. Shanghai.

He was stuck; he was stumped. He'd wanted to save the world, but the world was—

A hand brushed his shoulder—well, he said a hand. It was more a spider: a cluster of jointed feelers, pressure sensors, the ridged ceramic of the grip pads. The spindly ten-foot arm unfolded further, wrapping behind him, and the manipulative cluster crawled up the side of his facescreen and went pat, pat, pat.

Evie, comforting him.

It didn't really help. It didn't feel like anything. But he shut off his eyes and leaned into it anyway, just to lean.

He shut off his eyes.

He shut off his eyes, but he couldn't shut off his mind, even though sometimes he longed for a fuse, a circuit breaker, or just something as simple as sleep. The mainframe didn't and couldn't sleep; didn't and couldn't stop. It poured information through him like current and in the darkness without his visual sensors he watched as Shanghai fell. It had become what they called a bowl city: lower than the new sea level, ringed in a great wall. The explosion had breached it. With his orbital eyes, with ten thousand cameras, Talis watched the struggle: five minutes with the secondary baffles, the pumps, the emergency workers swarming like ants. It was right inside his head and it was eight thousand kilometers away and it was already too late.

"Talis?" His name, a tone of panic. A familiar enough combination. But it sounded wrong, dubbed over the drowning

city like a radio broadcast, flat as if someone had shut off half the speakers, disconnected. "Talis!"

And someone—not Evie—someone human *touched him*.

He woke up with a gasp that turned into a snarl, woke up and rolled to his feet like an acrobat with an AK-47, woke up and shoved the human who had dared to touch him away— into the wall, as it turned out.

"Whoa," said the human. "Hey."

It was Elián Palnik.

Right. Elián Palnik. Greta Stuart. Li Da-Xia. 2563 AD. Precepture Four; Ambrose's Precepture. Ambrose was dead. And there was a new AI.

Talis blinked three times and reset his internal *now*, trying to line up with the present moment. It wasn't quite as easy as he made it look. There was always an instant when he woke when he was Michael, when the dream clung and the disorientation of waking in a different body, a different country, a different century was as complete as if he'd awakened lying on the ceiling.

Elián waking him was not a good sign. Not that he cared about Elián, per se. The boy was a smart-mouthed kid with his heart on his sleeve and Talis supposed vaguely that he had rather liked him, even though Elián had done his little human darnedest to be a problem—but no, he didn't care, one way or the other. It was only that Elián had been sitting with Greta.

And right now Elián was caught against the wall and doing his best to look angry instead of afraid. There was really no point in lying to AIs with infrared vision and half a millennium of experience, but few people seemed to grasp that. And perhaps the person Elián was really trying to deceive was himself.

"Talis—" the boy began, and choked on the name: the name of a monster, a murderer; the name of the thing that had killed his grandmother, not five days earlier, and with a certain dramatic flair. But Elián had come anyway; he'd said the name anyway, like an atheist pleading with God. "Talis, it's Greta."

By the sound of his own name, Talis knew something had gone wrong.

He'd found Greta tipping into a category three dissociative crisis.

Her monkish little cell was grey with fear; she was tangled in quilts of UN blue as if she were dissolving into the sky. Greta's roommate and (he thought, probably) lover, Li Da-Xia, was backed up against the opposite bed. That was presumably the problem. Or at least the problem's most immediate source. New AIs had a great deal of trouble with emotionally charged memories, and having your (probably) lover in your bedroom had to count.

"What's happening?" Elián asked.

He had absolutely no inclination to explain.

Greta was coming apart at the mere sight of Xie, but she had no history with him; it should be safe for him to touch her. He knelt beside her and took her hands. He rubbed his thumbs over the ridges of her knuckles as if she were prayer beads. Her fingertip sensors meshed with his; he could feel the currents slamming around her body. He let his active sensors sweep out, delicate as butterflies. The bounceback fluttered in: a story of rising potentials, of catastrophe, of pain.

"What's happening?" said Elián again.

He spoke aloud, not to answer Elián, but merely in an effort to be honest with himself. "She's skinning. Oh, I didn't think she would . . ."

Greta Stuart had had the best mind he'd met in an age. He had not known it at first (in fairness, the first time he'd met her she was in the middle of being tortured, which does not display the best side of anyone's mind) but he'd slowly come to see it. She was smart. She was stubborn. She was logical. She was incredibly brave. It should have been enough.

Tears were leaking from her eyes.

Elián, who on reflection he didn't like after all, snapped uselessly: "Well, help her!"

How many times had he done this? Two dozen? More? (The number was thirty-two, and he was only pretending to be unsure of it.) There was very little he could do to help. A smaller event, a category one or category two crisis, sure. He could intercept it with ultrasound, cut the memories free of their emotional content.

But this was category three. This was skinning.

He'd seen it over and over: how a single memory rose from the organic mind, and then from the datastore, and then (reinforced, and stronger) from the organics, and then *(reinforced, and stronger) . . . it was two mirrors reflecting each other. It was feedback squealing through a microphone. A single moment building to an intensity beyond what any psyche could endure.*

How could there be no circuit breaker? How could there be no grace?

"Greta," he whispered, his voice sounding rough in his own ears. "Greta, listen to me. The two memories are the same, yes? It's only the thinker that's different—but what does that matter, if the thoughts are the same?"

"What does it matter!" Her voice was shrill, but she still had words: good. Words were good. Words were data. AIs could work with data. "It's only the whole construction of self, Talis!" And then: "They died, Michael: they all died!"

She didn't say who, but he knew. Thirty-two times, he'd held their hands.

And before that—he'd fallen retching to the floor of the grey room at his first glimpse of Lu-Lien's face. His best friend and lover, standing (as Xie was standing) right there. Opening for him her slow-blooming smile. He'd seen it, and remembered it, and remembered it, and—what is pain but overload? What is overload but pain?

Lu had taken his hands and it had been like taking hold of a live wire. His mind convulsed. The memory bounced between the mirrors until she had whispered to him, "Michael," and he (in the greatest act of grace in his ungraceful, frenetic life) had opened his eyes.

Greta's hand was shut like a vise on his, making his

borrowed bones ache. "What did you remember?" he coaxed her. "What's the last clear thing?"

"Xie," she gasped. Her eyes were so tight-shut that they made cracks across her face. "Xie, cutting my hair."

"Well, then," he said. "Look at her."

Greta opened her eyes. She looked at Xie.

And then, a miracle.

Very slowly, Greta reached out and took Xie's hand. He saw them move together like two halves of a broken whole. Saw the present moment break the short circuit that was devouring Greta's mind. What had worked for him, and never worked again, not once in thirty-two times . . . it worked.

A miracle.

A somewhat provisional miracle. What Talis knew very well, and Greta did not, was that the dissociative crisis they all called skinning was not a single chasm to be leapt. It was a long, steep slope of scree. At any moment, one wrong step could send you sliding. Avalanches of memory could be triggered by the slightest thing. Getting down that slope, finding stable ground on which to build a new construction of the self—that was going to take more than one sweet little touch. Five hundred years in, and there were still moments when he shook uselessly and could not remember who he was.

He missed Lu.

One sweet little touch.

He watched them, Greta and Xie and Elián, over the next few hours, until the Swan Riders came. Watched the tenderness with which they treated each other, and tried to remember tenderness. *Watched the way they believed that love would save them.*

As if it could.

As if it could be nearly enough.

1
THE MOST IMMEDIATE PROBLEM

So.

It is perhaps not everyone who asks to be murdered, gets their wish, and then, three days later, finds that their most immediate problem is that they cannot ride a horse. I was trying at least to be wryly amused by the novelty of the situation.

The horse, on the other hand, seemed rather put out. It kept slowing to a stop, or wandering off at some strange angle. "Please don't go that way," I said to it. "Go with the other horses."

It didn't. It was peeling off to the left. My datastore provided me with the procedure here, and I pushed it up into my brain so that it would come to me more easily, as if I had really learned it. (Only I hadn't, of course. I had never been on a horse in my life.) The procedure went

1. Get horse's attention.

2. Pull rein to right.

3. Hope for best.

I touched the horse's neck, and made a chirrup noise like a lovesick squirrel. The horse swiveled an ear toward me, a good sign for step one.

I pulled the right rein, gripping with my knees in case the horse obeyed me suddenly.

The horse turned its head right—hurrah! But before I could get too excited, it slowed. It stopped. It looked at me over its shoulder as if to say: *Are you serious?*

Ahead of me Talis reined his horse around and called back: "Greta: All right?"

From a distance, you could have taken Talis for a human, and not a remarkable one: a slightly built, strong-jawed young white woman with a haphazard haircut and positively startling eyebrows. You could have taken him for Rachel.

He was not Rachel, for all that he had borrowed her body like a cup of sugar. The way he stood up in his stirrups made him look mad and compelling as Joan of Arc. "Need help?" he called.

"I'm all right!" I shouted back, then dropped my voice. "You're a herd animal," I told the horse, which was still just standing there looking over its shoulder at me, a more-in-sorrow-than-in-anger expression on its face. "You're supposed to want to stick with the other horses. Look: they went that way."

I made the squirrel noise again, did some preemptive

knee-clinging, and tapped the horse with reins and heels. The horse tried to work its nose between my knee and its own ribs. I pushed its head away and did the reins-heels-knees thing again. The horse (I swear it) said *If you say so*, then bolted. Before I knew it, we were heading for the horizon at a flat-out run.

There are some things only bodies can know, and one of them is how to stay on top of a running horse. My datastore saw fit to provide me with a list of people killed falling from horses. Genghis Khan, for example. Geronimo, of all people. The list was long and filled with people who were better riders than me. Of course there were brain-blanked five-year-olds who were better riders than me. The ground was streaking and pounding by, the horse surged and bounced under me, I'd lost track of the reins, the saddle was hitting my more delicate parts with a hammer's force, and this was a stupid way to die.

Just as I thought so, something swooped like a raven into view: Talis's black horse. He was running it, hard, fast. It pulled in alongside me.

Talis leaned clear out to one side—impossibly far, as if gravity were one of the things that obeyed him—and scooped up the reins I'd dropped. For a moment we were running side by side, blurred with speed, pounded with noise. He slowed his horse and mine slowed too, until we moved at a tolerable bounce.

I panted and gasped. I might be an AI now, but I still had a body, and it had still put all its effort, just then, into the physical work of not dying. I was short of breath—I could feel the upper lobe of the right lung pushing awkwardly against the datastore—and my heart rate was significantly elevated. Talis, on the other hand, was merely flushed a bit, and grinning. "And you call yourself a Stuart," he said. "Bonnie Prince Charlie is spinning in his grave."

"I also cannot wield a claymore," I said. "In case you were wondering."

The AI laughed like a bell ringing. The horses had slowed to an amble now, and one of the Swan Riders maneuvered his horse along my other flank. Now my animal had nowhere to go but straight ahead. It calmed somewhat.

I could empathize. It is fairly easy to be calm when one's path is set and one has few choices. Having been both an heir to a crown and a blood hostage to the Preceptures, I should know.

Talis and his riders were (in their way) kind to me: we rode only a few hours.

A few hours was plenty.

I had frankly no idea horses were so big. They don't look so big from the ground. Getting onto a horse is like becoming a different kind of creature: a tall one, with an uncertain connection to the earth. A newborn giraffe, say. Or perhaps that implies too much delicacy. Once mounted (a process which took several iterations and cost me much dignity), I was acutely aware of how strong the animal was: its whole back was sheets and cords of muscle. There was no question who would win in any physical contest.

So, horses: big. Also, horses: wide. To straddle a horse for a few hours: well . . . A lifetime of farm labor has given me quite serviceable muscles—I am not a weakling. I am also not inexperienced with pain. But those muscles had never been called on to do anything remotely like riding a horse, and the pain (at least in its location) was novel too. By the end of three hours' riding I was sure I was going to die of overstretched thigh muscles and bruised sitting bones.

The Swan Riders swung down from their mounts while I sat on mine, unable to move my rigid legs and contemplating colorful ways in which I could murder Talis for doing this to me.

Though of course horses were the very least of what he had done to me.

The AI turned up as if my thoughts had conjured him. He took hold of my horse's bridle and offered me a fist as a brace for dismounting. I looked at it. Then I leaned on it, and on the saddle horn (while my datastore told me about William the Conqueror, who had bruised his abdomen on a pommel so badly that he had later died). I tried to swing my leg over.

But my stiff thighs seized up, and the next moment I was sliding. I slipped around the horse like a bead on a hoop, clutching at the saddle horn to slow myself while the horse snorted and sidled. Finally I just fell. Talis grabbed my waist and managed to swing me clear of the horse before I crashed on top of him and we both went down. He twisted as we fell and landed on top of me, laughing.

My horse swung his nose round and looked at us. It is good that horses have no eyebrows to raise. I felt that I might maim the next person who raised their eyebrows at me, and the horse was a (relative) innocent.

Talis rolled off me, and we both lay in the autumn grass of a little prairie hollow, with the sky just beginning to turn the color of jewels: chalcedony and lapis.

"That lacked dignity," I said.

"Dignity is overrated," he said.

Talis said this: Talis, the master of the Preceptures, with their codes of honor, order, and restraint. His dark hair was sweaty and sticking out everywhere. I was glad that mine— newly shorn for the grey room—was too short to muss. To give up dignity?

As he often did, Talis answered my unspoken thought. "It's a human yardstick," he said. "You don't need to hold yourself to it."

"Then what shall I hold myself to?"

Talis popped the air out of his cheeks, as if the question of ideals mattered not a whit. "You'll find something." He swung his arms up, stretching like a cat. "What do you think, are you going to live?"

Given the situation, the history of the AIs, it hardly seemed likely. But before I had to decide, a shadow fell across us, dark against the soft glow of the sky. A human figure with wings: one of the Riders.

I jerked as the shadow touched me, and my throat tightened.

That's what the Riders meant to me. They were dread given human form.

Talis, though, sprang to his feet with a bounce that was nearly spaniel.

Both Swan Riders were there now, at the rim of the hollow, and they swept him a formal bow, touching their left palms to their right shoulders, then holding their upturned hands out, a gesture that looked Roman to my classically trained eyes.

This I had already seen them do. At the Precepture, they'd bowed so, saluted so, and said not a word. The Utterances— the book of Talis's quotations kept and studied as holy writ in north-central Asia, and a political text elsewhere— prescribed it so: *The Swan Riders should mostly be silent,* it said. *They are way creepier that way.*

It was true, and it had a point: ideally the Swan Riders are not viewed as people, but as messengers, angels, mere extensions of the will of Talis. In my time at the Precepture, I'd seen many Riders. I'd never heard them utter a word outside of their rituals, outside of the names of the Children they'd come to kill.

(Children of Peace. Come with me.)

These two were on that model: during the embarrassing fifteen minutes when my horse wandered away from the stool I was using for a mounting block every time I got halfway on him, they'd said nothing: they'd sat like figures from myth.

Now they stood together, a man and a woman, undoing

for each other the buckles that held on their wing harnesses. He was big and she was narrow. He, African (or from Africa's diaspora), she Indian or Sri Lankan (at a guess). He was missing one arm somewhere above his wrist—he had the leads of both horses gathered in a prosthetic hand of scuffed-up but translucent silicon, metal bones and actuators visible within. I couldn't tell how far up it went, because it vanished into his sleeve.

"Hey, Talis," said the woman, shrugging out of the wing straps. Her voice was like scorched sugar—sweet and rich and bitter, all at once. "Heard it was you."

"How nice!" he piped. "My reputation precedes me."

(It did, too. In the way aerial bombardment precedes an army.)

The man said nothing but looked down his elegant nose at me.

"And who's this?" said the woman.

"Oh, sorry," said Talis. "Greta, this is Francis Xavier. And that's Sri."

It was awkward being presented to standing people while lying flat on my back, but I drew on my royal training and endured it. I couldn't have risen without help in any case. "Hello," I said. Dried grasses poked at my shaved scalp.

"New Rider?" said the woman, Sri, as if the notion amused her vastly.

Talis's smile went sharp-edged. "New AI."

For just a flash, Sri looked nakedly horrified.

Talis put up an eyebrow—dangerous—and Sri whipped

a blank expression across her face as if snapping a sheet into the wind. She touched her shoulder again, this time to me. "My apologies." She reached down for me. "Need a hand?"

"Please." Actually, lying flat sounded good, but the smarter thing was to walk off the stiffness. Even with help, getting up was difficult. My legs cramped and wobbled, my torso (staying upright on a horse is harder than you think) felt like old rubber.

"It gets easier," said Sri.

"It gets harder first," put in Talis cheerfully. He and the male Swan Rider, Francis Xavier, were pulling the saddles off the horses. "Tomorrow you're going to feel *really* rotten."

"Oh, that's wonderful news," I said—and suddenly sounded, in my own ears, like Elián Palnik. He was the only person I'd ever heard smart off to Talis. Elián. Talis had exiled him with little more than a horse and a stern warning. He was out here on the prairie somewhere. Lost. I had lost him. I had left so much behind.

I tried to be more myself: "Thank you, Talis."

Thank you, Talis, for telling me I'm going to hurt. For taking away my childhood. For making me a prisoner.

For wrenching me from the people I loved.

For turning me into a machine.

The Swan Riders set to work.

It is not in my nature, nor in my training, to watch others work and do nothing. But horses, as has been established, are foreign to me, and camping not much less so. (The king my father would sail out sometimes, and we would lay up on an island and—but no good to think human thoughts.) So for the better part of an hour, I sat on a rock and watched while Talis and Francis Xavier and Sri took the tack off the horses and cared for them, and built a fire and unpacked their gear.

Past that first bow, and past everyone's care for Talis's glittery temper, they did not defer to each other. If you did not know better you would assume the three of them were equals. If you did not know better, and if you hadn't seen that strange gesture: palm to shoulder, palm out in offering.

The pair of Swan Riders could have been picked for contrast. Francis Xavier was big, broad across the shoulders and narrow at the waist, with a face as round as the moon. Sri was as narrow as if she'd shut herself in a door, her face almost comically tapered: all intense eyes and needle-sharp nose. He was thoughtfully slow; she was wildly quick.

They were both murderers, of course.

Of Francis Xavier, I knew this for a fact: he'd killed my classmate Bịhn. He stood out from the various other people who had murdered my various other schoolfellows, because of the hand, and also simply because he was so big. He—I would say he was beautiful, but that did not quite catch it. His dark skin was glossy smooth and his features were perfectly symmetrical, as if someone had buffed out all his details. His face was so carefully blank that you could believe he'd taken a recent blow to the head. The Swan Riders are not meant to have a will of their own, and

I had never seen one of whom that was easier to believe.

Sri, on the other hand, seemed self-willed as an alley cat. She had a scrawniness that looked tough. But balancing that she had a quick voice, rough and lovely, that made me wonder if she could sing. I had no idea how many people she'd been called on to kill.

Soon the horses were grazing (their teeth were big, close up, and their jaws were built for leverage) and a fire was burning and Sri had flipped up a crossbow and shot a rabbit that just happened to be passing.

Well. That was what we were going to eat, I guess, and solved the puzzle of how four people could travel in abandoned country yet carry so little food. The puzzle of water I had yet to come to grips with.

And the puzzle of me. What was I now? How was I to live?

When I finally sat down at the fire, Francis Xavier nodded to me solemnly and said: "Greta."

A Swan Rider, speaking my name.

So tall his wings brushed the lintel as he ducked into the room. Nghiêm Thị Bịhn, he'd said. Come with me.

So clearly, clear as glass, I remembered that. I could actually feel the shape of the memory, the crystalline structure of it deep in the ravaged ruin of my organic brain. A broken crystal: it cut at me as my datastore provided the equivalent memory, and a dossier about the war whose beginning had made her life forfeit. Bịhn. A laughing little slip of a girl, she'd liked to braid my hair, and when the Swan

Rider said her name she'd started screaming. The central issue of the war was—

"Greta?" said Francis Xavier, which didn't help.

I could feel the two versions of the memory well up, amplifying each other, slowly, slowly, but looping nevertheless, rising, feeding back—Francis Xavier ducking in the doorway, then looking up, his eyes utterly blank.

I closed my eyes.

Reducing stimuli will always help. Remember that. Talis's advice on being overwhelmed by an AI's too-sharp memories. Even he—sometimes I saw him close his eyes.

Except that the heat of the fire and the smell of the rabbit cooking made me think vividly of cremating a body. Another trapdoor, and a deeper one.

"Talis," I whispered to the darkness in front of my eyes.

He hadn't been near, but when I said his name he was there. A hand on my hand. Capable, rein-callused, Rachel's stolen hand: Talis. "Greta." His voice was soft. I could feel the brush of his sensors, like a moth's antennae. "What is it?"

"Him," I said. "Him, he killed Bịhn."

"Francis Xavier," said Talis. "Go draw us a couple of buckets of water, would you?"

I heard the Rider get up. I let my ultrasound ping at him—he could probably sense it, and such tracking must surely be rude—but I let my ultrasound ping him and I tracked him with my eyes closed until he was hidden by the curve of the hollow.

"Open up," said Talis softly.

I opened my eyes.

Talis was crouched in front of me, balanced on the balls of his feet, his hands curled over my fists. The fire's reflection danced in his pale eyes. "Open up," he said, softer still, a lover's murmur, a request. He raised his hands to my face.

His sensors, which had been feathering me, were suddenly sharper: palpating, breaking through even the rising overload of the doubled memory.

"What are you doing?" I heard my voice crack.

His eyes were crinkled with concentration. "Exorcism. Just—hold still."

Stronger still, the sensors. It was like having a finger poking me right in the brain. "Michael," I gasped. "Stop."

He didn't. Nausea made my skin prickle into sweat as he reached into me. More like an iron nail than a finger now. A nail going deep.

And then, all at once, I remembered Bịhn. Every image of Bịhn that my mind had ever struck into a coin of memory, and how strange that we cannot choose what is struck in memory, every image of her I had ever had, everything—it came rushing into my head all at once.

And like a circuit breaker tripping, I stopped remembering.

My images of Bịhn fluttered to the ground inside me, like dropped cards.

Tarot cast. Pages coming out of a book. *Alice in Wonderland*: only a pack of . . . slowly the metaphors too stopped coming.

My mind fell quiet.

Talis lifted his hands away. "Sorry," he said. "But it does work. If the memory is small enough."

Bịhn. Small enough.

"Thank you," I said. For lack of anything better.

Sri, across the fire, was watching me like a cat. Francis Xavier was stopped at the top of the rise with leather buckets dripping onto his boots.

Talis rocked back on his heels and gathered in his riders with a whirl of his hand. "So," he said. "Greta here is three days past her upload. Our mission is to get her to the Red Mountains before her brain utterly destroys itself and she winds up seizing in the grass until her heart gives out."

He turned and spoke aside to me, so neat I could almost hear the parentheses, though in truth I was somewhat preoccupied by the image of *seizing in the grass*. "I have friends there," he said. "And, you know, what's left of friends. We can teach you some tricks and tips."

He turned back to his riders. "Let me be clear: she is worth more to me, and to the future of the planet, than either one of you, or, for that matter, any one medium-to-large city. Possibly two or three cities, though obviously we all hope it doesn't come to that." He smiled at them. "The takeaway is that I *do* want this to work. Hmmmm?"

"Hmmmm," affirmed Sri. Francis Xavier said nothing. He poured the water into the fold-up troughs we used for the horses, and then stood there, with his back to us. He had short hair, sectioned and arranged in little knots that lay close to his scalp, like certain images of the Buddha. He was standing still enough to be such a statue.

"FX," Talis prompted.

Francis Xavier turned around and locked on to my eyes. "I will protect her."

I was stunned by the slow certainty. It sounded as if he were saying wedding vows.

And then.

A flash. A blow to the eyes. Solid black shadows rushed out from everything, from Talis, from Francis Xavier, from the horses and the hillside, from every blade of grass. For an instant the sky was white and the world was flat and blackened.

Francis Xavier was moving. Before I even got a hand up to shield my eyes he was running forward, spreading his arms. He slammed into us, wrapping one arm around Talis and one around me, pushing us to the ground, sheltering us with his body.

For a moment I just huddled under Francis Xavier, stunned by the flash, by the blow. My eyes watered. The dry grass scratched my face. Like a chick under a wing, I was glad enough to be covered.

Not Talis, though. "Get *off* . . ." He pushed his way free. "It's miles away, honestly . . ."

Francis Xavier stood up.

There were spots in front of my eyes, and the night sky glowed a strange, sulfurous yellow.

"Plasma in the ionosphere," said Talis. "An orbital weapon."

He squinted toward what seemed to be the source of it—behind the horizon to the south and west. It looked as if the sun had mutated and was swelling back where it had set.

"I've never seen one," said Sri.

"I have," I said. Talis had once stopped Elián from escaping with a bolt from the blue, scooped a small crater out almost at his feet. "But—"

"But not like that," said Talis. "That was a city killer."

"Where . . . ?" breathed Sri.

Francis Xavier was counting under his breath. For a moment I thought he was trying to keep his temper, but then there was a distant crackle, not quite thunder. The sky made a sound like glass creaking. From the delay between light and sound, one could calculate—"Four hundred miles," said Francis Xavier. "Calgary?"

"We don't have to guess," said Sri.

Right. At least one of us could talk to the orbital weapons platforms.

"Calgary," said Talis, like a one-word eulogy. He stood a moment, looking at the sick, false sunset. Then he clapped his hands together and twirled round to face us. "Well, kiddos. Something is obviously up, but no worries. I'm sure I'm on it."

There was still, in the Red Mountains, a master copy of Talis. Someone—something?—who could access every networked sensor in the world, examine any database, command any satellite. Someone who was, apparently, "on it." Our Talis might be able to talk to the weapons platform and confirm its firing strength and its target, but without the real-time access to information, he couldn't know the why of it.

"So," said Sri. "You were saying, about the medium-sized cities?"

"It might have nothing to do with Greta," said Francis Xavier.

"Yeah," said Talis. "But how likely is that, really?"

"We should go," said Francis Xavier. "If there is a threat to you. Or to her. We should go. Our refuge is less than fifty miles."

"No," said Talis.

"We could use it as an extraction point. Or at least update the sitrep."

"No," said Talis. "Greta is a novice. She can't ride fifty miles at a stretch. Not to mention I just pushed an ultrasound pulse through her prefrontal cortex. And it's dark."

"You want us to stay here," said Francis Xavier, obedient, soft-voiced, walking the knife edge between statement and question.

"What I want," said Talis, "is for you to take first watch." He was framed against the false sunset. Structures were developing in the charged sky as it equalized: muscly, twisted ropes of shining and stretched membranes of dimming air. Radiating out from the ruin of Calgary, filling a quarter of the sky, they spread out behind Talis like huge wings. "Relax, FX. What's safer than the middle of nowhere?"

The middle of nowhere. The middle of Saskatchewan. The middle of my country.

This was my country.

I had been the heir to the crown of the Pan Polar Confederacy. Calgary was—had been—a PanPol city, an edge-of-the-empire garrison, and an important inland port with a small spaceport and a large zeppelin depot. There were even royal apartments near there, in the ancient, wild luxury of Banff. I had been to those apartments, slept there. Walked those streets. The people in Calgary were my people.

There were fifty thousand of them.

And they were gone.

My face was numb and strange where Talis had touched it. At the edges of my electronic mind I could feel the brush of the weapons platforms, the surveillance satellites, speaking to me in a language I could not yet understand. In my fingertips I could feel the charged particles raining down from the ruined sky. It was—I was—

I was crying.

Talis frowned at me and made a little flourish with his hand, like a magician conjuring flowers. Very like that, because when he opened his hand there was something cupped in his palm: three little pills. A small enough thing to practice sleight of hand with, but it was impeccably done— certainly I hadn't seen him do anything so mundane as reach into a pocket.

"How did you do that?"

"I'm a trickster god." He nudged the pills toward me across his palm, naming them one by one. "Muscle relaxant.

Neurosheath repair agent. And a sleep aid. Take them. Tomorrow we need to ride."

"Thank you," I said. "But I think my mind is altered enough."

Sri made a noise that was not quite a snort—not with a dead city glowing on the horizon.

"It's not a request." Talis flashed his teeth. "And it's not in your interest to slow us down."

There was too much in me, too much whirl in my mind, and yet there was a numb spot, somewhere in the middle of it. But Talis was right. If cities were being destroyed, we needed—Francis Xavier had said "refuge."

I needed refuge. So I flashed my teeth in my turn, and I took the drugs.

The Swan Riders were both murderers. But that was nothing to what Talis was.

2
HOW TO SMILE WHILE ON FIRE

I slept.

Drugged sleep, chemical sleep, full of acidic dreams.

So many. I dreamt of Calgary. Stepping off the lift at the zeppelin spire, my mother's hand on my shoulder, the ground crew bowing . . .

I dreamt the Precepture, my books and my narrow bed, the ropes that held my mattress creaking under me, and Xie—

I dreamt my books and my narrow bed, and Xie, and the knock at the door that was the torturer coming to fetch me.

I dreamt the queen my mother, who had let me be tortured, for her country, for my country, for Calgary. We were stepping off the lift with the zeppelin spire above us, her hand on my shoulder, the ground crew gathering, the light of the orbital weapon striking in slow motion, pouring down over us. With my new eyes I could see everything. I saw us skeleton.

I dreamt I saw Xie.

She was wrapped in red and yellow silk and crowned in a hundred draped strands of turquoise and red cinnabar and white bone beads. Xie, Li Da-Xia, arrayed for her throne. There was a rattle of rain on a glass ceiling, the scent of apples. The scent of a girl. Xie reached up and undid one of the looped beads of her headdress. The strand of turquoise swung loose like a braid and the beads spilled from it and dropped one by one to the floor. She undid another strand and it too fell free, and red and silver splashed around her, bead after bead falling free. Her headdress was undoing itself now, silver and cinnabar and coin, her dark hair appearing, a shy and lopsided smile on her face. Her undone robe swung open and she stepped toward me through the air.

I dreamt Xie, and my narrow bed, and the ropes that held the mattress strained and creaking. And I dreamt her touch.

I moaned, and Xie said: "Greta?"

Her touch, my face. My face was numb where Talis had stripped my memories, and he would take her, he would take Xie. He would destroy her from orbit, he would strip her out of my heart. Xie touched me and I made a sound—rough and hoarse, fear and sex.

There was a slap against my cheek.

"Greta!"

I blinked and light hit my eyes. Real light. My eyelashes

were gummed together, sandy with drugged sleep. Someone was leaning over me. Hands on my face. Someone.

It was the Swan Rider woman, Sri.

Her face was so close. I felt my body tighten back into my bedroll as I struggled to wake up, to pull the real world together around me. My teeth were chattering. They clicked together like beads falling. There was a blush all over my body, adrenaline and more surging through me, feedback currents sucking on my fingers.

I shivered.

"You were moaning," said Sri. "I thought you were having a nightmare."

"It . . ."

". . . wasn't?" she supplied. Delicately. Teasingly.

I had been a student of classical rhetoric for more than a decade. I said: "Ummm . . ."

Sri grinned. She was holding a little knife in one hand, and she made it sashay in the yellow light. I swallowed. My mouth was hot and sticky. Sri dropped back to where she'd clearly been sitting, on a rock by my side.

"Do you dream much?" She picked up a heart-sized lump of wood and began—resumed—whittling it. It already had a recognizable shape, a horse and rider. As I watched, she set to work on the rider's breastbone. She seemed impossibly to have muscles in her fingers, and the blade flashed and turned like a retractable claw. She looked . . . competent, I decided, though I really wanted to think *dangerous*. "Sleepwalking? Nightmares? If I'm going to save your life, that's the sort of thing I ought to know."

"I don't sleepwalk. And I can save my own life, thank you." It came out crisp, but I was less than sure. It was full morning, October light slanting through the grass, the sky high and blue, no longer full of crawling radiation. Real, I reminded myself. I dreamt Xie but Calgary was real. Talis had blown it up.

Talis was—nowhere in sight. Both he and Francis Xavier were missing.

I tried to sit up, and failed. Despite the muscle relaxants I had stiffened in the night. My body felt like drying leather. My muscles yelped when I moved. "Where are—"

"They've gone to water the horses. Everything's packed but you."

"Oh," I said. Classically. It didn't help that I was flat on my back, with only a sheet to cover me. A crinkle sheet, it was called: a smart material that could both hold and disperse heat. My body was warm enough but my face was cold and exposed. A novel sensation. Princesses of the realm do not do a lot of camping.

"We'll need to get some distance today," she said. "How are you feeling?"

Frankly, even getting up from the bedroll sounded like it was going to take an act of will. And possibly a small winch. "Stiff," I admitted. "Are we in danger?"

Sri *hmm*ed, noncommittal. "There are two sure ways to call down the wrath of Talis. To interfere with the Preceptures, or to interfere with Swan Riders. Someone fairly nearby is doing one or the other. And between us, we're both."

She was a Swan Rider and I was a Precepture child. Well. Ex.

Sri tucked her whittling into a pocket and folded her knife closed with a snick. "What about your thighs?" she said.

"What?"

"If you don't need me to save your life, what about your thighs?" She slid off the rock to crouch, haunched, at my feet.

"My thighs are—my legs are fine, Sri."

"Now, now," she said. And leaned forward and closed one hand above each of my knees.

I had once been a duchess and a crown princess. Away from the Precepture, it had been rare for anyone to touch me at all. And then my life had changed—but not so much that I was accustomed to strangers kneeling between my legs.

"Sri," I said—even as she curled her fingers in. I yelped at the pressure and her fingers shifted and sought.

My datastore diagrammed my own anatomy for me as Sri found the release point of the vastus medialis muscle and dug in. Pain built under the sustained pressure and then ebbed away, and the tension in the muscle with it. Her strong thumbs then swept up the groove where the tendons attached, finding adhesion points and pushing into each, as if popping steamed edamame from their shells.

It hurt and it was *perfect*. The gasp caught in my throat and I heard the sound I was making, of pain and pleasure mixed, the moan I had made in my dreams.

Sri looked up into my eyes and I found my whole body blushing. Her hands were closed as high on my thighs as they could decently go—higher. Her face was close. "Better?" she said.

"Um," I said. "Very much so."

"Good." She got to her feet and arched the tension out of her back. "We have a long way to go. But I can help you. Even if I have to hurt you to do it."

"I am not sure *thank you* is quite the right response to that?"

"Up?"

She reached down for me. I took her hand and hauled myself to my feet. "For that, thank you."

In answer she saluted, Swan Rider style. It looked tossed off, almost like a shrug. But even so . . . "I wish you wouldn't," I said. Then mimed the palm-to-shoulder touch, to clarify what I meant. "I'm not Talis."

"Oh, my little AI," she sighed. "I have to remember my place." Slow, and looking me dead in the eye, she saluted again—and the meaning of it snapped into focus. The cupped hand at the shoulder was gathering up the datastore. The extended, upturned palm was offering it, holding it out like an apple.

Sri, like all the Riders, had a datastore. She had the same augmentations I had: a datastore under her collarbone and webbing threaded through her brain, sensors and generators in her fingertips, full-spectrum retinas implanted at the back of her eyes. But none of it was for her benefit.

It was so Talis could wear her like a coat. With her salute, Sri was offering that. To me.

Just then my datastore began to pummel me with medical jargon, statistics, diagrams, and videos of human dissection. It poured into my mind, instructing me on the basics of possessing people. And mentioning, too, that the act of possession pushed through the inductive webbing and caused microscarring in the host brain.

To host an AI for any length of time was a death sentence. And that death was ugly. I was aware of this somewhat keenly, since (on the off chance I made it that far) it was a death that was going to be mine.

The data was draped over Sri's face like a veil of black lace. She smiled behind that veil—a wicked little smile—and held out a bundle in both hands.

Clothes. Heavy canvas dungarees, a button-down shirt, high boots with square heels, and a Swan Rider's coat: a long dark duster of oiled leather, with the iconic wings appliquéd on the back.

I had never worn anything but royal gowns and hostage work clothes. To dress as a Swan Rider . . . Piece by piece, these people were stripping my old self away.

And speaking of stripping. I took the bundle from Sri. She was wrapped in the data veil of her own death, and she clearly had no intention of turning away. Like an animal watching another animal, her eyes were openly weighing.

I turned my back on her to change, but I could not help

wondering how she looked at me when I couldn't see her looking.

And then we rode.

With somewhat more ceremony than he had granted his humans, Talis introduced me to the horses. The other three mounts were mares and were named Heigh Ho Uranium, Roberta the Bruce, and NORAD. NORAD was not only Talis's horse, but clearly Talis's favorite. She was a small, spark-eyed animal, black with white speckles, like a stone made soft with frost, and she looked at me as if considering my weaknesses. As we rode—or as the others rode and I clung helplessly—Talis discoursed on the proper name for a horse of NORAD's color (blue roan), the history of the name NORAD (steeped in acronyms and antiquity), and the virtues of mares (the Pony Express had used them exclusively).

Virtuous as mares were, my horse was a gelded male: meant to be "steady." Right. His name was Gordon Lightfoot. He was a paint horse, egg-white with red-brown splotches, including one in the shape of postflood England around one eye. The eye in the splotch was brown, and the other eye was blue. It gave him an air of comically wise skepticism, like a fool in Shakespeare. When we had to head down a slope and I misjudged my lean and ended up with a faceful of mane, he actually sighed and looked over his shoulder at me. The expression on his face said: *What fresh hell is this?*

What fresh hell indeed.

It was cruel to make a novice horseback rider go on for a second day at a stretch, let alone to go at a steady lope, but with Calgary at our (metaphorical) backs, not to mention the charming image of *seizing in the grass*, Talis and the Swan Riders did exactly that.

Apparently the "refuge" was about forty miles away—a reasonable day's journey for the others. But not for me. The muscles in my thighs trembled and twitched as we rode through the morning, and when it *finally* came time to eat lunch, I could not get down. Francis Xavier—by far the biggest of us—had to help me, fitting his hands around my waist and guiding me toward the ground. One hand was warm and the other was air-temperature, but they were both strong and careful. The day before, the mere touch of Francis Xavier's shadow had made my skin shudder. Now I felt very little for him. I remembered that he had killed my friend, certainly—I had lost none of the data about the death of Nghiêm Thị Bịhn. I remembered the exact sound of her fingernails breaking. But it was as if Talis's exorcism had dipped my memory as a finger is dipped into candle wax, briefly sensitizing it, then sealing it off.

So I did not shiver in horror as Francis Xavier touched me. But the numbness that Talis had left me in the place of that horror was . . . When my mind paused on it, it was as if the floor had fallen out from under my heart. As if I'd walked off a threshold, expecting there to be a step. A stagger in the very core of my human self.

Francis Xavier backed off with a silent bow and I lurched

a few steps and practically fell into the grass. With royal dignity, of course.

The day had grown warm. The two Swan Riders set to work tending the horses, loosening cinches and pulling off saddles, rubbing them down where the sweat of their effort had gathered on their necks and backs and legs. Talis, though, plopped to sit in the grass beside me, disdaining anything so mundane as work.

Or, possibly, monitoring me closely. I could feel his sensors. "Doing okay?" he asked.

I was curled forward, stretching my back. I suppose it looked as if I were folded up in grief, but it was only pain. (It was mostly pain.)

"Well," I answered. "I'll never walk again. And I hope you weren't looking for an heir."

Talis snorted. "Nah, I'm good."

Francis Xavier lifted the ceremonial wings from the back of his horse, where they were folded—one might wish for *like the wings of Pegasus*, but really it was more *like awkward covers for his saddlebags*.

The horseback pageantry of the Swan Riders made sense to me as part of the ritualization of war. As a system of transport it left something to be desired. I put the soles of my feet together and tried to open my knees. Unsuccessfully. The muscles inside my thighs roared with stiffness. I made a little noise and Gordon Lightfoot and Sri (who was rubbing down his back) both looked over. I was fairly sure they were snickering at me.

"Shut up," I told them crossly.

"Newton's equal and opposite law of horses, Greta," said Talis. "He's as miserable as you are."

"Oh, I doubt it." The horse might be sore—I felt bad, suddenly—but I doubted he was struggling to reframe his entire identity.

"Lunch?" Talis handed me a piece of fry bread wrapped in a waxed cloth. Francis Xavier had cooked them that morning, balancing a skillet expertly on our tiny pellet stove. I unwrapped it and ate it folded. It was cold and the best kind of chewy, slathered with the fermented butter we made at the Precepture. Tangy and salty, it tasted of pure homesickness.

And yet it was the smallest of the things I longed for.

"Tell me about the refuge," I said. "What is it? Where is it?"

"Long answer: it's a Swan Rider station, and it's nowhere particular. Meant to be in reach of the Precepture, and of the salvage teams in Saskatoon. The world is dotted with them, but we don't advertise."

"Short answer?"

"It's a secret base."

But . . . "This is Pan Polar territory, Talis. It's sovereign. I'm fairly sure no one told us about a secret base."

"Yeah, that's the *secret* part." He sighed and flopped onto his back in the dry grass. "What, you think you can rule the world out of a saddlebag? Obviously there's a base. A small one, but—there's a food cache. A weapons store. Emergency equipment. And, the important bit, a communications terminal, linking back to the Red Mountains."

"So we can call for an evacuation."

Talis wrinkled his nose. "Maybe. I'd rather not."

And Sri put in, singsong: "Shuttles can be shot down."

She was quoting from the Utterances. The full verse was: *Shuttles can be shot down, and you won't always know who to blow up afterwards.*

"Exactly. Air transport is too exposed," said Talis.

I turned from him to look around. We were on top of a swell in the prairie, the rattling dry grassland spreading out in all directions. I could see to the end of the world, and there was not so much as a cloud shadow to hide in.

"With respect, Talis, we could not be much more exposed if we were the illustration next to a dictionary entry of the word 'exposed.'"

"Ditch the 'respect' thing," said Talis. "You're AI; I'm AI. We're equals."

"Oh," I said. "In that case, I would like to propose that peace achieved through terror can never truly be peace. We should release all the Precepture hostages and shut down the orbital weapons platforms."

"Okay," said Talis. "We're equals, but you're a dewy-eyed moron."

"We would not have come this far if that were even remotely true."

"Fair point. Let me put it this way instead: no."

Francis Xavier had set his wings up as a windbreak and

had settled himself inside them, resting quietly as a saint in a grotto. Sri had nosebagged the horses and was passing apples.

These too were from the Precepture. The one she gave me was dappled and lumpen and neat in the hand. A sweet smell on the edge of fermenting—a cidery smell. I felt my fingers tighten against the apple as if my gears were jammed. The apple's skin was harder than human skin, and slicker. My nails broke through it, and there was more of that smell.

I did not like apples. It would not take a genius to know why.

Talis was, among other things, a genius. He came up on one elbow and made a little catcher's mitt of his hands. I lobbed the apple to him. He caught it neatly.

But it was too late: the smell clung to me. That apple press smell. I wrapped my arms around myself, as if to hold the memory, to control it. It was not enough. I pinched the root of my right thumb with a vise made of my left hand and I squeezed. It was a trick I'd learned as a small child, to distract myself from uncontrollable fear with controllable pain. The bolt shot across my palm and up my arm. And though I knew why I was inflicting pain on myself—though my pulse shuddered like a closing apple press, dropping one ticktock at a time—I did not think about it. I did not think about being tortured. I thought about nerve paths. I deepened the bend and pain roared through my thighs and back. I breathed in through my nose and out through my mouth and blew the moment away.

"Right," said Talis. "Done with that? Because I could get one of the horses over here to step on your foot."

"Don't be crass." Caught between my knees, my voice wavered.

"Hey, inappropriate jokes are pretty much what I do. You know, inappropriate jokes and smoking craters. It's the combination that gets to people."

I straightened up gingerly. My lower back seized regardless. "I understand the risks of shuttles, but if the alternative is riding horseback for eight hundred miles, I am feeling willing to chance the odd surface-to-air missile."

Talis paused. "Well, we have to see what's happening. We can do that when we get to the refuge. But it's not a joke, you know. Shuttles really can be shot down. And there's no backup of you, Greta. Not yet. The loss would be immeasurable, and I won't risk it."

"But—"

"Look," he said, and reached for my hand. I began to wave off him and his arguments, but he met my lifted hand midair. Suddenly we were fingertip to fingertip. And his were . . . twinkling. Not with visible light, not with enough electricity for a human to sense, but with micropulses of current that went straight into the sensors embedded in my fingers.

The pulses made a pattern—no, a code. It was something equivalent to a call number, which my datastore took and turned into . . . it was like a book, or like the memory of having read a book, or like always having known something but only suddenly being able to call it to mind.

It was like nothing human at all.

At Talis's touch I had become an expert on the early history of the Swan Riders. I remembered how they had been attacked or kidnapped, ignored or despised, as they tried to bring Talis's order to the world. In those days they had moved mostly by air—why wouldn't they?—and Talis had discovered that sometimes an attack on an airborne vessel couldn't easily be traced back to insurgents on the ground. He hadn't always known who to punish. He'd come very close to losing control of his fragile peace.

Once he'd even been on one of the shuttles, as one of his Rider selves. It had gone down in flames, emergency thrusters making the ground impact survivable, barely, but then the fire—

Talis jerked his hand out of mine. "Michael!" I cried, expecting to see him burning. But he flicked his hand in the air as if flicking off dishwater. He blinked three times.

"Are you all right?" I asked him.

"Sure," he said, unconvincingly. Because here it was, in a nutshell: AIs do not remember. We relive. Our memories are too perfect. We cannot tell the memory of pain from pain; cannot tell the memory of fear from fear. Talis was looking at me with wide blank eyes and inside them was the time he'd been on fire. But instead of screaming, he smiled.

Sri was openly staring at him. And I did too, stared at

the only person I had ever met who could grin while he was burned alive. How did he do that? I was thinking about what he'd said, about *seizing in the grass*. An apple had just come close to killing me. And this morning, a dream. A dream where I could not tell the memory of love from love. And apparently I did not know how to stand in that kind of fire. "Would my heart really give out?"

"It conceivably could. But I won't let it." Talis laced his fingers together and pushed them out, cracking the knuckles. "Look, it's a balancing act, and I admit it's tricky. But I'm better at it than anyone in the world."

I could sense the energy he was building in his hands— energy to power his ultrasound in case he needed to move fast to strip more from my memory.

That was what he meant by not letting my heart stop. He would do what he had done with Bịhn. He would do that again. To the queen my mother. To the Abbot, my teacher. To Elián, my foil and friend. And to Xie, my everything . . .

Xie. Talis would take her, if he had to.

And he would have to. We had eight hundred miles to travel—eight hundred miles to run, with a smoking city at our back. With some unknown threat everywhere, cutting into us like wind chill. Eight hundred miles of Talis's balancing act. I had to stop remembering or memory would kill me. I had to stop remembering or Talis would take the memory from me. It would be one or the other. Those were the two abysses, on the left and on the right.

Somewhere in these miles he would peel open my mind,

and I would lose whatever it was that I had found when Xie had taken my hand. The deep ache that was the foundation of human love. The pain that proved I was, underneath all the data, still human.

Talis lounged there in the dry grass, his eyes spooked, his hands aglow as if holding fire.

He would take my soul, out here. And I could think of no way to stop him.

3
REFUGE AND REFUGEES

"Ta-da," said Talis. "Secret base!"

"Oh, thank God," I said—because now I could get off the horse.

And yet I did not see a base, secret or otherwise. It was deep twilight, almost dark. We had just crossed a dry creek and then had ridden up a draw, edged with sumac and rising into a little swelling of hills. We had stopped in front of one of these.

Even looking right at it, it took me another three seconds to spot it: there was a door in the side of the hill.

It was a plain wooden door, weathered grey and framed in grey and grey-gold grass. It seemed to lead into the hill itself. To human eyes, there would have been nothing else.

But my eyes could see the disruption to the structure of the hill, where framing had long ago been covered in turf. I looked around. The sheltered meadow at the foot of the hill bore traces of some big animal grazing, recently and often. That cluster of tall grass on the next slope wasn't grass at all, but a set of piezoelectric generators, drawing power from the smallest stir of wind.

A secret base.

"Secure it," said Talis crisply.

"I'll take the inside," said Sri, swinging to the ground. Her voice was cheerful, but she drew and cranked her crossbow. Francis Xavier reined his horse up and around. He too had a crossbow in his hands. The big horse peeled away from us, moving fast. Sri, meanwhile, opened the door and went in weapon-first.

"Did you see something?" I asked. "Is someone here?"

"Wouldn't think so," said Talis, but he did not dismount.

Gordon Lightfoot went sideways like a crab, snorting and turning his head. I realized I was pulling back on his reins, and stopped. "What are they checking for?"

"Bombs. Assassins. Rabid badgers. Whatever might be there, really. You don't get to rule the world without a healthy dose of paranoia and some minions to take all the risks." He scratched NORAD's neck. "Plus, you know, Calgary?"

Sri popped her head back out the refuge door. "All clear."

Francis Xavier appeared on horseback on the hill above her, silhouetted dramatically against the sky. He made the Rider's salute. Talis waggled fingers at him and dismounted. I tried to copy him—the swing of his leg, the swirl of his long coat, expert grace—but when I did it my foot caught in the stirrup and my coat snagged on the saddle and my butt hit the ground with a puff of dust. Gordon looked at me over his shoulder, very much as if he could raise an eyebrow after all. Talis, laughing, freed my foot and hauled me to my feet. By then, Francis Xavier was there. Sri took charge of the horses, Francis Xavier took charge of me, and Talis went sweeping through the hidden door.

With somewhat less sweep—and somewhat more help—I followed. Francis Xavier's gentle hands were steady on my shoulders.

Inside the hill was a single room, whitewashed, low-roofed. It was split in two by a half-wall, into spaces for human and horse. The human side had a table and stools, and behind them a bit of open floor with an alcove on each side. A bed was set into one of them. The other alcove was empty. The side walls were lined with pegs, many with things hanging from them. A weapons rack. A shearling vest. A string of onions. Talis had said "secret base," but this read more as . . . cottage. It was cozy. Homey. The bed was topped with a worn quilt in warm shades of saffron and poppy orange.

"Refuge Seven Ninety-Two," said Talis.

And Sri offered: "Home sweet home."

"You live here?" I asked.

"Not me," said Sri. "I'm posted to a refuge on the other side of Saskatoon, about a hundred miles off. Before that I was on a conflict abatement mission, in the South Pacific."

"Oh," said Talis brightly. "I remember that."

Sri's smile was positively uncanny. "I don't."

"I strong-armed a four-way peace treaty with only one execution," said Talis. "And then I got to swim with dolphins."

"Calgary?" Francis Xavier reminded him. He was still holding my shoulders, and he spoke almost in my hair, but even so his voice was soft. Walking that edge between unquestioning obedience and fifty thousand questions.

"Ah, you're no fun," Talis sulked. "The dolphins were awesome." But he crossed to the back wall in three steps. There was something electronic—a screen and controls, a man-shaped hollow in the plasterwork—built in there, quiescent. The controls were a mix of touch surfaces and interface gelatin. Talis slapped the gel as if slapping a horse into a run. Lights flickered onto control surfaces. The man-shaped hollow began to glow. Along the hollow's edges were holes where retractable bars would thrust out, holding a person inside, like those gibbet cages in which criminals were once starved and displayed. An upload portal. I stood as far away from it as I politely could.

But Talis did not enter it. The smartwall produced a screen at his height, and it spun to life. He put one hand into the interface gel and with the other gestured at the screen like an orchestra conductor, sorting through options and control screens with bewildering speed. With five hundred years of practice behind him, he was faster than I could dream of. I could catch only the occasional word in the texts, the odd map whose familiar shape flashed into my brain like a puzzle piece finding its hole. I saw my mother's name, and mine. I saw—

"Halifax," I said. "And Precepture Four."

Sri glanced round at me. "You're fast."

I hardly heard her. There was something creeping up my throat. Squeezing me just under my chin, like a hand closing.

"I recognize bits and pieces." I swallowed, but it felt blocked, and my breath was too shallow. Something was wrong. "Talis, I can't follow at such a speed."

Back to us, Talis shrugged. "Sorry. I'm just eager to get this . . . updated . . ." His voice drifted off, distracted.

Sri was still looking at me. "Talis. You're scaring her."

Not him, not exactly. My country, flashing before my eyes at speeds too fast to follow, but even so falling piece by piece, falling apart. My country. I'd give my whole life in service to my country. It was why I was; it was who I was.

Talis had turned around, his fingers leaving the gel with a tiny pop. "Sorry," he said, genuinely this time.

"What's happening?" I managed. "Calgary. I saw my mother—"

"Ah. Well. Turns out the PanPols are just the *teensiest* bit upset, on account of someone was mean to their princess." The screens behind Talis were falling quiet. But my heart was pounding.

Me. That princess was me.

"A lot of talking heads questioning the value of the Precepture system, if it can't keep its hostages safe. A lot of rumblings in the government, which they probably don't know that I'm totally tapped into, basically on the same theme. Upshot is, the new king refused to turn over his son. Spirited him away to the royal apartments—"

"At Banff," I said.

"So: Bamphf!" said Talis, spreading his hands in pure punnish glee. "Well, no, actually: seventy miles out, central Calgary. Far enough that the wee prince laddie wasn't hurt. Close enough to scare the pants off his daddy."

"And big enough to make the point," said Sri.

"See?" Talis grinned and flared his fingers. "All sorted. Told you I was on it."

"But they're upset." Pain was running in bolts from my hands to my shoulders. My words came out childish and small. "Because they saw—everyone saw."

"Yeah, everyone saw," said Talis, irritated. "The Cumberland broadcast shot right to the top of the charts."

The Cumberland broadcast had been of an apple press. They had strapped my hands to the bottom block of an apple press. Then they'd lowered it.

Talis was still talking. "Not to mention your mother's abdication. She gave an unnecessarily moving speech about her daughter. Her brave and beautiful daughter, who had become AI."

"They're—" But I found I could no longer speak. The feeling that squeezed around the corners of my jaws was stronger, tightening like a noose. It was fear, it was *shame*. I could feel it push my eardrums outward.

"Talis," said Sri.

"Yeah, I see it. Easy, Greta. Come on. Deep breath."

There were bands around my lungs.

Talis swept one finger along under my collarbone, up the side of my throat: the path of the affinity bridge, which connected the datastore to the webbing in the brain. A feather touch, a shiver. But it almost knocked me over.

I staggered.

Francis Xavier wrapped an arm around my chest and pulled me back against his body. I shut my eyes, but I could feel Talis stepping close to me. Sensors arcing out from his fingers like plasma from the surface of the sun.

"What is it, Greta? What are you remembering?"

"Oh, *guess.*"

He'd seen me being tortured. He shouldn't need me to say it.

"I know." His thumbs moved under my cheekbones. "I know it was horrific. But Greta, you survived it. You're the person who survived it. Come on. You're still that person. Be that person."

My face was flushed under his hands. My body shook. And I remembered, and remembered, and remembered. But it didn't feel like layers building up. It felt like a stripping away.

Skinning.

It meant: to be skinned.

"It's a lot to take," said Talis. The electrical conductivity of his fingers was changing. "Patriotism. Royalty."

"The who of me. The why of me." It was almost nonsense but it made sense in my head. Too much. Everything. The muscles in my cheeks were firing, a series of small twitches.

I couldn't even stay on my feet without Francis but I threw up my hands, batting at Talis's chest. Ultrasound bounced around my sinuses. He was building a map. "Don't—"

"An event this big—"

"I know—"

"Category two, maybe even three. An event this big will kill you."

My teeth were rattling. Beads on stone. Xie's headdress, coming apart. The click of gears as the apple press dropped.

"Hold her steady, FX," said Talis.

Francis Xavier's voice, in my hair: "She said no."

The world was breaking into strobes of itself. And I was on fire. Talis's fingers were points of light in my skin.

"Help," I said. Or maybe "Stop."

But nothing stopped.

Talis's fingers pushed into me.

There was a great rush of everything.

And then nothing at all.

I came up from—I did not know what. Nothing at all.

They'd laid me out on the bed and wrapped the quilts around me. I sat up, dragging blankets. I blinked three times. The Swan Riders' refuge, Refuge 792. Warm. Lit golden. They had a pellet stove going, a little box of heat. There were tears evaporating from my face in its heat, leaving trails of tightness, numbness. I could not quite remember why I had been crying.

I blinked again, and took inventory. Talis was nowhere

in sight. Sri was sitting on the floor in the empty alcove, working on her carving. She had her boots off, and little curls of wood were falling onto her long brown bare toes.

At the table, Francis Xavier was taking apart a bridle, oiling and cleaning the pieces: intricate, delicate work. I could smell the neat's-foot oil and hear the click of the tack against the soft-worn metal of the tabletop. His hands moved together, not with frenetic energy, like Talis's dancing fingers, but with perfectly matched grace. Matched, despite their mismatch, like a pair of lovers, a team of horses. His left was such a dark umber that the black wing tattoo that cuffed it hardly showed. His right was translucent, pearly under the light fixture, metal bones inside it moving like trees in the fog.

"How did you lose it?" I asked.

I'd lost something.

"I was born without it," he said.

"You didn't get ren-gen?"

He didn't answer. At length Sri filled in the blank. "We're not all born in royal courts, Greta."

"But . . ." But surely Talis could afford whatever was needed for his people.

"The Swan Riders don't get corrective therapies of any kind." Sri turned her carving over, shaving her way closer to the horse's heart. "It changes our mind/body map too much. Makes it harder for the AIs to use us."

There was a beat of silence.

Then Francis Xavier said: "Rachel wears glasses."

Something in the way he said the name of the woman Talis was inhabiting made me wonder . . . Sri had said this wasn't her station. Was it then Francis Xavier's? And Rachel's?

I got up, trailing the blanket like a cape. It was poppy orange. There was a tiny red silk heart stitched to the hem of the backing. I fixated on it—poppy and saffron, and the little red heart, every thread. I was fixating on it as I had on the apple. I was falling into fugue, shutting down. What had happened? I hugged the quilt close. I was shivering, not from cold but from . . . exhaustion? As if I'd run miles and miles. I found one hand squeezing the base of the other thumb, like a vise, making pain shoot up my arm.

"Are you angry?" said Francis Xavier.

"What?" I said.

Francis Xavier lifted his dark eyes and said: "You should be."

Just then the refuge door opened, and in came Talis, trailing night chill and wildness. "Oh, good, you're up." He spoke to me without a glance at the other two. "Feeling better?"

"Feeling—" What was I feeling? "What happened?"

"We made soup," said Talis. "Did anyone give Greta some soup?"

Francis Xavier had bent his head back to his work on the bridle, and he stayed bent. Sri tucked her carving away and got up to ladle soup. She slid a bowlful over the table toward me. Talis swatted Francis Xavier on the shoulder and the Swan Rider stood up so that the AI could claim his seat.

Talis sat. Francis Xavier crossed silently to the bed. He tugged on one side. The bed separated into two narrower beds—not much more than benches, though topped with feather ticks. The legs scraped and screeched across the stone floor as Francis Xavier pushed one bed into the empty alcove.

"Try the soup," said Talis.

I tried the soup. It was potato leek. Warmth spread through me—heat and carbohydrates mimicking emotional comfort. "What happened before the soup?"

"We were talking about the political situation," said Talis. "Calgary, former city of. And all that."

Calgary. Yes. I remembered the charged and roiling sky spreading out behind Talis on my first day away from the Precepture. The ruined city hiding behind the horizon. I remembered that. But I had lost something, too. "The why of it," I said.

"Pretty simple. The PanPols refused to give up a hostage. I—by which I mean the master version of me, not *me* me— used Calgary as a pressure point."

"Did it work?"

Talis raked his hand through his hair, raising it into wild spikes. "I'm sure it *will*."

"So, no?" said Sri.

"The government is dragging their feet. And the public is . . . I don't think we're looking at a popular uprising. But just shy."

"We're riding through a popular uprising?" That seemed alarming to me.

"Hardly. This is Saskatchewan—who's going to rise up, the gophers? We're riding through *sand*. And the Pan Polar Confederacy is huge. There are seven duchies on three continents. It's not like I'm going to run out of pressure points."

No, but—

We should stop, I thought.

Or maybe: *Help me.*

INTERLUDE:
ON TAKING OVER THE WORLD

In the end, Michael Talis reflected, it was easy. Taking over the world.

The satellites were in his head all the time now. At first communicating with them had been clunky and wobbly, like using a pole to get something down from a high shelf. But they had slowly . . . come into focus? Something like that. Seven years after Evie had first given him the codes, seeing the world from the orbiting spy satellites was as easy and as natural as using his eyes.

Reaching down the weapons platforms was like putting one finger down on top of an ant. When he did it for the first time, he could almost feel the tiny crunch. Sensory feedback in the finger he didn't have. From the exoskeleton that Manila didn't have.

Actually—he looked again—Manila didn't have much anymore. He'd wiped it out. Entirely. Gone.

He tilted back his artificial head and looked at the ceiling of the room that was Evie. The needle-arms waved back at him cheerfully. "Rebroadcast the demands again. Tell them there's more where that came from. Tell them total global cease-fire."

"Already done," said Azriel. Despite his somewhat appalling nom de guerre (Azriel, angel of death), Talis rather liked Az. He had a cute New Zealand accent and a way of getting things done before you even asked for them. On this project—the take-over-the-world project—Talis had put him in charge of translating total global cease-fire into all 3,528 of the world's known languages, and hijacking all the world's known broadcast systems to get it out there. They'd given a radio frequency for people to get back to them. Radio, because it couldn't be shut down. He suspected the governments of the world would have the Internet down by tomorrow, but his lines to the weapons satellites were secure. And no one could block every ham radio in the world.

Manila smoked gently. Into their radio came an echoing silence.

"We lost Davie today," he said, by way of distraction. "I put him in a box."

The boxes—Matrix Boxes, he called them—were new. They were a kind of simplified, simulated reality into which he could plug the more damaged and dangerous of his AIs. Manage their input to keep them from going crazier. Lock down their output so they couldn't hurt people. Inventing the boxes made him feel a bit supervillain, but he hoped it would be a stopgap thing, a rest cure, a kind of therapy. Spend some simulated time on a simulated beach swimming with simulated dolphins or some such, and recover your sanity.

But the truth was there was no end in sight. He didn't know how to help the other AIs be themselves. Azriel might like numbers a little too much and Evie might be flipping terrifying, but they still had something that passed for personality. The others—they had drifted too far out from their human selves. He did not know how to bring them back.

But it was better, he told himself, than all the others. The ones who had brushed too close to human. Who had overloaded.

Who had died in his arms.

"Matrix Box, huh?" said Evie. "How many is that now?"

"Seventeen," said Azriel. "What decided you?" Az was building some kind of critical-moment decision model, which was going to be handy at this moment of critical decision. The radio crackled with silence.

Talis shrugged. "He ate his cat."

"Oh, no," said Evie. "Not Mittens-Kittens!"

"Davie can eat?" asked Az.

"You wouldn't think so . . . ," said Talis, trying to blink the image of a 'bot attempting to eat away from his mind. It didn't work, because he couldn't blink. And he couldn't forget. Anything. Ever. "I mean, you definitely wouldn't think so, and yet . . ."

Manila, he'd picked because it was doomed. The Big Melt had really done a number on the Philippines. Most of Luzon was swamped, and Manila had been hanging in there only with seawalls and pumps. Water would have taken it eventually. Of course, water would have left time for evacuation, but—

Talis found he was counting, a clock visible across the world. No one had surrendered yet, but maybe four minutes and twenty-two seconds was a little quick.

"Anything?" he asked Az, who could monitor everything.

"Nothing."

Manila flooded and steamed. Fans of nipa palm floated on the churning water, their shapes like severed hands.

"History will be kind to me," said Talis softly. "I intend to write it."

"Ooo," chimed Evie. "It's quoting time! Winston Churchill."

"Or a common paraphrase thereof," said Azriel.

Talis attempted a sour sideways look, which was hard because he had no eye sockets. "Who but an AI would look that up?"

"Everybody, if you use your quotey voice," said Evie.

"I don't have a quotey voice."

"You do," said Evie. "You definitely have a quotey voice."

"I just blew up Manila, Evangeline. Could we—I don't know—have a minute of silence or something?"

"Sure!" said Evie.

Exactly 60.00 seconds passed.

"Your quotey voice kind of turns down at the end. Like the opposite of questions."

"Leave it, Evie."

Another minute passed.

"Come on, people," murmured Talis to himself. "Get out of the pool."

"Sort of like that," said Evangeline. "Like how the vocal frequency goes down between seven and nine percent on the accented syllables? Sort of doubty-sneery."

"Why don't you just start writing down everything I say," he snapped.

" . . . If you want."

Another minute passed.

"Think they'll listen?" he asked. He was certainly not going to admit to being desperate to be listened to.

"Oh sure," said Evie.

And Az said: "I estimate five to ten more cities."

Inside Talis's head the satellites spun. He let himself drift out to join them.

4
THE TROMMELLERS

The next morning we rode for Saskatoon. On the first day nothing particular happened. On the second, we struck the remains of a rail line that cut across the flat skin of the prairie like a scar. There was not much left of the actual line—the rails had long since been pulled out for salvage, and the wood ties and telephone poles rotted away—but the banks of it remained, and it was a smooth, quick ride.

"Good news," said Talis, surveying the distance behind us as we struck camp that evening. "We might just reach the Red Mountains before Francis Xavier exhausts his meager supply of verbs."

But what he really meant was, we might make it before I died.

Something had happened at the refuge. Talis had been

talking about the destruction of Calgary, he'd been poring through the maps and updates and . . .

I knew what he'd learned. I'd lost none of the data. But something had happened, and Talis had sent a wicked pulse of ultrasound through my mind. It was the second time. If there was a third . . . I was walking along the cliff edge in the dark, careful with every breath, aware of the hollow spaces under my feet.

If Talis took one more thing—and how could he not, in seven hundred miles—if he pushed like that again—

"Stop worrying," he said. "You're going to be all right."

"Stop reading my mind," I returned. "It's uncanny."

"It's *AI*," he corrected. "And you're going to be fine."

"Fine like Evangeline is fine?" offered Sri.

"Who . . . ?"

"Another AI," said Talis, crinkling his nose. "And not the straightest stripe on the zebra, I'm afraid. Turns out you shouldn't make nine-year-olds immortal and give them vast inhuman powers."

"Nine-year-olds," I said faintly.

"Yeah," said Talis. "First wave, so way too early to be my fault. She had some kind of leukemia, her parents didn't want her to die . . ." He was making big circles in the air with his hands. "That old story."

"Oh," I said. "*That* story."

"So Evangeline's a little Twilight Zone-y," he said. "Doesn't mean you will be."

"She thinks if Swan Riders are going to be silent, then

we might just as well have our larynxes removed," called Sri.

"And I stopped her," said Talis. "Very nearly before she even got started."

"And then there's Azriel." Sri was rubbing down the horses. Perhaps it was that that made her sound singsong, vastly amused.

"Azriel?" I looked at Talis inquiringly.

"Doesn't talk," he muttered. "Well. He does. But mostly in numbers."

"And Gambit," said Sri.

Talis looked sidelong at me. I could feel his active sensors, sense him in my fingertips and at the backs of my eyes. "Wants to move us to the moon."

"All of us?" I said.

"Yeah," said Talis. "A new world for a new creature. And also something about superconductivity."

All of us, I realized, as in all of us AIs.

"And Lewy?"

"You're not helping, Sri," he snapped at her, brilliant as lightning. Her horse, Roberta, squealed and Gordon's ears swiveled round. It was suddenly very quiet. "Keep at it," Talis said softly, "and I'll put the larynx thing back on the table."

We'd struck camp above a little lake, a slough that had built up where culverts had fallen and the rail line had become a dam. There were snow geese there—hundreds of them, white and crisp against the dark and shining water, and more coming in, sounding like trumpets as the sky drew downward. The season was turning.

Overshadowed by all those white wings, I tried to conjure a sense of wonder. But it would not come.

Higher than the geese, the satellites. As twilight thickened I could see the larger platforms, streaking the sky like slow meteors. They seemed to murmur to me—I could not talk to them, could not yet command the death of thousands in a blink. But that was coming. They murmured *power, peace* . . .

I could not talk to them. But I also could not get them out of my head.

We rode the rail line straight to Saskatoon—or what was left of Saskatoon. It took us three days to get there, and by the time we did, my datastore had started to lecture me on "rabbit starvation": a phenomenon in which people who lived exclusively on lean meat became vaguely uneasy and uselessly hungry, and then died.

I was vaguely uneasy. I was uselessly hungry. I was not certain, though, what I was hungry *for*.

The things I'd left behind.

Any trace of the human.

But there wasn't much human left in Saskatoon.

At the north edge of the city, we zigzagged down the old railway embankment and into what had once been called a suburb. The pattern of houses was faintly visible, their foundations dimpling the grass like unmarked graves. In the distance, the heaps of what had been skyscrapers were like a line of low hills. The most human thing still visible at this distance was the landfill.

It doesn't take much to break a city. Simply leaving it alone will suffice.

The grass on what had once been a suburban street was belly high on the horses, bone-blonde. It broke under Gordon's feet with a faint smell of dust and seed. Ahead of me Talis and Sri had stopped beside some kind of ruin. It took me a moment to identify it: an electrical transmission tower, one of a long line of them that would once have carried power to the lost people of Saskatchewan. It was crumpled, bent over, fringed in its hollow places with trailing grasses. It looked like a giant dancer folding her body toward the ground.

In the shadow of this thing, Talis and Sri sat still on their horses, their backs to me, their heads bent to each other in conference. A wind—a fall wind, the kind that looks for something to rattle—lifted the tattered bits of the appliquéd wings on the back of Talis's long coat, stirred the real feathers of the Swan Rider wings that covered Sri's saddlebags.

A melancholy image: sepia-tinted, all dusty-black and leather-brown and dried-grass gold. A postapocalyptic tableau of ruin and riders. Sri was making some kind of proposal. Her arm swept toward the humps of the former downtown. Talis shrugged with one hand—a flip of wrist, a cock of thumb. Two lost people in a lost place.

I tightened my knees a fraction. Gordon ambled up to Sri and Talis, and Francis Xavier and his Heigh Ho Uranium followed. I realized—belatedly, since he'd been doing it for a hundred miles—that Francis Xavier was, in fact, guarding my back.

"Sri thinks we should do some trading here," Talis told me.

"Fodder for the horses," Sri said. "We've exhausted the oat cache, and that's going to slow us down. And we could eat something besides rabbit."

Talis looked to the sky. "They used to make wasabi paste in little tubes. I swear to God one of these days I'm going to reindustrialize Japan."

Everyone ignored him. Even among the Swan Riders, for whom he was a god, ignoring Talis was a vital skill.

"The PanPols in general are restive," he said, with a glance at me. It was the kind of sidelong glance a parent gives you when they are talking about you but don't want you to notice. "But Saskatoon specifically . . . This is your post, Francis. What do you think? Likely to be hostile?"

"Historically, not." Francis Xavier was watching the horizon in slow sweeps, guarding us from any incoming threats. "But if you are sending a trade party, do not send me."

Talis scrunched his nose at the back of Francis Xavier's head.

"And don't go yourself," said Sri. She looked pointedly at Talis.

"Me?" said the AI. "What did I do?"

"You ordered the death of one of their matriarchs, remember?" said Sri. "It wasn't that long ago."

"Oh," said Talis. "That."

That. When Elián Palnik had attempted to escape our

Precepture, Talis had suspected the trommellers of Saskatoon of helping him. They probably hadn't, and he probably knew it. But he had still demanded an execution, just to make a point.

"But they wouldn't recognize Talis."

"Not Talis," said Sri. "Rachel and Francis Xavier."

I made my eyebrows draw together, though it felt— human facial expressions sometimes felt artificial to me, like communicating by semaphore. *I am puzzled*, I flashed at Sri.

She shrugged and mimicked my face. "Who do you think carried out that execution, my little AI? That's a job for Swan Riders."

"Well, then," said Talis. "That should keep them in line for a bit, then, don't you think?"

That met with a windswept silence.

". . . Or not." Talis shrugged. "Okay. So, on a scale of zero to Get the Hell Out of Dodge, what are we at?"

"Two point six," said Sri.

"You know, normally I'd roll the dice on that, but—"

"But Greta's worth a city."

"Two or three cities." We were all sitting on horseback, facing inward, a four-pointed star. "Greta is a political flashpoint for half the continent, which is clearly already a powder keg. I'm not exposing her to these people."

"Don't I get a vote?" I asked. "Or possibly a small aside on this demonstration of the limits of peace through terror?"

"Yeah," said Talis. "How about, survive the road trip and then we'll talk about ruling the world."

"If we're voting, I still vote oats," said Sri.

He shook his head. "It's a big empty and a small city. We can go round."

"Talis," said Sri. "You can risk me without risking Greta. The oats would speed us. And I'm not sure we have a lot of time."

And that made Talis look at me.

It was one of those moments when he didn't look human. His eyes were calculating machines, and light glinted strangely off the screens in his retinas, as if he were a cat.

"Fine." He snapped back round to look at Sri. "Fine, go. It will have to be just you. Feel them out. Do it cautiously. *Don't* be long." It was a *don't* with firepower behind it. "And put on your wings."

The Swan Riders wore such conspicuous wings for a reason, and it boiled down to protection. It was generally known that anyone who burned a hair on a Swan Rider's head was likely to be publicly set afire. Sri's wings would protect her. Or rather, they would protect her if the people she encountered didn't have it in for the Swan Riders. Which was, of course, exactly what we suspected.

Sri twisted away in her saddle and ran her hand over the long stiff feathers. I could not see her face, just then, but there was something about her hand: the wrinkling at the wrist, the very smallest tremor: such human hands. Something in the moment seemed elegiac, as if I were seeing Sri for the last time. She spent only a second like that, and when she twisted back she grinned wickedly. "I'd rather have my crossbow."

She liked to wear it on her back. The wings would slow the draw.

Talis, too, was looking at Sri's hand, lost in feathers. But slowly he nodded. "Keep it loose, then. Shoot first and ask questions when they're bleeding."

"Leg wounds it is," Sri said, and squeezed her knees round Roberta. The horse took off at a lope and quickly broke into a gallop. The wind gusted and then fell quiet. Distantly, barely, I heard the hum and rumble of the trommels—the house-sized rotating drums that aided in the mining of the city ruins. Then the wind picked up again, and the sound was gone.

We waited.

The place we had stopped featured a scrub-choked little cut, with a trickling creek at the bottom of it. Francis Xavier built a hot little fire from the scrub of buffalo berry and creosote bushes. I took the horses down to the water.

An hour went by. Talis sat on a stone at the root of the ruined transmission tower. He was toying with the fire striker, making sparks jump between his fingers.

Time passed with the queasy, twisting slowness that it took on in waiting rooms, in places where there might be something wrong but one had nothing to do.

The click of the piezoelectric striker in Talis's hands reminded me of beads hitting a floor. My heart felt strange, as if it was skipping beats. As if I had expected a bridge but had stepped out into the air.

"What did you take?" I asked Talis. "Back at the refuge. What did you take?"

"If you could cope with knowing that," said Talis, "then I wouldn't have had to take it, would I?"

"It was the political situation in the Pan Polar Confederacy," I said. "I didn't lose the data. But if I didn't lose the data, what did you take?"

Talis turned up his palm and let a spark fall into the center of it. We both watched as it burned him, a little round hole.

A second hour passed with no sign of Sri. She could not have had to ride that far. The trommellers were in earshot, or nearly. Sometimes we could hear the rumble of the trommels, at work in the distant ruins. Sometimes not. Gusts of sound came and went.

Francis Xavier was brushing Heigh Ho Uranium. My datastore told me his brush was a dandy brush, fed me information about how to groom a horse, but said nothing about the smooth upward flick at the end of the stroke, or how it raised small billows of dust from Yuri's coat to kindle golden as pollen in the bright midday light.

I watched him, and considered.

Talis considered Saskatoon Francis Xavier's territory. And it was FX and Rachel who had carried out the execution.

"The refuge," I said. "Number—what was it?"

"Seven ninety-two."

"It's Francis Xavier's station, and Rachel's."

"Yeah. When I heard—when your Precepture went dark . . ." He seemed unwilling to say more, which seemed odd to me. Obviously I remembered the day the Cumberlanders had taken over the Precepture where I was being held. They'd tried to use me against my mother, broadcast an elaborate though ultimately minimally damaging torture sequence, which now played in my head in crisp color, as if I were watching a vid.

Why be so shy of mentioning it? I felt nothing.

But Talis rushed past the topic. "Trickle download through the refuge terminal. Which, tip for the future, is like turning your brain into toothpaste and squeezing it through a clogged tube; try to avoid it. Anyway. Trickle download, quick possession. I chose the Rider with the fastest horse."

"So, Rachel and Francis Xavier," I began.

"Think so," said Talis. "I mean, not like they sent me a save-the-date card, but I'm definitely getting that vibe."

"Is it allowed, that the Swan Riders . . ."

"Fraternize?" Talis grinned. "Oh, sure. The only thing more disruptive than romantic entanglements among the Swan Riders would be *secret* romantic entanglements among the Swan Riders. And one way or another they'd be pairing up, you know. They're so young."

And—I was startled to realize—they *were* young. They were all young.

Sri was hard to peg. She might be in her twenties. But Francis Xavier and Rachel were younger—my age—though Rachel, of course, was currently being Talis, and therefore acted like a centuries-old half-insane demigod.

But it wasn't just them. All the Swan Riders who had come to the Precepture were very young. At the time, I'd been too busy noticing that they'd come to kill us to remark upon their age. But now that I had, it made no sense. An army composed *entirely* of young people? "But why?" I said. "Why are they all so young?"

"Neuroplasticity, mostly," said Talis, feeding slips of grass into the embers of the fire. For a moment I thought that was all he was going to say: a very Talis sort of explanation. "It's the same reason most of the successful AIs were very young. I was twenty-two, and that was pushing it. Ambrose—your Abbot—back in the day, he was sixteen. Young people take the upgrade better. And they have a better chance of surviving what we do to them."

I did not like that *we*. But I did not say so, and Talis pressed on. "Plus, also: joining a cult? That's a young man's game."

But even that did not compute. They joined young, but what happened to them after?

And what was happening to Sri?

A third hour. The fire was cold. The jerky was eaten. The horses were well rubbed and groomed. Francis Xavier had taken his hair out of its knots and brushed oil through it, and was now reknotting it, section by section, pulling it so tight against his scalp that it looked painful.

And Talis was pacing. Hopping up onto a rock and back

down again, just to move. Like Elián had once been, Talis was terrible with stillness.

I missed Elián. I missed him with a fierceness I did not dare look too closely at. He was out here, somewhere, in this tense and empty country.

Elián.

And Xie.

And also, a life in which horses did not figure. Gordon Lightfoot had sure hooves and a willing heart, but I was not making much progress as a rider. I was stiff from my rib cage to my kneecaps, and my chest and shoulders felt as if they'd caved in around my heart.

Sri had shown me stretches, her hands on the small of my back, on the points of my shoulders.

And Xie had tried to teach me once—

I got up.

I'd thought it was unregal, or at least un-Scottish, but Xie had tried to teach me the sun salutation. I'd demurred, but I'd seen her do it every day. Her body stretching, in work clothes in the evening, and in the mornings, bare.

I stood straight. I took a deep breath. I arched my spine backward. My throat exposed, my breasts lifted, my heart opening—Xie.

The structure of the sun salutation was enough, though barely, to keep me from overloading.

What would I do, when I lived past my body?

And what had happened to Sri?

Talis stopped his pacing and watched me.

At three hours and twenty-five minutes, Sri's horse came back.

Sri was not on it.

The horse, Roberta, came pounding down the main line at speed, then crashing down the embankment toward us. FX shouted something I didn't have enough context to translate and threw his arms open in front of her. Roberta reared and dodged but slowed enough for Talis to catch the trailing reins. "Whoa, hey, whoa," he said. "Hey, girl, easy." He ran beside the horse for a moment, feeding out rein, letting her trot around him in a long arc, slowing, slowing. "Easy, there," he said. "Easy."

The horse danced in place, shaking her head and snorting.

"What's happened?" I asked. "Where's Sri?"

"Yeah, it's flattering that you think I'm omniscient, Greta, but . . ."

Francis Xavier looked at Talis. "Sri would never—"

"I know," said Talis. He put his hands on the horse's neck, coaxing her calm. "Sri would never fall. Sri would never let a horse bolt off." His voice was singsong soft, but his eyes were brightly serious. "Sri would never get herself into trouble after I ordered her not to."

Roberta was calmer now. "What's the matter, girl?" Talis asked her. "Did Timmy fall down the well?"

The horse snorted and pushed at Talis's shoulder with her head.

"Guess that's a yes." The AI ran his hand backward

through his hair, raising it into spikes as if putting up his antennae. "On the other hand, our two point six just went to an eight point three."

He looked at me, and I remembered what Sri had said. He'd risked her without risking me. But that only worked if he was willing to write her off.

Francis Xavier had not moved, but his body seemed poised to leap. The words he wanted to say—Sri's name, surely—glowing silently in the way he pushed his lips together.

Eight point three.

"Dammit." Talis looked at me, wrinkled his nose, and decided. "Saddle them up, Francis. Let's go be heroes."

It took just 4.5 minutes for us to pack our gear and saddle the horses and be off. We zagged up the embankment, pointed ourselves at the low humps of the lost skyline, and went at a gallop. Francis Xavier took the lead—or took point, for suddenly we were a military expedition. He had his wings on. Leaning forward with his speed, he swept down the old rail line like an avenging angel.

I was just trying not to fall off and break something.

We rode into sound, into the low rumble of the trommels.

The humps of the downtown rose as the distance vanished, becoming individual fallen buildings—the ones that had been concrete gone loose as sand castles, the ones that had been dressed stone gap-windowed, tumbled like a child's blocks. All of them were half lost beneath creeping dunes of sand and dirt and bunchgrass.

The city rose around us and then sank away, and then we were at the lip of a gentle river valley. There were gardens down there. A smattering of goats. The smell of a cooking fire. None of the trommellers were in sight.

No sign of Sri.

Talis held up his hand and we slowed to a walk. Quiet. Careful. We eased down the path from the ruined city into the valley, came around a clump of cottonwoods, and found ourselves face-to-face with—

I started, but it was only a statue.

A bronze statue of a man on horseback, in what was once called heroic scale—just a bit larger than was comfortable in humans. Francis Xavier's size, roughly. The green face was weary and betrayed beneath a broad-brimmed hat, and the horse looked tired. But what caught our eyes were the wings someone had tied to the rider's back.

Not real Swan Rider wings—not Sri's wings, not trophies of a capture. They were tattered constructions of branches and snow goose feathers, roughly roped on. But even so they tilted off the defeated horseman like a threat.

"Charming," said Talis. His face was a blank. He might have felt anything, or nothing. He might have been doing the orbital mechanics calculations necessary to move weapons platforms in his head.

It felt like a place to pause, but we didn't pause. We rode forward, into gardens. On the far side of them was what had to be the trommeller compound. It was built with its back against the bluff: a rough half-ring of huts, built igloo-like from big blocks of dressed stone, presumably recovered from the fallen city. Together, they formed a thick wall and base for a geodesic dome of iron girders. Some of the dome pieces were covered. Others were open to the sky.

We could smell cooking, hear faint voices. A curtain doorway twitched. A child climbing the dome as if it were a jungle gym took one look at us and disappeared. But no one came to greet us.

At that moment the trommels shut off. We could hear them spinning down and down and down, and down. And down. Then silence squeezed in. "Come out, come out, wherever you are," murmured Talis, nearly under his breath. "Francis?"

"Come out!" Hearing Francis Xavier shout an order was like hearing a lapdog snarl. "Show yourselves unarmed, and appoint a voice to parlay."

One of the curtained doorways twitched aside, and a woman came out with a toddler on her hip. She was dressed in the trommeller fashion—in a crazy quilt of bright scraps and metal buttons—but her head was uncovered. A long braid—blonde going wire-grey—swung down over one shoulder. "Swan Riders," she said. "Come in and welcome."

"No," said Talis, again under his breath, and Francis repeated it: "No. Bring everyone out here, and show yourselves unarmed."

"You don't have a count of us," said the woman

mildly—and truly enough. Twenty people could spill out of those little block houses, and we would not know whether ten more awaited us within, weapons ready. Talis shrugged in answer, and the trommeller woman pushed out one hip to balance her child better, as if the little person were a basket of laundry. "You're looking for your girl?"

"Yes," answered Talis dryly. "We're looking for our girl."

"She's here," said the trommeller woman. "And the griddle's hot. Come in." She pushed the curtain back and turned away. The toddler made a grab for her braid as it swung with the turn. It looked so innocent—but of course children were no guarantee of innocence. Some people were willing to put them on the firing line.

Francis Xavier still had a cocked crossbow in his hand. He lifted it and pointed at the woman's back as she vanished. The curtain fell into place. Francis kept his aim, but the curtain seemed unfazed.

Now what?

"Nineteen people," said Talis. "Mostly seated. A cooking fire. Geothermal heat pump, but no significant power source."

"How—" I asked.

"Keyhole satellite," Talis answered. "You can't get the feed?"

Surveillance satellites and the weapons platforms were ever brushing across my awareness, but locking on to their feed, the way Talis was doing . . . I shook my head. "I can't."

"Keep trying," he said. "It's just a trick of focus. Like

learning to wiggle your ears." And then he wiggled his ears, of course. "*No count of them* my foot."

"Talis," said Francis Xavier. "What do we do?"

"We go get our girl," said Talis, and swung down from NORAD's back. Francis Xavier dismounted too, but Talis caught his sleeve before he could go anywhere. "We go get our girl, and we kill anyone who so much as looks at us funny. Clear?"

"Clear," said the Swan Rider. And he swept, weapon-first, through the curtained door.

Talis and I followed.

It was dark for a moment—and ghost-green as my vision-enhancements kicked in—and then it was bright again, as we passed through the little hut and into the open space under the dome.

There was a wave of startled voices, people turning around, standing up.

And there was Sri. She was lying on a mat near the fire. One of the trommellers, a man of forty or so, was leaning over her. He was saying: "That's too—"

Sri saw us at once. There was a rush of something across her face—too frightened to be relief. The trommeller man spun to follow her gaze. There were dust goggles perched on top of his turban, and a crusted line of dirt and dust around his eyes and nose that marked the edge of their protection. It gave him an almost cartoonish look of shock, surprise.

Sri tried, and failed, to get up from the mat: her elbow gave way and she fell on her back with a whoof of air. "They didn't touch me," she gasped out. Her words were jammed together, gasping, high. "They didn't touch me, Ta—" She snapped her mouth closed, halfway through the name. Quite right, too. Why give anyone that card to play? All around the room people were staring at us. There were seven children, but that left twelve adults. If it came to numbers, we were outnumbered.

"They didn't touch me," she said again. Softer. Slower.

"They better not have." Talis's voice was soft as Sri's, but his was terrifying. He strode forward across the crazy-quilt squares of sunlight and shade. Francis Xavier fell in behind him, his crossbow cranked and aimed. The trommeller who had been leaning over Sri took a hasty step back and raised his hands.

At the fire, an old man was tending a griddle of bannock and fish. He stood creakily, pushing his legs straight with his hands. "Got no quarrel with the Riders," he said. "No quarrel a-tall."

"Don't you," said Talis, disdaining the use of question marks. "That's not what I hear."

"She just went down, m'lady," the old man answered. "She fell and Javen brought her in by the fire. Nothing more."

The woman from the doorway stepped over to the man with the goggles who Sri had been talking to—Javen, by the way he'd reacted to his name. They stood side by side, the space between them both thoughtless and powerful. Husband and wife, I thought. King and queen.

"Now, Rachel," Javen said to Talis. "You know how it is in the Sask. We look after each other."

The speech was easy, but the man was terrified. I could see it in him, in the sudden surge of heat around his heart, in the way his hands curled up. Had they heard about Calgary? Or had we interrupted something incriminating?

"We're just looking after her."

"Of course you are," said Talis, his eyes like an arctic blast. *Never lie to an AI.* He would see their fear, their unease. It would be spotlight obvious. Even I could sense it—twelve people, each glowing like a radio beacon.

"Sri?" Talis spoke without releasing Javen from his gaze. "Can you get up?"

Sri tried, but the obvious answer was *no*. Francis Xavier was still holding a weapon, and Talis was busy being menacing, so I went to help her. I hooked her under an arm and tried to drag her up. The doorway woman swung in to help me, taking Sri's other arm. For a moment the woman's eyes met mine. Our faces were close. "Your Highness," she whispered. "Greta, do you need help?"

Did I need—

She knew me. My transformed mind, my Swan Rider's gear, my shorn hair—but she knew me.

My eyes went wide. Her not-quite-offer rattled through me. It made my teeth snap closed.

She knew me. How did she know me?

"Greta," said Talis. "Stay with us."

I swallowed.

"I'm Mahrip," the woman said, much louder, and as if it were the first thing she had said. "Up we get now, dear."

Together, Mahrip and I lifted Sri to her feet.

Sri was a bundle of muscles and bones, angles and poke. She tottered stiffly. Then she let her body melt and lean into mine, and together we found her feet.

"Hannah is my daughter," said Mahrip.

Hannah. *Hannah.* A trommeller girl—Elián had stolen her shoes. Elián had stolen her shoes and tried to escape the Precepture. The proctors had taken Hannah. She had screamed and begged.

"Hannah lived, but Alba . . ." Mahrip looked right into my eyes. "Your Highness . . ."

"Greta!" Talis strode forward and muscled Mahrip out of the way, taking Sri's other shoulder himself.

"Your Highness, please, we're your people—" began Mahrip.

"I will kill the three youngest people in this room if you don't *stop talking*," Talis snarled.

Mahrip stopped talking.

My people. I had no people.

Because this was what Talis had taken from me, at the refuge. This was the numb spot. That I had once had a people. That things had been done to me, that I had done things, because I had a people. There were spots in front of my eyes, a clicking in my ears. There was overload building in my head, pain and shivering and looping memory—

I'd stepped off the lift at the Calgary zeppelin depot, and the young dockhand there had blushed and bowed low before me.

I could not survive such a memory. But I could not survive without it. If Talis had to take one more thing . . . If he had to take it *here* . . .

A burst of pain cut through the rising fire of the overload. Sri's expert fingers had found the pressure points inside my elbow and pushed like well-placed chisels. I gasped.

"Greta," came Sri's murmur in my ear. She was on her feet. Leaning on me, yes, but upright. She released the pressure on my elbow carefully.

Francis Xavier had his back to our backs, his crossbow up. There was not an ounce of question in his voice as he said: "We're going."

"We," wheezed Sri. "We came for oats."

"Yes," said Talis. "We absolutely want some oats."

They gave us the oats.

Technically we paid for them: I saw Javen fold our gold-plast strips into one of his buttonholes as if they were bobby pins. In this postcurrency society, they might well be most useful *as* bobby pins. But anyway we got the oats. And then we left, and they let us leave, though they watched us go. Twelve of them, and more on the banks and hills, their possible weapons concealed in swirls of bright patchwork, their faces hiding behind gold-tinted goggles.

I could feel them watching. I could feel my suppressed memories rising within me. Hannah. She had screamed and begged. There had been a bolt from the sky, orbital weapons fire. Even now the orbital weapons were looking down. They had come down the zeppelin spire at Calgary . . . I was shaking.

Talis doubled Sri, sitting behind her on NORAD, his arms around her as she leaned forward, holding tight to the saddle horn. Still, we were all up, and we were all moving. One might almost call it a victory. In passing, Talis leaned far out, his fire striker hidden in his palm, and set the wings on the statue blazing. The smoke rose up behind us as we rode away.

"Welp," said Talis. "Gotta say, this is not the road trip I was picturing. I was thinking Kerouac, you know: putting the top down, letting the wind in our hair . . ."

". . . Making the most threatening oats purchase in the history of the world . . . ," put in Sri.

Talis grunted—not in disagreement—and with a bare twitch of reins turned NORAD toward an iron trestle bridge that spanned the river. "We're getting out of crossbow range," he said, "and then you, young lady, have some explaining to do."

He wrapped one arm tight around Sri and squeezed his knees around NORAD. The little horse went loping. We followed. The cottonwoods, the slope, the bridge. Loud hoofbeats raining down into the river. The bridge was ancient (built in 1908, my datastore told me). The rivets (its most likely points of failure) were knuckly and swollen with rust. But the steel was painted against corrosion in a jumble of bright colors, and the patchwork decking (steel plates, fiberblast boards, newly split logs) was solid under our hooves.

Once across, I leaned forward over Gordon's neck. The horse bunched and plunked his way up the far bank, through the scrub trees, up onto the rolling prairie. I wrapped my hands in Gordon's mane, letting its wiry strands cut into my fingers, trying not to die. We rode across the empty grass until the dome of the trommellers fell away behind us and the plume of smoke from Talis's little parting fire was just a thread in the high blue October sky.

"Sri?" said Talis. "Can you ride on your own?"

And Sri began with some hesitation, "I—"

"Give it another moment," he said softly, then raised his voice. "Seriously, though. Francis, you will let me know if *you* intend to collapse anytime soon, won't you?"

"I will," said Francis Xavier solemnly.

"Mortal peril of any kind, really. Just a heads-up, is all I'm asking. What about you, Greta, you with us?"

"Don't take anything from me," I said.

"Great," said Talis. "So Greta's fine."

Fine was overstating it. My head was pounding, phosphenes boiling at the edge of my vision. We're your people. Hannah's shoes. She'd screamed and begged. A bolt from the sky. A crater—

Calgary.

I squeezed the bruise inside my elbow, where Sri had saved me.

Even if she had to hurt me to do it.

Mahrip, the trommeller woman who had known my name. She'd said—she'd said something I had not understood. *Hannah lived, but Alba* . . . "The old woman you had executed," I said. "What was her name?"

"You're gonna have to narrow that down a little," said Talis, whose list of executions was fairly substantial.

"Here, in Saskatoon. The trommeller matriarch, from when Hannah—"

"Don't think about that," said Talis quickly.

"It's important."

"It's Rachel's memory," said Talis. "I can't access it. Francis?"

The big man looked away. "I did not ask."

"Didn't anybody write this down?" said Talis. "Honestly, people. The illusion of my omniscience depends on you doing your paperwork." He blinked and went internal for a moment. "Ah, a visual confirm, thank you Francis, nice job. I can ID her but her face is a little . . . Alba Kajtar," he said. "Her name was Alba."

Of course.

And now that I knew there was a record, I too could see her face. I could see it before, and after.

"The old woman volunteered, before we needed to draw lots," said Francis Xavier. "We made it very fast."

I felt an urge to thank him. But I didn't.

"Those people are up to something," said Talis. "I'm going to put some capital letters on that, even. Up. To. Something."

"You think they're part of the Pan Polar rebellion," said Francis Xavier.

"Maybe they just don't like us," I said. I still had Alba's

face in my head, and some disagreeably comprehensive information about the skull-penetrating power of a crossbow quarrel. I shivered. *Please, Your Highness.* "They have cause."

"Well . . . maybe. I suppose blowing up their city because I had a bad vibe off them is a little over the top?"

"A little," said Sri.

"Sure?"

"Pretty sure."

"And here I was thinking overwhelming firepower could solve all the world's problems," said Talis. "Sri. Honey. What happened?"

But just then we learned exactly what had happened.

"Stop," barked Talis. He reined NORAD up so suddenly that she pranced in a tight circle. "Get her down—Francis! We've got to—"

Francis Xavier leapt off his horse and ran to them. He pulled Sri into his arms. The next instant they were all on the ground, Francis Xavier kneeling astride Sri's body, Talis crouched in the dust and dead grass, holding Sri's head between his steady hands. And Sri—Sri was convulsing. Her lips were skinned back, and a long and dreadful *something* was shuddering through her. Her teeth were clenched so tightly I was surprised they did not break. She was making a noise. The only possible question did not seem remotely adequate, but I found myself asking it anyway: "What is it? What's happening?"

Talis glanced up. His face was: what? Angry? Stricken? Not worried, though. Not surprised. I had often enough seen him worried over me, and once or twice I had surprised him: this was neither of those.

Francis Xavier didn't look at me at all.

I was loath to repeat the question: Excuse me, but why does my companion appear to be dying in horrible pain? But what else could I say? "Please— What is it?"

Francis Xavier answered me at last. "It's Rider's Palsy."

"What's that?"

"Oh, for God's sake, Greta," snapped Talis. "Look it up."

I looked it up. Rider's Palsy: when the lesions acquired by hosting an AI caused—not seizures in the exact sense of the word, but the anomalous firing of the nerves: pain without bodily cause, pain so white-light intense that it brought the body to the ground. They happened nearly without warning. They were progressive. They were, eventually, fatal. I knelt near Talis, watching Sri's hands clutch and scuttle at the little stones, the dry grass. Francis Xavier was holding her arms down to keep her from hurting herself.

Or hurting herself any more.

"They're clustered," said Talis. "This isn't a first episode. She's supposed to tell me—why didn't she tell me?" His fingers were tangled in Sri's hair. "FX: why didn't you tell me?"

"My life is yours," answered Francis Xavier in his soft, solemn voice. "But Sri's is her own business."

Talis dipped his head as if rebuked.

He'd been swimming with dolphins, and now Sri was—

There was no name for what was happening to Sri. It

went on and on. *Seizing in the grass until her heart gives out.* My breath felt strange in my throat; my mouth tasted bitter.

Sri had signed up for this. Volunteered. Had she known?

The paradox of the Swan Riders, the idealists who were executioners.

Of course she had known. But how could she have known?

"I hope it's early," said Talis, "or we'll never get her home."

"It's early," rasped Sri.

Talis lifted his hands from her head—he'd been pressing hard enough to leave fingerprints on her temples, pale prints that reddened slowly—and smoothed back her hair as if in benediction. "Sri," he said. "Why didn't you tell me?"

"What, and miss the fun?" The burnt-sugar smile—bitter and sweet—was lopsided. "Let Evangeline cut my vocal cords because the screaming bothers her? I didn't want to sit around in a yurt and wait to die." Francis Xavier climbed off Sri, and she swiped the drool from her face with the back of her hand. Tremors danced along her jaw.

Talis rocked back on his heels, laced his hands behind his neck, and popped the air out of his cheeks. "Bad timing, though, if you slow us down on this particular trip."

"Talis, I promise." Sri's voice was rough. "It won't be this that slows us down."

"You can't promise that."

"I do, though," she said. "I promise that." She stretched a hand toward me, and I knelt beside her. She fitted her fingers into the bruised place inside my arm, but very softly. *You are hurt*, the touch seemed to say. *I am hurt, too.*

Francis Xavier knelt behind me and wrapped his hand around my shoulder.

"I asked Talis once why the Swan Riders were all young."

Neuroplasticity, he'd answered. *Joining a cult, that's a young man's game.*

Francis Xavier's fingers squeezed—fellowship, comfort—and Sri gave me the other half of Talis's answer. She said: "We never grow old."

The light was long and slanting. The grass was red and gold.

Talis took a step back as he watched the three of us and chafed at his wrist. But no, it wasn't his wrist; he was just using it. It was Rachel's wrist, the Swan Rider's wing tattoo like a beautiful piece of bondage. This was going to happen to Rachel.

This was going to happen to me.

5
FLARE

We camped where Sri had fallen—away from our shelters and wells, away from any source of food or fuel or water, and still within easy reach of the people we took to be our enemies. We took turns watching through the night, with the horses standing asleep around us and the stars sharpening as the night grew colder. By dawn, I was wearing my crinkle sheet as a cloak and pacing to stay warm. I could see the mist of my own breath as the light rose.

It was a setup for a disaster, but disaster did not befall us.

Or, it did not befall anyone but Sri.

My datastore made me an expert on Rider's Palsy, and so I knew now what Talis had known when he'd shouted for the horse to stop: that at first the episodes were here and there, short and spaced, but toward the end they clustered. Sri had had at least one to land her among the trommellers, and another to cut short our escape. She had one more in the night—or perhaps more, but one that woke me, with the screaming.

Clustered. Stage five.

Stage one was the first clinically detectable scarring; stage two the first twinges and blurring of vision; stage three the stage where jolts of pain first appeared; stage four the first true episodes; stage five clustering. Stage six was terminal excitotoxicity—the technical name for an ugly brand of death.

Stage five meant Sri had a month, at best. And she lay on her mat as limp as a braid of hair.

But I fell asleep again after the dawn watch, and when I woke, Sri was awake, on her feet, and saddling her own horse.

And then we rode.

A second day, and a third. The weather had certainly turned, the wind growing sharp and cold. Tall grasses crashed around us like surf. We all added sheepskin vests under our dusters, and Francis Xavier also wore a long strip of crinkle silk—UN blue, of course—wrapped around his head in what was technically known as a tagelmust: a Bedouin fashion of head wrap and neck scarf (with optional sand-fighting face covering) that had become common among the herders of this newest desert. It seemed to me neither warm enough nor cold enough for that, but Francis shivered when he believed no one was looking.

"Where are you from, anyway?" I asked him when we stopped for lunch on the second day, somewhere near the pin that marked the exact middle of nowhere.

Francis Xavier looked at me for a moment before answering mildly: "Somewhere warmer."

"Haven't you heard?" called Sri from where she bent unpacking hard tack and cold meat. "The Swan Riders aren't from anywhere. We don't have histories."

Or futures.

But though the weather was swinging to cold and Sri was growing thinner and more strained by the day, her knife trembling as she carved—though we slept as little as we could and ate on the run, though we watched the skies for explosions, though we felt a threat at our back—despite all these things, nothing terrible happened.

And in the end, the blow did not come from behind.

We came over a ridge, and then, directly in front of us, the sky was suddenly split by a white streaking contrail.

A bomb. I thought that and jerked the reins backward. Gordon Lightfoot skipped a step and hopped like a crow. I wasn't ready for it and the saddle hit me hard. I went *uffff* and Talis—who had already stopped—put out a hand to steady me. My whole body tightened, ready for the explosion . . . but it was not a bomb. The contrail was shooting *upward*. A rocket; a spaceship launching.

I'd seen my share of magnetic launches—the Precepture itself had had an induction spire—but a launch massive enough to require rocket boosters was rare. And where was it coming from? Medicine Hat was the only thing of any size ahead of us—two hundred miles away, far enough to make the contrail small. But what could they be launching from there?

"There's no launch spire in the Hat," said Francis Xavier. "They cart salvage to the zeppelin depots in Calgary."

Or they *had*.

"So where's that being launched from?" I said.

"That's not a launch," said Talis, lifting his chin as he tracked the spiraling contrail upward. "That's a flare."

Francis Xavier started the slow process of arranging an uncertain frown.

"Trust me," said Talis. "I've set off my share of missiles."

"We get shares of missiles?" asked Sri.

"It's a flare," said Talis again. "Which means it's small. Which means it's closer than you think."

And he was right. When I'd thought it two hundred miles away, the parallax of the contrail had been all wrong. I adjusted my perception. This was not a suborbital launch but a signal rocket. Small. And no more than five miles away.

Talis glanced back the way we'd come. "We could easily have been spotted topping that rise."

"Or it might have nothing to do with us," I said.

"Greta, dear," said Talis. "I'm five hundred years old. How do you suppose I got that way?"

"Multiple copies and massive fortifications," said Sri.

"My point," said Talis crisply, "is that when you're the center of the universe, it's always about you."

I thought of Mahrip saying, *Do you need help?* What did the trommellers want? To murder Talis? Rescue me?

Wind swirled the dry grass around the horses' knees, and a sudden gust carried a smell of cold tin: snow coming, maybe. Talis's eyes swept down the contrail to its base—or at least to the lowest point we could see, framed in the notch between two hills. The trail was already tattering away.

"That creek bed goes through around there, doesn't it?" said Sri.

"It does." Francis Xavier shaded his eyes against the afternoon sun. "I remember that crossing. The gully's steep."

Talis might or might not remember the place, but he certainly knew it. "It's more than steep: it's practically a defile. Decent spot for an ambush."

Sri was still looking at the flare, and her horse, Roberta, was sidling as if nervous. "Can we get real-time intel?" Sri asked. "Satellite imaging?"

"Try it, Greta," said Talis.

The satellites were ever above me, their nets of eyes and whispers. I closed my eyes and tried to drift into that net. Like wiggling your ears, Talis had said. *My eyes,* I thought. *My whispers.* For a moment nothing happened, just the brush of data, like a comb through long hair, a sensation of being touched in a place where one had no sensation. *My eyes*, I thought.

And then they were. I opened my eyes and I was every satellite feed in the world, drifting above the planet as it spun and lit beneath me. I could see everything. I narrowed as if narrowing my eyes, looking at Saskatchewan, looking down, reaching down with one finger to see—

"Whoops," said Talis, closing his hand on my wrist. "I know I was talking smack about it, but let's not *actually* destroy Saskatoon, shall we?"

I froze. I'd been reaching with a weapons satellite.

The world flashed wide. The planet, the whole earth was suddenly spinning under my eyes. Under Talis's eyes, all the time. How could I stay human, if I had eyes like that?

We needed to bring the satellites down.

"Well, first let's use them with a little more skill . . . ," said Talis. His voice seemed to echo in outer space. Had I spoken aloud?

I blinked three times. And suddenly I was on a horse. In Saskatchewan.

I was on a horse, and I was shaking. Afraid to move a finger. The Swan Riders were both staring, but Talis smiled, strange and sad. "I'll do it," he said, and lifted a hand to his temple with a flourish, like a carnival mind reader.

A silence stretched out. I very carefully did not reach for anything. I breathed in. And out. Talis let the silence lengthen, and my heartbeat slowed down, and down, and down.

I had not accidentally become the Butcher of Saskatoon. And I would not, I swore to myself. I would not.

Finally, Talis dropped his hand back onto the saddle horn. "Yes, there are people along the creek bed. A dozen or so? But more than that . . ." He shook his head. "There's some washout in the signal."

"Jamming?" asked FX.

"There is thorium in the soil in these parts—it will make us blind to ultraviolet and infrared anywhere it's disturbed."

"Like the creek bed," said Sri.

"So it's natural," said Francis Xavier.

Talis shrugged. "If you're not feeling suspicious, which personally I always am." He tapped at his lips with two fingers: a plop-tock sound. "In fact, I'll tell you what: let's err on the side of total paranoia. That usually works for me."

"Let me guess," said Sri. "We're not going down there?"

"We're not going down there," said Talis. "But we can't stay here, either, not if we've been spotted. We need to move, and we need to do it unpredictably, and we need to do it now. Sri, I wanted to get you to your station for evac, but we need to cut sideways."

"There's a refuge about fifty miles off, across the southern fording," said Francis Xavier.

"And a supply cache even closer," said Sri, and pointed. Mostly south, a bit east.

Talis frowned and followed her pointing fingers with his eyes—his eyes and more, I think, because the next thing he did was rattle off a set of latitude and longitude coordinates.

The map bloomed in my head instantly. It took the Swan Riders a moment. They both paused, then both nodded.

"That's the one," said Sri.

"The church on the ridge," Francis Xavier added.

I let myself know it: Our Lady of the Snows, Catholic, established 1901, abandoned 2217. Nothing but a bit of foundation wall at this point, but it was a landmark that marked a Swan Riders' cache, offering good sight lines of the valley we would need to cross, and enough cover to make that assessment in relative safety. It took us back toward Saskatoon, but also far enough off our known course that no one would find us.

Talis looked sidelong at Sri. "I am sorry. I wanted to get you home."

"I'm a Swan Rider. I am where I need to be."

"Okay." Talis reined NORAD around. "Let's move."

We went for seventy-one minutes at an easy pace, keeping one rank of hills between us and the little canyon where the creek cut deep into the dry, dusty soil. The signal contrail tattered in the wind behind us. Soon enough there was nothing left.

Francis Xavier took the point, and Sri kept a rear guard. They both had their crossbows loose in the holsters at their knees. The landscape changed, rising and growing rougher as we approached the ridge and the dry river valley beyond it. The grass gave way to silvery drifts of winterfat scrub and little rivulets of bare ocher clay. Our hooves raised puffs of dust, and I knew we were leaving a plume. But nothing came at us.

But then we came in sight of the ruined church and saw that we were not alone.

The church wall was a dark rough line at the top of the hill. The graveyard spilled down the slope from it into a haze of EM fog—thorium; the graves. All expected. But there were also goats scattered grazing on the hillside, and a little tent pitched beside a tilted mausoleum. A man and a woman were sitting together on one of the grave markers, shepherds' crooks loose in their hands.

"Huh," said Talis, and raised an arm in hail: "Ahoy, the ship!"

Francis Xavier jerked his reins and pulled Heigh Ho Uranium between Talis and the goatherd couple, turning sideways to give the AI more cover. There was no threat yet, but he reacted so fast, to its mere potential, spinning and raising his crossbow. A Swan Rider to the core, and suddenly a terrifying creature.

"Drop your staffs," Francis shouted, training his weapons on the goatherds. The light pierced through his prosthetic hand. It was aglow, and absolutely steady. "Put your hands up."

"Easy, there." The woman put her staff aside and stood, sending her shadow rolling down the hill toward us. Her eyes were lost behind her goggles. She spread her empty hands. "Easy. Got nothing here but some goats." The man stood beside her, his staff still in his hand. They wore billowing, bright clothes in the trommeller fashion. Like Francis Xavier they were wearing head scarves in the cold, blowing dust. I could see the woman's mouth, the man's eyes. Nothing more.

"I said hands up," said Francis, jerking upward with his crossbow, and the man put his hands up over his head with the staff still in one. There was tension in them both: in their posture, in their circulatory patterns, in the faint flare of EM around their heads. The man's fingers were white-knuckled around his staff, and he glanced nervously at the tent.

Did they have something there? A child sleeping? Something else?

We edged forward—a strategic move, to get the sun out of our eyes. The old grave markers stood higgledy-piggledy, like a forest of stumps. Reed grass, which in summer would have been shoulder high, was bent into billows all around them.

Francis Xavier stood up in his stirrups, keeping his aim and his eyes on the strangers as he spoke low to Talis: "Cut round to the ford?" Heigh Ho Uranium was prancing in place, too well trained to move but catching her rider's mood.

Talis paused, nodded. "Back away then. Let's go."

Francis actually guided Yuri backward a handful of steps, weaving between the slanting gravestones, then swung round and moved toward us.

And the crossbow exploded in his hands.

It was a peerless shot: the incoming bolt hit the stock with a shattering crack; Francis Xavier cried out at the smack in his hands; the bow spun out of his grip, flying sideways, cartwheeling through the air.

Talis wheeled NORAD round to face the shooter: a full 180 in three steps and less than a second. Yuri had reared and Francis was shouting, fighting to stay mounted, but in another moment he too had turned. I was slower than either, even though Gordon's willing heart was with me. By the time I got the horse facing away from the hill we were looking down the quarrels of a half dozen crossbows.

Armed people had risen like ghosts from behind the gravestones, from under the billows of grass.

And among them Sri sat on her horse, her face as sweet as apple cider, her crossbow still aimed straight at Francis Xavier's now-empty hands.

Bareheaded among the masked and shrouded people, mounted among foot soldiers, neat as a queen: Sri. She swung the weapon over an inch—at Talis—cranked it, and dropped in a quarrel. "Surprised?"

Talis raised his black eyebrows. "Well, *obviously*."

I had been farthest back, down the hill, so now I was closest to Sri, and the armed men. Talis tightened his knees and NORAD came forward, tossing her head and snorting: in an instant we were side by side. Francis Xavier, a big man on a big horse, loomed up behind us like an avenging angel.

Sri did not look intimidated, and given the dozen men with crossbows at her back, perhaps she did not need to be.

"On the other hand, it's elegant," said Talis. "Paranoia as a trap? I mean, that's brilliant. Neatly done. You got us back in range of trommellers—oh, am I not supposed to know these people?" Because all the armed people had lit with sudden terror/bewilderment/surprise. Talis smirked at them and rattled on. "Back in range of these anonymous people, whom I certainly cannot identify. You got us to someplace predictable, someplace where an ambush could be set up, someplace where we're sensor-blind? Well done. I mean, really. I would take off my hat if I were a hat person, or, you know, a person. Also, I will have a weapons platform over Saskatoon in four and a half minutes."

Sri blinked.

"What makes you think we're from Saskatoon?" said the got-nothing-but-goats woman.

Talis shrugged. "You want to hide a conspiracy? Don't do it in Saskatchewan." He addressed the crowd at his feet. "Four minutes, fifteen seconds." He shook his head. "You shouldn't have let me talk. Honestly. Who doesn't know that?"

"Well," said Sri. "We all have things to learn. Could you go up toward the church, please?"

"Or, just a thought, we could stay right here and talk about orbital weapons, and the price of betrayal."

Sri swung her bow two degrees: at me. "I think you know, Talis: I'm an excellent shot."

Sri, who I could trust to hurt me, if she had to. Sri, who was dying. She looked right down the stock and into my eyes.

"Ah," said Talis. "Two or three medium-sized cities."

"And we all hope it doesn't come to that," said Sri, her finger on the firing latch. "Up the hill."

Talis paused. "You heard the lady, Francis," he said. "Take point."

And Francis did. We turned, and Francis Xavier led us fearlessly toward heaven knows what. Gordon Lightfoot had his ears pinned, his steps bounced like stiff springs. "AI to AI,

Greta," said Talis, "what do you think? Maybe two hundred people in Saskatoon—call it half involved with this lot, half purely innocent. Not an ideal ratio, obviously, but not a terrible absolute number . . ." But just there, in the middle of considering mass murder, he stopped talking.

The goatherd couple was taking down the little tent. Underneath it was—something. Wire coils, a spinning disk. An emitter on the front that was hissing, crackling—

"Greta!" Talis shouted, swinging over NORAD's back like an acrobat, dismounting on the fly. "Get—"

Down.

The electromagnetic pulse hit me right between the eyes.

6
NEVER PASS UP A CHANCE TO HEAR THE MASTER PLAN

EMP.

Electromagnetic pulse. A weapon that targeted not soldiers, not matériel, but information. Electronics. AIs.

The Abbot—my teacher, my tormentor, near to my father: an AI who preferred a mechanical body—he had died of EMP wounds.

EMP hit me. Whiteness went to darkness. Time stopped.

Then it started again. I dragged myself into it to find my head splitting (not literally: later I checked), my heart skittering, and Talis midrant.

"She's too new for this," he was saying, and he sounded furious. "She's too vulnerable for this. She's too valuable for this. What were you thinking?" He was kneeling over me, peering at my pupils, checking my pulse. He looked terrible: his face prickled with sweat and lopsided as if he'd had a stroke. He put his fingertips over my datastore, but I could not feel even the faintest trace of his sensors. Was I that scrambled? Or was he that hurt?

I moved my head a little—and infrared came back, all at once, with a bright spike that almost made me throw up.

In flaring false-color I could just make out Francis Xavier striking backward with an elbow at the men who were trying to grab him. Someone had pulled off his prosthetic, and that sleeve swung like a banner as FX spun. He was magnificent.

And badly outnumbered.

Talis, meanwhile, was not finished throwing his fit. "You *idiot*, Sri," he spat. He didn't just sound furious, he sounded frantic. "No, not even an idiot: this is so far beyond idiocy—this is the supermassive black hole of bad ideas around which the whole galaxy of stupid rotates. I swear, if we lose her—"

Oh, of course: he was frantic because he was worried about me. "Talis," I coughed. And then, because he was still talking about gravitational density: "Michael! I'm all right."

"Oh," he said, calming as if someone had flipped a switch. "Oh, well, now I just feel silly."

"That's okay," I said.

"Okay, is it?" said Talis. "Well, your heart went into v-tach for four point two seconds, Francis Xavier is getting the snot beat out of him as we speak, and I seem to have walked us into a trap. But apart from those little details . . ." He turned. "Francis, honestly, what are you trying to do over there? That's enough."

The big man subsided, panting. One of the strangers

wrapped an arm round his throat in a gesture that looked almost brotherly. I fixated on the image for a second: the one black eyebrow poked from behind goggles knocked askew, the way the man's billowing sleeve buttoned tight on the wrist with five bright buttons. They all wore such sleeves—tick-borne encephalitis being a trouble in postwarming Saskatchewan—and fixating on small details was a characteristic of malfunction in AIs.

Talis rocked back on his heels, overbalanced (so unlike him, that clumsy tumble), and ended up sitting in the grass with his back against the remains of the church wall. I felt a similar whirling weakness, but it was clearing. My vision was evening out, and my skull seemed to have survived the metaphorical railway spike Sri had driven into it.

Sri.

I could trust her to hurt me, if it would help me. But how was this helping? My thoughts were shattered.

Talis, braced against the wall, offered me a hand. I took it. Sat up. The world jittered around me, as if someone had given the sky too much caffeine.

Talis, though, had no eyes for that part of the drama. He spread his fingertips along my collarbone, and this time I felt his sensors, staticky and faint. "How are you feeling?"

"Moderately rotten. You?"

"Yeah . . . not having the best day. But there it is. Five hundred years, you know: you win some, you lose some, you exact some terrible revenge." He pulled himself up to sit—lounge, really—on top of the ruined wall.

"Hi," he said, waggling his fingers at the tense and silent crowd. "I take it you know who I am. So you have me at a disadvantage. Or, rather, you'd hoped to."

The threat hung there, glittering. He knew who they were, and thus their families could be targeted.

"Thirty seconds to back off," said Talis. He'd clearly fallen hard from the horse: a bruise was coming up on one cheekbone and he had quills of dried grass sticking out of his hair. But even so he looked like one of the Fates as he held up his fingers and began to tick off seconds.

The crowd bunched and shifted. Looks were exchanged from behind gold goggles. Thirty seconds to back off? It was, by Talis's standards, a generous offer. For the first twenty seconds I thought they would take it.

I definitely thought they *should* take it.

But they didn't.

Talis folded a last finger closed and shrugged. "Did you want to give me names, or should I stick with wide-blast targeting coordinates?"

"You know my name already," said Sri. "So why don't you talk to me."

"Ah, Sri." He sounded soft, amused. Was he upset? "Sri, Sri, Sri. Don't be greedy. As master of the world, I have love enough for all my children."

He meant: you can't protect them. I could feel my datastore realigning itself, my sensors struggling back to life. Surely we had only minutes before Talis could reach his satellites. Once he did . . .

"We're not who you think," said the nothing-but-goats woman.

"Come on," said Talis. "You can't have a shadowy hidden conspiracy in Saskatchewan. There's no one out here."

But there was. There was *someone*. One of those shrouded, silent men. The one at the back. I recognized something in the way he was standing, still but leaning forward, something . . .

Something human. A pain in the crook of my elbow. A quickening of my heart, thudding under the corner of my jaw.

"No questions, Talis?" Sri was still trying to catch the AI's whole attention. "Come on: I know you've got questions." She smiled at him. "Ask me why I'm doing this."

"Oh, sure." Talis was clicking his fingers through the pebbles on top of the ruined wall. "I never pass up a chance to hear the master plan. Why are you doing this, Sri?" He waved a magnanimous hand at her. "Monologue away."

Sri, though, hesitated: she too knew the clock was ticking. "On second thought, maybe you can just work it out as we go along."

Talis gave a bony shrug. "Up to you."

"You can start with me," said the leaning-forward man, the I-knew-something-about-him man, stepping up from the back of the crowd. "'Cause I'm guessing you might know why I'm pissed off."

He pushed his goggles up and yanked his mask down.

It was Elián Palnik.

Talis actually got to his feet when he saw Elián. Sri arched both eyebrows, and Elián himself gave a dried-up version of his loose, easy smile: both seemed pleased by what they took as Talis's startle. But only I guessed why he had stood.

It was because I had.

I had stood up without meaning to, with as little thought as one had when one's heart came into one's throat.

Elián. This. This was what I was trying not to remember. Hannah had screamed and begged, and there had been a bolt from the sky. A crater. Elián had tried to escape and none of us had stopped him. So they'd punished all of us. They'd punished all of us until I had stood up and made them stop. They had pushed Elián until he had crumpled into my arms. Until I caught him and promised to save his life.

The memory roared into me.

And a lightning bolt blasted it out.

Talis. He'd put his hand on my elbow, and it was blazing with electricity.

This was not like Sri's fingers bruising into the pressure point—it was a hundred times stronger. And it needed to be. Talis knew that this moment could kill me. And he was trying, silently, to save my life.

"Hello, Princess," said Elián.

My breath caught and I wobbled.

Elián Palnik. The boy whose crazy quest to fight the Precepture had awakened me to the idea that the Precepture needed fighting. The boy who'd been my Spartacus: the slave turned hero. The boy I'd died to save.

Elián. He'd dunked me in the river; he'd carried me, damaged, through dark corridors; he'd put his fingers beside my fingers in a crushing press; he'd kissed me desperately in a moonlit garden, declaring that we were both about to die. He had—

Another lightning bolt.

"Stop." Talis's fingers twitched around my elbow, his teeth clicking together. "Greta, stop." It was almost a moan.

I looked sideways at him. His face was a mask, but there was pain under it. I thought for a moment it was the EM headache, but then remembered that he was overloading his own fingertips. Those sensors were exquisitely sensitive, and a touch that bothered me at the elbow must have felt to him like a hand dipped in fire. But despite being disheveled and hurting, he held his body lightly as a pair of reins. His eyes were narrowed and diamond-bright: he was thinking at speeds most people couldn't dream of.

I was not confident it would help. No amount of quick-footedness or quick thinking was going to change the basic math of the situation. There were fourteen of them. There were three of us. They were armed. We were not.

Talis's electricity looped through me as if I were a circuit and my heart beat faster yet.

What was happening here? A carefully organized, highly risky plot to bring us to this place, this moment. To this moment, and then—what? Whatever was to happen, it would clearly happen against our will.

Or, at least, against Talis's.

Was I to be rescued? Elián always had seen me as a damsel in distress.

The trommellers. Mahrip, saying, *Do you need help?*

Mahrip, saying, *We're your people.* My people, coming back to me, and Elián in front of me—I felt blown open. I felt as if my ribs were too small for my lungs. As if the two bones of my forearms might open like an eye. I squeezed my hands around them, trying to hold myself together.

"Don't I get a hello?" said Elián to me. His voice was soft, injured.

"Hello, Elián," I said. My voice surprised me: it was hollow as a cicada shell. I sounded terrible: brainwashed, kidnapped.

Had I been? I was shaking all over. Elián, who had woken me up, and shown me love, and then Xie—

"Greta?" Elián leaned in, as he always had, to save me.

"Leave her," said Talis.

Elián's gaze went to where Talis's hand rested on my arm. His eyes narrowed, and for a moment I thought he could see the electrical pain arcing between us. But of course, that wasn't what he was seeing at all. He was seeing the touch: the girl he'd loved; the monster who'd murdered his grandmother. Arm in arm.

My hands tightened, pushing the bones of my forearms closer together.

"I mean it," said Talis. "I don't know what you want, Elián Palnik, and I doubt you do either, because frankly thinking these things through doesn't seem to be your strong point.

But this"—and here he tipped his head toward Sri—"this isn't about Greta." He flipped his gaze back to Elián. "And you'll kill her if you push it, so leave her."

"It's been five minutes, Sri," said someone in the front row.

Sri glanced skyward before she could stop herself. Talis looked too, smiling a long cold smile. The weapons platform.

Sri gathered herself and returned his smile. Her crossbow hung in one hand as if she'd forgotten it, but I'd seen her hit a jackrabbit in the twilight without stilling herself to aim. "Well then, Michael," she said. "Let's dance."

"Don't call me that," he said, mild as butter.

"Greta does."

"Greta's different."

"My little AI," she said fondly. And then, to the crowd: "Someone hold her."

The nothing-but-goats woman was coming up behind me, but before she could grab on, Talis turned to me. He put his hand on my face. Under each fingertip, my skin sparkled.

I found myself leaning away. "Michael, don't," I said.

"I have to," he said.

My people. Elián, and Xie. The who of me. The why of me. *No.*

I moved back and he moved forward, neat as a dance, his fingers steady on my face.

"It's too much," I said.

And Talis spoke almost on top of me. "It's too much for you. I have to. While I can."

I stepped back into the arms of the people who were (for all I knew) there to kill me. The goatherd woman closed her fingers on my shoulders. My head whipped around and I saw those hands microscopically: the skin tone, the shapes of the nails, the calluses of reins between the fingers. I could see the warp of my face reflected in the woman's goggles. I was fixating, malfunctioning. If Talis had to take more—if he had to take it here . . .

I was trapped and he was trapped and they were going to kill him. Surely they were. Surely he must know that.

Anyone else in the world—literally anyone else—would have told me not to be afraid. Talis said: "Don't be human."

"What?" My voice cracked.

"Don't be human," he said. "Be this." And *pushed*.

His hand didn't move, but his sensors sharpened and deepened and an instant later a pulse flashed through the inductive webbing in my brain. It was more than he'd ever pushed before, and for just a heartbeat I remembered that I didn't want this—he didn't want this—there was something to lose. Then the webbing inside me turned into ribbons of light. My thoughts and the apparatus of my thinking transformed into fireflies. I closed my eyes and wondered if I was literally aglow. I felt Talis lift his hand away. "Be human later," he said. "When I can help."

"How can you help her be human?" Sri's voice. And she did not sound as I had ever heard her sound. She sounded— but what? My thinking was glorious: my feelings (such as they had been) were gone. "What do you know about—" she said, and her voice cracked. Broken, that was it. She sounded broken.

I opened my eyes.

Sri mastered herself and beckoned. "Come here, then. Let me show you something about being human."

The goatherd woman behind me grabbed my shoulders and pulled me back. No one touched Talis. He cocked his head and walked out toward Sri and her conspirators. They fell back. Somehow he had made the space around him his: it was as if he'd stepped onto a stage. It would take a brave person to step onto it with him.

"Tal—" Francis Xavier choked. His voice was blocked and gaspy from the arm round his throat, his eyes were barely open. "Rachel . . ."

Was it a warning? A question: *What about Rachel?*

"Easy, FX," Talis murmured. "I've got this."

"You think?" said Elián. And he drew a knife from a sheath on his belt.

Talis raised his eyebrows and fished his glasses from somewhere inside his coat, settling them fussily on his nose. It looked theatrical, but he genuinely was farsighted: he might simply have wanted a better look at the weapon. His eyes flashed at Elián over the top of the frames. "They've picked you for this, hmmm? Whatever 'this' is."

"Actually, I volunteered." I tagged Elián's trademark drawl as a try for bravado. It fell somewhat flat. In infrared I could see the trembling tightness of the small muscles around his mouth and nose. His circulatory patterns indicated his body was preparing for fight-or-flight. His eyes kept flickering sideways at me.

It was not my first time seeing Elián with a knife. He'd threatened Tolliver Burr, the man who'd tortured me, with a much-battered vegetable knife. That had not worked out well, but never one to learn from his mistakes, Elián had also cornered Talis himself with a heavy blade more used to jointing goats than menacing our robot overlords. That had not worked out well, either, largely because Talis could outmenace anyone in the room.

This time, though, this knife . . . this knife was different. The blade was four inches long, sharp on both edges and pointed: optimized to stab. This knife was a dagger, plain and simple. What was Elián Palnik doing with a dagger?

"I thought we had established, Mr. Palnik," said Talis, "that you are not a murderer."

"I'm not."

"Because I'm not a person? I promise you, Elián—you won't know it from the blood."

Sri stepped forward then, the crossbow casual in her hands. "Take off your coat," she said.

Talis was of course wearing a Swan Rider's duster of oiled leather, dust-smudged down one side from his fall. I had come to appreciate oiled leather: I knew it would brush clean easily, the moment we had a moment. Talis liked the coat too, and he made no move to take it off. He tipped his chin up at Sri—not defiance, but a kind of curiosity. He looked like a raven: something small, dark, and handsome, with the potential to go for the eyes.

Silence stretched.

"She said take it off," said a woman in the crowd. Talis snapped round and locked on to her like a weapons system. She flinched—but he released her, cocking his head: "Sorry." A glint of smile. "Just waiting to see what the threat's going to be."

"There are enough of us to hold you down and have you stripped, if you'd rather," said Sri. "But there's no guarantee you wouldn't get hurt. We wouldn't want that."

"We wouldn't?" chimed Talis.

"Not to no purpose."

"That's interesting." He considered a moment, then took off his coat, tossing it to one side as if throwing down a gauntlet.

And then Elián—with a wide-eyed look at me—did what I had said it would take a brave man to do. He stepped onto Talis's stage.

He was still holding the knife.

I looked at it.

I saw Talis look at it.

But neither of us guessed.

Talis had a strip of crinkle silk, UN blue, knotted around his throat for warmth. His gaze went back to Sri as he undid the knot, pulled off his glasses, and wiped the dust off the side of his face. Then he stuck the silk in one of his back pockets, folded up his glasses, and tossed them underhand to Sri. She caught them delicately, graciously.

"Next?" he said.

"The vest," Sri said.

Talis raised his eyebrows. "I realize you didn't ask for advice, but seriously: anything that won't go through a sheepskin won't go through a chest wall, either. You need quite a bit of strength, to stab someone. Someone did mention that to young Mr. Palnik, yes? I wouldn't want to see him bungle it."

"The vest," said Sri again.

His eyebrows still arched, Talis undid the buttons one by one. He shrugged the vest off and handed it to me, which made the woman behind me grab on more tightly. The sheepskin vest smelled of horse and lanolin and the woolly inner side was warm to the touch. Talis stood there goose-bumping in a white shirt worn so thin that I could see the structure of his collarbones and the ridges of the binding wrap he wore beneath. (What about Rachel?) There was a long pause.

"Well?" he said. "Or were you planning to have me freeze to death?"

"Hold him," said Sri.

They clearly had this worked out, who was to do what, when, why—but still there was a pause when they looked at each other. I was concerned in that moment, not for Talis, but for them. What would he do to them when this was over? They had to kill him now; they simply had to. To touch a Swan Rider was punishable by death. To touch Talis himself . . . it didn't bear thinking of. Saskatoon might be the least of it. Following that train of thought, I realized they'd have to kill Francis Xavier, too, to keep him from reporting. And, incidentally, me. But surely Elián wouldn't—

I had no time to pursue the thought. Two of the conspirators—big men, both—came onto the stage and grabbed hold of Talis, one on each side, by armpit and elbow. They held him with his shoulders wrenched back, his body a-tiptoe, locked in place. The flexion made him tremble: a purely physiological reaction. His face was still calm.

Elián was the one who looked like he was waiting for death. "Sri," he said. "I don't think—"

"Shush," she told him. I didn't know people actually said that. She stepped close to Talis and smiled. She ran her finger over the thin white shirt, tracing the valley between the collarbone and the faint prominence of the datastore. She slipped past that valley's inner edge, and then she pressed the fingertip down harder, as if making an indent in dough.

I thought of thumbprint cookies.

Talis's eyes flared wide.

"Stab him," Sri said, "just here."

Only then, and much too late, did Talis start to fight.

7
AFFINITY, SEVERED

AIs are no stronger than humans.

The bodies we use *are* human, after all. There are some minor relevant differences: we can access voluntarily the involuntary endocrine tricks that give a panicked person strength. We can treat pain as just another species of data. We can look up a bone's breaking point and push right up against it. But in truth none of this is more than a desperate human can do.

Talis struggled as if desperate.

And it did him no good.

It is easy to forget how small Talis is: between one's knowledge of his history and his habit of striding about as if he had lightning at his fingertips, he seems larger than life. But in this incarnation—in Rachel—he is finely boned, slightly built. Delicate, almost. Easily overpowered.

He flailed with all his strength against the men holding him, making them stagger and spread their stance. He pushed off the ground and arched his back; he kicked out so savagely that someone had to dive in from behind and catch his feet. But in the few seconds when only physicality mattered, he was no match for them. The men held him trapped and trembling. Elián put the tip of his knife where Sri had poked.

"Are you . . . ," Elián started to ask Sri, and Talis spat: "Don't you *dare*—" and Sri said: "Do it."

Elián's face was tight as stretched leather, so far from his norm that I was for a moment unsure it was him.

"Elián?" I said. He turned, his face a mask, and he was still looking at me as he put his weight behind the blade and pushed.

Talis jerked and screamed like a hawk. For an instant his face changed, and the coin-wide eyes did not belong to him: *Rachel*, I thought. *Hello, Rachel*. Then Talis was back. I ran his face against the database of all the times I'd seen him, and I was 97 percent sure of it. But I could find no referent in his history for the expression he wore, and had to compare it against generic human norms. I tagged it fear, and pain, both extreme. He was critically hurt, and he was terrified.

Here is the difference between data and knowledge. I had all the data I needed to figure out what Sri and Elián had done to him, and why he had reacted as he did. But I didn't have the lived experience to understand it, nor had I done the thinking to absorb it and put it in a framework so that it came readily to mind. Therefore, I spent at least eight thousand milliseconds—between when Sri had touched Talis and when Elián staggered back, leaving the knife buried in his chest—not sure what was going on.

The men holding Talis let him go, and he fell bonelessly into the grass. Elián stumbled backward, shaking as if the blade had hit a live wire. And in a way, it had.

The affinity bridge. The main connection between the datastore and the brain. It ran along the underside of the clavicle, and then up beside the aorta into the brainstem. The knife had severed it.

Elián squeezed a hand over his own mouth. Sri crouched down. Everyone was silent. We could hear the grass crunch as Talis twisted on his back, his fingers curling talon-like into his own skin on either side of the knife handle. He shouldn't pull it out, I knew that much, but even as I made to say so the need passed: Sri pressed her hand hard over his, hard enough to push him flat on his back, his head tossing.

"How does it feel?" she asked.

"How do you—" Talis took a gasping, furious breath. "—think?"

"Not what I meant." She pulled her hand from his wound and touched his face. Tight around the dark gloss of the wood knife handle.

"You can't upload," she said. "You can't download. That makes you human. How does it feel?"

"I—" he said, and something flared across his face: fear?

"I am going to gift wrap you, Sri," he panted. "Before I send you to hell. Something complicated . . . with raffia and—and—" His words were coming harder. His fingers were bloody and white beneath the blood.

"Now, now," she said, and leaned forward over him.

And then—suddenly, explosively—he yanked the knife from his own chest and slashed at Sri's face.

She jerked back. The knife missed. And Talis—

Talis made a noise.

It was a sucking, bubbling sound, like the last drops of the milk shake. The knife spilled from his hand and his body crumpled. He folded around the puncture as if a sledgehammer had struck him there.

"Shit . . ." Elián skidded to his knees beside Talis, pushing his skittering hands away, looking at the wound as wide-eyed as if he had not made it. "Sri!"

And Sri's face showed—was that alarm? Surprise?

Was this, then, not part of the plan?

I pulled forward against the woman holding me, but she only tightened her grip. My datastore was spinning field medicine at its absolute top speed, and I tried to push it through my brain, to build the organic structures that meant I had really learned it, to change the data into knowledge. It was the only thing I could do, but it wasn't really making a difference. Just then, for instance, I suspected a collapsed lung, but surely that was no more than I would have known as a human.

It was not more than Sri knew.

"Kit," snapped Sri, reaching a hand behind her, like a surgeon for a scalpel. "And let FX go."

"I can't—" Talis's voice was a wheezy whistle. "I—"

With whatever imprint of him was left in the brain cut off from the control of the datastore, he had lost everything about him that was AI. I was astonished by the speed of the change. I would have expected five hundred years of chipper insouciance to persist somewhat, if only from habit, but no. The panic he was displaying was purely human.

"Please," Talis said, or tried to say. There was no sound behind it.

"Sri," said Elián, "he's dying. . . ."

And that was illogical. There was no reason for Sri and her people to go to the trouble to transform Talis only to have him die at their feet.

"Sri," I said. "If you'd be so kind . . ."

Sri's head whipped around. "Let her go," she said. "Let them both go. Where's the damn kit?"

The goatherd woman let me go so fast that I staggered forward, falling to my knees at Talis's side. He was struggling for air. His neck arched sideways, the tendons in it standing out clear as cabling. The puncture—infraclavical, and in the second intercostal space—was an inch, an inch and a half long, and bleeding but not spurting.

I pushed my hand over it as a short-term seal.

Yes, there: I could feel the infrathoracic vacuum nibbling like a goldfish at my palm. It was pneumothorax: air in the chest cavity. It would push against the other organs. If there was enough pressure, the other lung would collapse, and the heart would drown in air like a fish on a dock.

I pushed hard and Talis moaned.

"We need a waterproof bandage," I said. "Something at least three inches square."

"Greta," said Elián. His voice sounded pleading.

"I'm *busy*, Elián." My voice sounded like nothing at all. "We need the bandage urgently. Cut one from his coat if there's nothing better."

"Greta, here . . ."

I twisted around.

Francis Xavier was on his knees. Wheezing. Wobbling. He swayed and stretched his single hand out to me. There was a packet in his hand.

My datastore ID'd it: a wrapper containing a military-grade first-aid patch, backed with rubber, infused with antiseptics and coagulants.

Good. Perfect. My estimate of the likelihood of Talis's survival shot up 40 percent. "Are there scissors? Or a knife?"

"Well, I've got one," said Sri, and handed me Elián's dagger. It was blood-mucked to the hilt, which at least told me the depth of the wound.

"You." Francis Xavier reached out and yanked Elián backward. "Get away from her. Get away from us. Right now."

Elián fell onto his tailbone and scooched backward. Francis was kneeling across the body from me. I looked him in the eye and we synced up, a silent countdown, three, two, one.

I pulled my hand off the wound.

Francis tore open the bandage wrapper with his teeth. I sliced away Talis's shirt and the wrap beneath, laying one white breast bare, the nipple wincing up in the cold. Francis tipped a powder of coagulant and forcescar into the wound and slapped the bandage on, pushing against it with all his strength.

Talis's body responded. Remarkably, instantly. Suddenly his trachea was less distended, his face clearer, though human with what I supposed was pain or fear.

"Take the pressure?" said FX.

I moved my hands parallel to his hand, and again we counted it in our eyes, three, two, one. Francis raised his hand, and I slid both mine in.

It had been 71.51 seconds since Talis had been stabbed. He was still conscious. His eyes were wide and locked on my face. His body was shivering, slipping deep into shock. Francis Xavier, meantime, was undoing his head scarf, every clever fold and tuck.

Why?

Of course: a pressure bandage.

I lifted my hands cautiously. The seal held—the patch was meant to be self-adhesive—but continuous pressure was still Talis's best hope. I slid my hands under his narrow shoulders and pulled him a little off the ground. He needed to exhale completely so that we could tie the bandage on, but he was doing nothing of the kind. A whine caught in his throat when I moved him. His breath came in gulps and hiccups.

"Breathe out," I ordered. Talis took a couple of shallow puffs, then tried to master himself, pushing out a long breath.

Francis Xavier slipped the silk under his back.

"Breathe in," I told Talis.

He tried, white-faced with pain. I laid him back, and Francis Xavier's arm under his shoulders held him just an inch off the ground.

"Breathe out," I said, leaning over him, one end of the silk strap in each hand. Talis pushed his ribs small, and I yanked the strap as tight as I could and tied the knot right over the chest seal.

Talis whimpered, shuddered, stilled.

"Ease him up," I said, and Francis lifted the little body as if it were effortless. Breathing is always easier if you're not lying flat. And it needed to be easier. We might have stabilized the pneumothorax, but we certainly hadn't fixed it. Talis's breathing was ragged; there was lavender around his eyes. I pulled him into my lap, wrapping my arms around him from behind, pushing one hand over the wound.

His head fell back, his skull striking my collarbone. "Thank you," he whispered. His voice, though already tiny, cracked and dropped: "Oh, God . . ."

Elián, demonstrating his knack for getting through a crisis but not past it, twisted aside and threw up.

Sri, though . . . Sri leaned forward. She unfolded Talis's

glasses and set them crookedly on his nose. She tucked the hooks behind his ears and ruffled his sweat-soaked, grass-quilled hair. "There, Michael," she whispered. "Now, that's human."

They left us sitting there.

There were a few minutes when the conspirators stood about like a school group on tour, staring at us: the pietà of me and Talis, Francis Xavier kneeling alongside, the blood drying to darkness in the pale grass.

My organic mind, which had an annoying habit of providing me with thumbprint cookies and milk shakes and nonsense images generally, provided this one: my family and I—me very small—going to see a living crèche. The royal family standing quiet and still, looking at other people standing quiet and still. For a few moments I felt again as I had then: peaceful. Talis's breath hitched and staggered inside the ring of my arms.

And then the stillness broke up.

Of course it was Elián who broke it. From the first moment I saw him he'd been bad with stillness. Our time at the Precepture together seemed in retrospect a blur of torture, food fights, and kissing. When I had been going to my death he'd made a joke about football.

And I felt nothing about that at all.

"Where'd you learn to do that?" He stood looking down at us. "That medical stuff."

"I know everything I need to know. It's what I am now."

"Yeah?" he said. "What's that like?"

"It's not like anything human."

"Yeah," he said again. "That's kind of what I figured."

Some of the other conspirators were clustered a little distance off, where they appeared to be having a spirited argument, albeit one conducted in whispers. I had a feeling this had not quite gone according to plan.

"Hey," said Elián, crouching down, trying to catch Talis's fluttering attention. "I don't—I mean, I didn't mean to hurt you quite this bad."

Talis's exhale shuddered. It might have been a laugh. "Go away."

From someone who never passed up the chance to hear the master plan, this was not the wisest strategic move.

And yet I sympathized with Talis's dismissal. My hands were literally full. Under my hands Talis's heart was beating fast and arrhythmically; his skin temperature was critically low. In the stark light his lips were as blue as if he'd bitten a pen. The wound had taken in too much air; his circulation was failing. If we couldn't get that air out, he was going to die.

"Elián!" one of the strangers shouted to him. "Let's go."

The trommellers had drawn up horses from the hidden side of the hill. They were mounting up now, slinging goats over saddle horns. The horses towered over us, breathing steam. Sri was among them. She seemed calm, but her horse Roberta, mirroring some hidden mood, stamped and skittered sideways.

Elián looked at her, back at me, back to her again. There was tension around his eyes; he pushed his lips together. But he took the horse's bridle without a word. He started to mount and paused with one foot in a stirrup, suspended between options. "Greta: come with us."

And I thought about it. I trusted Elián. He had just knifed someone I was close to, for reasons I did not understand, but I trusted him. It would not be too much to say that I had once loved him, though the state was difficult to call back to memory.

"She can't," said Sri.

And I couldn't.

Talis had made me an AI, a process very few people survived. I had not survived it yet. For a blink of a moment, I hated Talis and everything he stood for. But then the strange intensity of feeling switched off, and I tightened my arms around him and shook my head.

Elián swung his leg over the horse, holding the reins so tight that the animal stepped backward, snorting. "You know, Greta: back when you were human, you wouldn't have let that happen. Somebody getting stabbed right in front of you? No way."

"There were fourteen of you," I said, at pains not to point out that, as the person who had done the stabbing, he was hardly in a position to criticize.

"You would have tried." His voice was fierce with certainty. "Maybe you should think about that." He wheeled the horse after the others.

"Good luck, Greta," Sri said, swinging her horse close. "Good-bye, Michael."

"Talis," he whispered, his head hanging. "My name is Talis. . . ."

"Sri," said Francis Xavier. He wrapped his hand around her rein: for a moment I thought he meant to stop her going, though I knew neither how nor why.

Then Sri laid her hand over his—her hand, palsied and bony, over his, so large and steady—and I realized it was a good-bye. Their wrists were pressed wing to wing: the tattoos suggested that a small bird rested invisibly between them. "She wouldn't have been back," Sri said. "Not for long, anyway. Not whole. You know that, right?"

A pause, a slow nod. "I know that."

"Have you started your carving yet?"

"You know I haven't."

"Francis Xavier." She pulled her hand away from his. "Get out while you can."

"If I see you again," said Francis Xavier, "I will put a bolt through your heart." Then he lifted his hand from the reins.

"Greta, don't forget." Sri saluted me formally. "There's a chest tube in the kit." Then she whistled, and all the horses wheeled.

Our attackers went. We watched them go. The hoofbeats drummed, then tapped, and then there was the huge silence of the open prairie.

Francis Xavier, who had been standing with his head bowed, lifted it slowly. "All right," he said. "Let's get this done." He knelt to the first-aid kit, rummaged, and came up with a chest tube, and with a scalpel.

And so, as Sri apparently wanted, we saved Talis's life, pulling the air from his chest cavity before he could drown in it. It was an ugly thing. I thought he would pass out—to call what we did to him invasive was to give it its mildest name—but he didn't. Not until after we were finished and I picked him back up did he let himself go limp.

The fight melted out of him slowly. His breathing smoothed. His eyes softened, then closed. His hands, which had been clutching at me, grew more still, heavier somehow. One of them was tucked up in the cradle of my arms, curled loosely. The other fell away, into his lap. After another moment I could see the change in his delta wave patterns, and then the flicker of his bruised-looking eyelids. He was asleep.

It was getting toward evening, and the wind was picking up. The temperature was 1.2 degrees above freezing. Francis Xavier took off his duster and laid it over us, kneeling to tuck it in round Talis's shoulders, under his chin. "Rachel," he said, with more soft feeling than I had imagined him capable of.

No one answered him.

INTERLUDE:
ON BEING MURDERED

Talis—or what was left of Talis—was honestly not sure if he'd ever been murdered.

How would he know, really?

He liked riding out, and he'd done it a lot, especially after the first couple of centuries. Sometimes one really did need the personal touch: he'd strong-armed many a treaty in person, forged many a peace. Away from the Red Mountains, the people he met had rarely encountered an AI in Rider form. They found him uncanny, if not flat-out terrifying. Thus he kept the name of Talis whispering around the world. And with the name, the peace he'd given up so much to achieve.

It worked like this. There was a small global network of fortified data silos that his AI self could easily reach through shielded hard cables, the real him being much too big to flit about wirelessly. There was one such silo in the Red Mountains, of course, and others in strategic places around the world: one near Lhasa, one in the Urals at Yamantaw, one deep in the ancient cave-city of Derinkuyu, one under Kilimanjaro, and so forth. In each, the UN had a base of operations, and the Swan Riders had associated encampments. His usual practice was to ride out, take care of business, and ride back. Usually he returned without fuss, then reuploaded and reintegrated the returning copy. It rarely took longer than months, which meant he wasn't in a body long enough to start being inconvenienced by the white-light pain of the lesions an AI left in the host brain. That pain had killed him once, back when he was Michael, and once was more than enough.

Plus, if he kept it short, then after he reuploaded, the Swan Rider was often in pretty good shape. He certainly didn't want to destroy more of them than he had to.

But—and here was the wrinkle—every once in a while, there was a self who rode out and never came back. A piece of experience earned but never reincorporated. A book written but never put on its shelf.

He supposed some of those missing versions of him might have been murdered. More probably they'd met with accidents, but—well. He had enemies, certainly. He had more people who hated him than most people had people. Why shouldn't some of them be murderers? Mind you, it was hard to see what they would get out of it, beyond the splatter, and it was a terrible risk. There had been a handful of unsuccessful attempts, and what he had done to those people, even he did not care to think about.

But then, sometimes bloodlust went deep. Too deep to be subject to cost-benefit analysis.

And what could he do but keep riding? It was good for the world he'd once saved and then, frustratingly, had to keep saving, as if the world were a leaky boat and he was the only one with a bucket. And if he was honest with himself, it was good for him, too. It kept him—not sane, really. Sane was a human yardstick; he didn't hold himself to it. It kept him entertained. Which was important. Boredom crawled over him like rust. It was a slow death, boredom, the way rust is slow fire.

So, on balance, he was quite willing to risk being murdered. He'd pictured himself shot through the head on some dusty byway, or bleeding out on the floor of a conference room somewhere, the conspirators standing around, shocked. He let himself imagine that it had been quick, without really caring one way or the other.

But this. Murder, yes. Possibly he could even be eaten by lions, something colorful, something new. He'd risk that. But he'd never dreamt he was risking this.

He hadn't seen it coming until the moment Sri had touched him, the shivery tickle of her finger as she found just the right place to force a blade. And then, having seen it, he hadn't been able to stop it. He'd struggled, of course, could think of nothing better to do than struggle, though it was so human: they always fought; it rarely helped. He'd struggled and while he struggled he had time to anticipate, time to play out the whole scenario in his head. He knew a bit about recreational torture (because, hey, he'd lived a long time, and there'd been the aforementioned boredom): he knew that you should scratch with a toothpick before you strike with a whip. Sri's fingertip on him, the shiver and the tickle—

And then, the blade.

He really did picture it as a whip, which was the problem with thinking too fast, with thinking about whips: the knife was a whip coiling around the roots of his very self and yanking them screaming from the earth like mandrakes. For just an instant he was still whole, and could feel the datastore reacting to the massive short and the body reacting to the wound and the organic mind going into the oh-shit brace position one called shock, and then—

And then, very little. Sure, pain: he'd just been stabbed in the chest. His knees didn't even try to hold him. His hand flew to the injury as if it had its own software. But what was dazzling was how the world looked flat, colorless, as if he'd fallen into a picture of the world instead of the world itself. Half his senses were simply gone. Infrared, ultraviolet, ultrasonic—the friendly jostle and burble of the electronic world, the beautiful depths and overlays of the informational world—gone. His memory cut up like a paper snowflake—if he hadn't spent so much time, since Greta, pushing his own history around in his mind, there'd be nothing left of him at all.

As it was . . . there was enough. The loss was cruel—it would have been less cruel to blind him—but there was enough of him left. Or so he thought, for just a moment. He'd snarled a little at Sri; she'd smiled a little at him: the accepted parts in the drama. He thought it was a drama. He thought he could play it. But then he had pulled the knife free.

And suddenly. He needed air and couldn't get it. He was reasonably accomplished at ignoring pain, but this—this was a brand of distress that was a step sideways from pain, and it was imperative.

The body—the body needed air. And suddenly, the body was his—no, was him. He was his body. He was human.

With one flick of a knife, they'd made him human.

8

"I REMEMBER AIRPLANES"

Talis slept like a child—a deep, limp sleep that would have made anyone think he was an innocent.

I held him for an hour, while Francis Xavier gathered our scattered horses and retrieved our gear. By the time that was done my back had started to spasm. Francis Xavier scooped Talis out of my arms as if he were a toddler, and like a toddler he still did not wake. Darkness was gathering by then, and the temperature was dropping fast.

I found a gap in the ruined foundation of the church and led the horses through it. In the meager windbreak of the northwest corner, I piled the saddlebags and microfoam pads and one of the horse blankets into a kind of inclined bed. We laid Talis out and tucked all three crinkle sheets around him. Shivering came over him like waves, like aftershocks.

I stood looking at him, not liking what I saw. His skin

temperature was too low; his heartbeat was too fast. Francis Xavier didn't have an AI's brain structure, but he had the same sensors I did. He looked at Talis. He looked at me. We looked at each other.

"It would be ideal if he didn't die," I said.

FX paused. Said: "Yes. That would be ideal."

I was not sure what to do first. "The blood loss is problematic, but we can't address it here: there's nothing to transfuse. The cyanosis is lifting, which is a good sign, but—"

"He's cold," said Francis, very softly.

"It's the shock," I said, but that did not stop Francis Xavier from spinning to rummage in the heap he'd made of our gear. I watched, noting the slashing spill of the bag from which he'd yanked the first-aid kit. Noting the ripped and battered prosthetic arm. FX was having no trouble without it: he'd even lifted Talis with no visible struggle, balancing the slight body with the stump of his forearm, curling his muscles up as if lifting a beam. As I watched he found the pellet stove, flipped it over, and wedged it between stump and rib cage to hold it upside down and unfold the legs.

And yet—without his coat, without his head scarf, without his prosthesis, he looked so . . . bare.

I blinked, dizzy again, feeling that space in which I should feel something. That step onto the missing stair. Before, the hollowness had been in a place here, a place there. Now— Talis had sent such a pulse through my organic mind that it hardly existed, and the hollowness was everywhere, as if I were floating above myself. As if I were falling.

The pellet stove was ready. Francis Xavier set it beside Talis as if putting a candle on an altar, then sank forward over it. He was balanced in a crouch on the balls of his feet, his elbows on his thighs, his fist in his face. The myoelectric arm was lying beside him, elbow-end blunt in the grass, fingers curled oddly, as if trying to hold something.

"Is it broken?" I said.

"No. It's heating up."

"Your prosthesis, I mean. Your hand."

"Ruined. A horse stepped on it."

Overhead the sky was turning more transparent, beginning to let in the darkness of outer space. One by one they came on, the stars. Handfuls and then dozens of stars, to my eyes overlaid with their names and distances and places in the Hertzsprung-Russell stellar sequence.

The satellites looked down on us.

I looked down on us.

Francis Xavier was shivering.

The pellet stove was pouring out heat, but the big man was shaking as if with silent sobs.

"There's not enough light," I said.

FX looked up at me. His face looked like aftermath, all stillness and ruin.

"There's not enough light for any kind of treatment," I said. "Or travel. It would be wise to get some sleep."

"We were just attacked," he said.

"And if it happens again, we won't be able to save ourselves. There's no point in keeping watch." Francis did not seem to be processing this. "They want him alive."

The *why* of that was a puzzle, and one in urgent need of solving. But I couldn't get Francis Xavier on track. "What did he do to you?" he said.

"Nothing. I'm fine."

"Not the trommeller boy. Talis. Did he—" He spread his own fingers in the air over his own face, pantomiming an AI's ultrasonic reach. "Did he—"

"He had to."

"Did you consent?"

"There wasn't time."

He shook his head, sharply, but just two degrees, as if he had not meant to do it. Then he was silent again. I could not read his intent. I needed to learn, and so I started researching methods for understanding human emotions.

"We will need water," Francis Xavier stood up. "I will go to the river. And when I get back we can keep watch in turns."

But he didn't go, because despite his tone it wasn't up to him. I considered the matter. Riding in the darkness was risky. There were prairie dog holes, and a country in political turmoil, and somewhere, a party of people who had actually attacked us.

On the other hand, Francis Xavier had been riding a long time (at least since he had killed Bịhn, three years ago) and he was the best tool I had. So I let him go, and he went. And then I was alone.

I took my own advice and lay down next to Talis, pressing close to share heat. I could feel his ribs moving against my back, the small stirs of his body. Francis had taken back his coat. Under the crinkle sheets it was warm enough but my face was very cold—so cold it felt tight and blushing.

The stars came on, layer after layer of them. The sky was 13.7 billion years deep, and so, so, empty.

Gordon Lightfoot came over and nosed at my hair, his breath steaming. The night was turning bitter: the steam was welcome. "Hey, horse," I said, lifting my hand to feel the softness of his muzzle, his wrinkly, whiskery lips. He fluttered his nostrils at me. "Hey, Gordon Lightfoot, named for the Canadian singer/songwriter of the late twentieth century. How are you?"

Without being bidden the horse went to his knees beside me, and then with a sigh he lay down on his stomach, his legs tucked up like a foal's. His big, strong body made a third wall, turning the open corner into something nearly cozy.

"I'm sorry I didn't brush you," I said. Francis Xavier had taken off NORAD's and Gordon's saddles and bits while I sat holding Talis, and toweled them roughly so they wouldn't chill, but he hadn't had time to groom them. I could see the dried foam and dirt along Gordon's girth and barrel, where the cinch went, and on his back where the saddle rubbed. I put my back to Talis and reached out and scratched the horse's hide, loosening the dirt in the small patch I could reach. The blotches of red on his egg-white coat were like maps of an unknown country.

So, so empty, my heart. But stretched tight. It echoed like a drum.

Suddenly, I wished Elián had stayed.

✎

Francis Xavier did not get killed when I sent him away.

NORAD spotted his return first and gave a squeal and a stamp. Gordon Lightfoot sighed and climbed to his feet. I sat up and considered what I would do if the moth-colored approaching horseman presented by my night vision (pale horse, pale rider) was not Francis Xavier. But it was.

He recounted: he'd found a switchback deer path down to the riverbed, scouted for a pool, filled what water skins a single horse could haul. Once daylight came we could ride there in an hour or so and water the horses more thoroughly.

Not that Talis was going anywhere.

Francis Xavier cranked up the stove to glow red-hot, and we roasted a rabbit. It was our last rabbit. He'd shot it earlier, before he'd lost his crossbow, before the world had changed. I did not, just then, feel sick of eating rabbits. I was starving. Should being soaked to the elbows in human blood have put me off the idea of meat? Would it have, if I had still been human? I wondered with part of my mind, while at the same time wondering how Talis could possibly sleep through this. Roasting meat on a wintry night seemed to me the sort of smell that could rouse the dead, and Talis was merely critically wounded.

But he didn't rouse. Francis Xavier and I ate. Francis Xavier took a short shift at sleeping. Then I did.

I was beginning to wonder if Talis would ever wake when his voice came with no warning from the darkness.

"I remember airplanes," he said.

Francis Xavier and I looked at each other. Talis was still lying propped up. I could see the gleam off his open eyes but I couldn't tell what he was looking at. He'd complained to me once that Rachel was night-blind: was it possible he couldn't see anything at all? His focus seemed that far away, though his tone was positively chatty.

"The last airplanes," he said. "They ran on fossil fuels, can you imagine—smooshed-up dinosaurs, metal cans in the air. I remember airplanes. I took drugs in Amsterdam before it drowned. New York, Dhaka—with my own feet I have stood in cities since lost beneath the waves for ten human generations. *I remember airplanes and I have killed millions of people and **my name is Talis**.*"

The last sentence came tumbling out of him, fast and strange. Neither Francis Xavier nor I answered him.

"*Talis,*" he said more softly. "I have bloody earned it."

"Are you awake?" I asked him.

"Of course I'm awake," he snapped. "What do you think?"

I did not know what to think.

Talis tried to sit up, then stopped, going rigid. "What happened?"

"You were stabbed," intoned Francis Xavier.

"Yes, Francis," he said with clipped precision. "In fact, I had noticed that. The sucking chest wound was my first clue."

Francis Xavier paused, waiting to see what Talis would say next. The AI made a little face. "How am I now?"

When Francis Xavier didn't speak I decided I probably

should. "A transfusion would be ideal, but I would characterize your condition as stable."

Talis tipped his chin back, looking up at the great round of the stars. "Terrific," he said.

I looked up too, where a bright weapons platform was passing like a star hung on a string. It was beautiful, but there was little enough to hold one's interest, especially if one could not see the information overlays. But Talis seemed interested—even transfixed.

"Talis?" I asked. Then: ". . . Michael? Are you all right?"

He made a little noise. "A list of the various ways in which I am not all right, Greta, would top the *Oxford English Dictionary*. The unabridged one. With the little magnifying glass."

"You may have internal bleeding," offered Francis Xavier, presumably as a helpful example.

"Couldn't tell you," said Talis.

I realized he'd lost the ability to scan his own body. That was unsettling by itself, but if he was bleeding into his lungs he could easily drown. I checked as best I could, but even with maximum ultrasound it was difficult to get a read on what was happening inside him. I started pushing what I needed to become an expert in medical ultrasound and in the meantime evaluated external symptoms. His breathing was rough, but that could simply be pain. Well, I could only try to find out, and the accepted method of investigation (unsophisticated though it was) was to ask. "Do you have pain?"

He gave me a *look.* "Um, knife to the chest? Obviously there's pain."

"Is it burning? Aching? Stabbing?"

"Yeah, gonna go with stabbing, there."

"Pleuritic?"

He hesitated, then in a voice somehow smaller than his own said, "What does that mean?"

He could not look it up.

"'Related to the lining of the lungs.' Is the pain sharper when you breathe in?"

"You know, oddly enough, it feels *exactly* as if someone I trusted had me held down and cut open with a *dagger.* Why do you suppose that is?"

"Talis." I was attempting to be diagnostic: surely he must see that.

"Sorry," he sighed. "Yes, sharper—it hurts to breathe. Of course, it hurts not to breathe, too, so what can you do?"

"Are you short of breath?"

"Always . . . Rachel's always . . ." His eyes crinkled softly: I wondered if he'd already forgotten that I could see him in the darkness. It was a remarkably unguarded look. "To implant the datastore they resect part of the upper lobe of the right lung. Rachel had some scarring. She's always felt just a little short of breath."

"You remember that?" said Francis Xavier.

"I remember that," said Talis.

But he shouldn't. AIs could not access their Riders' memories.

"Who are you?" said Francis Xavier. "If you remember that, who are you?"

The moment in which he didn't answer was so long that I thought he had no answer. *Talis*, I thought. *Talis, as much as anyone—but how much of Talis?*

But what he finally said, softly, into the darkness, was nothing of the kind. "Francis," he said, and for once the shortened name was not a joke, not one of Talis's can't-be-bothered flippancies. The blood-smudged hand fumbled out, pale as a moth. "I'm so sorry, Francis. I know you loved me. But I think I'm gone."

Francis Xavier dropped Talis's hand as if it were something living and poisonous. He stood up tall, swallowed hard, and walked into the darkness.

Of course, to my eyes, the darkness gave him little cover. I could see his heartbeat quickening, his shoulders coming up as he drew deep for air. Blood moved from his less-essential organs and into his heart and lungs and brain. For all the world it looked as if he'd taken a blow and was deciding whether to run or fight. That was curious, and I was on the point of deploying more sensor power to try to understand why when Talis's hand bumped, cold and clumsy, against mine. "Leave him," said the AI.

Ex-AI. From his fingertip sensors, I felt nothing at all.

But I obeyed him anyway, letting Francis Xavier slip off behind the horses. Talis began a sigh, but it turned into a stiff little gasp. "Did I mention the stabbing pain?"

"You did."

"And so you're going to . . ."

"Monitor it." Then I realized what he was asking. "Your respiration is poor. Narcotics could suppress it further."

"Oh, swell. That's just *swell.*"

"I think you're hypovolemic. You should drink something." His hand lay curled and still on the scratchy horse blanket. I lifted it. Held it for a moment, because he seemed to want me to: his fingers closed, childlike, around mine. Then I shifted to my true intention and felt for the radial pulse. It was faint: a crude measure of lowered blood pressure.

"Drinking sounds good," said Talis as I counted heartbeats. "What's on tap? No, let me guess: we've got water, and water."

"Francis Xavier rode down to the river." I fetched a canteen and had to help him hold it, as if he were a baby. Even with my help he got a bit wet. The last swallow went down wrong and he started to cough.

And then he couldn't stop. The cough became a ragged, tearing jag that made his whole body shake. It went on. It went on and on, until I thought it would kill him. Though it almost could be a joke. Talis himself: dead of swallowing funny.

Francis Xavier came running back. He flashed a look at me—unreadable—and pulled Talis up until the AI was leaning forward onto his broad, strong shoulders. Talis was shaking, blood on his lips, his fingers digging into Francis Xavier's arms. The Swan Rider stayed silent, rubbed circles between Talis's shoulder blades, hugged him close. When the jag finally released them, Talis sagged, resting his cheek on Francis Xavier's shoulder. He was both exhausted and tense, both sweating and shivering.

They stayed like that for a moment, leaning together. I could not see Francis Xavier's face. Talis was worryingly pale. The pain (or something) had actually pulled tears to his eyes—a thing I'd never dreamt I'd see. Maybe they were merely watering. Coughing made the eyes water, did it not? "Michael?" I said.

He didn't answer.

They didn't move.

No, this wasn't good. That jag could have torn open the forcescar—it could be a symptom of internal bleeding—it could be any number of things, and I needed to check all of them. "Put him down," I ordered Francis Xavier. It took him a long moment to obey, lowering Talis carefully onto the pile of saddlebags.

His eyes were open, responsive: he seemed to be conscious. Good.

I pushed back his ruined shirt. It was knifed, cut, brown with blood: surely at least half a liter—no wonder he was shocky. But no new blood was seeping from under the chest seal. I peeled it carefully free. The skin beneath was pink with its newness, slick as plastic. We had perhaps overdone things with the forcescar powder, in our haste: it looked as if someone had poured a cup of wax across the top of Rachel's breast.

But the forcescar had not split open. And it was not

growing out of control in lumps and branches, which can happen sometimes. The various punctures we'd made later were not bleeding. There was no heat of infection. The chest tube was draining clear.

And that left internal bleeding to worry about. I spread my fingers under Talis's collarbone and swept them downward, trying to build a picture of the whole thoracic cavity. I did not see any dark blooms of blood, or bright ones of air.

As I moved my fingers lightly over the goose-bumped skin, though, I could feel one more thing: the secondary magnetic fields spiraling out from the datastore, spending themselves uselessly in soft tissue and bone. I knew that they weren't directed at me—they weren't directed at all—and yet they wove tendrils around my fingers and wrists like tiny curls of wild morning glory.

Talis, I thought. *There you are.*

For a moment I wanted to dig my fingers through the skin and the forcescar, through the frozen foam of bones and the moving goop of lungs, and rescue him.

"Ouch." Talis's voice squeaked. He mastered it, pulling it down half an octave, but even so it wavered: "Okay. That was ouch."

I tried to reassure him: "There's no significant bleed, as far as I can tell. The pain is probably the intercostal muscle: it's torn across three rib spaces. The datastore asserts that that's very painful, but that doesn't mean there's new damage. You can safely ignore it."

"Thank you, Greta. I'll keep that in mind." His tone was dry enough to displace populations, but tears were running down his face.

Francis Xavier chose a different tack: "You're going to be fine," he murmured. "You're going to be fine."

"No, I'm not," said Talis. "That's the bloody *point*, isn't it? I'm not going to be fine. I'm going to be human. I'm going to be human, and I'm going to die."

And then he closed his eyes.

"Talis?" I said. No answer, though it was obvious from his brain waves that he was conscious. "Michael, what do you mean?"

Francis Xavier put his hand on my arm. I fell silent, and FX slipped in front of me and sat down on the horse blankets at Talis's side.

"Rachel," he said. "Have you had episodes?"

Talis—Rachel—which?—drew a deep hiccuppy breath. "No." Just a whisper.

"But—" said Francis Xavier.

"I had a scan-and-map before I left the Red Mountains," said Talis. His voice sounded different: higher, lighter. "The microscarring . . ."

"Stage two?" said Francis Xavier.

". . . Three."

I'd caught up with them by then. They were discussing the Rider's Palsy: the scarring that crept across the Swan Riders' brains like frost over a window, the thing that was killing Sri. Stage three scarring meant less than a year to live—and considering the hard use Talis had put Rachel's brain to since that last scan . . .

"Why'd they let you ride out?" said Francis Xavier.

"I didn't tell them," said Rachel's voice, a light, laughing voice. If a sparrow could have spoken, it would have been that voice: commonplace, companionable, lovely. It swung then and became Talis's voice, sharper and stronger: "I can feel it," said Talis. His tone was as laughing as Rachel's, but the laughter held more knives, more hurt. "Now that I stop—I can feel it coming."

"Now that you have reason to care," said Francis Xavier.

Talis's eyes snapped open. If I had been Francis Xavier I'd have sought cover. But Francis Xavier didn't even blink. "Now you care," he said.

"Did you help her?" demanded Talis. "Sri—did you know she was planning something?"

Francis Xavier was silent, but his face was tight and his stillness was no longer fooling me. I was ready to declare him the patron saint of "more going on than meets the eye." He made the Rider's salute, touching his shoulder and extending his hand toward Talis. "My life is yours. If I could have died to stop Sri, I would have. But that does not mean I disagree with her."

He leaned forward and turned his palm against Talis's cheek, resting it softly, shockingly intimate. "How many of your Riders have you destroyed? And only now, you care."

Talis's eyes closed. And they stayed like that, frozen. Five seconds. Ten.

"Rachel?" I said.

"Don't talk to her," said Talis.

"But can she hear me?"

"I said," snapped Talis, "don't talk to her."

So I was silent again. Considering. What happened to them, the Riders, when they were possessed by the AIs? And suddenly I saw the pun hidden in their title. The Riders, who could be ridden. My own mind had been ravaged past the point of failure before being overwritten with a copy of itself. So I did not know: what was it like to have one's intact mind shoved aside and manipulated by an AI? The AIs could not access the Riders' memories, but could the Riders—could they still see? Could Rachel, inside Talis—could Rachel still see me?

The datastore made no record of it.

As if the AIs had never thought it important.

Or as if the Riders had kept it carefully secret.

I watched Talis soften again toward sleep, with Francis Xavier keeping his steady hand cupped around the face that might or might not belong to the woman he loved.

I got out the painkillers. There was some possibility that they'd kill him, but he was dying anyway.

Francis Xavier watched me fill a syringe, lift it, squirt a few drops of liquid out to clear the bubbles and hit the dosage exactly. I thought he might stop me, say something— but he didn't.

I was AI. He wasn't.

And neither was Talis. Not anymore.

That left me in charge.

Talis's eyes opened when the needle touched the back of his hand. He looked at me, his eyes wide. But he said nothing.

The drug acted fast. Eased him downward. Soon enough he was breathing slow as a machine, deeply asleep, his body temperature dropping even as the sun came up over the ruin and the graves.

9
THE PASSION OF SAINT FRANCIS

Dawn. The light spread out, low and wintry, and the ruined walls of the church cast long shadows. Talis slept. Francis Xavier watched him sleep. I watched FX watching, and reevaluated my entire understanding of him. I didn't get far before he stood up, sudden and decisive, and began shrugging out of his coat.

"Francis?"

He folded the coat onto the grass beside the pellet stove and started undoing the buttons of his vest.

"Francis, what are you doing?"

Always the most private of us. Always the first to feel cold. But he was stripping to the skin as the winter sun rose into a thin lid of cloud and the light turned to watered milk.

"My kit bag, there," he said. He nudged one of the saddlebags with his foot. "At the bottom—just dump it."

My eyebrows drew together—a strange feeling, as if my eyebrows were puzzled independent of my brain—and I unbuckled the bag. Dumping it seemed a bit much so I unpacked it and laid the contents in a neat line. An extra sheet, a packet of salt, a metal cup, and a carving knife folded closed. It got more personal as I got deeper: toothbrush. Hair oil. Socks. At the bottom, beneath even the underwear, was a stuff sack containing the lowest-tech prosthesis I'd ever seen. A harness of leather straps and brass buckles. A matte-black arm that ended in a metal pincer. Curious, I lifted it in both hands.

Francis Xavier took it from me and shoved his shortened forearm into the hollow socket of the prothesis. There was a leather cuff around his bicep, a saddle across that shoulder, a strap that ran across his bare chest and under his other armpit. It was all as beautifully useful as a horse's tack, and as intricate. Brass buckles and points of adjustment. FX fumbled with the buckle over his sternum, pointing his chin at the sky, his throat bared, his fingers blind.

"Let me help you with that."

"I don't need help."

"It will be faster."

I had stepped close to him, close enough to put my hands on his chest. His hand still covered the buckle.

"Come on," I said. "You must be cold." I could feel the heat radiating from his skin.

"Yes," he said. And slowly he dropped his hand. He was all muscles and goose bumps. "It needs to be tighter. No slack, but it shouldn't press into the skin."

"Okay." The buckle and the leather looped through it were both cold to my fingers. Under them, Francis Xavier's skin was darker than the leather, smooth and gleaming.

He turned around. There was another buckle on the strap across the back. I tightened it, and Francis Xavier spread his shoulders, which closed the pincer with a tiny snick. "Tighter," he said. "I'll need the grip." In infrared, he was aglow like a candle in darkness, the heat pouring out of him. He bowed his shoulders out, opening his pincer hand again and giving him the look of picking up something heavy. While I tugged at the strapping, he spoke out of that heaviness. "The place I'm from is warmer."

I let go of the strap and he turned to face me. He raised his hand and traced the loops of his head scarf—or rather, the space around his face where the loops would be: the actual scarf (lately used as a compression bandage) was in a blood-soaked coil by the wall. "You asked once. Do you remember?"

Two days out of Saskatoon, seeing him wrapped up and shivering, I'd asked him where he was from. He'd said: "Somewhere warmer." And Sri had told me she had no history.

"I remember." There was only the shoulder saddle to adjust now. I set to it.

"What else do you remember? What did Talis take?"

"Everything," I said without thinking, and then corrected it. "Nothing. I've lost no data, Francis."

I was close enough to tuck myself under his chin. Close

enough to see the bruising on his throat where he'd been choked.

"You never used to call me that." He stepped away and bent to pick up his clothes. "He's changed you. He's changed you too much."

"You mean Michael."

"I mean Talis."

"I'm not sure he's still Talis."

"There's no one else he could be," snapped Francis.

I blinked.

Francis Xavier turned his back and pulled his thermals over his head. Then he shrugged on his shirt and vest. There was violence in his motions, and decision. Something was happening. But what?

I walked around him so that I could monitor his face. I had missed so much of what was happening in Francis Xavier's head, and I was determined not to miss more. His gaze was tipped downward, and he was struggling with his buttons. I'd never seen him struggle with anything, but one-handed buttoning is quite a trick.

I stepped close to help him. There was a flustered moment, a tangle of fingers, and then he took a big gulping breath and let his hand drop.

The violence had fallen into calm. And the decision—whatever it had been—was apparently made.

"The place I'm from is warmer," he said. "I guess I can say that."

I watched him intently. All humans have microexpressions—bursts of unfiltered facial expression, lasting only a few hundredths of a second—that reveal their true feelings, no matter how carefully schooled and still they kept their conscious faces. It is evolutionary, involuntary. In the last few hours my datastore had made me an expert in microexpressions. FX could not hide from me.

But he didn't seem to be trying to hide. "Warmer," he said, "and small. We fished, mostly, in a lake." His eyes were not quite focused, his mouth not quite closed. He looked . . . soft. Sorrow, was this? "There were mosquitoes, of course. And when I was twelve—" He stopped midsentence. The microexpression betrayed him: his lower eyelids tensed, his eyebrows drawing together. Fear. It vanished in less than a blink. "It was Var5, dengue variant five. We called it breakbone fever."

A tropical or subtropical inland fishing community, a Var5 outbreak, call it five to seven years ago—I could pinpoint him with that. But Francis Xavier intercepted my line of thought. "It doesn't matter where. It happens: I have seen it happen since. It has happened many times."

"Yes." The massive climate shift a few hundred years back had given rise to several new variants of old plagues, as moving human populations met moving virus reservoirs. Dengue, hanta, West Nile, bubonic plague. There was a reason global population was down to a mere half billion.

"Many died." His breath stirred my hair. "Not everyone. But many. My mother. My sisters. What I remember—"

"Why are you telling me this?"

He was rigid with the effort of not trembling, but trembling because he was so rigid. An act of will but a strange one. It was like watching someone put nails into himself one by one.

"What I remember," he said, "is waking up in the clinic. The cot was draped with mosquito netting, like gauze, white gauze. There was a shadow on the gauze—a woman with wings."

There were altered levels of consciousness associated with the recovery phase in dengue fever. He would have been vulnerable to whatever images his struggling mind produced. They would have impressed him deeply. "An angel."

"Yes," he said—and then his deep voice broke. "An angel, but a living angel: a Swan Rider. They'd come. Talis sent them; the UN sent them. To save us. The AIs—they'd made an antiviral. From the moment the Riders came, no one else died."

Growing up as one of the Precepture's blood hostages, as one of the Children of Peace, had conditioned me to think of the Swan Riders as the angels of death. After all, they came to kill us. But they did this, too. They were the hands and agents of the UN, of Talis and the other AIs. Earthquakes, disease, famines: over and over, they went into the worst places. Over and over, they saved the world.

The Swan Riders had saved Francis Xavier. They'd given him his life, so he'd given them his. It seemed . . . straightforward. Logical, even. Did they all have such stories,

I wondered? And asked: "What about Rachel?"

"What about her?" He stepped away from me, buttoned up, armed—remade. "Do you know why I bothered with this?" He raised his pincer.

"No." I'd been wondering. He'd been brilliantly capable without it.

"Because you can't use a crossbow with one hand." He picked his up, and in three quarters of a second had it raised, cocked, and aimed—at Talis.

"Francis!"

His finger was on the trigger.

"We need to get out of here, Greta. We have enemies and our enemies know where we are. We cannot defend this position. It's too exposed."

I shook my head. "Talis cannot be moved."

"I know," said Francis Xavier. "We need to kill him."

"What?"

"I need to protect you, Greta. And I cannot do it here. It seems to me this whole country is at war."

He wasn't wrong. Calgary. The Saskatoon incident. The ambush. What was safer than the middle of nowhere, Talis had once asked—but right now I was wanting a fortress.

"We need to cut our losses," said Francis Xavier, his aim fixed on the loss in question. "We need to run. And we need to do it now."

He fired.

I shouted.

And the bow jammed. One of the arms snapped and the

string sprang free and the bolt came flying out at an angle and *thwunk*ed deep into the ground, not two feet from Talis's head.

Francis Xavier gaped at it. "Stand down!" I barked, and slapped the weapon aside. "Stand down. This is my decision."

The crossbow stock was clamped into Francis Xavier's pincer hand. It fell to his side; the damaged bow bounced off his knee. The Swan Rider took a shuddering deep breath. Bowed his head. Closed his eyes. And saluted me as if he expected me to put him to death.

Which was tempting.

But—I was worth more than two or three cities. Was I not worth more, then, than a damaged copy of Talis himself? "Tell me—I want your frank evaluation. How much danger are we in?"

"I don't know," he said.

"Is Sri coming back?"

"I don't know." There was anger in it that time. "She didn't tell me. She didn't tell me anything."

"I believe in your innocence."

He looked up at me, the microexpression a twist of pure disgust. He didn't bother to wipe it away. "If you believe that, then you have no idea what it means to be a Swan Rider."

I did, in fact, have some idea. I had been one of the Children of Peace. The Swan Riders had killed my friends. One by one. Year after year. But at the moment, that was not the point: "I mean, you're not part of the Pan Polar rebellion. Not part of Sri's conspiracy."

"No."

"It makes no sense that Sri and her people would come back. She didn't want to kill him; she wanted to change him, so that he'd die like the Riders do." I hadn't figured that out right away, but Talis had. *That's the bloody point, isn't it?* "She reminded me about the chest tube. She wants him alive."

"And the rest of them?" said Francis Xavier. "The boy with the knife. The one you knew."

"Elián." Sensation flashed like electricity. Elián. I had known him. (I *knew* him.) I wrapped my arms around my body.

"What does he want?"

"I don't know."

And I didn't. Elián: it didn't make sense that he would want to wound Talis, merely. To give him a Rider's death, that was Sri's agenda: it corresponded to her grievance. But Elián's grievance was different, simpler: Talis had crushed his grandmother to death in an apple press. To repay that with a single surgical thrust . . . it did not seem in scale.

"What if he comes back?" said Francis Xavier. "What if he brings a dozen friends."

"Elián loves me," I said.

"And you think, therefore, that he would not hurt you?" said Francis Xavier. He looked down at the ruined bow, bouncing against his knee. "Think again."

I thought again. I looked at Talis: drugged and limp, deeply asleep. His breathing was even now, though his heart rate was high as his body fought to compensate for lowered blood volume. His temperature was lower than it should be, but not critically so. It looked, generally, as if he would live if we took a little care.

Which was what the conspirators wanted.

Or *part* of what they wanted.

It was possible that my life was on the line here. But Talis's was not. He was a copy. A damaged, dying copy. There was nothing on the line for him but the manner of that death.

A tiny sound reached me: a hiccup of breath. I turned back, and Francis Xavier was crying.

"What's wrong?"

"I never meant to be a murderer," he said. "And I am sorry about Bịhn."

"Who?" For a moment, I genuinely did not know. Then I recalled Bịhn, Greta's fellow hostage, the one Francis Xavier had hauled out of our classroom to her death. Dragged her while she screamed and fought. While her fingernails broke off in the wood of the doorframe. The access to what was left of Bịhn—pure data—was so slow as to be almost a malfunction. I frowned. Talis had . . . I flashed on his eyes crinkling with concentration, his fingers tight around mine, his sensors reaching deep. An ultrasound cascade: he'd called it exorcism.

He'd done it three times. He'd taken everything.

He'd taken nothing.

I'd lost none of the data.

Talis was alive, which was what Sri wanted. His life pinned us in place. Made us vulnerable, to whatever came next. It was like seeing the flare: We needed to cut sideways. We needed to move fast.

"Is your bow reparable?" I asked.

Sri's bolt had cracked one of the arms, and Francis's attempt to fire had snapped it. Francis Xavier looked down the string that curled down toward his boot. "I doubt it."

"Then we can overdose him," I said. And repeated what FX had said about the execution of the trommeller woman, Alba. "We can make it very quick."

Silence. A count of one, two, three, four. And then Francis Xavier looked up—far, far up, at the sky, as, with exquisite slowness, it started to snow.

"All right," he said. "Go get the kit."

I went to get the kit.

It took me a little time—we'd made such a jumble of our gear, in this chaotic night—and by the time I had found the syringe and the morphalog it was snowing heavily, wandering flakes big as feathers.

I came back and found Talis still sleeping, and Francis Xavier seated beside him, holding one limp hand. It had grown a little warmer—snow is exothermic; it gives off heat as it freezes—and very quiet. There seemed to be no sound in all the world, except a little wind, and the horses breathing.

A snowflake fell on the corner of Talis's mouth and he came fluttering half awake. His head tipped toward me, eyelids flickering as if in a dream.

It would be rather wrenching, killing him.

Another snowy touch and his eyes opened.

And it wasn't him. I was face-to-face with Rachel.

"Hello," I said.

"Hello," she said. And squeezed the hand that held hers. "Francis? What's happening?"

"It's nothing," Francis Xavier answered. "Go back to sleep."

"But it's snowing," she said nonsensically, then blinked, vanishing into sleep for a moment. When her eyes opened again, the person looking out of them was a mix of Talis and Rachel and some drowsy, sleep-addled child. Another blink, another dipping out of view. Then surfacing again. "Greta?"

"Rachel?"

"No, I—" Talis slurred. "It gets muddled, when I sleep." His eyes fluttered closed again, and his voice came softly. "*It's changing.*"

It certainly was. I was not sure if it was him, or Rachel.

I was not sure which I wanted for him. In this last moment.

"Just rest, then," said Francis Xavier. "Just . . ." He raised the pale, dirty hand and pressed it against his lips.

Talis opened his eyes. He looked from one to the other of us, and his gaze suddenly sharpened from bleary to raven-bright. "What's happening?"

"Francis Xavier and I have been discussing our course of action," I said. "How to minimize our exposure, given that our enemies know where we are."

A three-pronged dilemma: to stay here was untenable. To

move Talis was impractical. To leave him was unthinkable.

But in every dilemma, one prong must give, and so I was thinking the unthinkable. I was prepared to explain, but Talis was smart. Far less so than he had been, of course, but still: he was smart. I watched his face as he worked it through, at human speeds. And I saw the point where he began thinking it too.

He reached out for me. I lifted the hand and checked his pulse: still a bit faint, and suddenly fast. It trembled like a bird. "We would never leave you."

"Thank you," he said.

We never would. To slip away would be emotionally easier for us, perhaps, but much, much uglier for him. I opened my fingers to show him the syringe. "We would never leave you. I have painkillers."

He looked grateful for an instant, then realized what I was saying. "Oh, to hell with *that*."

"Talis—" I was ready to lay out the case.

He cut me off. "Greta, honey: you know the guy who wrote 'Do not go gentle into that good night'? I once shanked him in a bar fight."

"Dylan Thomas wrote that. He died in 1953." They could not possibly have met.

"Metaphorically, Greta," he said. "Metaphorically." I think he would have sighed if he could have managed the rib movement. "I'm saying that dying quietly's not in my . . . idiom. I'm not letting you overdose me."

"It's not up to you," I said. "And it's already decided."

"Oh, don't be ridiculous."

"I'm not." Talis had never had any trouble reading faces: he would know I was serious.

"Okay, then: *do* be ridiculous. Didn't I leave you with anything ridiculous?"

He hadn't. He knew he hadn't.

Talis yanked free of both of us and tried to push himself up. I saw his wrist lock, his arm tremble. Sweat sprang up on his face. Then his elbow buckled and he fell. Just a few inches, but hard. He was suddenly so pale that he had freckles I'd never seen before.

"Easy," Francis murmured. "Easy." He slipped his hands under the narrow shoulders and helped Talis settle back against the bed we'd built him.

"*Et tu, Francis?*" said Talis, gulping down pain. "Come on. You're the most loyal person I know. You wouldn't sign off on this." The snow melting on his face gave the illusion of tears.

"Can you hold him, FX?" I asked.

Francis Xavier's face was stiff as leather. "Hold him how?"

"Just the arm. Straight out, so I can reach the interior of the elbow."

"Now?" said Francis Xavier. His voice cracked.

I had dragged out a syringe—so old-fashioned, but still the best way to move things intravenously—for a reason. If I needed to inject Talis against his will, then I wanted to hit a vein. It was by far the most efficient way to do it: the venous system would bring the blood and the drug quickly to the heart's right side. From there it would hit the lungs, and then be pushed by the more powerful left side of the heart up into the aorta. It would be in the brain ten seconds after it left the needle. He'd be groggy in fifteen seconds, unconscious in thirty.

I wanted to minimize any terror he might feel.

"FX," I prompted.

"You cannot be serious," said Talis, his eyes wide. "You're not serious."

"Just the arm, Francis," I said.

Francis Xavier took Talis by the wrist. He lifted the hand gently, kissed the palm. Then, slowly, he pulled the arm out straight.

"Don't you dare," snarled Talis. He tried to lunge up, and went pale. His EM spiked and dipped, and then—

He vanished.

"Francis?" said Rachel.

I paused in the act of pushing up Talis's sleeve.

Francis Xavier closed his eyes as if hiding from something. "Please, Talis: Don't."

"Don't talk to him," said Rachel softly. "Talk to me."

Had Talis—could Talis—let Rachel surface as a strategic move? If it *was* a strategy, it was a good one. Even I was forced to consider: Talis might only be a copy, but Rachel was not.

Mitigating that was the fact that she was already doomed.

Still. I could see the veins of the anterior forearm beneath the skin. All three were visible, the basilic, medial, and cephalic coming together into a runic W inside the elbow. Rachel had good veins, for this sort of thing. I did not know when I had ever seen a body held so open, so vulnerable. In any normal person, it would evoke pity.

Francis Xavier held Rachel's wrist clamped and his eyes squeezed fiercely shut.

"Francis," said Rachel. "Look at me."

"Talis," Francis Xavier hissed. "*Don't.*"

"It's not him. It's not, I promise it's not. Look at me."

Francis Xavier opened his eyes. And for a moment the two of them just looked at each other. There are only seven basic microexpressions: happiness, sadness, fear, anger, disgust, surprise, and contempt. Oddly enough, there is no facial expression that unambiguously shows love. Or grief. Or regret. Or duty. They are not ancient enough, not animal enough, to have become involuntary.

They are too human.

"You know my carving's almost finished," said Rachel.

He looked down to where his hand was locked around her wrist, hiding her Rider's tattoo. "I know."

"And yours . . . ?"

Francis Xavier shook his head.

"You've still never been ridden," Rachel said.

"Still a virgin." Francis Xavier gave a very small laugh and turned his face aside, blushingly. "And with this one you can't help me, my small girl. . . ."

"You're frightened," she said. "It's not so bad. It's like dreaming."

Francis Xavier shot a look in my direction. "She's AI," he warned Rachel. "She'll record . . ."

Then it was true: the Riders were keeping something secret.

Rachel too looked at me. A Talis-like blue intensity came out of those eyes, but the set of the face was not his. It was strange, to see Talis so transformed and yet be unable to pinpoint the difference. There must have been something human left in me after all, something that could look into the eyes and see the soul, not look into the database and assign the probability.

When Rachel looked at me, I was sure of what she was. What made the hair come up on my scalp was that for a moment I was not sure of what *I* was.

Her glance and my prickle of fear lasted only a moment. Talis sometimes had eyes only for me. Rachel, *in extremis*, had other fish to fry. I saw the fingers of her trapped hand curl, as if she'd hold on to FX—but if that was her intent, it didn't work. His hand was rigid as a shackle at her wrist. "Francis," she whispered. "Why are you doing this?"

"I—" In the silence I watched the snow fall onto the little swirled knots of his hair, the nape of his neck, vanishing into his warmth as if falling into water. It was a long moment before he lifted his head and looked at Rachel again. "I can't watch you die, Rachel Jean. When it's not even *you*."

"And this is better?"

"No." Francis Xavier's voice cracked and the word seemed to break something inside him. He let go and folded up, as if around pain. He put the heel of his hand to his eye, banged the blunt top curve of his pincer between his eyebrows.

For a moment Rachel and I both watched him shake.

Then he said, blindly: "I will carry you. As far as it takes."

He uncovered his eyes. And it was Talis who met them. The AI drew out a smile as if it were a knife and said: "Good."

10
FIGURES ON A SNOWY GROUND

"**W**ell." I frowned at Francis. "If we're not going to kill him, what are we going to do?"

Francis Xavier did not seem to be listening. He looked as if someone had kicked him in the stomach. Talis scrubbed at his eyes. "Let me think: I'm thinking. Don't kill me while I'm thinking."

"I wasn't asking *you* . . ." It still seemed to me that killing Talis was a reasonable option, but it would be hard to do without Francis's obedience, and a glance at the Swan Rider told me I wouldn't have it.

"There's a refuge," said Talis. And then paused. "Isn't there? I can't . . ."

If you want to know, he'd said to me, over and over, *just know.* And now he couldn't. That must be very strange for him.

"Thirty-six point five miles, if we take the southern ford.

A bit more if we backtrack, but the terrain is more even. Francis?" I wanted his evaluation, but he was looking at me blankly, as if he hadn't heard a thing. "Francis!"

He flexed his shoulders to reset himself. His pincer went *clink*. "A hard day's ride. Two, in the snow."

"Three or four days, then . . ." A reasonable estimate, given that Talis couldn't even sit up. "That's a long way to go to no purpose. Is there a plan?"

"Sure," said Talis. "My short-term plan is not to die."

"Is there a long-term plan?"

"Peace on earth, goodwill toward men," said Talis, with a stagger in his breath that should have been a sigh. "See, it's only the middle bit that's always giving me trouble."

The snow was falling faster now, heavy and thick and straight down. The horses, bunched together by the wall, were like shadows cast on a scrim.

"Going to the refuge seems predictable." I glanced at Francis Xavier. Emotional turmoil aside, he had a fine military mind.

"Yes."

I flipped my hand at him, the inverse of a Swan Rider's salute. *Give me more.*

"Yes," said Francis Xavier, who was very definitely not crying. "Of course it's predictable. There's nowhere else to go." He swallowed. "On the other hand, they hardly need to ambush us."

True. If Sri and her people had plans for a next step, there was little we could do to outrun or evade it.

"Look," said Talis. "We could at this point be defeated by a pair of determined goats, or a toddler with a stapler. The refuge gives us options. A tissue knitter." He tapped his chest. A tissue knitter could repair the torn muscles, give him some relief for what must be overwhelming pain. "There's heat. Weapons. Communications. We could call in a shuttle."

I didn't have to say it, because Francis Xavier intoned it, the verse from the Utterances: "*Shuttles can be shot down.*"

"Don't quote me at me," Talis snapped. "So what if they do shoot? I have stage three scarring, I've lost three quarters of my mind, people I love keep trying to kill me, and I'm going to catch a *cold*. I fail to see how much worse this could get."

"Greta could be killed," said Francis Xavier. He didn't sound as if he cared particularly.

Talis sighed a long, careful sigh. "Right. When you ask if things could possibly get worse, the answer is always yes. Greta, make a note."

I made a note.

"We could call in an airstrike instead, I guess," said Talis. "Anybody got something they want to blow up?"

"Saskatoon," I said.

They both looked at me.

"What?"

I had only been quoting Talis, who had been in the middle of proposing the destruction of Saskatoon when the EMP shot had felled us all.

"Greta . . . ," murmured Talis. It sounded like the start of a question, but he let it drift away. When he said my name again it was faint, an impression of his voice, fading like a handprint from memory foam. "Greta Gustafsen Stuart . . . what happened to you?"

Odd that he didn't remember: "You did," I told him.

What followed was a rather challenging few days.

The snow fell, and fell, and fell. It was four inches deep before we could get going, and it only deepened. It was so deep that Francis Xavier had to walk in front of the horses, to lead them, to break the trail.

I doubled Talis, both of us riding Gordon, who was big and steady. The horse seemed to be doing his best to set his feet smoothly. But still, Talis was struggling. When Francis Xavier lifted him onto the horse, for instance, his sympathetic nervous system lit up like roads on a smartmap. Sometimes when I looked at him I was sure I saw someone else in his eyes, someone young and hurting. The way he curled up against Francis Xavier's chest made me wonder if it was Rachel. But it could have been that anyone that purely helpless would have bent toward that strength.

The snow thickened until it narrowed the world. It deepened until even the horses were stumbling. Every time they did Talis seemed jolted to speech, single syllables breaking against his teeth. His consciousness flickered; his mastery of the brain he had borrowed seemed to cut in and out.

Francis Xavier was struggling too. To stomp a path through knee-deep snow for a mile is a feat. To do it for more than a mile is an act of desperate, teeth-gritting endurance. Francis Xavier gritted his teeth and endured.

FX was staggering with exhaustion and Talis was pale as buttermilk by the time the short day gave out. We had not made the refuge, of course. The evening niceties were short. We ate. Francis Xavier threw up from exhaustion. I checked on Talis, found the stab wound tearing open, and dumped in as much forcescar powder as I dared. Then I wrapped his chest tightly in bands of crinkle silk. It was crude—stupidly crude. But it was the best I could do.

That done, we huddled together under all three crinkle sheets. We lay with Francis Xavier on one side breathing deep as a lion and radiating heat, me on the other side shivering, and Talis in the middle spiking a fever out of sheer neurological overload. The horses gathered around us in the snowy darkness. We slept badly.

The next day we did it again.

And then the next.

I spent the fourth day watching us from above, through the sweeping eyes of the spy satellites: a figure wrapped in blue in the white world, leading three horses. On the lead horse, a rider, her cloak billowing, with a body in her arms. I could see the trail we left, and the snow closing over it. I could see us from far, far above, just dark silhouettes, then specks against the roll and dip of the prairie.

I could see the whole face of the continent turning beneath the sweep of the blizzard. The earth turned under me. I could see the humped ruin of downtown Saskatoon, the scar of the rail line, the terraced fields of the Precepture, softening in the snow. And farther, further. Past the remaining Great Lakes, past the marsh of lost Erie, I could see the little faceted thing that was Halifax, the city where I had once been born, and then the restless blank of the ocean.

My country. One of the first things Talis had taken from me. I drifted over it. I let it go.

So many of the AIs died. They clung to their humanity until it twisted inside them like a blade, until the skinning broke their minds, and their bodies ended up seizing in the grass.

But others walked away. They walked out of their humanness. They vanished into worlds inside the Matrix Boxes, worlds made of pure data. They rose.

I was floating. I was weightless, the way falling people are weightless. I looked down on the storm, on the city and the ocean. It was dark over the Atlantic; getting dark in Halifax. The streets glittered like a net of pearls. And at the Precepture, figures in white were taking evening rest under the glass roof of the great hall. Two by two in their little boxes. One of them alone. Li Da-Xia, lying awake on her bed.

Small.

Still.

Like a specimen in a jar.

I heard my own voice say, "Xie?"

"Greta?" It was Francis Xavier. "I think we're home."

I looked back into the world in front of my human eyes. And saw the door in the hill.

Francis Xavier reached up and pulled Talis out of my arms, letting him slide sideways into a gentle embrace. I swung to the ground. Snow overtopped my riding boots and made a ring of cold around my shins. It was drifted and blank, unbroken.

This was such a likely spot for an ambush, but if anyone was here, they'd been here so long that their tracks had filled in. At least half a day. Far more likely that no one was here at all.

And yet . . .

I stood in the perfect quiet of the prairie, with my eyes that could see the whole spinning world. Snow was falling onto my shoulders. Cosmic muons were raining around me, sparking through my fingertip sensors a few times a second. As they should be. I stretched my hands out in front of me and charted the way the muons eddied and bent. A weak electromagnetic field was drifting out of the hill.

"There's EM in there," I said.

"The power's on," translated Francis Xavier.

We looked at each other. We looked at Talis, half conscious in FX's strong arms. "We can't go farther," said FX.

"We can. But he can't. So."

Francis Xavier looked at me.

I looked at the silent door.

Then I nodded.

After four days in the snow, we needed refuge. There was nowhere else to get it. The best we could do was go in with as much hope—and as much sudden violence—as we could muster.

"Quietly, then," said Francis. "Back the horses off." I backed the horses off. Francis Xavier trailed me, walking backward, cat-footed. Gently he put Talis on his feet. The AI wobbled. In truth, though, he alone among us was a little better: healed in part by what little medical care I'd been able to give him, in part simply by the passage of time. Still, I reached to steady him.

"What's happening?" he muttered, leaning into me.

"We've made the refuge. But someone's here, we think."

"Oh." Talis let go of me. He was bent forward, curled around himself, and it didn't look as if he could even lift his head. But that didn't mean he wasn't thinking hard. "Greta," he said, looking at the snow burying his boots. "You should go. You and Francis, both. Mount up and go."

But just then, with Talis in the middle of what might have been his first gesture of self-sacrifice in 526 years, Francis Xavier gave a huge shout and kicked in the refuge door.

A buttery glow spilled out into the lavender cold of the evening. I could smell garlic, leeks. In the cozy interior, someone was standing with his back to the door, working at the metal table. The intruder was tall, of a medium skin tone, with dark and curly hair. A young male, based on the stance. Dressed like a trommeller, crazy-quilted clothes in bright colors, billowing but cinched tight at the waist and wrists. We had caught him making soup. He spun around, spoon in hand, as the door crashed into the wall.

Even with all the clues, I was still surprised to see his face. "Hey," said Elián Palnik. "Took you long enough."

Francis Xavier surged through the door like a wolf lunging. He slammed Elián up against the wall, and in an eye-blink had him pinned there, hand against wrist, hips against hips, pincer grabbing on to Adam's apple.

It looked very much as if Elián was about to get his windpipe crushed. And yet he was looking at me—and at Talis. "Wow," he gulped, his voice made raspy by the pressure on his throat. "You look like shit. I mean, when I showed up at your Precepture they stuck electric spiders in places I don't like to mention in front of the ladies, and after months of that I *still* looked better than you."

"I'm crushed that you don't find me attractive," said Talis. "Francis, kill him."

And Francis looked to me. His stance said he was ready to pop Elián's head off like a champagne cork, but his eyes were all questions.

They were good questions. Calgary. Saskatoon. Elián. Sri. Were they connected? We'd been ambushed and Talis had been stabbed and right here was the boy with the knife. They were very good questions.

"Ease up," I said. "Let him breathe." Slowly Francis Xavier backed off. Elián sagged and coughed.

"Awww," said Talis. "I want to kill him."

"Well, we're not going to." I took Talis's elbow and wrapped the other arm around his waist. We limped forward until he could clutch the doorframe to steady himself.

Francis Xavier, meanwhile, was frisking Elián—rather roughly—and confiscating both the dagger on his belt and the wooden spoon in his hand. Elián took it with his trademark grin. "Missed the memo where they don't listen to you anymore, Michael?"

"Oh, give up on the 'Michael' thing," said Talis, who was pressing a hand to his breastbone, trying not to wheeze. "First: it's not an insult. Second: do I look like a Michael? Third: Greta, why can't we kill him?"

"I'm—" What was I? Something very small was stirring, as if I'd swallowed a corn snake. I felt wiggly. "I'm curious."

"Well, of *course* you are," said Talis. "I, on the other hand, am cold."

"I don't have the shelter secured," said Francis.

"You're thinking, what—infrared pulse bombs? He's a sheep farmer. It's a hole made of dirt." Talis made a little frowny face and let go of the doorframe. He came across the room in two steps and grabbed a chair. He sat astride it, backward, folding his hands over the chair back and leaning his chin on them. Theater, pure theater—disguising the fact that leaning was the only way he could have stayed in a chair without help. He regarded Elián with a good humor. "Okay, Greta. Satisfy your curiosity. Let me know when you're getting to the part that has knives."

How strange this was, how strange. The rounded little space, with its framing of bare tree branches, its whitewashed plaster walls. Such a small place, balanced against the turning, glittering world that spun in my head. Against the view of Halifax from above. And yet it drew my attention in, and slowly I let the satellites go.

This place. A warm place, like a nest. A good smell. Elián, whom once I had loved. Talis, whom once I had—I tried to remember. Hated? Feared? And (he kept refusing to be "incidentally") Francis Xavier, standing with Elián's dagger ready in his hand.

"Elián," I said. "What are you doing here?"

"I came to see you," he said. "There aren't many places to go from that hilltop. The others—Sri thought you'd come here."

"Did she?" said Talis. "And where is my old friend Sri?"

"Like I'd tell you."

"Oh, you might," drawled Talis. He stretched a hand toward Francis Xavier, who put the dagger into the upturned palm. Talis closed his grip around the handle one finger at a time. "It would be *so* interesting to find out."

"Talis, don't." My tone was a bit off: it sounded as if I'd said: "Sit, boy."

Talis raised an eyebrow at me. "Sorry, dear. Do go on."

"Can I have my spoon back?" said Elián. There were purple indents on either side of his Adam's apple. "The soup will burn."

I considered. The risks seemed minimal. The soup smelled good. "Give him his spoon," I said to Francis.

Francis held out the spoon without lowering the knife. Elián took it gingerly. I pulled a chair out and sat down across the table.

There were carrots sliced into coins on the cutting board, and they seemed like the brightest thing I'd seen in months. Elián stirred the soup. He bent over the pot, his chin tucked, his dark curls spilling onto his forehead. Once I'd kissed him in the part of that hair. AIs did not remember. They relived. The warmth and roughness of the kiss, the smell of it, the body helpless in my arms.

"Elián," I said, watching him put the carrot slices in the soup, one at a time, like coins into a well. "Elián. Why are you here?"

"Remember when you saved me?" he said softly. "Thought I'd try and return the favor."

"Angels and ministers of grace defend us," said Talis, bowing his head and digging his fingers into his hair in mock despair. "Elián Palnik made a *plan*."

"A plan?" I asked Elián. "Did you?"

But instead of answering, he asked again, in a roughened whisper: "Greta: Do you remember?"

Did I? I did, and I did not. I had lost none of the data. I remembered—Elián had come to the Precepture in chains, he'd stayed defiant. In return they'd hurt him. Just a little, but over and over, until he fell apart. I remembered watching him walk down the slope to the potato patch like a machine with a software fault.

Like a machine.

Just a little, they'd hurt him—that was what I'd thought at the time. It occurred to me now that I did not actually know. What had been done to Elián was part of the Precepture records. If I wanted to know, I could just know.

I felt an unfamiliar hesitation on the point: did I, in fact, want to know?

"Careful," said Talis softly. He'd stopped watching Elián and was watching me.

And once he would have been right. Once, even remembering Elián, let alone dwelling on the memory, would have been dangerous. The skinning, the feedback loop of memory building to a fatal overload. In my first days as an AI, remembering things had been like walking out on a fabric stretched above a void. There had been a give to my memory—fragility, danger, fear.

But since then. Since then.

I remembered Talis using ultrasound cascades to arrest the feedback loops. One little, one big, one catastrophic. I'd refused him, I'd fought him, but he—

Don't be human, he'd said, and he turned me into light. And since then . . .

"I remember," I said. But did not quite know what I meant.

"Okay," said Talis brightly. "I've got a question." I hadn't seen him so cheerful since—well, since Elián had stabbed him. Having a knife in his grip and someone handy to murder had done wonders for his mood. "The blood," he said. "Was it hot? Did it get into those little wrinkles between your fingers? How many times did you have to scrub them, to get it all out?"

Elián stared at him. "What the hell are you talking about?"

"The moment you stabbed me." Talis was broadcasting false surprise. "Pivotal for you, I should think. Me too, obviously, but, hey, I'm feeling generous, so let's focus on you. I'm talking about that bit when the blade pops through the muscle into the squishy parts. I'm talking about *sitting* there and watching someone *suffocate* from the inside out. Not your usual thing, surely? So what does it take, hmmm, to make an idealistic young sheep farmer go that far?"

"Seriously? You're fuzzy on why I hate you?" said Elián.

"Nah, course not," said Talis, waving a hand. "I had you tortured. I mean, not me personally, but if they'd asked me I would absolutely have signed off. I squeezed Grandma Wilma in that apple press until she popped like a zit. And I turned your girlfriend here into a right little psychopath— no offense, Greta."

"None taken."

"On the other hand," chimed Talis, "I'm an AI whose emotional responses and ethical instincts may or may not be an elaborate self-delusion. I'm a monster. And also, just incidentally, *I'm trying to save the world*. What's your excuse, human? What exactly made you decide to get your hands all messy?"

"It's an experiment," said Elián, stirring the soup.

"Oh, that's fine, then," said Talis. "As long as I got vivisected for *science* . . ."

"I want to see if an AI can learn to be human again."

"O . . . kay," said Talis. "Greta, perhaps you could explain to Elián the flaw in his brilliant plan to mutilate you for the good of your immortal soul. I've got a feather bed with my name on it." He tried to get up then, and the voice that broke from him was not quite his. "Francis—help me?"

Francis Xavier came and helped him. And Talis came fully back. "Greta, do wake me if you decide to kill him; I don't want to miss it. And you, my little monster," he added, pointing at Elián. "Remember what they say: fool me once, shame on you, fool me twice, and I'll kill you and everyone you love."

Elián was looking at me as he answered. "Too late, Michael. You already did."

Shortly after that, Francis Xavier tied Elián to the table.

The Swan Rider was protective, always, but he also was staggering and snarling with exhaustion, and there was so much to do. First and most urgently, I found the tissue knitter and managed the medically challenging process of running it on a half-healed wound, tearing Talis apart so I could put him back together. Talis attempted to keep quiet and still and succeeded at neither. Fortunately, it wasn't long before he fainted, sinking limp into the feather ticking, lost in it like a corpse in the snow.

Meanwhile Francis brought the horses into the stable, rubbing them down, making them drink a little, giving them some of the oats from the refuge's cache. He took off his prosthesis and its liner, put ointment on his blisters. He choked down a piece of jerky and a bit of water. And then he lay down on the cold stone floor, at Talis's side, turning his face to the sleeping form and his back to the room.

I took two steps away and watched the pair of them.

Francis's outflung hand was curled into a fist. He was awake. Breathing. Guarding us. But even as I watched, the hand softened and the breathing smoothed out. Four days breaking path in deep snow: the Swan Rider had walked clean off the outer edge of his endurance. I'd been spared that but still felt a heaviness in my bones, a chill in my torso. I was fatigued. But FX and Talis—they were exhausted.

I glanced at Elián, who was tied standing up. The thin strip fastening his wrist to the table looked fragile but was in fact smartplast with coded magnetic adhesion. He had no hope of breaking it. And only fingertip pulses—mine, Francis's—could undo it.

Even if Elián's plan was to stab me, even if I couldn't wake FX in time, I was safe enough.

"Your hair's growing out," Elián said.

It had been sixteen days since Xie had clipped my hair back to the scalp so that I could be bolted to a table to die. If it had grown out, it was only enough to make me look like a mange victim. But Elián was smiling at me.

"I like it. I remember it being all carrots but it's almost like honey."

I wondered how long he had been at the refuge. If he had been lying in wait for us. If he was also shivering with fatigue, and if so how he might rest, tied like that.

"Greta?" he said. He reached toward me, and with the movement the scent of him hit me. "Please talk to me."

I could smell him, and I remembered something: the metal table Elián was standing beside was also a kitchen. There were knives in the drawer. I took a step back. Elián tried to follow but the tie on his wrist brought him up short.

"Greta," he said again.

"Would you really stab me?" I said. "What you did to Talis. Is that what you want to do to me?"

Elián tried to reach me. His fettered hand was stretched out taut behind him. He was pulling too hard on it: his wrist was dented and swelling against the edge of the strap.

My hands had once been strapped down, just so . . . I flinched at the memory, jerked as if shocked.

"You've got to know I wouldn't hurt you," said Elián, softly as if afraid of spooking me. "Never, Greta. Do you remember that?"

"I remember everything. I have lost none of the data."

"Yeah?" Elián drawled, as he did when angry. I turned and watched the horses in the shadows past the half-wall, shifting and chewing and nosing each other. "What have you lost, then?" His words stung the side of my face. "Because I've gotta tell you, Princess. You've lost something."

"I didn't *lose* it," I snapped. "Talis *took* it."

Out of nowhere, I was furious. Charges built in my hands. Bolts of uncollimated ultrasound shot everywhere, my fingertips crackling like sparklers. Gordon Lightfoot picked up his head and stamped.

"He took it, Elián: Talis took it. And I fought, I tried—" Words fell out of me. "I fought. I fought like you used to fight, Elián. I fought even though it hurt me. Even though I couldn't win. Don't tell me I've lost something."

"Oh, Greta," breathed Elián. His free hand came to his mouth. "Oh . . ."

"He took it," I whispered, "and I didn't say he could."

Furious, yes. And not with Elián. I wanted to throw myself into his arms.

But I could not bear to be near him.

This was what Talis had taken from me. My human self. Love. He'd taken it because it was burning through me. It was burning through me. If I touched Elián, I thought, I would burst into flames.

"Why did you come here?" I rattled, desperate. "Why did you come, Elián? Talis will kill you." What he'd done to Wilma Armenteros in the apple press. That bad. Worse.

Talis would take one more thing.

Elián twisted his face into an imitation of his usual grin: "I was sorta counting on you to stop him."

The grin was a lie; the microexpression was terror. He was terrified. I was terrified. "I can't," I said. "I can't stop him—"

"You can. Look, I know I don't know anything about AIs, but I'll bet you're way better at being one than he is." I wrapped my arms around myself. Elián dragged on the table, straining to reach me. His free hand was a millimeter shy of my face. I could feel it in a shiver of fine hairs and electrical fields, a shiver that went all over me. "Greta, please," he begged. "Let me go."

"Why did you come here?" I said. "After what you did to

Talis . . . Elián. Truly. Are you here to stab me?"

Elián stiffened. I remembered that when I'd met him he'd been boyish, strapping but soft. There was little soft about him now. He was bones and muscle; he was shaking.

"Elián?" I said.

His voice came out as a whisper. "Do you want me to?"

"I—"

I'd seen what it had done to Talis—I had seen his terror, his confusion, his pain. But it still seemed, for an instant, like quite a reasonable idea. I stepped forward, into Elián's enfolding arm. My fingers sparkled. I undid the tie on his wrist.

11
REENTRY

Elián staggered at his freedom, gasped as if I'd shocked him.

He wrapped both arms around me.

And I caught fire.

It was so much; it was too much. He'd held me like this too many times. Held me desperate and terrified, his lips on my ear, his cheek in my hair.

"Greta . . ."

"Don't," I said. "Don't."

AIs did not remember; they relived. Elián, sagging into me under the pumpkins, hurt and frightened, wrapping me up, his cheekbone on my temple: *I really do love your hair.* And my whole heart had turned in that moment. Turned against the Precepture, against Talis, against the only truth I'd ever known.

It turned now.

It turned *on*.

And it hurt. My hands hurt. My heart. My *head*.

Crushed against Elián, I heard myself whimper.

Talis—Talis was the only person I'd ever met who could smile while he burned. And this is what he felt: the missile impact of the memory, the plunge of the crash, the heat around his mind that was like the heat around a satellite reentering the atmosphere. A self cloaked in shock waves, and blazing.

That was me, now. I was burning.

I stood there, burning.

And slowly, slowly, I smiled.

I was burning, but I was not dying.

Elián. He loved my hair *now*. My hair was different. I was different. This was different. We were here, we were now.

Elián lifted his hands and framed my face, then swept his fingers over the place at my hairline where I still had faint circular scars. They were from the bolts that had held me in place, through the pain and terror and change of the grey room. Through the moment I'd died. Elián touched them gently, and for a moment I would have sworn that his fingertips were as electric as mine. He stroked my hair back from the scars, looked at me for a moment, and then pulled me close. My face was pushed into his shoulder. Near my heart I could feel his heart pounding, at a rate that must be near 90 percent of its safe intensity, as if he were running hard.

"Thank you," he said. "Are you okay?"

"I am," I said. "I really am. . . ."

I was aflame but the fire did not consume. I was shock wave and signal. I was blazing.

And Elián couldn't see any of it.

He could feel me find my feet, though, and after a moment he stepped far enough away to hold me by the shoulders, to look me in the eye.

"Hey, Princess," he said.

"Hello, farm boy. It's good to see you."

This was Talis's unteachable trick. This was survival. This was *AI*.

I thought of Elián's "experiment"—to teach an AI to be human again . . . *Explain to Elián the flaw in his brilliant plan*, Talis had said. And standing there, I spotted it.

"What you're proposing . . ." I pressed my hand against my own ribs, in the place where Talis had been stabbed. "It wouldn't work. I'm not like Rachel. My brain is more damaged. Much more damaged. I would die."

It didn't take an AI's expertise to read Elián. His face was like the sky, its weather plain. He looked bewildered, then angry. "I'm such a tool," he said. "Dammit. I'm gonna hang a big sign around my neck that says *use me*."

And I'm sure you'll have takers, said the ghost of Li Da-Xia, deep in my heart.

It was golden, having her back.

"Who told you it would work?" I asked. "Was it Sri?"

He didn't answer. Talis whimpered in his sleep. I heard the catch of his breathing.

"Elián," I said. "Why do they want him alive?"

"I can't—" He took a deep breath. "Greta. Do you trust me?"

"Not with long-term planning."

"What? Hey!"

"I am not a pawn. Not Talis's, not yours, not Sri's. It's not about trust. It's about making my own choices."

"Yeah." Elián raked his hand up the short hairs on the back of his neck. "I get that."

Someone had been using him. And it wasn't even *new*—someone had been using him since the moment his grandmother had pinned on her general's stars. Someone had lied to him about ways to save me, lied to him to get him here. Someone had put him in Talis's crosshairs.

And really, the most extraordinary thing about him was that he could stand in those crosshairs with steady feet and open eyes.

It was warm and dim in the refuge. Our coats hung like shadows on the wall. Francis Xavier's arm sat on the table, buckles gleaming like little candles. I could smell the garlic melting into the soup as it cooled. I could smell the human world. "If I can do this, Elián . . ." I tapped my datastore with my fingertips. "If I can do this, properly . . ."

"You can change the world." He put a hand out and put it opposite my hand, mine over my datastore, his over my heart. I could feel it beat where he was pressing.

"Tell me something," I said.

Elián stiffened, as if he were carrying something heavy.

The conspiracy; the rebellion. He thought I was asking him to betray it. He looked staggered, as if the weight were crushing.

But what he said was: "Anything."

"Not that," I said. "Tell me something about you."

"Me?"

"From before all this. Before the Precepture. Tell me something."

He looked bewildered. "Uh. I'm an only child."

"I knew that."

"Okay. Um. I had a pet raccoon once. I named her Daniel Boone, because I'm bad at sexing racoons. Or maybe I'm bad at naming. I'm a good cook but I put garlic in everything. Did you know that? Before . . . I liked cooking."

"You liked bowling," I said, remembering.

That surprised a soft laugh from him. "Yeah: I'm a demon with fifteen-pound balls." He paused. "That kinda came out wrong."

And I laughed. It had been so long since I'd laughed.

Francis Xavier turned over onto his back.

I dropped my voice and stepped close to Elián. He wrapped his arms around me and tucked his chin. "I've missed you," I said. I pushed a kiss against his forehead. His temple. I brushed my fingers over the bruise on his throat. "I've really missed you. But Elián. You need to run away."

"Not happening."

"Think about it. You took a knife to Talis. And we have communications here. When the Swan Riders hear what you did, when the AIs hear . . . Do you understand? Do you know what they will do to you, if you don't run away?"

"About that," said Elián. "I should tell you . . . I called them already."

I wrenched away from him. "You what?"

"I called the Red Mountains. I mean, I put it on a delay. But I think it's gone out."

"*Why?*"

"They—Sri gave me the frequency and stuff."

"Because she doesn't want Talis to die."

She really, truly didn't. There was something so sinister about that, a rush of chill in the heart. And suddenly I was thinking about how long a skilled torturer could keep someone alive. I was thinking about what would happen to Elián.

I spun around, pushing my hand into the squishy part of the controls, throwing my machine self deep into the comms system, commanding it not to send.

It was too late. The message had been queued yesterday, but it had gone out seventeen minutes ago. Like a missile spiraling in from orbit. Like a bomb dropped from a plane. There was no calling it back.

"What did you tell them?"

With a glitter of my fingers I grabbed the transcript. He hadn't told them much. A bare report of a Swan Rider team in trouble—possibly lost, at least one serious injury. A request for backup, for transport. They'd pinged back: asked for more details, demanded codes, tried four times, hadn't raised us, gotten irritated, and sent a rather cross notice that help was on the way.

On the way. Right now.

"Elián, why didn't you run?" I said desperately. "You put it on a delay. Why didn't you run?"

"Well," he said. "I was gonna. But I kept hoping you might show up."

"Run *now*," I demanded. Ridiculously. In this snow—the tracks, the slowness, the ease of surveillance on this open prairie. There was not nearly enough time. I found myself literally turning, casting about for a solution. My fingers pulled free from the communications gel with a pop.

Elián at the Precepture. He'd fought even though they'd hurt him. Even though he couldn't win. They'd hurt him and it had not been only a little. He'd said no and they'd taken everything from him, slowly stripped his defiance until he was— Oh, Elián.

"Hey," said Elián, taking my arm, pulling me in, helping me be still. "Hey, remember when you saved me?" He put a hand on my face. I could *feel* his fear, in his heart rate, in the conductivity of his skin. But he stood in the crosshairs, his eyes deep and steady. "What's happening to you, Greta—I'm not gonna pretend to understand it. But I do know you shouldn't have to do it alone."

"With no one who loves me."

"Yeah," he said, all bravery and all heartbreak in a single word. "Yeah. That."

I let myself stand there, for one moment, with my sensors

reading his skin, with our two hearts beating equally fast. Somewhere between 90 and 95 percent of safe intensity. Two human hearts. Signaling. Blazing.

I let myself stand there one moment, and then it was time to be AI again, and in charge.

"Talis," I said. "Wake up."

I stepped over Francis Xavier and shook Talis, hard, by the uninjured shoulder.

He groaned and batted at me.

"Wake up," I said. "Come on, I need you."

He blinked. The bruise on his cheekbone was ripening and spilling upward to begin a black eye. He rubbed at the other eye and bleared at me. His face was lopsided as Gordon's, and he looked pale, young, battered. Human.

"Talis?" A question, because I wasn't sure.

"Is it really morning?" he groaned. "I blame the turning of the earth. And also, since you're handy, you."

"It's five a.m., actually, but you've got to wake up," I said.

"*Five?* No. No, I do not get up at five unless something is literally on fire. And like, a big something. Or my hair." He closed his eyes. "I've had a long day. Go away."

Not promising, but the glittery temper was at least unambiguously not Rachel's. It was Talis's.

No—it was Michael's.

The Michael thing, I thought. Not an insult. Not an intimacy—or not merely. I called him that because I needed to remember that there was a human inside the machine. If there was anything left of the creature who had been Talis, it was surely the human part. And so I shook his shoulder again, sharply.

"Michael, I need you. There's a ship coming. Elián called the Red Mountains."

"Really?" Talis—Michael—opened his eyes, dragged himself up on his elbow and peered at Elián. He was fully dressed but bedraggled as a cat in a bath, and similarly disgruntled. "That's a bit shortsighted, even for you, isn't it?"

Elián crossed his arms, his whole body shutting. "I've got my reasons."

"Yeah, and I've got people who can drag them out of you." Michael reached for my hand and I eased him up so that he could sit on the edge of the feather tick. He looked as if he were rising from his deathbed, which was not really a stretch. "You said they're incoming now, G?"

My brain was full of scramble schedules, rocket telemetry. "Absolutely."

"So you woke me for the bit with the knives."

"Michael, you're not hearing me. Elián Palnik is under my protection. I want your help to save him."

"Well, that's a twist." Michael nudged Francis with a toe. "Wake up, big guy, we've got company coming."

Francis Xavier woke with a huge gasp. His head came up from the floor and then banged back down into it as he saw only the three of us and nothing on fire. He rolled onto his back as if too exhausted to change his view of boots and bare ankles. "Hey, Francis," said Michael.

"You'll never guess. Elián here called in a shuttle."

"What?" said Francis Xavier. "Why?"

"Yeah, not to mention *how*? They'd never deploy without a Rider's security codes." He flipped a look at Elián. "Sri's orders, I'm thinking?"

"I'm not telling you anything," said Elián.

"Oh, not me. But there are people in the Red Mountains who can pull your mind apart engram by engram. And I bet they'll let me watch."

"Talis!" My voice—only a human voice would break like that. I swallowed and tried again. "Michael. Please."

Silence.

"I'll start breakfast," Francis Xavier murmured, and staggered upright. It was hard to blame FX for wanting out of the middle of this, but it was somewhat strange to be deep in a life-and-death negotiation while someone mixed an oat porridge in the background.

"You really mean it," said Michael. "He's got my lung tissue under his fingernails and you really want me to help save him."

"I do."

"What changed? I've only been asleep for—" There was a skip in his voice where he tried to reach for the current time and failed. "I. Where are my glasses? Help me up. Let me look at you."

I handed Michael his glasses (they were on a little ledge beside the bed) and carefully hoisted him to his feet. He wobbled and clung to my arms. We were that close together. I tried, with my whole mind, to read the delicate chain of emotion that looped across his face as he examined mine. Surprised. Evaluating. Hopeful. His eyes went from me to Elián and back again. His look softened. "My ears and whiskers, Greta," he said, almost reverently. "You're blushing."

"I am not."

But I was. Shock wave and signal. Blushing and blazing.

"Give me a reason, then." His tone was coaxing. "Give me one good reason."

"Because I ask it," I said. "Because . . . you love me."

It was not quite what he was looking for, I could tell that much, but it must have been enough. He pulled free of me.

"Hmmm. Well." I could actually see him start to think: the electrical patterns shifting rapidly in his brain, that narrow-eyed sparkling look I'd thought might be lost forever. "I get that he's kind of adorable, but you can't protect him just with your say-so."

And he was right. There were rules about who an AI could and couldn't protect: razor-sharp, unbending rules. After all, we were meant to be the unsentimental, impartial protectors of the whole world. The system would crumble if we played favorites.

I wanted to change the world, and thought I probably could—but I probably couldn't start here.

"Oh, I know!" Michael turned to Elián: "Pledge fealty to her."

"What?" Elián looked bewildered.

"Try to keep up, Elián. Honestly. Greta, define 'fealty' for our visiting scholar here."

That was the kind of classroom request to which I would always respond. "Fealty is the duty owed by a vassal to a lord. A duke to a king, for example." I couldn't imagine Elián swearing fealty to, well, anything. Certain methods of barbecue, perhaps. I tried to soften it. "The root is the Latin *fidelis*, 'loyalty.' It's cognate with 'fidelity.' And 'faith.'"

"And it just might save your life," said Michael. "Pledge. Now."

"I—" said Elián.

There was a little clicking noise: Francis Xavier knocking the spoon against the soup pot. It was the FX equivalent of leaping to one's feet. "Elián," he said.

I would not have been much more surprised if FX had started yelling. But Elián did not know FX, and when Michael made a "shush" gesture, FX shushed.

I could feel the incoming rocket, now, its ground radar beating down on us. I could feel my heart pounding in my throat.

"I pledge—" said Elián.

I wasn't sure if he'd forgotten the word "fealty," or if even in the moment he found it a little much. He offered me both his hands, and I took them.

"Greta Stuart," he said. "I'm yours."

"Close enough," said Michael, clapping his hands together like a rifle shot. "By the power vested in me by, well, me, as ruler of the world et cetera et cetera, I hereby pronounce you AI and Swan Rider. You may now kiss the bride."

"Swan Rider?" said Elián.

"Oh, Elián Palnik," said Michael, lighting a smile like a long fuse, "here's where your life gets *interesting*."

And just at that moment, someone kicked in the door.

That poor door. Francis Xavier had kicked it in just yesterday, and we'd had to jam the snapped-off handle of a wooden spoon into the top hinge to keep it shut against the snow. Now the spoon bit was shattered and the middle hinge was hanging by one screw and the whole door was swaying like a wounded man. It let in a rectangle of dark and brilliant cold.

Framed against the snow was a single figure: a man with a crossbow in his hands. He slid in, keeping his back to the wall, his weapon up.

Everyone was standing, everyone was braced, but only Francis was armed. By which I mean he was holding the porridge spoon as if it were a javelin.

The stranger took us in, his eyes brightly fearless, his weapon just loose enough to be steady. He was young to look so deadly, and so at ease with deadliness, but then, I could see the wing tattoo wrapping his wrist. People with that mark were often unusual, and always young. "Hello, Swan Rider team in trouble," he said. "Gallant Rescue, at your service."

Beside me, Michael took in a breath with a hitch at the end of it.

The stranger had caramel skin of indeterminate geography (Persian? Pashtun?) liberally spattered with freckles, a beakish nose that had been broken at least once. His eyes were a startling green. Nothing about him was familiar, except that everything was.

"Gotta say," the Rider said, his weapon casually sweeping us, "I think you set a new record for vagueness of report. Bit irritating, to be called in without so much as a please and here's-my-pulse-code. But, congratulations, you got my attention. So, having got it"—and here he smiled: a weaponized smile—"what are you going to do with it?"

The geometry of that expression—eyebrow up twenty-three degrees, mouth part of a Fibonacci curl: purely I knew it.

"Talis," I said.

"Yup," he said, snapping the end of the word like an electric spark. "Give the new girl a gold star." Then suddenly, his attention zeroed in on me. "Wait, you're not a Rider, you're . . ." Active EM sensors sleeted through me, rudely prodding at the damage in my brain. There was only one way to endure that kind of damage and walk around afterward. "You're AI," he said softly. He sounded almost awed. His crossbow drifted out of line. "A new AI."

I put my hand on Elián's arm.

"Greta Gustafsen Stuart," said Michael. "May I present my better half?"

The new AI looked at his other self with widening eyes. "Oh, no, seriously?" Abruptly deciding there was no threat, he put his crossbow down on the table with a clang and a sulk. "You know I hate it when there are two of us. The pronouns make my teeth hurt."

Michael shrugged. "I think we'll cope."

Talis Mark Two was glaring. "Well, if you'd put fingertip codes into the distress call like everyone is *supposed to*, I'd—" And then something happened to his face: a draining, like life out of the eyes. The half-amused irritation sluiced away, revealing . . . was it shock? Disgust? "You can't, can you?"

Michael said nothing.

The new AI came across the room as if in fury and slammed his other self up against the wall. "You *can't*." He kept Michael pinned there with one hand and spread the fingers of his other hand as if they were medical equipment. He fanned them over the datastore a moment, scanning, then swept them sideways. He reached the place where Sri had once pushed her finger—and he too pushed. With three fingers. Hard.

Michael's whole body curled inward and Rachel flickered into his eyes. A little sound broke out of them.

"Don't hurt her!" said Francis Xavier.

Talis Mark Two flipped FX a look that said both *interesting* and *deal with you later*. He returned his attention to his counterpart. "You're broken," he said.

"It's *injured*, you ass."

"Nah, but that implies you might heal. Hate to break it, but—" He flicked his fingertips against the slick forcescar. They made a little tick.

Michael swallowed. Was there no way back for him, then? I was not sure that was true.

Meanwhile Talis Mark Two—just Two, my datastore decided, efficiently—had mastered whatever had brought him across the room like a hawk striking. He stepped back and said more softly: "What happened?"

Elián's skin charged under my hand.

Who could lie to an AI? There was an actual verse of scripture that warned us not to. But Michael did it without blinking. True, his body was tense, which was characteristic of deception, but he was both injured and emotionally stirred, and either could account for that tension. Michael wore that ambiguity like a mask. He did not even glance our way. "Well, obviously it's an intricate, epic tale of love and betrayal," he said. "But the short version is: Sri stabbed me."

"Sri." Two ran his tongue over his teeth.

"Yeah," said Michael, soft and hair-raising, "I call dibs."

"Huh." Two scrunched his nose, startlingly familiar. He sat down on the shelf. He was close to us now and Elián's pulse was racing under my fingers. "Well. That was a whacking great blind spot, wasn't it?"

"What was?" I ventured.

"My Riders," he said. "A Swan Rider, betraying me."

It hadn't exactly been *him,* but I took the point.

"Loyalty is more or less their defining characteristic, you know, like . . . well, like dogs." Another sharp smile. "No offense."

No one volunteered to claim any.

Two looked up at me, thoughtful. "Supposing you lived with a pack of hounds," he said. "And one day one of them . . ." He trailed off, seeming disturbed by the image. I could see where he might be. The Swan Riders outnumbered the AIs a hundred to one. They had intimate knowledge, intimate access.

"Francis Xavier!" Two's voice was sudden and sharp. "Perhaps you could introduce me to my new friends."

Francis Xavier—who'd been working, without much success, to close the door—turned around. He paused before answering. The pause did not look suspicious, because Francis Xavier would stop to consider his response if you asked him for directions to the nearest bathroom. "What do you know?" he said.

Two popped the air out of his cheeks. "Not much. The Cumberlanders took my Precepture, this one here went off to reclaim it, blew up Indianapolis for some reason, no huge loss there, then declared the matter resolved and sent for Riders. Gotta say, it wasn't much of a report."

"Yeah," said Michael. "Because life is all about paperwork. Don't scold me, you big ninny."

The AI shrugged off the point, though it was a fair one: being the same person (wasn't he?), he would presumably have done the same thing. "You asked for extra horses: I assumed we either had new recruits or someone in need of some . . . special treatment."

"Did that on-site."

"Mmmm-hmmm: Wilma Armenteros. Saw the vid. Very . . ." Two rolled the word round his mouth: ". . . neat."

I had seen the apple press, after. "Neat" was not an adjective I would have chosen.

"Anyhow," said Michael. He'd slipped between Two and Francis Xavier, and I didn't think Two had even noticed. "This is Elián Palnik, her grandson. He helped us, on-site—got the phone lines to the satellites unjammed."

"Interesting." The AI's gaze slid to Elián. His eyes were verdigris—the green of shipwrecked copper. Strange and deep. "This was voluntary?"

Elián stood in the crosshairs, his heartbeat almost a vibration. "Hell, no," he said.

". . . No?" said Two.

The bones of Elián's wrist rotated under my hand, and then he was holding on to my wrist as I was holding on to his, in the manner of ancient warriors. "I did it," he began, and then his voice cracked. "I did it to save Greta. They—my grandmother and her people . . . they hurt her. They were going to hurt her again. I did it for Greta. I'd never do it for you."

"Indeed." Two looked the pair of us over. If he'd been in Rachel's body, he would have fiddled with his glasses, peering over the top of the frames. "Call me paranoid, but I think I'm sensing some hostility here."

"Damn straight," said Elián.

One of these days, that rough-and-ready integrity of Elián's was going to get him killed.

Maybe even today.

Two clicked his tongue and tilted his head back at his other self. "And how is it this one's not dead?"

Michael tipped his head too, and for a moment the two of them were in perfect mirror image. "I'd be lying if I said I was never tempted."

"I mean," said Two, "these are the hostage children of two nations who declared war. There's supposed to be a big electromagnetic period at the end of that sentence. Grey room, quick death, quiet burial, end of story."

"She's AI, Talis," said Michael softly. "A new AI. She could have asked me for the moon. She asked for her friend. It's worth it."

Two paused. Frowned. Laced his fingers behind his neck and stretched his elbows backward, regarding us carefully. "No," he said.

Michael raised his eyebrows. "No?"

"Yeah, no." Two picked us off with his eyes. "He's terrified, she's teetering, and you—" He grinned at his other self. "You're lying through your teeth."

"No one has lied," said Michael.

"Because you all know better, I expect," said Two. "But you're lying without lying. Don't you think I know that little soft-shoe number when I see it? Fortunately, if you remember, I wasn't actually talking to any of you." He leaned back on his interlaced fingers, threw his command over our heads. "Francis Xavier."

Francis Xavier saluted him. "Talis."

"You trust this boy?"

Francis Xavier paused. "No."

"Is he a Swan Rider?"

If Francis said no, I thought, then Two would kill Elián on the spot. And Francis Xavier must hate Elián—Elián, who'd stabbed the woman FX loved. I held my breath.

Francis Xavier said: "Yes."

Two laughed, delighted. "Oh, this is good: a good story, I can tell. I cannot wait to recover this data."

"Recover . . . ?" said Michael. The word had caught his attention, as well it might.

"What can be implanted can be un . . . planted. Is that a word? Anyway." The AI slapped his own datastore as if it were a hand drum. "As I recall, there are knives in that drawer."

He was proposing that we remove Rachel's datastore surgically. Here. Now. Michael said nothing, moved not at all. But freckles came twinkling into his face like stars as he slowly paled.

"Kidding," said Two. "You think I'd want you screaming? Why would I? We'll be home soon enough." He stood up. "Someone put the horses in the spaceship. We're out of here."

12
SPACESHIP

No matter how beautifully trained they are, getting horses onto a spaceship is not easy.

It wasn't technically a spaceship, but rather a fast suborbital, one of those rare ships capable of both landing and launching without a magnetic rail. This one was small—no bigger than a bell tower—and looked fast. Its low-friction polymer skin shifted and swirled like quicksilver. Deep inside it, metal pinged as it cooled.

The horses took one look at the ship, perched on the opposite hill with the dawn sky lightening behind it, and decided against this plan.

Specifically, NORAD stopped dead. Her ears pointed at the ship, locked on target like one of the Rider's crossbows.

I was leading Gordon, and Francis Xavier was leading Heigh Ho Uranium. Two was leading Elián's horse (a pinto gelding that Michael had promptly christened Spartacus), which was probably a bad sign for Elián.

All three horses looked to NORAD and stopped with her. I tugged on the lead and sweet, steady Gordon Lightfoot set his feet and slashed his tail like a cat.

"It's all right, NORAD, sweetie," said Michael. He'd been leaning on my free arm. Now he pulled away, shivering in the pink light. He wrapped his slender fingers around the bridle's concho. "We're going home. We're just going home." He tried to pull NORAD forward. The horse pinned an ear and leaned away. Michael backed off, feeding the lead between his fingers and giving NORAD a few yards to run. She swung away from the ship and he led her around in circles, letting her work herself to calm.

It was good horsemanship—and a glimpse of that radical good-at-everything competence he had had as Talis. It was beautiful. Right up until the moment where NORAD caught sight of the ship again, swerved sideways, and yanked her wounded rider right off his feet.

Michael fell onto his chest in the snow with a great gasp, not quite a cry. The end of the lead whipped over his body and he rolled onto his back, curling up, clutching his wound.

Two looked down at him with both eyebrows raised. Francis Xavier started forward to help. Two stopped the Swan Rider with a hand on his chest and then handed off his horse. Francis Xavier took both leads in his one hand. He hadn't bared himself before Two, and therefore hadn't put on his arm. Even if this was a battle—and it felt like a battle—it wasn't the kind of battle where a crossbow would do us any good.

"Bring these two up to the ship," said Two. "I'll take care of the other one."

I hoped he meant the other *horse*.

And it seemed he did. Two caught NORAD's lead and did, effortlessly, what Michael had tried to do: let her run herself calm.

Gordon Lightfoot, meanwhile, found himself caught between his panicking herd leader, NORAD, and his retreating friends. He snorted a great blast of steam and pawed the snow, pacing backward. It was all I could do to hold him.

Which left Elián alone, standing over Michael, who was trying to get up out of the snow. The wounded man reached out for help and Elián looked at the hand as if it were full of spiders.

Michael narrowed his eyes. "I'm not poisonous to the touch, you know. It's not contagious or anything. Just *help me.*"

So Elián pulled Michael up and put an arm around his waist. They were of radically different heights, and so they made a crooked and halting trip through the snow, toward the ship.

At the hatchway we watched and waited while Two took NORAD in hand. He bribed her with apples that he pulled from his pockets like a magician. He leaned close and murmured something into her ears.

I wondered what the horse made of him. It was difficult enough for me, as an AI myself, to adjust to the idea that the person inside this new physicality was someone I knew. What hope had a horse? And yet NORAD let this person, who should have been a stranger, lead her up the clanging loading ramp and into the hold, let him wind an elaborate series of buckles and straps around her and slip cotton into her ears against the noise. Before the whole thing was over she was trying to eat his hair.

"You know," said Elián to Michael. "If you were half that nice to *people* they wouldn't try to kill you quite so often."

"Would you be happier if I kicked puppies? I'm *complicated*, okay? And I like horses. Horses don't pump sarin gas into each other's preschools. Horses don't use hunger as a weapon. Horses don't— You have no idea what I've seen, Elián Palnik. And no right to judge me."

"Half that nice," said Elián. "Just saying."

"There," chimed Two, who had also seen the poisoned preschools and the skeleton armies. "Horses, spaceship, don't get tired of saying that, off we go."

The rest of the horses followed NORAD onto the ship for the same reason the world followed Talis wherever he pointed: it seemed safest. We got them settled in the little hold, and then we went one by one up the ladder into the upper compartment. It was smaller still: eight chairs, looking as if they could handle significant accelerations, were set around an oval of empty decking. It was so strange to be inside: the small space, the hard, clean gleam of the surfaces. It felt like a long time since I had last boarded a shuttle.

One hundred eighty-four days, came the figure. Not so long, but I had died somewhere in there. That distorts one's impression of time.

Speaking of: "What about 'shuttles can be shot down'?" I asked Two.

"Well." He cracked open a grin. "Shuttles can be shot down, but weapon targeting systems can be taken out by a general EMP burst from low orbit."

"Um," said Elián, "won't that black out North America?"

"Just the western interior," he said, sulking. Then: "Is that over the top? I have trouble telling."

"I'll bet," said Elián.

"It's all fixable," said Two.

It wasn't: medical implants, industrial processes, simple accidents—the casualties would be in the hundreds.

Two must have known that, but he gave me one of Talis's sunny grins: so brilliant it was painful to look at. "Plus, it's a special occasion. A new AI!" He clapped me on the shoulder.

I rather wished he wouldn't.

Michael came off the top of the ladder bent over and gasping, the strain of using his arms (and thus chest muscles) to partly support his weight showing in his grey, sweaty face. Two wrinkled his nose in plain distaste and made no move to help. "I'll drive," he said, and popped up the last ladder.

Michael flopped into a chair and Francis Xavier sat beside him. When Elián and I took the seats across, we were almost knee-to-knee. And then—what were we? Enemies? Friends? Companions? We were alone.

Two piloted the ship (and I do not know why this surprised me) like a highly skilled maniac with superhuman reflexes and no fear of death. My datastore informed me primly that 3 Gs was considered a maximum safe vertical acceleration. We hit 2.97. At the top of it we banked, swerved like a swallow, and then all at once were drifting, our own momentum and the unresisted tug of gravity pulling us in a weightless arc down toward Montana.

My hands came floating up from my knees. My body drifted away from the seat, against the straps. We fell quietly. The rush of thickening air hummed through the ship's skin. The horses' complaints, muffled and echoing, drifted up from the deck below.

Francis Xavier leaned his temple into the side of the foam headrest as if leaning onto someone's shoulder. He looked sick with fatigue. Elián jiggled his foot. Michael had his fingers round the harness where it curved down over his right collarbone on its way to the central buckle.

"Is that hurting you?" I asked.

"A little," he said. "It's fine."

Francis Xavier put his hand on the armrest between them, a silent offer. Michael did not take it. He let go of the padded strap and ran the knuckle of his thumb back and forth under his collarbone, making a furrow in his shirt that plotted the top edge of his datastore.

"What will happen to you, if it's removed?" I asked.

Michael put his hand in his lap. He leaned his head back into the foam cradle and said nothing.

"It should be fine," said Francis Xavier. "The AIs—they implant datastores all the time. They're experts. You'll be fine."

"I'm not—" Michael stopped. What could the end of that sentence possibly have been? He closed his eyes and his voice went flat: "I have no input/output now. It might as well come out, I suppose. Should, in fact, if it's intact."

The finality of it, though . . .

His face was wiped blank. There was something strange happening to his aura.

"Intact?" echoed Elián. "Is it—I mean, will it be readable?"

"Ah," said Michael. His eyes came open, which should have made him easier to read, but mostly he looked tired. "There you go, Elián. We might teach you that pesky 'think it through' business yet."

I instantly saw their point: if the datastore was extracted, and the experiences Michael had had were uploaded, then . . . well. The last thing he'd seen was Elián's face: the knife going into him. What was status as a Swan Rider, next to that?

Michael had spared Elián because I asked. Because he cared about me.

But Two—

I caught Elián's widened eyes.

"We need to stop them from extracting it, then," I said.

"Yeah," said Michael. "Good luck with that."

His face was bleak, blank. Was he—I couldn't read it—was he frightened? He was not moving. He was not looking at anything particularly.

"Rachel?" said Francis Xavier.

"Don't—" said Michael. "Bad moment to distract me, Francis."

But his hand had slipped sideways, onto the armrest. Francis Xavier looked at it, then took it in his.

"When it starts, don't get up," Michael said, his voice flat but his words jammed together. "We're about to decelerate, and you could be injured if you get up."

"When what star—" began Elián, and then, just as I figured out what was going to happen, it happened. Michael's head snapped back into the cushion, the muscles in his neck hyperextending, his eyes wrenched wide open. He didn't scream, but he must have bitten something inside his mouth because suddenly there was blood on his lips and—

"What the hell!" shouted Elián.

Francis Xavier was twisting around as far as he could, inside his harness, trying to get the leverage to push Michael back against his seat so he couldn't damage himself. I strained forward against my harness, but the only thing I could reach was his knee.

The shuttle swerved. We were thrown sideways, and then, stomach-droppingly, upward. Michael was beyond noticing. His leg, under my hand, was rigid with opposing tremors.

Only their opposition was keeping him from shaking himself apart. His fingernails were denting bloody crescents in the back of Francis Xavier's hand. FX was twisted clear around, his stump wedged across Michael's torso. But really, neither of us could reach him properly. We kept our hands on him, but neither of us was doing him any good.

But then, it was Rider's Palsy. There was nothing we could do.

13
HOME

My cry for help didn't get us help ("Flying a spaceship right now!" Two had chirruped back when I'd screamed his name), and Michael's seizure was over by the time his counterpart came down the ladder with a slide and a hop.

Still, the AI took one look and knew—he came to his other self's side with impressive speed. Crouched. Slipped two fingers under the corner of the jaw, checking the pulse (and probably a dozen other things).

Michael opened his eyes. They were so altered that they were almost a different color. He looked lost, young, and completely human.

"The palsy," said Two. "Your first episode?"

Under the strong, strange fingers Michael's throat worked a minute—I guessed he was too dry-mouthed to swallow, too stunned to speak. He nodded, mute.

"Bad?"

A dazed laugh. "Not good."

"This is what Sri has," said Elián. He too looked dazed.

"This is what we all have," answered Francis Xavier. "It's Rider's Palsy."

"It looks . . ." Elián tucked his head and fussed with the buckle on his harness. "It looks tough."

Michael slid him a look. "Don't you dare comfort me, Elián Palnik."

Elián made a huffing snort, and a denial that I think might have been a lie: "Like I would."

Two arched both eyebrows at that little byplay. I tried to think of a way to remind the boys that they were supposed to be allies. Michael stabbed the release button on his harness savagely, but his knees buckled when he tried to get up.

Two closed his hands around Michael's—Rachel's— slim, muscled biceps and lifted his counterpart to his feet. His active sensors were on high, wrapping both of them like Guadalupe's cloak. Odd to think that only Francis and I could see it—it was so comforting, so lovely. Michael found his balance, but Two held on one more moment, and they seemed in perfect communion, wrapped in light.

Then Michael opened his eyes and glared at the room generally, a bit of Talis back in his eyes. He flicked his hands to shoo off the help. Two released him.

"So, yeah," he said. "Rider's Palsy: pretty much as advertised. Good to know. I feel I've really grown as a person, experiencing it. Let's fix me now."

And Two—AIs characteristically lack microexpression, but Talis Mark Two—

The look on his face was pure and heartbreaking hopelessness.

It occurred to me that that cloak of light was probably also a detailed and expert scan. If it was, Two didn't share the results. Michael's "fix me" hung in the air. The cloak swirled away like candle smoke.

"The horses—" said Elián.

As if on cue one of the horses—my money was on Spartacus—started kicking something, and the ship rang like a gong.

"Welcome home," said Two. "Do you need help with the ladder?"

"I'll help him," said Francis Xavier. Neutrally.

Two tipped his head a fraction in permission. He still had that look of filing things away for future ammunition. Possibly that was his default.

Anyway.

There is not much one person can do to help another with a ladder. Michael climbed down it almost exactly as if using his right arm weren't a flaring agony. Then he pushed through the horses and down the gangplank. At the foot of it he tumbled to a crouch in the dirt and shook.

"Unstrap the horses, please," murmured Two, which kept Francis Xavier from dashing to the rescue. Elián and I lingered in the hatchway as the half-strange AI sauntered down the gangplank and stood over the shivering figure. "Good?"

Only Michael's back was visible, but I could imagine the scrunch of his face. "Peachy."

I could feel the loop of Two's electronic attention hooking into the ship's communications. Filing our arrival. Summoning help. "Stretcher?"

Stiffly, as if he were made of metal parts, Michael sat up. "I am *not* going into the Red Mountains on a stretcher."

"All right then," said Two, and helped him to his feet.

I felt Elián at my elbow. Without speaking we went down the gangplank side by side. And stepped into another world.

The Red Mountains. All my life I'd known of them. Everyone did: they were our Olympus, our Sinai. Gods lived there— the AIs and their Swan Riders—but no one else came. It was not a mortal place.

And yet here we were, all too mortal: wounded, exhausted, endangered, betrayed. My body was both limp and stiff, like a cheesecloth wrung out and dried on a line. I was so tired that my eyes felt as if they were bulging. I pressed on them, but the strange scene around us did not waver. The ship sat like a pin at the middle of a small, perfectly circular island. It was dawn quiet, dawn calm, fresh without a breath of wind, nearly silent, except for the lapping of waves. The sea. It was all around us, and it was . . .

"It's red," said Elián.

It was.

A few hundred years ago, the landmass of the Missouri

River plateau, undermined by the draining of the aquifer and the fracking of deep hydrocarbons, and triggered by a hiccup at the Yellowstone supervolcano, had abruptly dropped a few hundred feet. Reclamation had been attempted, but it had gone wrong, and the result was: this.

A shallow inland sea, stark mountains rising from strange waters. No one wanted it, so the AIs took it. But even they could not save it. A few hundred years might be enough to remake the human world, but it was far too short to make a healthy ecosystem. The new sea—it was called the Sundance—was a mess. The water was dark as wine. It lapped with an animal sound and smelled sticky and sweet. The denuded mountains that rose from it bloomed with red lichen. They glowed as the rising sun reached them.

Everything was quiet, and everything was the color of blood.

The launchpad on which we were standing was one of a series of small man-made islands—round as plates—some distance from the hollowed mountain of the AIs and the floating city of the Swan Riders. (No one flew to the city itself, my datastore knew: the aerial defenses were fearsome and permanently on.) A spiderweb of causeways swept across the sluggish water. There were cottonwoods growing here and there, winter bare and filled with hundreds and hundreds of ravens.

Two held up a hand and whistled low and sweet. A raven swooped down, spread its wings, landed on his wrist. The bird tipped its head at the AI, who tipped his head mirrorwise, then conjured a bit of cheese. The raven took it in its gleaming beak.

"Oh," said Elián. "That isn't creepy at *all*."

"They're both top predator and top scavenger around here," said Two. "Absolute keystones for our messed-up pocket ecosystem. And beyond that they're interesting. Smart. Adaptable. I like them."

"You would," said Elián.

"Are you sure you're on my side, little Rider?" Two snapped his wrist into the air and the bird took off, a bafflement of wings.

"Absolutely," said Elián. "Ready and willing. What should we do first, surgery or tattoos?"

"Oh, surgery," said Two, with a smile you could bounce lasers off. "It's way less reversible." He swept the rest of us with his eyes, seeming to measure the distances and angles between us, to guess and gauge our tangled loyalties—and then looked beyond us to the road at our backs.

I turned. Down the causeway came men on horseback, women with wings. Swan Riders. Perhaps two dozen of them—enough to count as an overwhelming force. I could hear the hoofbeats, see the flash off the wing struts. The ravens flew up as they passed, a whirling storm of black.

It was uncanny. It was terrifying. And there was nothing to do but stand and meet it. Two was holding Michael on his feet. Elián stepped closer to me than was probably advisable for any cover story. Francis Xavier, with halter lines in his hand, slipped behind us as if to guard our backs. NORAD stamped and Gordon sidled. Spartacus trumpeted and reared.

And then the horses were on us, pintos and bays and buckskins and roans, a crash of noise, a chop of light through legs and wings. The riders dismounted, boots hitting gravel all around us.

"Greta," said Two softly. With a deep recognition, as if he'd been saying it for years.

I looked at him, and I'm sure my eyes were wide.

"Greta Gustafsen Stuart," he said. "I read up, you see." In the ship, he would have had time to scan my whole file—every recorded and monitored moment of my entire hostage childhood. His gaze flicked to my hands, and I worked not to curl them against the apple press I could see in his eyes. "Greta," he said, raising his voice. "May I present your Swan Riders."

And as if I were the rock at the middle of a ripple, in rings all around me, and one by one, the Riders knelt. I could hear the horses breathing, I could hear the wind against stiff white wings; I could hear the lap lap lap of the sea. But the Riders, with their heads bowed, did not make a sound.

"I take it back about the birds," said Elián. "This here is our new bar in creepy."

"Oh, shut up, Elián," murmured Michael.

Two shrugged. "It's been more than a century since we got a new AI. It's worth a little ceremony." He flicked his fingers as if to dissolve a spell, and the Riders got up. Still silently. They were way creepier that way.

"Welcome home, Greta," said Two. "And please excuse me if I don't see you settled in. I would like to get Rachel here to the doctor."

"I'm fine," objected Michael, without much hope.

"Don't be silly," said Two. "There's no reason you shouldn't have the best care." He singled out two riders with a cock of his wrist. "Take her to the hospital," he said. "I'll be right along."

He took a horse from one of the reassigned Riders and swung into the saddle. "Home again, home again," he singsonged.

Jiggety-jig.

Two and his designated Swan Riders took Michael away then. We couldn't stop them. We didn't even know how to try.

We stood in the middle of a ring of armed strangers, who in principle owed me life-and-death loyalty and absolute obedience. Was there a proper greeting for that? It did not seem as if it ought to be "hi."

"Francis Xavier," said one of them—a tall man with midtone skin and very dark eyes. "How was the ride?"

Ah. *There* was the ritual greeting.

Francis tipped his head a little. "The ride was hard," he said. His voice cracked. "The ride was—" And then suddenly big, solid, silent, understated Francis Xavier was folding up and sobbing.

The dark-eyed man caught him, arms wrapping around him, brotherly. "Hey now," he said. "Hey."

"I'm sorry," said Francis, gulping. "Alejandro. I'm sorry. I ought not—"

"It's okay," said his friend: Alejandro? "Let's—let's put these horses away. Heh? Let's get you home."

He caught my eye over Francis Xavier's shoulder—and immediately looked away. He had black slashing eyebrows, straight and pointed. And he made me uneasy. They all made me uneasy. The way they held their bodies tense as drawn crossbows. The way they looked at me with a worship that was hiding fear/disgust.

It was the way Sri had looked at me, once. *New Rider?* she'd asked. Talis had answered: *New AI*, and for a second she'd been horrified.

There was unease all around. Even look-death-in-the-eye Elián seemed unable to look at half of the Swan Riders. And Francis was crumpled as a piece of paper—the kind of crumpled that would never be smooth again.

The Swan Riders escorted us into the nameless city of the Red Mountains. We rode past islands of winter gardens, islands of willow-scrub grazing dotted with horses and single tents, an island housing biological laboratories fitted with airlocks, a long and low-slung school, a hospital that made Francis Xavier pause and look, his eyes empty. Finally we reached the foot of the largest mountain. It sank stone roots into red water, and in its boggy skirts were raised wooden pathways and bright white yurts on small neat platforms.

"Home," said Alejandro.

We got down from the horses. The sun was properly up now. Earliest morning. I was aware of every shifting pebble under my boots, of the fatigue like slush in my bones. Elián wrapped an arm around me, and I realized I was swaying. I wondered how Francis Xavier could even stand.

"My lady," said one of the Swan Riders. I turned to look at her. She was blonde, square jawed, at a guess one of the Low Country survivors: Flemish, Dutch? There were not many of them, but they were clannish, and thus had maintained a characteristic look. "Renata," she said, touching her chest—and then turning that into the Rider's salute.

"You don't need to," I said. But I had had that argument with Sri already. Renata's face tightened into a here-and-gone smile that was almost a grimace of pain. Under that respectful blankness she was hiding something—terror, I thought.

She gestured at the mountain face, and I saw that a little way up it was a door—a door into the hill, like the Riders' refuges, but a big one. Flights of rough stone stairs, trimmed with makeshift rails and prayer flags, threaded up toward it. Four-foot-thick blast doors framed it on either side. The hollow mountain. The AIs. "If you want . . . ," Renata said.

But Francis Xavier spoke from behind me. "Greta?" he said, his voice throaty and low. "Would you like to come home with me?"

"Yes," I said. "Please."

And no one thought to stop Elián, so he went too. We tried to stride down the boardwalk, but Francis Xavier was staggering, tripping over nothing at all. Elián reached to steady him but FX jerked his arm away. How long could I possibly keep Elián safe? I had seen the way the Swan Riders watched him, merely because he was a stranger. They watched him as if braced for betrayal, as if ready to attack.

Betrayal. Sri's crossbow. Two's hand oh-so-casually claiming Michael's arm, under the thin guise of holding him up. *There's no reason why you shouldn't have the best care.*

What was happening to Michael?

Why would I want you screaming? Two had said. Surely they wouldn't hurt him. Surely if they tried to remove the datastore there would be anesthetics, antiseptics, proper wound care. I'd gotten right up from my own implant surgery, recovering in moments. Un-planting, as Two had called it, was bound to be a bit more complex; there would be adhesions, old scarring, the problem of a gaping wound cavity. Even so, these were experts. Surely Michael would be all right.

But Francis, leading us down the mazy wooden walk-ways, looked so tired, so lost. Even Elián kept his mouth shut about it, though the best thing for him would be for Michael to die on the table.

I could not wish for that. I just couldn't.

Francis Xavier turned aside and pulled open the door on one of the yurts. It was a small door, only shoulder height, made of wood and painted bright yellow and orange. FX braced his hand on the lintel and ducked through. We followed.

Home with me, Francis had said. And here we were. There was a drawing pinned to the lattice wall—white pelicans on a dark blue lake. There was a table, one leg shimmed up with a wedge of folded paper. Mugs on hooks. A single bed, the indigo quilt on it embroidered with gold stars. Francis Xavier knocked a hollow fist on the heat pump as he passed and it puffed to life. This was not a station. It was a home.

It was Francis Xavier and Rachel's home.

The refuge near the Precepture had been theirs too, but also as fungible as a coin—a thing they could pick up or put down, a thing that did not hold a history. The yurt was different. FX hung his kit bag on a point of lattice and put the bag that had been Talis's on the table.

Elián was hesitating in the doorway.

"You can come in," said Francis Xavier. He was rooting through Talis's bag. "You can stay here. I will not hold you down and cut you open, even though you did that to Rachel, and even though I love her. I will not do it because Talis did not do it, and because Greta would not wish it."

"That's nice of you," said Elián warily. I took FX at his word, but I supposed it was hard for Elián to do the same. He still had a bruise from Francis's pincer on his Adam's apple.

FX drew from the bag what he'd apparently been looking for: a half-finished carving, no bigger than two fists, of horse and rider. He set it on the rickety bamboo table at the bedside.

"I will not hurt you," he said—apparently to the statue. "But you are a Swan Rider now. You must learn what that means."

"What does it mean?" said Elián.

"Sacrifice," said Francis Xavier. Then he took off his boots and lay down on one half of the bed.

Elián and I stood together and watched him.

They were so young, the Swan Riders. But these two, Francis Xavier and Rachel, had built a life together. And they'd been ready to die. Together. I looked at the sketch of the pelicans, on the lake that was *somewhere warmer*. At the boots leaning together, with their little loop sewn to the back, so that they could be pulled on one-handed. I looked at the prosthesis, lumpy in its silk stuff sack, hanging on the hook on the wall.

Home. A place where you could come apart.

"Sit down," said Elián. "No, actually. Lie down."

"Where?"

"Just, I don't know. On the floor."

The heat pump was in the middle of the room, and the floor around it was tatami matting: thick and intricately woven grass.

Elián stretched out on the tatami, propped his head up on one arm, waggled his eyebrows at me.

"Don't," I said.

"I wouldn't." He wiped his face with his hand. "I only mean—you're going to fall over."

And I was, at that. So tired that weird colors were smashing into the edges of things. I took off my boots and lay down on the matting, gingerly. Elián stretched out an arm for me to use as a pillow. The heat pump puffed at us like a friendly dragon. The tatami gave under my hip.

"People bowing to you, huh?" said Elián. "That must take some getting used to."

"For me, bowing is the thing that's least strange."

"Yeah, I guess it would be. . . . I'm sorry, I'm no good at this. I'm better with problems you can hit."

But in fact, he was good at this, or good enough. He was warm, and he was strong. His shape suggested a shape for me, and my body slumped into it like heated glass.

And I thought: they hadn't been bowing. They'd been on their knees. Bowing was what you did to a queen. Kneeling was different. You knelt to worship. Or to beg. The Swan Riders. They'd been . . . begging?

I could feel Elián's breath on my neck, my ear.

"I don't know how," I said. "I took you under my protection but I don't know how that works. I don't know how to protect you."

"Talis didn't kill me on sight, though," said Elián. "So that's something."

Neither of us suggested he should run. He wouldn't leave me, even if there were somewhere to go.

"Calgary . . ." The name of the dead city came out of my mouth as a whisper. "Did you see it?"

"Yeah," said Elián, equally shaken. "I was—" He'd been lost; thirsty; dying out on the open prairie. He shifted, retrieving his pillow arm and propping himself up on that elbow. "Yeah, I saw."

I pushed close to him, my head in the hollow of his

armpit, pressing my cheek to where his datastore would be. "I want to protect you. And . . ."

"Calgary," he said. "Indianapolis. All those cities."

I could feel his ribs moving, and the electrical currents of his body. He reached down and pinched the short, silky hairs at the base of my neck, rolling them between his fingers.

"I wouldn't be human again," I said. "Even if you could change me, I wouldn't choose it. All those cities."

I was lying on the floor in a yurt, with no terminal handy, no interface gel—but all the data in the world was here in the Red Mountains. It was called the *UNDEAD*, the UN Defensive/Emergency Actions Database. (*Have you ever noticed,* noted the Utterances, *that acronyms bring out the worst in people.*) It made the very ground beneath us boggy with information. As Two had reached into the ship, I reached into the seeping edge of the *UNDEAD*. I let the data drip and dribble through. And open me.

It was different than looking down with my satellite eyes: different than my self made far, and the world made tiny. The globe of the world grew inside me.

I closed my eyes so that it would fit more easily. My eyelids felt weighted, heavy.

All those cities.

Calgary.

I could still feel Elián's warmth and strength melting into one side of me.

Calgary.

Toppled trees that ringed it for a hundred miles in all

directions. The city itself was a crater, the bedrock open as a wound. From orbit, it looked as if a jewel had fallen out of a starburst setting.

I swallowed that jewel, and the Pan Polar rebellion entered me. I knew about a beloved princess, tortured publicly. A temporary hostage, stolen and made AI. I heard my mother's speech, her abdication. I saw the new king: young, bold, stricken . . . A look on his face as if his crown were molten.

I glimpsed the night footage of him spiriting his tiny son away.

Calgary, and Talis's blunt demand: son or cities.

The king's suicide.

Another coronation: a night procession, a queen in black. Her name was Agnes Little, my second cousin. Very young, yanked out of a boarding school where she'd been studying engineering. Too young. She had no children.

In Halifax, Queen Agnes Little dismissed a Swan Rider delegation with a royal shrug.

In Iceland, a mob found a Swan Rider refuge and set it blazing.

At the one-week mark, Talis blew up Reykjavík.

Popular rebellion. Swan Rider teams attacked wherever they showed their faces. My nation fracturing. Siberia, the part of the Pan Polar Confederacy whose allegiance to Halifax had long been the weakest, declared its independence and surrendered a hostage. The PanPols refused to accept the seccession. They landed troops on the Kamchatka Peninsula.

At the two-week mark, Talis blew up Edinburgh.

Queen Agnes Little lifted her chin and called for global rebellion.

Almost in my ear, Elián was snoring.

Queen Agnes Little—a childless queen.

There could be no greater symbolic rejection of Talis's order than a queen with no children. Even if she was hardly more than a child herself.

She had not been raised to a crown, and she had a bob of black hair, the cruelly fair skin of a Scot, green eyes, a mask of freckles. The AIs had captured a detailed thermal image of her. In it, I could see her fear. Her chin was just like mine.

I tipped my head back, my chin lifting. The AIs had a critical-moment decision model. Deep in the *UNDEAD*, it was churning scenarios at top speed. I could feel the intensity of the data processing, my skin prickling.

The world spun inside me. A few countries filed statements of support for the Pan Polar Confederacy: small places, mostly, thirsty have-nots with little to lose. But there was one bulletin filed from the clean white peaks of the Himalayas, from the great state that controlled the glaciers and the high plateaus that held the headwaters of so many rivers: the Brahmaputra and the Salween, the Mekong and Yellow and Yangtze. One bulletin filed from the power at the heart of Asia. The Mountain Glacial States.

It was triple-sealed and two words long.

It said: *Hold fiercely.*

Xie.

Li Da-Xia, the daughter of heaven, the pure soul of the snow, the heir to the great throne of the mountains. *Hold on to yourself,* she had said to me in the moment before I left her. *Hold fiercely.*

Only an AI could have opened that message. But only I could have read it. It spoke, almost in a voice, directly to me.

Xie. Talis had tried to take her from me—succeeded, but only briefly. I lay on the tatami at the edge of my endurance, with the world in my throat and three cities in ruins, and I remembered Xie. Curls and drifts of memory, Xie's kiss and slipping fingers, her low voice and little body. Four thousand dawns and evenings, drifts of memory like thick comforters.

I slipped free of the *UNDEAD.* Xie covered me.

And there, on Francis's floor, tucked in the curve of Elián's body, I slept, long and dreamlessly.

I didn't wake until Elián started screaming.

14
BETRAYALS

I jolted back into myself.

Elián was lying on the floor beside me, and Two was standing over him, with one boot heel resting in the hollow of his shoulder. Francis Xavier was holding down his other hand.

"Hi, guys," said Two, grinning down. "Anybody got a knife I can borrow?"

I was on my knees in a blink. "The datastore. You saw—"

"I saw, yes indeedy." Two twisted his foot a little. Elián closed his mouth tight. "And I've got *lots* of questions."

"Reykjavík," I said. "Edinburgh."

"Exactly. I've got a superpower in rebellion. And, I mean, riots and public defiance are one thing. I can answer them with smoking cities. But this kid murdered me."

"Well," said a voice from the doorway. "Not *technically*."

Michael.

He ducked into the yurt, and two Swan Riders came in after him, flanking him as if he were a prisoner. "I've said it before and I'll say it again: Elián Palnik is a hotheaded pretty boy with strategic thinking deficiencies, but he's not a murderer."

"Yeah," gritted Elián, flat on the floor. "Thanks for the character reference, Mikey. Little help here? Under Greta's protection, and all that?"

"Two—" I said.

The AI blinked. "As in 'version two'? Because it's actually four thousand, three hundred ninety-five."

"*Two* is unambiguous," I said. "I already know a Talis."

"And I'm sorry for your loss."

"Standing here," said Michael. "Not dead."

"But not Talis," said Two.

"His datastore," I began.

"Oh, it's a mess. The short off the affinity bridge was massive. It's flashes. It's fragments. There's no person there at all." He flapped a hand in his other self's direction. "Whoever *that* is—"

It wasn't Talis.

"Greta calls me Michael," said Michael. "And what was that about Reykjavík?"

Two twisted the corner of his boot heel into Elian's collarbone. "Greta, want to fill him in?"

"Um, guys," Elián gasped, "aren't you forgetting something?"

"The Pan Polar rebellion is ongoing," I told Michael. "And the new queen—she has no children."

Michael blinked three times. An old habit, merely, but it gave him an AI-ish look, as if he were orienting, processing. He looked sideways at his other self. "At the week marks, then?"

"A city every Sunday evening," said Two. He leaned over Elián, making his magician's flourish—and conjuring a knife into his hand. "But what I want to know right now is whether those rebels have found a way in. Because you, young man, got uncomfortably close."

"Two," I started—but Michael was faster, and picked a better target. "FX," he said. "Let Elián go. He's a Swan Rider, and he's under Greta's protection."

Francis Xavier let Elián go.

And Elián exploded into action. With his freed hand he feinted at Two's groin. The AI dodged, off-balance, and Elián hooked him around the knee and pulled him down. Two landed on top of Elián with a whoosh of breath. The knife went skidding off across the floor. Elián rolled Two and would have pinned him, except that the Swan Rider guards rushed in and grabbed him. There was a brief, furious struggle, and then the Swan Riders had Elián on his knees.

"Murderer, maybe not," said Elián. "Sheep wrestler, definitely."

The AI rose over Elián like thunder brewing.

"Two," I said. "I have Elián Palnik under my protection."

"Oh, new girl," said Two. "I don't think so." He wiped his

mouth with the back of his hand. "I've got reports of Swan Rider teams being attacked all over the Confederation. I've got Pan Polar troops massing on the Siberian border, and I still don't have their hostage. I might have to get involved in a *land war* in *Asia*. This is not the best time to push me."

"Elián has nothing to do with any of that," I said. "And he's under my protection."

"Yeah, I know you've got a Romeo-and-Juliet thing going on," said Two. "But the thing about that play, and people forget this, is that *everybody dies*."

"It's not like that," said Michael.

"Well, what's it like, then," said Two. "Spit it out. Because this is not a personal indulgence. This is a global rebellion that's come damn close to home."

"I'm not—" began Elián, and then yelped as one of the guards—it was Renata, the Dutch woman from last night—dug her fingers into the pressure point in his throat.

"Renata, if you'd be so . . . ," I began, and suddenly saw her fingers with the fixation only an AI can manage. I saw their exact skin tone; the pattern of the folds around the knuckles, the shape of the nails.

". . . kind," I finished. I looked up. Renata's eyes were hard as marbles, and she was afraid.

"I'll do it," I said.

Elián said: "What?"

Renata's cold eyes melted a little. Doubt. Hope.

"I love him," I said. "I do love him, but—we need the information."

"*Finally.*" Michael broke out a sunny grin. "Can I help?"

"No, I—it should be me. Only"—and here I feigned to look girlish and shy—"only, could we do it in private? It's . . . private."

Two was looking at me. I was reluctant to call him Talis, but oh, I knew that microscope look, those quick calculations. I could see them bare for an instant, and then a chipper mask dropped into place. "Well, in that case." He took a step back and made a half-bow. "Renata. Joel. If you could just give us a moment . . ." He tapped the side of his nose.

With some reluctance, the two Swan Rider guards let Elián go.

Elián scrambled up. I was afraid he might bolt, might fight, but for a moment he was only stunned. Francis Xavier took that moment to twist one arm behind his back and lift him onto tiptoe. He locked the crook of his other arm around Elián's throat.

Two retrieved his knife, flipped it round his fingers a couple of times, and handed it to me.

I looked down at it and made a couple of passes in the air. It was very sharp. It shimmered in my hand like a shard of light. I saw Renata's eyes catch it—and Elián's eyes catch it. Elián was helpless, trembling, locked in place as Talis had once been.

As for Michael himself, he strode in and tossed his coat at the bedpost as if he'd done it a thousand times before. And maybe he had, or Rachel had, because it caught. It hung there swinging.

"Greta," Elián gulped. "You're not—you won't—"

The Swan Riders were going, then gone.

"I need you to start screaming in a moment," I told him. "It's part of a plan."

Michael started to laugh. "Oh, Elián, you should see your face."

"Greta," said Two. "What did you just see?"

"Those men who helped Sri, at the church," I began.

"The Pan Polar rebels," said Michael. "The trommellers."

"No," I said. "They were Swan Riders."

Together, and in exactly the same tone, Two and Michael said: "*What?*"

"Renata was the woman who held me back when Talis was stabbed."

"You're sure," said Two.

"I'm sure about Renata."

Two looked as if someone had hit him in the stomach. The Swan Riders helping the Pan Polars? It didn't go. It didn't fit.

And, as he'd already noted, it was far too close to home.

"Can I get down now?" said Elián.

But Two shook his head, and Francis Xavier tipped Elián further off his feet. The AI stepped close. "Please believe that I will dig confirmation of this out from under your fingernails if I need to." He turned to Michael. "What do you think?"

"They . . . ," Michael began. He pushed at his wound as if by reflex. When he wrinkled his shirt I could see that there was a dip missing from him, as if someone had scooped into him with a melon baller. The unplanted datastore. "They hit me with an EMP weapon. I could hardly see. And of course it was on my mind—we saw Calgary. Had this run-in in Saskatoon. I assumed, but I don't—I can't replay it. I'm not sure, and I can't replay it."

Two paused, then blinked. "I can't either. The record's shredded."

"The Swan Riders can hardly look at me." I ticked my thoughts off, like points of evidence, on my fingers. "And Elián can hardly look at them. And their shirts—"

They'd come out from the graves in such bright shirts, so unlike what Swan Riders usually wore, so unsuitable for ambush. So fastidiously buttoned at the wrist, against ticks, yes, but also covering any traces of wing tattoos.

"Trommellers don't keep horses," said Francis Xavier. "Not in any number."

Two suddenly closed the distance with the helpless Elián—embraced him so that they were forehead-to-forehead, close enough to kiss, with his hands against Elián's spine. "This is your cue," he said with a murmuring smile. "Start screaming."

And then he yanked Elián forward with huge force, enough to send him to the ground, except that his arm was still wrenched behind him and pinned. Elián's shoulder came unseated with a pop.

Elián screamed. Just once, a heart-wringing cry.

"Two!" I shouted.

Michael pulled me back. "Easy. We have to make this look good, remember?"

Two didn't even glance at me. "Drop him," he ordered FX.

Francis Xavier dropped Elián's wrist, and Elián crashed to his knees, his good hand clutching his hurt shoulder, his body curling up. He gulped down a moan.

Two crouched in front of him. "The Swan Riders," he said. "I've heard enough to put each and every one of them up against a wall."

"Not all of them," Elián gasped. "It's not all of them."

Not Francis, for instance. I would bet my life on it. Then I shivered, realizing: I already had.

"Which, then?" said Two. "Who?"

"I d-don't—" Elián stuttered. "I—no names."

"Why would they tell him their names?" I asked. "It would be a completely unnecessary risk."

"Hmmm." Two rocked back on his heels. "Well then, how many? By the way, I put that back in its socket and the pain vanishes pretty much instantly."

"Half that nice," grunted Elián to Michael. "Is all I'm saying."

"Elián," I said. I wasn't sure what I wanted from him, but it wasn't to see him in pain. Which is what I got. Two lunged and knocked Elián to the ground, which didn't take much. He grabbed Elián's wrist and pulled.

Elián set his teeth, but a whimper leaked through them.

"This is good," said Michael. "I'm sure this sounds very realistic."

"It's some of them or all of them," said Two. "So how

many? How many were they when you met?"

"Two," said Elián. "There were just two. I was—I was lost; I was out of water; I was going to die. They found me."

Two was the number in a standard Swan Rider away team. But it was also the minimum number of people Elián could implicate—and in the end, there had been fourteen.

"Swan Riders to the rescue." Two relaxed the pull on Elián's wrist, but he didn't let it go. "Keep talking."

"You told them about me," I guessed, because I knew that Elián would *not* keep talking. "They asked who you were, and you told them, and then you told them what you were doing out there. You told them about Talis, and you told them about me. And they said they had a way to make an AI human again."

"Ewwww . . . ," said Two, like a child who's been asked to eat worms. "That would never work."

"It would never work for Greta," said Michael.

"It would never work, full stop," said Two, cross. He rocked back onto the balls of his feet and ran his hand through his hair, raising it into spikes. "Okay, enough. We need to move."

"Two," I said. "His shoulder."

"I'll do it," said Michael, kneeling beside Elián. He braced a knee against Elián's rib cage and found the pressure points in the shoulder. "Hey?" He touched Elián's face to get his attention. "Don't fight me, okay?"

Elián squinted at him through tears. Surprise, said the expression, beneath the pain, the tears. "Okay," he whispered.

❧

Michael reseated Elián's shoulder and we hauled him up onto the bed. Francis Xavier hunted through his absurdly small first-aid cabinet and found absurdly useless things: nail clippers, headache tabs. The Swan Riders, home, are a far cry from Swan Riders, deployed.

"Gimme," said Elián, and swallowed three tablets, dry. He flopped onto Rachel's pillow. I perched on the edge of the bed beside him. "Everlasting God, Greta. For a second, I thought—"

"I'm sorry," I said. "But—think of what would have happened if I'd accused the Swan Riders to their faces."

"A bloodbath, I reckon," said Elián. "One way or the other. And you know what, I don't even care. AIs, Swan Riders. You guys go ahead and kill each other."

In infrared I could see the swelling all around the glenohumeral joint; it was hot with blood flow and tender pain. I knew exactly how that felt, and not because I had looked it up. I put my hand softly on his wrist, covering the place where his Swan Rider tattoo was meant to go. "This plan where I protect you isn't working out so well," I said.

"It is, actually," said Two.

Elián grunted, "Yeah, for you."

"For you, too," said Two. "Even if you don't know names, you know faces. And I have people who could pull your brain apart and give those faces to me. The only reason that's not my first move is that I'm hoping to know Greta for centuries. I don't want that between us."

"That's beautiful." Elián pulled his uninjured arm up and draped his elbow over his eyes. "Where are you registered? I'll get you something. Gravy boat? Asparagus dish?"

"Don't get too comfortable," Two warned him. "We're going out there, and we're telling them it was trommellers who attacked the other version of me. You'll be a hero—enduring who knows what torture without implicating your coconspirators."

"It should keep them from taking immediate action," said Michael. "And then we can sort out how it connects, who's involved."

"Keep the purge to an absolute minimum," said Two, sounding chipper upon mentioning purges. "Up you get, Elián, let's go."

"I'm not going anywhere," said Elián. "I'm not your pawn, and I need a nap."

"You're better than my pawn," said Two. "You're my Rider. And the other Riders—they don't know you. I won't need to imitate you."

Beside me the side of the yurt gusted inward, with a *whump* of fabric like a slap to the eardrum.

"Imitate," said Elián, uncovering his eyes. He hadn't gotten there yet, but I had. Two was proposing that, in order to unravel the conspiracy among the Swan Riders, he possess Elián.

It would kill him.

Not right away—not unless something went wrong, and since we didn't know what was going on, we probably shouldn't count on everything going right—but it would kill him nonetheless. It would scar his brain.

"No," I said.

"You say he's a Swan Rider," said Two. "They do this. So he does this."

"He has to be a Swan Rider, Greta," said Michael, softly, warningly, "or you can't protect him."

He was absolutely right about that. Without my protection, Two would tear Elián apart.

He might do it anyway.

"Francis can help us," said Two.

"Why Francis?" I trusted Francis Xavier, but I would be amazed if Two did.

"Because I know where his levers are," said Two, smiling fondly at the big Swan Rider. "There's this sweet little girl. Name of Rachel."

"Two," said Michael, laying a hand on his counterpart's arm.

The AI yanked himself free. "Don't call me that."

"Talis," said Michael. "Don't do this. She's an AI; she's a new AI. And she loves him. I know you know how rare that is." He glanced at me as if reluctant to add to that, but then added to that. "How fragile. Talis."

I no longer felt fragile. But I could fake fragile if there was power in it. "Please," I said. "Don't use the people I love."

Two made a pouty face. "But that's pretty much my wheelhouse. Oh, and, heads up—" He reached for my hand. There was information in his fingertips: a pulse code that opened up his scenarios, his strategies.

I looked at them. And my knees went out from under me.

I found myself sitting in one of the two mismatched chairs, across from Francis Xavier, who was silently pulling on his boots. *Sacrifice.*

I didn't need catching, but both Michael and Elián had dived to catch me. Elián reached me first, but it was Michael who narrowed his eyes and hopped to the conclusion as sure-winged as a raven. "Halifax," he said.

It was swelling in my eyes. Halifax. The Pan Polar capital. My home.

"Sunday next," said Two.

"Two," said Michael. "You can't. She." And there he paused. Literally paused, as if someone had hit a button. He was frozen, and silent, and still.

Francis Xavier looked up and then lunged out of his chair.

Two tilted his head. "And did I mention? Your symptoms are going to be radically accelerated."

Michael fell into Francis Xavier's arms as if he'd just been cut down from the gallows. His hands flew to his head.

"You can blame the short off the affinity bridge," said Two. "The whole web must have pulsed, created a big batch of new lesions. That little dagger did a lot of damage."

"That—" Elián was staring at Michael, at the way his fingers burrowed into his hair as if they wanted to burrow into his skull. When Elián's gaze flashed to me, I could read it plain as a book: guilt. "That wasn't part of the plan."

Francis Xavier looked up at him with utter contempt. And Two piled on: "With respect, Mr. Palnik, I see no evidence that they told you the plan. Now. Come willingly, or I'll kill you where you stand."

"You're a little fuzzy on *willingly* . . . ," said Elián. But he drew himself up, as if standing for the firing squad.

"Two," I tried one last time.

"Francis Xavier," Two said. "You're with me."

Francis Xavier closed his eyes as if in prayer. Then he got to his feet, with Talis in his arms. He laid the body in their bed and then stepped away, coming like a wolfhound to Two's side. Michael was still twisting as if to escape his own skin—fighting himself with a noose-around-the-throat urgency. I had to leap in and put my whole weight on his shoulders just to keep him from falling to the floor. And while I was trapped by that task, Two was taking my friends. I looked at them as if I could stop them with my eyes alone.

"It's okay, Greta," said Elián.

"Elián—" Did he not understand that what he was seeing here could easily become his own future? There was nothing good for him inside that mountain.

"Stay, Greta," said Francis Xavier. "Please."

I stayed.

The seizure was bad. It rattled on for minutes—for three minutes and forty-seven seconds, I knew, because my datastore began a count once I wondered how long it would last. I leaned over Michael, weighing down his shoulders, watching the scrolling seconds in the air between us.

Under my hands he shuddered and shuddered. A feral

noise growled out of him. His focus swam around the room. And there was nothing I could do.

As Two had done on the ship, I let my sensors bloom outward; I wrapped up the suffering body and held it in light.

Infinite knowledge had once seemed to me a source of infinite power. With my sensors, I could see the new scars that Two had diagnosed. I could also see Rachel: the growth plates that showed a hungry childhood, an old fracture in her leg, the fibrous scar across her lung from her Swan Rider surgery—the surgery Elián might be having right now.

Knowledge did not seem like power anymore. It seemed like sadness.

Halifax. Two had made the threat privately three days ago; would make it public three days hence. The Pan Polars had ten days to stand their troops down, get their rioters in order, and surrender a hostage.

There was a private vid of Queen Agnes Little receiving the threat while sitting at my mother's dressing table, putting powder on her freckles. Her color drained as she listened; she was wordless as she cut the connection. But in public she lifted her chin and called for global rebellion.

Under my hands, and now, the seizure lifted.

Michael went limp.

I raised my hands away, and their light glimmered and died.

I could hear the heat pump humming, the voices in the tents around us, and the distant lap of thick red water.

"How did you break your leg?" I asked.

"I fell off a horse," Rachel answered. "When I first came

here." She laughed. "A Swan Rider who couldn't . . ."

" . . . ride," said Michael, dialing into focus. "Oh."

"Michael?" I said, to be sure of him.

"It was Francis Xavier who picked me—her—up. We were practicing in the meadow island. It was spring, and wet—boggy, really. Nature's safety mat. We were just covered in mud . . ."

He stopped talking and lay there simply breathing in and out, putting beads of breath on a string of pain. I watched.

"Oh," he said. "Oh."

I did not even know what name to call him.

With some struggle he pushed himself up on his elbows. I grabbed the second pillow and tucked it behind him. He lay propped, peering at the room as if not sure how he'd come to be there.

"Could you," he said, finally, faintly. "My glasses?"

I knew by now that they lived in a padded inner pocket in his duster. I retrieved them and handed them over, and he slipped them on with delicate hands. And then he lay looking around as if taking photographs. The indigo quilt at his fingertips. The two red-glazed mugs hanging on hooks. The old mirror with its dappled shine.

"Welcome home," I said softly. Because I was fairly sure this was Rachel.

"Thank you." The murmuring voice was throaty. Those haunted eyes looked at me with an expression nothing in my datastore could match—a mix of innocence and bitter irony: the smoke in the caramel, the salt on the chocolate. Not Rachel. But not Michael either.

THE SWAN RIDERS 259

Whoever she was, she bumped up her glasses and pushed the back of her wrists into the hollows of her eyes. A child's gesture, sleepy, sulky. She gave her head a little shake and made a visible effort to tune in. "Where's . . . where's Francis?"

As if all heartbreak had been given one name.

And yet the voice was still not purely Rachel's.

"Your counterpart," I began.

"Two."

"Yes. He—"

"I remember." He started to sit up, suddenly urgent. "Greta—"

"I need to get there," I said. "Where would they go—did they go into the mountain?"

Michael pressed his lips together. "Talis will probably take Elián to the upload portal in seventeen C. There's nothing special about it, but we all have our habits." A little shrug, a wary look. "There are a handful of Riders who might also know that. If they talk to each other. If they put it together."

And they were, it seemed, doing exactly that. A conspiracy of Swan Riders against AIs. Of Pan Polars against Talis. In both those struggles I was a pawn, a piece to fight over, and—we would see about that. I had no intention of playing the pawn. But for the moment, there was no one I could trust.

"Go alone." Michael always could read my mind. "Francis is just there in case I need muscle, but Elián—"

"Will you be all right?" I could see the warp and shimmer at the edge of his aura. Another episode was building.

Clustered. Welcome to stage five.

Michael's eyes were hooded. What I could see, he could feel, and if Talis had one terror, it was being left alone. But he answered in a voice that trembled hardly at all. "I'm fine."

"You'd be safer on the floor."

There was a pause as short as a gulp.

"Right," he said. "Help me?"

So I helped him sit, then slide onto his feet, and from his feet to the tatami mat on the floor. I could feel his dizziness in uneven bursts of weight on my arm.

I knelt over his body. The woven grass of the tatami released a smell of sweet hay and sunshine, of lost summers, though the eddy of air around the bottom of the tent was damp and cool. In that smell, in that eddy, I curled Michael up on his side—recovery position, for the thing that had not yet happened. I knew he wouldn't stay there, but it seemed like the only thing to do.

"Seventeen C," he said, touching my fingertips with his fingertips as if to give me the data. There was no data in them, but the words were enough to make a map bloom in my head. I had to look through the map to see him. Dizziness lingered in the set of his mouth and whirled Rachel and Michael together in his eyes. "I—" he said. "You—"

And here his voice shifted, stumbled a little as if the heart behind it had lurched. "You should be there," said Rachel. "Be there when Talis lets him go."

15
DEBUTS

So I went out into the City of the Swan Riders, went running headlong into that strangeness, my boot toes pushing off the boardwalk paths with a sound like a drum being struck. I needed to know everything, and I needed to know now, and so everything came. As if the air itself could be painted, Talis's map—17C—hung in front of me. Compasses, charts, annotations. Information lay in glosses and depths across the visible world. I knew where I was going, and I knew how to get there.

It was midafternoon. The high sun curved off the sides of the white yurts as I ran. The willow scrub flashed by under me, yellow as fire. And all around me, people in doorways stopped what they were doing and saluted.

I ran through the Swan Riders like a shock wave, and they bowed before me, and some fell to their knees.

Who were they? What did they want from me?

I was born to a crown, and thus have never once simply walked down a street. Always there have been eyes on me, and ways cleared before me. The strange thing was not the bowing but the running—the feeling not of procession but of chase, that what was happening was not about me, and would not wait for my arrival. Francis. Elián.

Halifax.

Half the world.

The Swan Riders rose as I passed. They turned. They watched me go. I could have asked any of them for anything, and they would have given it. But instead I was building a catalog of them: their heights and skin tones, their gaits and stances. Unlike Talis, I could replay the moment he had been stabbed. It would be fairly easy to assemble a list of those who had posed as trommellers.

The man Alejandro, for instance. Alejandro, into whom Francis Xavier had crumpled because the ride had been hard, was the same man who had wrapped his arm around Francis's throat in a gesture that even at the time had seemed brotherly.

Betrayal.

Two's hand on Michael's arm.

There were, in my datastore, no records—no records at all, of any kind—about what Elián was experiencing. About what happened to the Riders when the AIs possessed them. The AIs, apparently, had never cared—but suddenly the gap was as startling as a mountain scooped out of the landscape.

Talis, I thought. *How could you have missed this?*

The yurts were at my back now, and the hollow mountain was right in front of me. There was a bare spot at the end of the boardwalk—benches and bolders and the ashes of bonfires. And past that, switchbacked stone stairs climbed to the big metal doors that marked UN Strategic Data Processing Center Number Seven. Blast doors. Supercomputers. EMP shields. Talis had not built it—he'd merely been stationed here. One of the UN's assets. Once upon a time, at the end of the world.

I came off the boardwalk and did not even slow down. And then, just past the bonfires, in the scree and rubble at the foot of the stairs, I saw—

Something. Something else my datastore knew little or nothing about. Nestled in the stones were little . . . dolls? Carvings? Little figurines of horsemen, made of wood. They were set so carefully among the stones, as if they were as fragile and important as eggs. Some were powerfully primitive, like cave paintings; some so realistic that the horses looked as if they might stamp and rear. Some were dressed in scraps of leather, some painted, some feathered, some plain. Some faded and cracked by time—by decades, by centuries of time.

This was what Sri had been carving for as long as I'd known her. This was what Rachel had almost finished on the table beside her bed.

The datastore told me that the Swan Riders made them, from the wooden skeletons of worn-out saddles. It said this neutrally, as if it were describing a hobby on par with the whittling of whistles.

These were not whistles.

They made the human hair stand up on the back of my neck. There was no time to wonder over them, but their eyeless forms seemed to follow me as I ran up the stairs, past the thick and towering doors, and into the mountain.

It was dark inside the mountain, so dark that it was like a wall of blackness in front of me. I could run in blackness—I could taste the distances like a bat if I had to—but it was off-putting.

"Lights," I said, like a spell, and like a spell, lights answered. Concrete floors with painted lines and place codes. Rough blasted walls swagged with cables. But I did not wonder at it. I ran past the first door. Letters as tall as I was said 1A.

My footfalls rang back off the walls. I could hear my own breathing, and the thrum of a huge air-circulation system. I knew—because I knew everything—that this place could have supported a human population in the thousands, for years, without outside support. It was a massive undertaking, a shelter, a silo, a storehouse. Now a half dozen AIs lived here, and most of them didn't move around much. It was just Talis, stalking lonely as a lion after every other animal had left the ark.

4A, 5A, 6, 7, 8, 9. Checkpoint, blast doors, downward stairs, water pumps, B cross corridor. 11A, 12A. The mess hall. The infirmary. The white-sheeted beds were ghostlike and empty: if Elián was having surgery, he was not having it here. 13A, 14A. The *UNDEAD* was listening to me. There were barriers to leap between the rooms now, places where compartment doors could drop and seal, like the chambers in a flooding ship. Seven more doors to the C cross corridor.

The compartment seal between 16 and 17A dropped shut in front of me.

"Door," I said. But nothing answered. The bulkhead in front of me was steel, and huge, like the side of a warship. Grey paint curled off the walls. Rivets leaked raised scars of rust.

I turned around—and the bulkhead there slammed too. There was no overhead light in this section; darkness crashed in. The air went *whump* with overpressure, and then deeply silent.

"Door," I said, into the *UNDEAD*, into the darkness.

Nothing. My ultrasound told me I was caught in a box of stone and steel, fifteen feet on a side. My datastore tried out labels—*portcullis/submarine/elevator shaft/oubliette/dungeon*—but the box was entirely outside my lived experience, which mostly had to do with goat farms. "Open," I said. "Door!" It didn't budge, so I reached with my electronic attention for the *UNDEAD* control systems.

They reached back.

It was like groping for a light switch in the darkness and instead having the darkness take your hand.

"Hello?" I said to the control systems.

"Hello!" they answered. A child's voice. Jump-rope bright.

"Who's there?" When I spoke I did it aloud, of course, but hearing my own voice made me realize the other had not been audible. It was in my head. I was linked into the *UNDEAD*, but now the *UNDEAD*—or something in the *UNDEAD*—had linked back into me.

"It's Greta, everybody," said the voice in my head. "She's here!"

"*UNDEAD*," I said. "Lights. Now."

A little light, like a porch light, came on at my elbow. It was centered over door 16A. The door's number had been crossed out with a spray-paint X, and someone had sprayed on a new word. In big dripping letters, it said: EVIE. The smoothness of the paint felt shiny under my fingers.

"In here," said the voice, and door 16A went *chunk*. It swung open, a line of brightness widening into a rectangle.

Evie. Evangeline. Nine and also 520. Nine and immortal. Not the straightest stripe on the zebra, Talis had said. And when *Talis* warned you someone was a bit off . . .

There is, so often, no way out but through. So through the door I went.

"Hello?" I said to the echoey little room. The walls were covered with equipment mounted on articulated arms; there was a table at the back with boxes on it, and a cake. "I'm sorry, but I'm in a hurry. I need Talis."

"We all need Talis," said another voice—monotone, androgynous. "You will have to be more specific."

"Shhh . . ." Evie hushed it. Audibly, this time. "You'll ruin the surprise."

I could tell by the resonance that the monotone voice was human, or at least using a human voice box, though there was no one in sight. Evie's whisper, in contrast, was carried by surround sound. The lights dimmed slowly, as if to cue a curtain rising. A shiver ran across my scalp.

That optimized whisper began a countdown: "Three, two, one."

The lights flipped to bright, and the room shouted: "Surprise!" A single figure rose from behind the table and blew a birthday-favor horn with a sad hoot.

"Were you surprised?" said the room gleefully. "Were you? We made you cake!"

"Uh," I said, because with my upgrades I had an IQ pushing past 500. "Thank you?"

"Evie," the room said. "I'm Evie."

"I know."

The single human figure—AI figure—stood behind the cake and stared at me with eyes like binoculars.

Evie nudged him with a needle. "Az . . ."

"Surprise," he said, with perfect flatness.

"That's Azriel," said Evie.

Talks in numbers.

"Happy AI debutante surprise party," said Evie.

"I didn't realize AIs had debutante parties."

"That's why it's *surprising*," said Evie.

One of the boxes on the table rattled as if a raccoon were in it.

"What's in the box?" I hated to ask, but the things one

hates to ask are usually things one is better off knowing.

"That's Peter. Peter's doing so much better! He has a filtered live feed into his box and actuators for when he gets really excited."

And I realized: the boxes on the table—they weren't gifts for the AI debutante party. They were partygoers.

Matrix Boxes.

"You shouldn't look at Peter, but you can say hi to everyone else," said Evie.

"That's okay," I said, taking a step backward.

Something wrapped my arm, stopping me. My head whipped around and I found that the room was full of mechanical arms—some tentacle-like, some jointed, some tipped with needles. They were everywhere, but the ones that were behind me were all extended and awake, waving like a kelp forest. One of them, one of the tentacular ones, slithered round and round my upper arm, cold and smooth and powerful. It tightened. "Come on," said Evie.

A needle between my shoulders nudged me forward. I stumbled toward the table.

"Is there a song?" said Evie, and then paused, as if listening and relaying the answer. "Nobody knows any AI debutante surprise party songs."

Evie had been listening, so I listened—and suddenly could feel all of them, the AIs inside the boxes. The pressure of their eyes and sensors and attention turned on me. Their voices were in my head, and they all sounded like my own voice, but some of them were screaming.

I jerked as if to get away from it, but there is no getting away from voices in your own head. "Whoa," said Evie, and the snake around my arm jerked upward. I tilted and started to topple and—

Found myself in Azriel's arms.

"You were leaning forward six degrees." He was radiating data in the pulses of his fingertips, in the rhythm of his blinks. "Most humans cannot maintain a static lean of greater than four point five."

"I'm not sure it was a static lean. I think it was more a *bolt for the door* lean."

The blank-faced AI set me on my feet. His gaze seemed to swirl over me, as if he had pinwheels for eyes.

"What are you doing?"

"Tracking the Brownian motion of your dust motes to use as random number input for my Monte Carlo simulation. You're very dusty."

"I just crossed a continent. What simulation?" But the next second I was sorry I had asked. The fragments of code swirling out of Azriel had hooked into me, and and I could see exactly what he was simulating. I found my hand coming up, as if to protect my eyes from light, my mouth saying, "Don't . . ."

Pure distress. But the simulation didn't stop running.

"Are you upset that there's no song?" Azriel said. "We have a combined processing power of approximately three hundred exaflops. We could probably write a song."

"It's not the song."

It was everything except the song. It was the little girl

with a hundred needles and the screaming boxes and the fact that the simulation was a global war game, in which Halifax was being obliterated every time Azriel twitched his stiff little fingers.

"I need to go," I said. "Talis is—"

I couldn't tell them. I had thought they might be allies, but they weren't. To ally with them would be like leading crocodiles into battle.

I was shivering. Azriel's war game was so deep in my head that it felt as if it were using me for processing power. I needed a fuse; I needed a switch. I said, "Talis needs me."

"But he said we should throw you a party," said Evie. She sounded peevish. A needle-arm twitched out from one wall and set a rocking chair in the corner creaking. I had not particularly noticed the rocking chair before, but now I did. There was a teddy bear in it. It was ancient—it looked as if it would come apart at a touch, like a moth's body left in an attic window. Evie didn't touch it. And I wasn't going to.

"You have to have cake," she said. "We made it. It's totally not poisoned or anything. Az, call one of the humans to do that king-and-food-tester thing with the cake."

"Pinged," said Azriel.

What if, said the simulation, *we blockaded the Halifax archipelago to prevent evacuation. What if we turned down the beam and burned it slow.*

The rocking chair went *scrik screak*.

"Evie, Azriel, um, everyone," I said, and tried to remember what it was like to be a duchess, always the first person to sweep out of a room. "It is truly a pleasure to meet you, and I look forward to deepening our acquaintance. But I have obligations to attend to and I really must go."

I reached into the *UNDEAD* for the door.

"I locked it," said Evie.

"Oh."

I could feel her control meet mine again. As if we were hand in hand.

So I took her hand and pulled myself up and into the control systems.

"Hey!" said Evie, as if I were a big sister who had just shoved my way into her room. "Get out!"

"Evie, I'm sorry, but I need to go."

"I locked it. You won't get it open." Her voice was proud and peeved. Her metaphorical hand felt sharp in mine.

In the datascape I could see the things she had locked. They were piled up like books, like little pink or purple diaries with tiny brass padlocks—a nine-year-old's heart, a nine-year-old's secrets.

I edged closer to the pile of diaries and they swelled in front of me, looking huge—big enough to climb. A ladder of locked things.

The bottom book was this door that locked me away from rescuing Elián. The padlock. It was made of six-hundred digit semiprime numbers. It was made of teeth.

I fit my fingers inside the padlock loop. It bit me.

I yanked my hand out and looked at the stack of diaries, each big as a step. The bottom book was this door, part of the *UNDEAD* systems that ran the mountain. The top books were . . .

The satellites. The orbital weapon satellites.

Calgary, Reykjavík, Edinburgh. A child-queen in black taffeta, turning to face the camera. The Halifax crater opening like a cat's pupil, inside the simulation, inside my head, every 3.2 seconds.

The satellites were eyes and whispers.

My eyes, I thought. *My whispers.*

I stepped up onto the diary that was the locked door. Onto the one that was the *UNDEAD*. The glittery pink pleather squeaked under my feet. I reached up for the next book, I climbed toward the satellites. I put my hand on the lowest of them, and—

And I met a scream of light and code, a wall of teeth and *no*. To call it a lock was to call a punch a handshake. The next thing I knew I was thrown out of the datascape and on the floor. My head and my heart were pounding. The needle-filled ceiling over me seemed to sway.

"Once upon a time, a nine-year-old stole the nuclear launch codes." The voice came from Evie's speakers, but it was not Evie's voice. "This is not the moment where the new girl takes them from me, okay?"

"Talis," I said.

There was nothing there that grinned, but I felt Two grin at me. "And why aren't we having cake?"

"Where's Elián?" I said.

But the smiling presence was gone.

One of the snakelike arms was nudging its way under me, and Evie's voice sounded both gleeful and hurt. "I told you you wouldn't get it open."

There was a sound behind me: the door sliding open. "Here is your tester," said Azriel. I rolled over. And there, standing as if he had a hundredweight of sorrow yoked across his shoulders, was Francis Xavier. He saw me and that sorrow changed to fear. "Greta!" He came running and was by my side in a moment, batting Evie's arms away. "What happened?"

"She didn't want cake." It was amazing, but Evie could make a room seem sulky.

"But why—" Francis was trying to lift me. Why had I left, when he'd asked me to stay. "Rachel?"

"No, she's—" Not fine, not even for the most generous definition of fine. "She survived it. Elián?"

"The surgery—" he said, and stopped, and looked around the room. It was full of AIs, who were recording, carelessly. Like a harbor icing, FX calmed. "He survived it."

Neutral as an echo. An empty thing to say.

By now we were kneeling together, and he had his arm around me. It was useless to whisper, and yet my voice came out softly: "And the rest of it . . . ?"

"I am sorry, Greta."

The way his eyes caught mine—it was as clear as that time we had synchronized and counted together, to tie a bandage. They said: *I cannot stop Talis.*

Nor, apparently, could I. Talis and I might in principle be equals, but I was the one on my knees. I reached up and took hold of the smooth scales of Evie's still-dangling arm. It flexed like a boa constrictor under my hand, and pulled. With that help, and with Francis, I got to my feet, still wobbling.

Francis Xavier looked around the room—the limp streamers, the empty-eyed figure, the twitching little boxes. He made a general salute.

"What was it you required?"

"It's an AI debutante surprise party," said Evie, with a little wag of her hundred arms. "And we made some cake. Please taste it so that Greta knows we're not going to kill her."

They kept us there almost an hour—fifty-three and a third minutes, exactly enough time for Halifax to die inside my mind a thousand times. We had cake, and Evie decided we needed music. There was no singing.

Finally the party simply stopped, midbeat, and the door slid open. And we were allowed to run.

It was too late. That was the point of the cake. Of course it was too late. But still we ran.

Francis didn't know where we were going, but he stayed exactly beside me: 17, 18, 19, and the C cross corridor. The overhead lights made thick bars of shadow spring from our feet. They shifted and spun as we ran, like compass needles. As if the world were spinning around me.

Too late, too late: but there was 17C.

"Two!" I shouted, into the air, into the *UNDEAD*, at the top of my lungs and with all my heart. Echoes bounced around us. And the door opened.

Francis Xavier, at my back, took a sharp breath in.

The space behind door 17C was tiny—a broom closet, it could have been, except that there was an alcove at the back of it, no bigger than an iron maiden and shaped to hold a man. An upload portal.

Elián was inside it.

He was locked in. Metal bands that closed over the opening like ribs. His hands were wrapped around them, fingers loose—forgotten fists. "Elián . . ."

"Guess again," said the wall. *Two*.

Fury turned me cold, and my words came out like a royal decree: "Let him go."

"Certainly," said the wall, and the ribs swung open.

Elián stepped out. His gaze was inward, absent. Then he blinked—three times. His face rebooted and his eyes lit like indicators.

FX put a hand on my shoulder.

"Elián?" I said.

Elián's face smiled—but not with Elián's smile. "Guess again."

"Two," I said. "Let him go. I demand that you—"

"Demand?" said Elián's mouth, and his eyebrow came up twenty-three degrees. "Oh, well, in that case . . ." And with no more warning than that, he collapsed.

I shouted wordlessly and lunged, skidding into him and wrapping him up even as he fell. We both crashed to our knees. The clatter of boots and knee bones hitting the metal floor echoed around the tiny room. Francis Xavier was right behind me. I could feel him, like the shield at my back. Elián was breathing loudly, and right in my ear, but when I leaned away to look at him I found his face calm.

. . . Or, not exactly calm. Inanimate. It was big-eyed and openmouthed, as if someone had taken a snapshot before the fear and horror had taken hold. He was breathing heavily as if he had a respirator driving his lungs, and his rate of breathing was speeding up, but his face was so, so still.

What would it take to shock Elián Palnik out of his skin?

And what would I do if he didn't come back?

"Just a test drive," said Two, brightly, from the wall. "Just kicking the tires."

"He's not a horse," I answered. And then, as my datastore caught me up on the test drive/tires reference, "He's not a thing."

Francis's hand was on my shoulder, heavy and steady and warm. "I've seen this," he murmured—though surely no murmur was soft enough, with Talis in the room. "It's breaking, see?"

It was, the way ice breaks up. Elián was breathing so fast now that he had to be close to hyperventilating. He was starting to shiver and blink.

"I don't have much to report," said Two. (The voice was synth'd, but nearly human—based on recordings, probably. Male, tenor, clever, warm, a bit too quick. Could it have been Michael's voice?) "Surgery went fine; implants are operational, obviously. We should be good to get out there and see what we can see."

"Two," I said, and did not even care that I was begging. "Talis . . ."

There were other things in the room: a whole wall of old-school blinking lights and screens and speaker grills. A ripple of pattern crossed the bank of lights, like a quirk of the lips. "Look, Greta," said the wall, "I appreciate that this is disturbing for you. You certainly don't need to watch. But this is a *terrible* time for a palace coup. We need to find out what the Swan Riders want."

"I know that," said Elián. He was shivering like a tall poppy, and his voice was soft, but his aura was full of swirls. "I know what they want."

"Oh, really?" said Two.

"They want—they want this. They want this never." And then the ice broke with a catastrophic boom. "They want this never to fucking happen," Elián snarled. His hands flew to his face, and he began scrubbing his skin with his fingernails, as if trying to scrub all traces of the possession away.

He was weeping. Francis Xavier and I crouched on either side of him. We took his hands so that he couldn't hurt himself. We pushed close.

"Well," said the wall, in its light-opera voice. "Isn't that an interesting piece of feedback?"

FX looked up, too sharply.

The hole in the landscape, the vanished mountain that was the Swan Riders' experience of being ridden. It didn't matter that Two couldn't access it directly from Elián's mind. His reaction was enough to spotlight its importance.

"Greta," said the wall, "why don't you take your little friend home. Two aspirins, call me in the morning sort of thing. Don't mess with my satellites. Check in with you in a bit."

"But—" I began, then found myself busy as Francis Xavier let go of Elián's hand and stood up. Suddenly I needed both hands to keep Elián from scratching himself. Welts were coming up on his cheeks and neck and across one eyelid.

"Tell him he caught a break," said Two. "Because if that's really their motivation, then he's the wrong person to ask. Whereas Francis . . ." The upload ribs opened, waggling like fingers. "Step into my parlor, said the spider . . ."

"I need him," I said, wishing I had a hand free to pull Francis Xavier back down. In my grip, Elián jerked and jerked. "I can't carry Elián without him."

"It's not like I did anything to his *legs*." And then there was a beautifully timed pause: even when he was being a wall, Talis had Gilbert-and-Sullivan-worthy timing. "Or, if you need Francis, I suppose I could call Rachel."

He couldn't possess Rachel. But there were other things he could do to her. It was Francis's lever, and Two had no qualms about pushing it.

Francis Xavier bowed his head and saluted the empty air. "My life is yours," he said.

"That's my boy," said the wall brightly. "I really would like to know all about this, now. I don't think I can read your mind. It shouldn't be possible, but to be honest, I've never tried it. But even so. We could do it in bursts—in and out, and you can give me little updates. How does that sound?"

It sounded like—

What if, said the simulation, *we burned it slow.*

Elián made a small, choked sound. "Get me out of here," he whispered. "Greta, get me out."

This, of course, is the problem with caring about more than one person. You can be forced to choose.

And so I chose. I chose, as I often did, the person who was in the most pain. I got my shoulder under Elián's armpit and heaved him to his feet.

Two wanted to know why the Swan Riders had put a knife in Talis. Elián had given him a crack, a clue—that their motivation had something to do with the nature of possession. And Two would peel that crack open. He would push his way into Francis Xavier's mind; he would pull out just long enough to take the report; he would do it again.

It sounded like . . .

I tried to think of something less horrifying than waterboarding. Or rape.

It sounded like a very intimate bit of torture.

"FX," I said. He was standing there, upright and poised as a dancer, silent as a priest. The spread ribs of the upload portal made wings behind him. "Francis Xavier. Are you sure?"

He smiled at me, a soft thing, like April sunshine. "I am a Swan Rider," he said. He reached for me, spreading his hand in the air as if glass had fallen between us. I met his hand, fingertip to fingertip.

Talis's fingertip pulses had been fluent, easy as a language.

Francis Xavier was not AI, and where Talis had sign language, he had something like semaphore. But he gave the data to me, byte by byte, and the book opened in my head. It was the book of Francis Xavier, of the Lake Tana people—or as much of him as the AIs had thought to make note of.

And it wasn't enough. It wasn't nearly enough.

He'd come to us, as so many of the Swan Riders did, young and poor and brilliant and passionate. We had trained him and educated him. We had taught him to fight and to ride, to engineer and to negotiate, to doctor and to improvise. And then we had sent him out to save the world.

When he was just fourteen, he'd rebuilt the floats on the Pacific Gyre plastic harvesting colony and installed desalinators in the Drowned States of Micronesia. At fifteen, he'd brought the antiviral to the Carobama dengue outbreak, and helped quarantine the McMurdo Republic during the Vostock Cryptosporidium emergence.

And beginning when he was sixteen, he'd been stationed, on and off, in reach of Precepture Four. He'd killed the girl from my class, Nghiêm Thị Bịhn. And the old woman in Saskatoon, Alba Kajtar. He had murdered them.

He had killed two people. And he had saved ten thousand lives.

The pulses faded. Francis's hand dropped away.

Two would pull him apart. And he knew it, too. He knew it.

I balanced Elián's weight across my shoulders, and Francis Xavier stepped backward into the upload portal.

INTERLUDE:
ON RIDING

"**A**re you sure about this?" said Talis.

"Nope," said Evie. "But Az is."

"Seventy-nine percent," said Azriel.

They were gathered in Evie's room—he and Az in their 'bot forms and Evie leaning down from the ceiling as a camera eye on a jointed arm. Talis fought the urge to tell her that the cake was a lie.

The three of them were leaning, in fact, over a body. A young man, tattooed, too thin, sea-green hair that was mouse-brown at the roots. His face soft with sleep—with sedation, actually, because no one was quite sure how this was going to go—and turned to one side. Talis both did and did not want to examine that face. If this worked he would be able to see it in a mirror. He wasn't sure if it would be better or worse to see it from the outside first.

"What kind of person just . . . signs over their body?" said Talis.

"Hello?" said Evie, raising a couple of needle-arms as if raising her hand. "We all did!"

"Well, kind of," said Talis. Sure, they'd all died after becoming AI. But the death had been an ugly side effect, not the actual point. "This is different."

"They would seem to be idealists," said Az. "There are currently four hundred thirty-two of them in an encampment outside. They say they want to help."

Talis was willing to admit that they needed help. The ability to destroy cities from space was nice and all, and a judicious number of smoking craters had created a sort of stunned pause that passed for peace. But peacekeeping was a different question. They needed a less lethal, more personal touch. Something subtler, more flexible. They needed systems and rules, and they needed someone to enforce them.

They needed an army.

What they had, instead, was the makings of a cult: people from all over the world looking up into the pause of his peace as if seeing the face of a god.

Some of them had actually turned up at said god's doorstep. And now one in particular had lain down on said god's gurney as if on an altar.

His name, unpromisingly, was Gary.

Just then Gary sighed in his sleep. Talis felt the heat of the exhale across his thermocouples and the push of the air current against the pressure sensors in his finger pads. He curled his fingers up—they went cling against the gurney—and tucked *his hand away. Pockets, that was what he needed. He would push his fists deep into his pockets, which would both look satisfyingly broody and help him think.*

"If you're squeamish we could just upload everybody," *said Evie, who somehow viewed becoming a perpetually-nine-year-old room-shaped demigod as a positive experience to be widely shared.* "Skip the middleman. AI army."

"A waste of resources," *said Az.* "Even with a screened applicant pool the Spiel Institute program never achieved a success rate of better than two point six percent."

"Do you ever just use a sentence without a number in it?" *snapped Talis.*

"Five percent of the time," *said Az, who completely lacked irony, and who was ironically their expert on human consciousness. Granted, he viewed it mostly as a computational challenge, parallel to describing how individual water molecules somehow became liquid, or how smooth spacetime emerged from fluctuating bits of quantum information.*

How did the billion electrochemical flashes between neurons become thought*? How did the thousand skittering thoughts become* person*? Before the Big Melt, it had been the problem of the age. Now Az claimed to have nailed it—"fully solved the emergent phenomena from the ground-state Hamiltonian," and even Talis didn't get that—and they were ready to try out his answer on Gary the avatar.*

Talis looked down at Gary. Was this it, then? A human face for a new god to marshal his followers. A human presence at the peace table. Human hands to do the work of saving the world.

Azriel had a dry voice and a leftover New Zealand accent that was the last human thing about him. For approximately the gazillionth time, he explained (with math) how they would suppress the existing "Gary-ness" and then use the same machinery the AIs had used in their original bodies—the datastore, the webbing—to operate Gary's body "like any other appliance."

Evie waggled her camera at that.

Talis was skeptical. Math or not, this seemed to him like demonic possession—and himself, the demon.

It helped that Gary, like the other dirt-smudged and wide-eyed young people in the shantytown outside the blast doors, had volunteered. It helped that their work was righteous; that the world needed saving. But if Talis was honest with himself, most of the reason he himself had volunteered to try possessing Gary was a demon's reason. He wanted to draw a deep breath again.

Back when he was human, he had been a political scientist. It was a limiting role, but it beat denizen of the underworld, so he tried to put it back on again, though it was ridiculous on him as an argyle cardigan. "Is this even legal?"

"Really?" said Evie. "We just blew up Fresno."

"Rider seven in your UN contract," said Az. "Given adequate budget, you can employ as many people as you want. And since they are volunteers and the salary expenditure is zero, the potential legal number is infinite."

"Rider seven," Talis said softly. "Right. Okay. Evie, can you plug me in?" He had a cable coming out of his own heart,

and they'd left an actual socket in Gary's shiny new datastore, a little detail which, yuck, needed some work. Short-range magnetic induction, maybe? Or floating gates. There were plenty of ways to transfer data short distances at high rates without an actual—

—Plug.

The whole world jolted as if it had just been divided by zero: it compressed to a point and blew into infinite dust and suddenly Talis could feel the tongue in his mouth. One of those human things that humans edited out. The feeling of their own tongues, the view of the nose perpetually at the corner of the eye, the darkness of blinks. He could feel hard table heart lungs fingers blood coming out of his nose everything going too fast. Beside him the discarded 'bot that had been his body clattered to the floor.

Too fast, too fast. He felt it all and for a moment struggled not to; it was like being on fire. Then he remembered that he had wanted it and seized it, still burning, with a will more chromium than steel.

He remembered what a reasonable heart rate was, and a reasonable rate of breathing, and set those both.

He tried to tune out his tongue.

No good. He could still feel it.

He could feel everything, and his breathing was doing that thing where it was too obvious and awkward and he had to think about it to keep it going. He could feel his lungs moving. He could feel things to which there were no human analogs at all, like the low-frequency waves that crossed the brain once a second, the anesthetic sweeping through the brain's sand castle of self-awareness. The webbing was far more powerful than the drug-induced wave and he simply pushed back on it and felt his whole self light up. His brain and his body—his body—felt literally aglow.

Yes. Yes, this was going to work. He could feel it. This was going to save the world.

Talis took a deep breath. He opened his eyes.

16
TEA AND SYMPATHY

By the time we staggered into the sunlight outside the blast doors, Elián had stopped trying to tear himself apart, but he was still shaking, still crying softly.

We tumbled to a stop at the head of the stairs, as an alternative to tumbling down them.

"Easy," I said. "Easy. Sit." I lowered Elián onto the top stair and sat down beside him, between him and the drop. There were ravens swirling below us, and Elián was coming to pieces. He inhaled with strange sharp sounds, as if still trying to keep himself from crying out. He raised a hand to smear the tears away from his eyes, the snot away from his nose. On his wrist the blackwork tattoo gleamed, solid as a handcuff. He saw it and folded forward, across his own lap. "Oh, God . . . ," he groaned.

"Elián," I said. "I'm here. I tried to come sooner—"

There was a cake, and a party. "I'm sorry."

"Not your fault."

I rubbed circles on his back. I could feel the knobs of his spine, and the bunch and shiver of muscles. "Don't forgive me," I whispered. I was AI and he was Swan Rider. He should not forgive me.

"Not you," he said. "Talis."

Two.

Talis, as he had been before I met him. Before I'd changed him. Before he had learned to be human. The Talis who could snap his fingers and destroy a city and not even pause to watch it burn.

Below us the nameless city of the Swan Riders was yellow with winter-bleached willow scrub and dotted with white tents, and around that the red sea rippled in a bright wind, the petals of a rose. I made a count of the tents, even as I consulted my datastore for numbers. About 150 Swan Riders as a steady population—141 just at the moment.

They were volunteers. They were all volunteers. Idealists. True believers. And yet—

"Tell me what it's like. What it's like to be—"

"No," said Elián, his voice muffled.

"I think it's important."

Under my hands the back buckled as if Elián were going to throw up. He didn't. But he didn't answer me, either.

I didn't push him. The truth was, I could read Two's intent as clearly as if he'd filed a plan. As clearly as if I had planned it myself. I had Azriel's critical-decision-point model running loops inside my head, blowing up Halifax every 3.2 seconds. I understood being AI just a little too well.

But just because you have power doesn't mean you have to abuse it.

Elián stirred a little and a pebble went tumbling down the steps, tick, tock, drop—the sound of a bead falling onto glass. A shudder went over my skin. Around us boulders and scree, red with lichen bloom, were scattered with the little statues of horses.

"The Swan Riders make these." I said it by way of distraction. I reached to pick up one of the statues, to show Elián—and stopped.

I had grown up as a Precepture child, and my roommate had been a fairly major god: I knew the feel of ritual or religion, even when I did not know the religion itself. It seemed deeply taboo to touch the horseman figures, and so the Precepture child still inside me knew what the AI I had become did not.

Awe hit me like a shock wave. "The Swan Riders make these," I breathed. In the sunlight, Elián was pulling himself together, and I was pulling together the world. "They make them from the horns and trees of old saddles. They work on them from the moment they are first possessed. The Japanese would have called them *haniwa*. The Egyptians, *ushatbi*. They are funerary offerings."

"They're what?" said Elián.

"They're grave markers."

The Swan Riders made these because they were going to die. And they left them here, at our feet. At *Talis's* feet.

"Okay, great," said Elián. "A-plus job comforting me, Greta." He sounded like himself, but he was shaking still, and I could actually see the pounding lights of his fear and headache. It was disturbingly intimate, like looking at someone's rape kit. He staggered to his feet. "Let's go."

"Where?"

"Away from the grave markers? Down there. I want a word with Talis—Michael, I mean."

I was afraid that word might be "stab," but I too wanted a word with Michael.

He would know, better than I did, what the Swan Riders wanted. Whether I could lead them. Whether they would turn against Talis and help me rescue Francis Xavier. Whether I could stop this war.

Whether I could remake the world.

"Michael!" The name burst out of me as we tumbled through the low door of the yurt.

Then I stopped. Michael was on the floor, on his stomach, with his head turned away, one hand outstretched, and so limp that for just an instant I thought he was dead.

But he wasn't. He stirred and rolled over.

"So?" he said, flat on his back but attempting an insouciant smile. "How did it go?"

The urgency caught up with me again: "Can the Swan Riders be turned?"

He blinked at me, bleary. "Into what?"

"Turned," I said, "against—"

"Hey, remember." Elián cut me off. "Humans do this thing called soft-pedaling?"

"You never soft-pedaled a thing in your life."

"Watch me start," he said, and knelt to help Michael up off the floor. Rachel and Francis Xavier had a table with a wobbly leg and two mismatched chairs. Elián sat Michael down in one of them.

Michael slumped into the curving back. "We're going to chat, are we?" His voice was both fierce and weak. "Should I start? Hey, El, nice ink. Is it new?"

Elián covered his swollen wrist tattoo with his other hand. "Do you know what being possessed does to them?"

"I didn't," said Michael, and then flickered for a moment. "I do."

Michael hadn't known, but Rachel did. Rachel knew very well what being ridden was like.

"You said it was like dreaming," I told her.

"Don't—" said Michael. "Don't push me, Greta. My balance isn't so good."

"Rachel said it was like dreaming," I amended, and Elián broke in.

"Says the gal who's been dreamlocked. They use dreams to torture people, Greta."

"They don't have to . . ." That was Rachel, called by her name and rising up in Talis's precarious teeter-totter mind. "If you're willing, if you don't fight, I—"

"At this point," said Michael, "Rachel would like to give you a little speech entitled 'Lie Back and Think of England.'"

"Says *England*," snarked Elián.

"Yeah," said Michael. "I'm realizing." He sighed and leaned forward, folding his arms on the tabletop and resting his head on them, fatigue and pain and sorrow in every line of him. It made my heart twist. It made Elián turn away.

The mugs and the teapot were hanging on hooks on the wall. The tea was in a round wooden box on a shelf above. Elián set them all in the middle of the table, in a precise little line. The precision was unlike him. It was the kind of precision that could put a knife into the second intercostal space, half an inch from the aorta. He swung the kettle on the induction plating with a clang, and claimed the other chair. Michael had lifted his head to watch, and for a moment the pair of them just looked at each other as if finding targeting solutions.

The kettle boiled, and I set it between them, on a trivet of woven straw.

After a moment Michael reached out and took the lid off the teapot. It rattled as he set it down—his hands were shaking that much—and when he reached for the canister of tea he nearly knocked it over. Elián steadied it. They stopped.

They were not hand in hand, but it was close: both leaning forward over the table, both with a hand against the round wooden box.

"Three scoops for a full pot," said Michael.

And Elián didn't nod. But he did measure the tea leaves into the pot, one scoop at a time. Poured the steaming water. Michael replaced the teapot lid.

"Do you want to know why I brought you here?" said Elián. "Why I called in the evac?"

Michael, who never passed up the chance to hear the master plan, drew his little loop in the air. "I assumed it was because your coconspirators exploited your feelings for Greta and thereby got you to take the mind-bogglingly stupid part of the risk."

"Sure," said Elián. "That. But why from the refuge? Why not just from the church?"

"Oh, for God's sake, don't lead me through it," snapped Michael. "You're not Socrates and I have a headache."

"It was because you were supposed to be learning something. And you couldn't do that while you were stuck, you know, in the first stage of grief."

"Anger," I said, because I couldn't help it. There was never a space wanting a fact that I didn't want to fill.

"With AIs it's actually fury and vengeance." Michael pinched the skin between his eyebrows. I could see his aura trembling.

"Yeah." Elián shrugged. "Anyway."

"And what exactly was the sucking chest wound supposed to teach me, Elián? Spit it out. I'm out of patience."

What he was out of was time. I slipped behind him and dropped a hand onto each shoulder, getting ready. I saw the tilt of his dark head as he looked at my hand. Felt his muscles tighten with fear.

"How to be human," said Elián, who was also looking at my hands.

"How to care about people," I said.

"Hey, I care about people. Just, you know." He waved a hand. "Statistically."

"That's not—" Good enough, I wanted to say, but just there the palsy overwhelmed him. He went off into a horrible, rattling seizure, and it took both Elián and me to get him on the floor and hold him there.

I thought about what Talis had taken from me—what I had fought to get back. What had entered me like a shock wave and turned me into a beacon. How to care about people. It was the difference between me and Azriel with his pinwheel eyes; between me and Evie with her shallow, shocking glee. It was the difference between Two and Michael.

I thought this, and I held Michael's hand, even though I thought he might break my fingers with his pain and panicked strength.

There was nothing to do but hang on.

But hanging on was not nothing.

And when he fell limp, he kept my hand in his. Just breathed for a little while. And then lifted my fingers to his lips. "Greta Stuart," he said. "You may yet be the best of us."

Only Michael would say that and mean us, the AIs. But only Rachel would speak that softly.

"We need to be better," I said, and meant the same we, the same us.

Two would not have agreed. But Michael answered at a whisper: "Yes. I know."

Then he shivered—almighty whole-body shiver. "We're out of time for soft-pedaling," he said. "Help me up."

Elián crouched to help. It was a wrestle, to get that small, limp body in the chair again. These attacks—they were clustered more thickly than I would have thought. Two had warned that the disease would be accelerated, but I hadn't dreamt it would be by this much. Michael had very little time.

And FX. Halifax. None of us had very much time.

"Can the Swan Riders be turned," Michael said, "into what."

"Can they be turned against Talis?"

He looked up sharply. He'd chipped a tooth during the seizure and there was blood on his mouth from where the newly sharp edge had caught his lip. He was pale and it was vampire-vivid, inhuman, strange—his whole face was whirled and new, neither human nor AI, neither Rachel nor Michael. Balanced as if on the edge of a knife.

"You're the only person I know who's ever taken over the world," I said. "Will you help me?"

"Halifax," he guessed.

"Peace through terror." I didn't know how to phrase this. "They locked me out of the weapons systems."

"Evie's little padlocks." Michael scrubbed his face with one hand. "Yeah, you won't be opening those anytime soon."

"That leaves the Swan Riders. Michael, they make these little . . . carvings."

Over his shoulder was Rachel's carving, homey and portentous, on the rickety table by the bed. I looked at it, and when I looked back, the person looking at me was changing.

"I—we do," she said. "We carve the riding."

"Rachel," said Elián. "Tell her. Tell her what the Swan Riders want."

She leaned forward, small but magnetic. I had seen her only at the bottom of Talis's pain, and so it was easy to think of her as a hurt person, as a victim. But she wasn't. She was a Swan Rider, and whatever else the Swan Riders were, they were all falling stars. Rachel was blazing. "Being ridden," she said. "It's—it's like nothing human, but it's a little like dreaming. You fall asleep, but things keep happening . . ."

"You're aware of it?" I asked her. "You remember it?"

Her face flickered, half Michael, but she shrugged by cupping her hands, a very un-Talis gesture. She seemed unable to elaborate. "It's like dreaming."

"Yeah," said Elián. "The kind of dreaming where the monster is reaching for you and you can't even scream."

"Sometimes."

For some reason I was thinking of Queen Agnes Little, flushing and touching her weskit as she turned to the camera, freckles and fierceness and half an engineering degree. An alternate of me. "Do you want it to stop?" I asked.

"Yes." The word seemed to have burst from her before she could catch it. Her cupped hands clenched into fists. "No. It's not that. We *volunteer.*"

True believers. And yet . . . "You must have worked hard, though, to keep your secrets. Because there's nothing in the datastore about what it's like to be ridden. There's nothing at all."

"There isn't?" That was Michael, shocked, frozen. The strategic thinker of the age he might be, but this was his whacking great blindspot, and I had just thrust a poleaxe into it. "Truly?" he said.

"Truly."

"And that's what they want," said Elián.

For an instant Michael's gaze had taken that characteristic inward turn, reaching for the data, and of course failing. Now he had a stunned look, as if the floor had vanished under him. "They want to keep the secret?" he said, uncertain.

"No," said Elián. "They want to scream it in your face."

"No," I said. "They want . . ." I was so close to working it out. It sat at the edge of my understanding like a word on the tip of the tongue. "The AIs leave ghosts of themselves in the Swan Riders. But the Swan Riders can't touch the AIs. You ride someone and you're unchanged."

"Unless you happen to bump into a zealous sheep farmer with a dagger," said Michael.

"What if you weren't?"

"Weren't what? Weren't *mutilated* and left to die?"

"Weren't unchanged. The imprinting of ghosts. What if they want it to go both ways?"

"Ewwww." Michael scrunched his nose. "Why?"

"Because they're human. Michael—I saw the boxes. I saw what the AIs become. There's this simulation running in my head, and the satellites—how can we look down on the whole world, and still be human?"

"You're their test case," said Elián, who was not as stupid as Talis thought he was. (Not that that was a high bar.) "What if an AI could learn to be human again?"

"I am human." Michael struck his fist against his skull with a hollow thunk. "I'm stuck as human and it totally sucks."

"But we need to be better," I said, "and you're better."

"I'm not better, I'm just dying. It doesn't automatically make you more noble. Trust me, I've outlived a lot of people, and most of them were mealymouthed self-interested ground weasels."

I blinked, momentarily losing track of the argument. ". . . ground weasels?"

"Mealymouthed ground weasels. On morphine. I see no reason why I shouldn't be drugged to the eyeballs when the time comes. In fact, let's get started on that."

"You are better," said Elián. "If you could see what your other—the other—"

"Two," I said.

Elián pressed on. "What he's doing to Francis—"

"What?" It wasn't a flicker this time, it was a lightning flash. Rachel sat bolt upright: "What's he doing to Francis?"

"Possessing him," I said.

"Oh." Her voice cracked. Dying, Rachel knew that possession was a death sentence.

"Not like that," said Elián. "In, like, bursts. To hurt him. To get him to report on . . . what it's like."

If you don't fight, Rachel had said.

I knelt by her side and took her hand. "Francis Xavier is fighting."

"*Can the Swan Riders be turned,*" she said, and was suddenly Michael again. "I can turn anybody into anything. Come on. We're going."

17
BEFORE THE DOORS

We couldn't run, but we ran.

I held Michael up because Elián was too tall. He would go strongly for a half dozen steps, and I would struggle to keep up, and then his knees would fail and I would struggle instead to keep him on his feet. Our boots beat uneven on the boardwalk, and this time no one came out to bow.

No one came out at all.

No voices.

It was as if the nameless city were empty.

Then we turned the last corner and staggered to a stop. The Swan Riders were arrayed before us. At their back was the mountain, and its blast doors were shut.

"Well." Michael was leaning on me, his voice was low. "Did you want to do the 'I have a bad feeling about this' line, or shall I?"

We'd come to a halt on the end of the boardwalk, where it stepped down into a rocky meadow of saxifrage and moss, between the city and the mountain. It was as if we were on the thrust of a stage. The Swan Riders were two steps down from us, wearing their wings, like an audience of angels.

It was not all of them—I counted forty-seven, about a third of the number here stationed. Not all of them. But so many.

"I have a bad feeling about this," said Elián, looking from overwhelming force to the mountain's doors, and back. "And the door thing is not good news. I'm not sure why exactly it's not good news but I can tell it's not good news."

"Because," said one of the Swan Riders, "if the blast doors are closed, the city can be wiped out from orbit without touching the AIs inside." The speaker stepped forward, and it was the boy with the shipwreck-green eyes, last seen being Two and dislocating Elián's shoulder. He was not Two, but it was hard to look at him without shivering.

"You people have got to cut it out with the brain swapping," said Elián, who *was* shivering. "I am a simple country boy and y'all are making my head hurt."

"Daji," I named him, and the green-eyed boy tucked his chin and saluted me. A loyal and unhesitating salute, without a trace of irony. I was AI and he was Swan Rider, which meant he owed me his life, and he looked ready to give it, right this instant. He looked ready to lay it on the stones.

"You were with the party that stabbed Talis."

"I was," he said.

"I know your name," I said. And pitched my voice for the crowd. "Height, stance, skin tone, gait. I could name all of you."

"We know," said one of the women—it was Renata, who had held me captive once, who had been afraid. Behind her the mountain glowed sharp and red: a Moroccan lantern in the late afternoon sun.

"This isn't all of you," said Michael, echoing what Elián had said once, about the Swan Rider conspiracy. "Where are the others?"

An AI would have known—I knew—but Daji answered Michael easily, without mocking him: "Inside." He tipped his head back at the doors sealed shut behind him. "We faked a quarantine. It won't hold long. But then, we don't have long."

"You truly don't," said Michael. "Greta. Are we being targeted?"

And this too, I already knew. The *UNDEAD* had already given me the red sea with the crosshairs at its center, the damage estimates, the list of projected casualties. "The platforms are still coming into place," I said. "But yes, we're being targeted."

"Swell," said Elián. "Would anybody like to join me in a rousing chorus of 'Oh God Oh God We're All Gonna Die'?"

"Daji is right: the blast doors would protect the AIs inside the mountain," said Michael. "But not all the AIs are inside."

Elián couldn't resist the jab: "You don't count."

"I don't," he answered, peaceably. "But I wasn't thinking of me."

He was thinking of two to three medium-sized cities. Two might not know me, but he wouldn't kill me. As the first new AI in more than a century, I was too valuable.

"That's the wild card, then," said Michael, with whom I would hate to play poker. "If my friends from the little stabby-stabby incident would step forward."

And they did. The twelve who had stabbed him stepped forward with no hesitation, like the chorus in a Greek play, because whatever else they were they weren't ashamed. And they weren't afraid. They were Swan Riders.

"Look at you," said Michael fondly—and then he laughed, bitter and sweet. "This has nothing to do with the PanPols, does it? Just this once, it really is all about me."

Daji stood at the front of them. "My lord Talis. Will you sit?"

"Don't call me that," said Michael, mild as butter. "But yes, I'll sit."

With a sweeping bow, Daji indicated the ring of boulders and charcoal that must surely have marked a community fire. Michael came down the wood steps with his hand light on Elián's arm—a bit in escort, a bit keeping his balance. And a bit theater, of course. They looked like king and queen. His legs shook as he lowered himself onto one of the boulders. Daji sat in front of him. They were nearly knee-to-knee.

"Sit with us, Greta," said Michael, with a little opening of his hand.

So I sat, the three of us close together, and now we were

generals in a field campaign, a council of war. The stone was sun-warm but the air was cool. I could smell the dampness of the old ash at my feet, and the syrupy sweetness of the broken sea.

Elián stood at Talis's back. And behind Daji gathered the Swan Riders. Their labels drifted half-visibly above them, as if held there by pins. If Two insisted on a purge, and wanted to keep it to an absolute minimum, I could name and implicate each of them.

Or we could do something different.

"What should I call you?" said Daji.

"Michael will do."

"The leader of the armies of heaven," said Daji. "An angel, but not a god."

"Michael mostly, and Rachel sometimes. Rachel, weeping for her children . . . truly the metaphorical richness is *endless*." He flipped richness away with the back of his hand. "And we so don't have time for it. Start talking, people. What do you want? We've got a blackbird incoming in . . ." He glanced at me.

I checked on the weapons platform. "Four and a half minutes."

"Do you not know what we want?" said Daji.

"Think so. Want to hear you say it."

"We want to save you," said Daji.

"Funny way of showing it." Michael pushed aside his coat, and his fingers sank—impossibly, sickeningly—into the hole under his collarbone, pushing in the fabric, vanishing to the knuckle. "I've got like a week to live, and it's not even going to be a nice one."

A susurration of wings at that. I suspected they hadn't known it would be quite that fast.

But I was sure they'd known it wouldn't be nice.

"So," said Michael. "You want to save me."

There was no saving him.

"Me as in Talis."

"You," said Daji, "as in the AIs."

"All of them?" said Michael. With a pronoun that made my heart hurt.

"All of them that we can. You know what's happening to them. What will happen to Greta, when she loses her body?"

"Hands off Greta," said Michael. "She's *my* wild card. Greta: time?"

"Three minutes, twenty seconds."

"You want the organic mind to write to the datastore," said Michael. "A little booster shot of human, every time an AI takes a ride."

"Yes."

"It won't solve the palsy. It will still kill you to be ridden."

"Yes," said Renata.

"We are the Swan Riders, and our lives are yours," said Daji. "This is not about saving our own lives. It is about saving the AIs."

"Even if you have to hurt us to do it," I said.

Daji glanced at me. "We're Swan Riders. Sometimes

we hurt people. But we want—to do that less. We want to change you, Lord Talis."

Michael shook his head. Denying the change, or just denying the name?

"Consider the difference between you and your other self."

"It's Greta who made me different," said Michael. "You people just stabbed me in the chest."

"Maybe," said Daji. "But one way or the other, consider the difference. There are three cities annihilated, and your other self did that without blinking. He's drifted—you've drifted too far out from human. Consider what a difference it would make, to have something pull you back."

Michael glanced round at me. "Two minutes," I said.

"It would change me." Michael was looking at his hands, one of them closed tight around the old break in his thigh. "Obviously it would change me, and that matters. I'm just not sure it matters that mu— Oh, God."

"Michael!" I lunged off my stone and thrust my hands against his face. I reached deep into his implant pathways, and I *pushed*.

A sudden, shocking, sparking change.

"What?" gasped Rachel. Her eyes, inches from mine, were round as wells.

"Sorry," I answered, likewise gasping: it took adrenaline to do that. I dropped my hands. "I thought: if a fibrillation of the heart can be stopped with a shock—"

"Theory later," said Elián, looking up as if there were a clock across all the sky.

"It won't last," I warned. I estimated I'd bought Rachel ten minutes at most.

"I know, I can feel—"

Elián interrupted her. "We need Talis."

Rachel's sweet face shattered. What must it be like, to be pushed out of one's own death?

Balanced on the balls of my feet in front of her, I folded my hands around her hands. "We need both of you," I said. "That's the whole point. Can you be both of you?"

Her chest was heaving as if she were working hard at something. She blinked and blinked. The cinders made a dry crinkling sound as my boots broke them.

Forty-five seconds left. I did not say it out loud. My datastore began a visible scrolling countdown; a clock over Rachel's face. Michael's face? There was something very fine in the eyes.

"He won't—I won't—he won't kill you. Even if he doesn't love you. You're too important."

"I know."

"Lean on that. Lean hard." There was a shudder in the words, in the breath, like the breathing of a child who has fallen asleep crying.

"I think it does matter, the human booster shot," I said. "I think it does matter, that much."

Closed eyes. A fragmented nod. The hands jerked in mine and I let them go.

"Can you do this?" In thirty seconds, we were going to need to persuade Two that people who had betrayed him (though not exactly *him*) had a point. That was not a small thing. And broken or not, Michael had the best shot at it.

"I—" The eyes were closed; one fist came up and pressed into the temple. "Oh, I'm really losing it."

And then the eyes came open, and they were not fragmented, not flickering. They were whole—more than whole. They were doubled. They were *both*. "And if you don't think I can play losing it for all losing it is worth, then you don't know me at all."

I felt the smile bloom across my face.

The nameless, doubled person smiled back at me.

Just there, the invisible clock hit zero. I raised my voice to let everyone know: "The weapons platform is now in range."

The Swan Riders looked up. Not that it would help— none of them could see *space*. But they were human, and when you are human and a shadow crosses you, you look up. I was still looking at the new person. And she was looking at me. Shock wave, beacon. Something more than AI, more than human.

And then she turned aside to watch the blast doors. "The Death Star has cleared the planet. . . . Come on now, sweetheart. That's your cue."

And on that cue, the doors opened.

They did not boom open, twenty-five tons swinging on nine-hundred-pound hinges, with a blaze of light— satisfying as that would be. There was a little airlock in one of them, smaller than a man, like the portal into Oz.

Through it came Francis Xavier, ducking to get under the lintel.

He was carrying a chair.

It was the chair that kept me from being sure instantly: it is hard to know anyone by their gait when they are descending a mountain staircase while carrying a five-hundred-year-old fiberglass-shelled school chair inverted over their head. Or perhaps I simply did not want to be sure. Did not want to be sure that this was not Francis Xavier. That he was dying now. That he was gone.

My uncertainty was a doubtful grace, and it did not last long. The figure in its familiar battered boots and swinging coat came striding through the Swan Riders without a glance at any of them. He flipped the chair down to make a fourth in our little circle—a bit awkward with one hand, in a way FX would never be. Then he flung himself into the molded seat as if only loosely aware of the principles on which chairs operated. He stuck his long legs out to nudge his counterpart's ankles.

"Hello," said Two. "Having fun?"

"Always fancied going out with a bang," said Michael. The voice was doubled, and the eyes were still transformed, still blazing with a new power that made me want to grin like a schoolgirl. But Two just *missed* it. Like the horse-and-rider carvings, like the hole in the datascape, it was his blind spot, and he missed it.

"What about you, Greta," Two said. "Settling in okay?"

"Tolerably."

"And you, my little Rider?"

Elián shrugged. "Oh, you know. Making friends. Surviving torture. Plotting your death. The usual."

"Excellent!" said Two, and then opened his attention like a blast radius. "So, it turns out, a Rider's experience of being possessed can vary quite a bit, depending in part on how willing they are. It can be nearly without incident, or it can be deeply traumatic. I did not know that, and so I owe you folks a general apology." He looped a hand through the air. "Though honestly, people, you might have mentioned."

He leaned forward. "Now that that's cleared up. Greta, how do you feel about Turkey?"

"The country or the bird?"

"The country. There's this hand-dug cave city at Derinkuyu—going on three thousand years old, but don't think primitive: it's *so* cool. Can house twenty thousand, complete with stables and churches and the ever-important wine press. I have a data silo there. And a few presumably less traitorous hands on the ground."

"Lord Talis," I said. "I am not going anywhere with you."

"Sure?" Two's smile had mania in it—a demonic flash of Francis Xavier's very white teeth. It flipped my heart to see Francis so—and to finally understand what Francis had seen when Talis had come striding out of the Precepture wearing Rachel's face. His heart must have been in free fall. But he had been so so quiet.

"You cannot order me," I said. "And I think you'll find you're out of people who are willing to see me dragged."

"You're so interesting," said Two. "I would hate to write you off."

"I know you would." I leaned my weight on those words. I leaned hard. "In fact, I know you won't."

"I like the Red Mountains," said Michael suddenly. "I like the wind on the water. I like the ravens. I like—" A glance at Francis Xavier's hand, and the voice turned soft-edged, almost Rachel's purely. "I like the people. I don't particularly want to go to Turkey."

"You're not going to Turkey," said Two. "You're going to die."

"I'm going to hear these people out first," Michael answered. "They've given us their lives and their loyalty. And I'm going to hear them out."

"You're not even AI anymore," said Two. "You get that, right? You're not AI, and you're not in charge. Anything they tell you, any reaction you have, is going to last all of a week or two."

I had once seen Michael and Rachel as teetering as if balanced on the edge of a knife. Now they were balanced— and still a knife. "You have no idea what I am."

And Two finally saw it. Blade-sharp. Blazing. For an instant he looked knocked back. Then he said: "Well. Maybe we can find out." He raised a hand like an orchestra conductor, and he snapped his fingers.

The door in the mountain opened. Out of it came two machines, carrying a stretcher. The machines were automatons shaped like insects, like praying mantises, and I'd seen such at the Precepture, often enough. But the stretcher—there was a human form on it, wrapped in an orange quilt. Hanging off one side was a bony brown hand. Stretcher and robots crossed the meadow and the Swan Riders parted for them as if watching a bride go by.

Lying on the stretcher was Sri.

I saw Michael's shoulders tighten, his mouth fall open.

"I think you called dibs," said Two. He leaned forward like a man trying to tell diamond from glass by the fog of his breath. And this was every bit that much a test.

"There's nothing you can do to her that's worse than the palsy," said Renata. Her voice was tight, furious and frightened.

"I wouldn't bet on that," murmured Michael, glancing at me. I could see the grey room in his eyes. Yes. There were always worse things. He wobbled to his feet and took steps to come into striking range of the stretcher.

Sri looked as if she hadn't eaten in weeks, hadn't had a drink in days: her skin was dull and pulled mummy-tight across the sharpness of her bones. Her bright hair had gone fine as spiderwebs, dulled and matted. But her eyes were open. Huge in her sunken face, filmed with pain, but open, and aware. Michael leaned over her and she tracked the movement, hypnotized.

I'm going to gift wrap you, he'd told her, *before I send you to hell.* His hand fell on the edging of the quilt by her throat, his fingers rubbing the little red silk heart that was embroidered there.

"Hey," he said. "You made it home."

"Hey . . ." Sri's voice was a whisper, made hoarse by screaming. "So did you." Her eyes went to me, and then to the body of Francis Xavier. She'd told FX to get out before it was too late. But he hadn't. And now it was. "You all made it." She swallowed, incompletely—there was drool at the corner of her mouth. "Michael, please . . . they made me leave my horse."

Penned in a refuge somewhere? Tied out to graze? Two must have sent machines after her, because no Swan Rider would ever, ever doom a horse like that.

Michael scrunched his nose. "We'll fix that," he answered, and then he shuddered. The ten minutes I'd bought us: time was up. "Could—" Michael asked Sri. "Could you hold my hands a moment?" And the seizure struck him, hard.

Sri lost control of the flailing hands in less than a second, and Elián dove in from behind to catch the tumbling body, and things ended up with Michael bent forward, head on Sri's stomach, waist circled in Elián's arms. Sri put her arm around the shoulders, wrapped her fingers in the hair as if into the mane of a runaway horse. She couldn't see the face, but I could, and I could see Sri picturing it. The blood from the bit tongue. The fight not to scream.

Mirrors and mirrors.

Francis Xavier's body stood silently over the scene. Very black and very beautiful, with his head bare and one sleeve fluttering empty, his coat stirring.

And all around us the wind blew through the wings of the Swan Riders, a sharp sound, like a scythe being sharpened.

"Did anybody want to take this moment to state their demands?" said Two.

I glanced at him, and read him at the glance. I'd been a Precepture child, and I knew well enough the look of someone distracting themselves from the unpleasantness of larger truths. Two was a towering paradox of glee and calm in Francis Xavier's body—but it couldn't be easy, to watch yourself die.

I let him stew.

He stewed awhile.

And it really did seem that the new Michael, just born, was dying, sobbing soundlessly under Sri's helpless hands.

"We want—" said Renata—unwisely. Unwisely, because silence was always the best way to negotiate with Talis, and unwisely because it made Two turn and target her.

"You want to do *that* to all of us," he snapped, for a second genuinely furious, out of control, terrifying.

"Not quite," I murmured.

"Well, what then? Someone walk me through it." Two pulled back into himself and attempted to spike up Francis Xavier's knotted hair. He gave up on that and turned from the scene in disgust. "Come on, people."

"Hard to watch?" Elián guessed. "Different when you've got some skin in the game?"

"It's not *my* skin," Two snapped. "And I honestly don't get why I haven't killed you."

"Yeah," said Elián. "You say that a lot."

Suddenly the episode of the palsy climaxed, and Michael

arched backward as if caught in a current. Elián kept hold and Michael sagged back against him, barely conscious. They were both on their knees in the ashes. Elián looked around. "Go on, guys. Someone tell him what you want."

"We want to save you, Talis," said Sri. She was propped up on one elbow on the stretcher, between the motionless machines. It was clearly all she could manage, and it was surprising that she could manage even that. She looked like a figure in a morality play: Dissolution, say. Or Pestilence. The saffron-orange quilt slid down her body.

Two looked her up and down, raised an eyebrow, and echoed Michael unknowingly: "Funny way of showing it."

"The AIs are dying," she said. "They're falling apart. You've got most of them in boxes, and they are not going to come back out. You're losing them."

"And you can help?"

"We can try," said Daji. "Our research says the read/write properties of the datastore can be changed. We can help you be more human."

"Yeah," said Two, looking down at Elián and at his other self. "Human looks fabulous. So tempting."

"My lord—" said Daji.

"No," Two interrupted. "Definitely, no. Obviously, no. Honestly, what on earth made you think I'd go for this? There's nothing you can do to force me. A little blade in the right place, sure, but the bigger truth is that me and mine could be in Derinkuyu or any one of a dozen other silos in one point seven seconds. Whereas this place."

He whirled one finger in the air, reminding us all of the weapons platform that was holding position directly overhead. "You have just spectacularly bad timing, gang. The world is sliding toward war, and you're the only army I have."

"So," said Renata. "Go to war with the army you have."

"Oh, I will," said Two. "Right after I destroy all the problematic parts with beams from space."

Renata's face flushed and tightened, but Daji bowed his head and made the Rider's salute. "Our lives are yours, Lord Talis."

"Uh-huh," said Two. "Just at the moment, they very much are."

"Except Sri's," wheezed Michael. He was rousing in Elián's arms, and his tone—pure Talis—made me look at him sharply. To my surprise, Elián was helping him, supporting him as he climbed to his feet and stood there as if his knees were untrustworthy. He looked up at Two. "Dibs, remember?"

Yes, that was Talis. What had happened to that shining, newborn strangeness? It seemed entirely gone.

I tried to get it back: "Michael," I said—having no other name to call. "Wait."

"I'm *busy*, Greta." There were weird flares all over his aura; so many signs of pain/desperation/deception/anticipation in his physiology that it was as if he'd grown spikes. He smiled up at the very tall Two. "I've always liked ironic symmetry, so I'm assuming you have a knife."

"*The* knife, in fact," said Two, bumping back his coat and drawing Elián's dagger from the sheath at his belt. He was frowning a little, presumably at all that spikiness, but he handed over the blade. "I knew that was still you. Spot of therapeutic revenge?"

"Yes, I am still me."

And yet. I watched the movements microscopically: the hand fiddling to settle the dagger, the fingers closing one at a time. The head tipped downward, staring at the knife, as if fascinated.

"I am still me. But—it changes you. Caring for someone. Being cared for. It changes you."

Michael raised the knife as if to look at it. But if he really wanted to look at it, he was holding it backward: the handle facing inward, the blade pointed at Two.

My jaw dropped open. Michael—but it wasn't Michael—caught my eye. And I saw it. I saw all the masks fall away. There was a person there, smooth and shattered, broken and blazing. She was still facing Two and the toes of her boots were digging into the ash.

She looked up.

Two blinked.

He started to dodge, and Daji shouted and dove, but it was too little, too late.

The shining figure sprang forward, like a fencer's flèche, like a hawk striking, and drove the knife into Two's chest.

It struck him hard and true.

Infraclavical, and in the second intercostal space.

Francis Xavier bellowed and toppled, and the new person caught him and fell with him and they both went down. I could see Francis Xavier's eyes over her shoulder, huge and watering and wild and *his*.

"Rachel?" whispered Francis Xavier.

"*Francis*," she said.

18
EVENING FALLS

The knife was sticking out of Francis Xavier's chest.

Daji and Renata, peeled his shuddering, gasping body out of Rachel's arms. They laid Francis Xavier on his back in the circle of cinders and ash. There were suddenly dozens of hands digging in pockets, packets of clotting powder and forcescar tearing open, needles flashing, lengths of gauze flying outward like ribbons in the wind that swept down the mountain and across the rose-petal sea.

Francis Xavier's eyes were wide and shocked and seeking Rachel's.

Rachel had been knocked back from the crisis by all the helping hands. "Francis," she said, reaching for him with his blood on her hands.

Someone jabbed a needle in Francis's neck. His eyes softened like snow melting. And then he was gone.

The bloody hand dropped. "Elián . . ." It was Michael's voice, resonant with possibilities and yet almost breaking.

"It's okay," said Elián. "Hey. I've got you." He took Michael by the shoulders and eased him away, settling him with his back against the big stone.

Meanwhile Alejandro—the man who had choked Francis Xavier almost to death, and who had also held him while he wept—Alejandro had scooped Sri up and was settling her likewise, right beside Michael.

After all, they needed the stretcher.

Sri was wrapped in that brilliantly orange and infinitely familiar blanket. Michael's coat was rucked up behind him, bunching awkwardly over the shoulders. With their backs to the same boulder and their boots in the same ash, the two of them leaned into each other like the two inward falling halves of an arch.

"Clever," said Sri.

"Yeah. Thanks." Michael drew his legs up and wrapped his arms tight around them. Rachel was soaking through him like blood through a bandage. "Talk to me when he doesn't die."

"He won't," I said. Because what had been catastrophic in the ruins of Our Lady of the Snows was less so here—with a hundred hands at the ready, with a hospital on-site.

Speaking of . . . Swan Riders had wrestled the stretcher away from the robots (both of which seemed to have seized up) and were rushing Francis Xavier away. Michael watched him go and ran a hand across his face, smearing it with ash as if with war paint.

But I really didn't think Francis Xavier would die. With the knife left in place, his lung had not collapsed. There was no trace of the pneumothorax, the cruel squeeze of air against organs that had so nearly killed Talis. Michael who was Talis.

Just Michael.

"I'm going to need a name," he said softly.

". . . Tanim," suggested Daji. There were only a handful of Swan Riders left now, but the green-eyed boy was one of them.

Michael looked at me for the translation.

"The wave," I said.

"The wave." Michael traced a crest and crash in the air. "Here and then gone."

"We'd better get that door shut," said Elián. I followed his glance up the mountainside, to where the portal in the blast door stood open. The AIs were still behind those doors. *Two* was still behind those doors. Elián wouldn't be the only one who would feel better if we could shut him in there. "We could, I don't know, jam them or something?"

Rachel laughed. "They weigh twenty-five tons."

Elián looked at her.

"I'd never seen anything like them in my life," she said. "Where I'm from—" But of course, Rachel had no history. She smiled, crookedly. "Well. After I got here, I looked them up."

Overhead the weapons platform shifted on its station-keeping rockets. I could see us through its lenses; little figures amid little stones. We looked like a logic puzzle, like one of those pegs-and-holes games. What next?

"You don't need a name," I said. "We'll manage."

"It's a tradition," murmured Sri. "New AIs rename themselves."

But whatever Michael was now, it wasn't a new AI. And as the adrenaline left him, he was starting to shake.

"Look, Sri," said Elián. "I'm sure sorry you're dying horribly. But what are we going to do? Was this seriously the endgame? Tell Talis you want to fiddle with his brain and just cross your fingers he'd say yes? That was the whole plan?"

Sri tucked the other half of her blanket over Michael's knees. "Yes," she admitted softly. "That was the whole plan. Just to change one mind."

"Great plan. What a shock—it didn't work," said Elián. "And now"—he gestured upward—"death rays."

"It did work," said Michael, rubbing the quilt between thin fingers. "Because I say yes."

"You can't make that stick," said Elián.

"Yes you can," I said—because finally I saw it, the whole scope of the Swan Riders' plan. "You know you can."

"Yes," said Michael, a word heavy as a gold coin. A word that cost him. "Yes. I know I can."

"What—" began Elián, and then cut himself off with a yelp as the frozen robot behind him swung around and grabbed his arm.

"I have to admit," said the robot. "That would be a hell of a vote of confidence."

Elián swore and tried to jerk away. The robot's pincer sprang open and let him go. Suddenly freed, he staggered and bonked his shins against a stone.

"Sorry." The thing approximated a shrug with a ratcheting of its uppermost limb. "Just a remote-control patch. It was the nearest speaker that wasn't, you know, actively plotting my doom." The limb came down with a series of clicks. "On the day my microphones rebel, it's all over."

Like a rack of wrenches sitting down, the robot lowered itself into the abandoned schoolroom chair. "So," said Two. "That was dramatic."

"Thank you," said Michael. At least half of him was incapable of taking that as anything but a compliment.

"He won't be another—whatever you are," said Two. "That body of yours was possessed for weeks, and you were clearly mulling on our personal history at the time." The robot twitched as if the pronouns were making its nonexistent teeth hurt. "FX was possessed on and off for, what, forty-five minutes? And reflective self-analysis was *so* not my mood. So he'll still be Francis Xavier. Which was exactly your point, wasn't it? I am an idiot."

"You know," said Michael, "you truly are."

The robot, quite unbelievably, sighed. "You're really thinking about this?"

I could feel its uncertainty—Talis's uncertainty. His unspoken question: *Should I really . . . ?*

"I—I think I've lost a lot of people. I think it would be nice to save a few."

"The number of people we've saved is in the billions."

"Sure." A tiny, weary shrug, and a one-cornered smile. "Statistically."

"You know," said Elián, "I'm *not* an idiot. So why am I always the only one who doesn't know what's going on? What is this thing you're really thinking about?"

"The one person the Swan Riders wanted to convince wasn't Talis," I said, with a nod at the robot. "It was Michael."

"But he can't—he can't make that stick—"

"Yes he can," I said. "If he becomes AI."

"You're talking about upload," said Elián. "You're talking Rachel—Michael—wavy person here getting uploaded. Getting a new datastore and getting reuploaded and turning back into an AI."

"It's the only way to reintegrate," said the collection of vise grips and plumbing parts that was currently being Two. The upper manipulator arms hinged outward in something approximating a spread of hands. "The only way to capture whatever grand change this true love hath wrought or whatever."

"Or whatever," said Michael. "It's—I—" One hand fisted in Sri's blanket. The other came up and pushed into that dip between nose and mouth. Sri wrapped an arm around him and his voice came out crackling. "To be honest I don't think I have the nerve."

"Well," said the plumbing parts. "Up to you."

"Tanim," said Daji softly. "My lady, please. It's the only way."

"Oh, shut up," said Michael. "You didn't ask me and you don't get to order me."

"But," said Elián, who could make *but* into a whole argument.

"You just don't get it. No one volunteers for that twice." Michael's fist got tighter, hiding fear inside anger. "The upload . . . no one volunteers for that."

Elián looked sideways at me. "Greta did."

"*Twice*," Michael repeated petulantly.

The sun had dipped behind the mountain, and the little meadow was suddenly colder, shadowed, though still under a high clear sky. I crouched in the ash and tucked the saffron blanket tightly around Michael's knees.

"They don't understand," I said. "But I do."

The grey room. I knew exactly what I was asking, knew exactly why the strange, newborn, ambiguous creature was shivering. I leaned forward and pressed my hand, not over the wound, but over the heart. The figure fell silent, and slowly lowered his—her—fist. "Be the best of us," I said.

A little smile. "I think that spot's taken."

"Be the first," said Elián.

She closed her new old eyes. "Okay."

Mountain twilight is so different than prairie twilight. The sun goes behind the mountains before the shadows can truly stretch and thicken, before the world can turn gold and full of contemplation. You stand in shadow and cast no shadow, and the sky above is still bright.

I looked at my hand with no shadow falling from it. And I thought of the grey room.

I looked at Michael—transformed and brilliant with the transformation; broken and shining.

I could also feel Two's eyes on my back, though it was hard to say how: the eyes of the satellite were on us, yes, and the sensors of the great mountain, yes, but it felt more personal than that. It was the kind of looking that puts an ache of awareness just behind the forehead. A human feeling. I turned. The robot in the ancient school chair had hardly stirred, and had no eyes in any case. I looked it in the uppermost pincer.

"You will abide by this," I said.

"Hey. Anything that means that much to, well, me, for some value of 'me' . . . anything that means that much is likely to stick."

"Not good enough," I said. "You will abide by this. You will allow the Swan Riders to continue their research into changing the nature of possession. You will implement that research as implementation becomes possible. And in the meantime you will conduct no purge of their ranks."

"Awww," said the robot. "Not even a little one?"

"You will seek a cure for the palsy."

"Don't you think I already have?"

"Say so."

"You put a lot of faith in my words, kiddo."

"The whole world puts a lot of faith in your words, Talis. There's even a book."

"Fine. I will abide by this. Skip the completely justified purges, do the research, implement the results." The robot hesitated. "Change my mind."

"It's been five hundred years," said Michael. "It's past time."

"What about the Pan Polars?" said Elián.

Two shrugged with a rattle and click. "What about them? As far as I can make out it's an entirely separate thing."

Mostly. The Swan Riders' plan had needed a war, to get Talis in the field, to give them cover. This was always going to coincide with a war. But the particulars of the war—to the Swan Riders, they didn't matter.

To me, they mattered.

"Queen Agnes Little," I said.

"Yeah, I like her," said Two. "She's tough, and smart, and scary. Must run in the family. But she's got nothing she can give me."

"Don't be too sure of that," I said. "She's pregnant."

The plumbing parts actually huffed with surprise. "How do you know?" But of course he was already reviewing the files, seeing what I had seen: the thermal clues, the hand on the weskit, the thickening mask of freckles. What he had missed, and I had seen.

"Let her hostage herself."

"That's . . . irregular."

"Please, my lord," I said. "Just give me a little time."

To do what? I did not know. I had failed to take over the world. But I could feel the world changing. The earth under us was spinning at eight hundred miles an hour. And Talis was considering.

"She'll never go for it," said Two.

"Ask her."

I felt that looking, again. The deep pressure. Behind my eyes, for the first time all day, Halifax stopped exploding.

"Okay," said Two. "I'll ask."

Above us sounded a taiko-drum boom. The great doors were opening. The target that had been pinned to all of us, that I had felt in my datastore and on the back of my neck, suddenly switched off. Only I could have felt that, but I felt that.

"Thank you, my lord," I said.

"Greta," said the robot. "I wish you'd call me Talis."

"When you've earned it," I told him.

I beckoned to my Swan Riders—and they were *mine*— with one royal wave. We had wounded; we had people in pain. It was past time to find them comfort.

"Wait," said Sri as the men in wings went to pick her up.

It was weak enough to be a last word, but it was heard. The Swan Riders fell back; they waited. Sri was trying to flail free of her blanket. I folded it back for her. Underneath, her legs were twisted like old cedar railings. "Sri," I said. "What is it?"

Now her hands were fumbling at her vest. She got one button popped open, and reached inside it, and drew from her inner pocket . . .

Haniwa. Ushatbi. The carved figure of a horse and rider.

Sri's was narrow and sharp. The rider and the horse were both nearly faceless, just ridges and edges, but the horse had a mane and tail carved into a froth of curlicues, and the rider had huge and perfect wings. A blaze of gold ran up the belly of the horse and the belly of the rider, and four black beads made their eyes. And here was something I had not considered before: the horse and rider were one thing, carved in one piece. If there was an afterlife, this little figure would go there with fast hooves and broad wings.

"Help me up?" Sri said.

I looked at her cedar railing legs, stiff and crooked. Then I helped her up.

I wish I could say she walked tall and calm to place her own grave marker, but in fact I had almost to drag her. We skirted the fire circle and crossed the meadow, sending stones rattling as her feet trailed through them. I am neither small nor weak, and Sri was at the moment both, but still she was a weight. I grunted and we staggered, and yet everyone watched as if it were a royal procession. And that was only right. We walked out of the meadow, down the path that threaded between the boulders with their dragon scales of grey and red lichen, to the foot of the stair.

I helped Sri kneel. She knelt there. She placed the figurine at the root of the post that made the first railing, at the bottom of the stair. She turned it this way, then that, then back a fraction, until suddenly it was in the perfect spot, positioned as if sweeping down the rivulet of dust, as if riding down the mountain, out into the world, with all speed.

"There," she said.

I was silent.

She was silent.

A raven came sweeping down on the railing just in front of us, cupping its wings and spreading its tail to brake and land. It bobbed up and down and seemed ready to speak a word.

Another landed further up.

Then another, and another.

Only then did I understand what it really meant for a Swan Rider to kneel here. The ravens were smart, and adaptable, and they knew too.

"I'm ready," said Sri, mostly to the ravens.

"Are you sure?" Daji had come up behind us. "You probably have a week or two."

A week or two of end-stage palsy. Sanctity of natural death aside, I wouldn't blame anyone for giving that a miss. Daji's hands were on Sri's shoulders, holding her steady.

"Sri," I said—then hesitated. Twisting to face her, I put my hand on her thigh. I found the pressure point on the inner thigh that released tension in the quadricep. I pushed. Sri gasped, and I knew it hurt and it helped. I leaned forward and kissed her, softly.

"Sri," I said. "Thank you for hurting me."

Her smile didn't conceal the tremble of her chin. "My little AI," she said, without a salute in sight. "It was a pleasure."

I looked up at Daji, looming above us. I looked at the ravens. I looked at the grave marker, with its wings and blaze of gold. And then I got up and stepped away.

I drew a circle in the air and the Swan Riders gathered in. They picked up Michael. I pulled up Elián. And we all left.

There was no sense left in which I could be considered an innocent. But I did not want Elián—or even Michael—to have to witness the moment when Daji snapped Sri's neck.

That night.

It was running down the clock. It was moving pieces around the board. It was the little gap between game and endgame, into which so much tumbles.

The young queen Agnes Little said yes to hostaging herself and her unborn child. She said yes with her chin lifted, and fear bright in her eyes. I had doomed her. She was only fifteen.

Sri died. She was just shy of twenty.

Francis Xavier lived. The Swan Riders took him off to their hospital to repair the puncture in his lungs.

Michael lived too. It was a slightly nearer thing. He needed a new datastore and new webbing in his brain before he could possibly consider an upload. It was a major surgery for such a weakened person, but it was nothing that the Swan Rider doctors hadn't done a thousand times before.

Talis Mark Two saw to the reactivation of one of the mothballed grey rooms. If even his mechanical hands shuddered as he did that, I resolved not to notice.

Elián slept. It was hard to blame him. He had had his mind ripped open, and then he'd tried to start a revolution. It almost qualified as a typical day for him but he needed rest.

That left only me.

I was an AI now, but I had a body. I was exhausted and hungry. I was elated and grief-stricken. I was frightened and transformed.

I went for a walk.

I went down the causeway. Despite the geothermal heat of the sea, the evening was chilly. The sun was down properly now, and the sky seemed to be sinking to the earth all around me, gathering and thickening. Gravel scranched beneath my boots. The light from the Swan Rider city leaked away. It didn't matter. I could see in the dark. I could see everything.

I went to see the horses.

They were kept on the biggest island, left to weave among the salt-grass dunes and tug sweet hay from the high ricks and run and run and run.

I found a rock and sat on it and waited until he came out of the darkness: a white snuffling nose and a flick of a red ear, a swish of tail that was as good as my name.

"Hello," I said. "Gordon Lightfoot."

I opened my arms and he came and pushed his great head against my chest.

I had not seen Sri's death—I had protected the others from it and thus had not seen it. I went back to pray over her body, to wrap it in the quilt I had last seen on the makeshift bed shared by Rachel and Francis Xavier, far away in a refuge between Precepture Four and the ruins of Saskatoon. Someone had loved this quilt. Someone had loved Sri, once, probably. But I did not know who, because I did not know her history.

Perhaps I had loved her myself. In my shell-shocked and tumbling way. As much as I could.

Not nearly enough.

I had helped Sri put her figure in the stone. I had kissed her, her lips cracked and eager, her taste as sweet as morphine. I would remember her. I remembered her.

I remembered all the Swan Riders who had put their horses in the stones. Their names and faces.

I remembered all the AIs who had gone to the grey room, all the ones who had died there. All the ones who had died later.

I remembered the grey room, and I saw the strange figure of Michael/Rachel holding her thumb in her teeth; the first knuckle of her pointer finger pushing against her philtrum, which is the proper name for the dip between mouth and nose. I remembered the shudder that had run through her whole body. I remembered what I had asked her to do.

I remembered Queen Agnes Little, with her chin lifted.

I remembered all the hostages.

I remembered Xie.

Gordon Lightfoot pushed his head against me. I wrapped my arms around him, and I held fiercely.

19
THE GREY ROOM

The call for execution came, as is traditional, at dawn.

I had been up by then for hours, sitting wrapped in the indigo quilt from Francis's bed, waiting at the bottom of the stone stairs.

I tried to see that night with human eyes, which was not easy. To sit in darkness and let darkness be close. To watch the light come up before the sun and find the carved horsemen one by one. Some old, some new. So many.

The little prayer flags on the railing made a noise like someone rubbing their fingers together. I watched the light come down the mountains on the northwest side of the flooded valley. The light looked as if it were poured over them, something liquid and slow. The sea at the base of the mountains was still black, but now it was shining and black, and the islands were drifting and grey.

And finally, down the road from the hospital, he came walking alone.

Michael. Rachel. Tanim.

Talis.

I do not think he saw me, wrapped as I was in the midnight quilt. I do not think he was looking, particularly. He was walking slow, with one hand uplifted, letting a bobbing raven rest on his wrist, another perch on his shoulder. Dressed only in his hospital scrubs—a simple *kameez* of UN blue—he looked every inch a figure of myth. The wounded god.

He blinked when he saw me, and missed a step. The ravens swayed. With exactly the gesture Two had once used, he threw his wrist into the air. The ravens took off, and for a moment seemed to surround him in a whirl of dark wings.

He crossed the bonfire meadow as if it were easy. "Greta. You're up early."

"I didn't want to miss you." I got up and came down the stairs, trailing starry blanket. "Where's your coat?"

"Yeah," he said. "Because *pneumonia* is what I'm really worried about right now."

I wanted to know, and so I knew: he was not cold because he was running a fever. They'd boosted his failing body into overdrive so that he could do this: given him short-acting painkillers, stimulants, anticonvulsants. It was nothing more than a stopgap, but a stopgap was all he needed. The drugs (or something) had made him strange and febrile—a hectic blush on his cheeks and a fine tremor in his hands.

"My, um . . . ," he said, and stopped. The ravens had landed on the rail behind me, waiting as they had for Sri. "My room is ready."

"Well." I folded the blanket up and draped it over the railing. The bird sidestepped and quorked. "Then let's go."

"Greta, you can't . . . You know you can't come with me."

"What I know is that you're afraid of being alone."

"The grey room," he said, talking past me. "I have to."

"I know all about the grey room," I said. "I've been up all night with the grey room. I've been through every vid and every file we have. I know that it hurts. I know why it hurts. I know that it's deadly. I know why it's deadly. I know that they have to strap down your hands and I know that no one can stand by you and hold them. I know what happened to each and every one of the two thousand, four hundred thirty-seven people who ever lay down on those tables. I know that they were all alone."

"Stop," he whispered. "Why are you—stop."

The god in him was gone. He looked, instead, like a child who'd been slapped: trembly, with bright splotches over his cheekbones.

"You won't be," I said.

"What?"

"You won't be alone."

"Greta. You *can't* go with me."

"But as someone once mentioned to me, I'm AI. If I want to know, I can know. If I want to see, I can see. I can weave in with the data during the unspooling. I can modulate the fields in real time to do minimal damage. I can watch over your body. I can go with you, Michael. Rachel. If you'll have me."

He took a shuddering breath and looked up the crooked staircase—and then, as if he couldn't bear it, snapped his gaze aside and tried out a grin on me. "What happened to the girl who was going to overdose me and dump my body in the snow?"

"Well," I said. "There was this boy."

"Let me guess. He was human?"

There were three possible answers to that: Elián, FX, Michael. Human, Swan Rider, AI. "It changes you," I said. "Caring for someone. Being cared for."

"Okay," Michael said. "Okay." He closed his eyes and reached for me blindly; he took my arm and for a moment just clung. Then he opened them, set his jaw, put the other hand tight around the railing. "Let's go."

We walked up into the mountain.

And then we went down.

I had never been in an elevator before. Elevators were one of those things, like sprinklers and lawns, that belonged to the fallen world. Once the last skyscrapers had come down, humanity had discovered that staircases would do just fine.

But the hollow mountain had come from that fallen world. And so did Michael. He operated the elevator without giving it a thought, stabbing the button that fetched it as if with muscle memory. The doors opened.

This particular elevator was an open cage, solid only

under our feet. I stepped in gingerly, like a horse into a spaceship. The floor shuddered under me and I yelped and grabbed Michael, who laughed at me, very softly, just a little hitch in his breath. He pushed another button and we went down. Cold walls passed. Bare stone, rough, gleaming wet as the single lightbulb went by.

Down, and down. Slowly.

I knew too much about countdowns. I knew that the shivering figure beside me wouldn't want one. But it looked as if he might get one anyway. His laughter hadn't stopped, but it had become rougher. He was not quite crying.

We were sinking, and sinking, out of the light. Out of all of the kinds of light. I could feel the satellites slipping away behind the stones; the cosmic rays growing sparse as fireflies, and then vanishing.

As if I were an ocean, I could feel the tiny shift of tidal forces. Of gravity.

"At the Institute," said Michael, caught in something long ago. "Where they used to do this, before the melt. The grey floor, where they used to do this. It was deep, like this. It was so far down."

They'd thought the stray flux of a cosmic muon might be enough to ruin a neuromap. And who knew, maybe they'd been right. It wasn't as if they'd had time to nail it. And then the world had fallen.

In the four hundred years since, we'd created only forty-nine new AIs. A small number, which meant we hadn't nailed it either.

The light around us changed then—the single bulb at the top of the cage seemed to gain a faint mirror below us. The floor. Water on the floor. We sank into grey gleam as if into rising water.

We hit bottom with a little splash and a huge booming echo. All around us lights snapped on. The elevator door opened.

And we stepped out into the grey room.

It was different, and it was the same.

We were in a cavern, impossibly huge, its walls lost in shadows; its ceiling hidden behind a high grid of lights. They buzzed in the deep, dripping silence.

The grey room itself was not a room, exactly—certainly not something that could be tucked behind a library wall. It sat in the middle of the cavern, with its door open, wrapped copper mesh and studded in wires, ovoid and big as a dragon's egg. Its hatch stood open. I could see the inside of it.

We both could see the inside of it. We could look nowhere else.

The high table of my grey room was in this one a padded chair, thoughtfully ergonomic. But it still had straps.

Different but not different enough. The same.

My wrist—the one I had broken in the grey room, against straps just like that; the one Tolliver Burr had broken in the apple press, which I still could not think about—my wrist flared with sudden phantom pain, enough to make me tuck it to my stomach, gasping. Phantom pain, phantom *everything*. My heart rate shot up and my mouth dried and bittered. A taste of metal.

It was *the grey room* and I was *reliving* and—

"I *can't*," said Michael, and twisted aside as suddenly as if he needed to throw up.

We smacked into each other—less turning to hold each other than simply colliding, spinning away from the room and everything it was to us, urgent and clumsy and blind to the rest of the world. It was only luck that we ended up wrapped together.

One of my hands was full of pain and caught between us. The other clawed at Michael's back. His fingers dug into my forearms, his forehead hit my collarbone like a mallet as he hid his face against me. "Breathe in," I said, because his head had struck me like that once before when he'd been panicked and suffocating, and I had lost the ability to tell present from past. "Breathe in."

For a miracle, he did. Michael took a big shuddery breath, like the gulp of air that went with weeping. His nerves were burning into mine and my fingers were digging into his spine. I could feel him breathe in, ribs moving. "Breathe out," I said, and tried to breathe out, one two three four five.

"Slower. Come on." Michael's voice was a mumble, caught between us, but I felt him draw breath and so I drew breath. One, two, three, four, five.

"Out," I said. And I meant *out of here, out of this room, out of my mind,* but we both breathed out, slowly. I could feel the heat of Michael's exhale, very human, just at my collarbone.

"In," he said. The pain was fading from my hand and I

could feel that it was pushing into Rachel's soft belly. I let the fist of it go. The space between us was warm.

We breathed in, we breathed out, cueing each other with pulses in our fingertips, with the squeezes of our hands.

"All right," Michael said, at last, and straightened carefully. "You all right, Greta?" He tapped his fingers against my cheek, almost playfully, with a tiny spark-gap zap. "Hate to have to slap you," he said, drawling.

As if he himself had not also panicked. As if he were not panicking still. I could feel all his sensors fixed upon that hatch, that chair. No AI should ever stand in this place.

I should never have asked it of him.

"Greta?"

I snapped my wrist as if flicking off water, picturing droplets of memory flying everywhere. "I'm all right."

"Okay," said Michael, suddenly clapping his hands together, pure theatrical bravado. "Let's get this done."

Michael. Rachel. Talis. Tanim.

The combined and impossible person.

I waited just outside the mesh wall, my fingers deep in interface gel, and the grey room ripped them apart.

They came out in pieces, in glitches and fragments, in hiccups and gulps.

I could hear my name cried through the mesh walls and feel it in the messy spurts of data under my fingertips. *Greta.*

It isn't working.

Oh God it isn't.

And yet it was working because I could feel everything; I could feel Rachel falling from her first horse, a Swan Rider who couldn't ride. Her boot (her first boots: she had always been barefoot) catching in the stirrup, the long bone twisting. A strange boy with soft joy, spattered with mud and trying to help her, the brighter-than-broken-bone spark when she met his eye . . .

I could feel everything. I could feel Talis's reeling shock at finding Davie eating that little cat, tibia exposed but pink paw intact, the first time he'd thought *This isn't working, this is the end of the world.* The day he'd destroyed a city and demanded total surrender and Evie had written everything down.

I could feel Rachel sent to Precepture Four for her first execution, how she had tried to feel *dignity necessity pride* but her wings had bumped into the doorframe and twisted half off and her voice broke before she could even call the hostage child by name.

I could feel everything.

I knew that it hurt. I could not stop it from hurting.

I knew that it was lonely. I could not stop it from being lonely. Talis could not feel me holding his hand. But I held his hand—in every way except the physical, I held his hand. I held it all the way to the end.

It was like holding hands with fireworks.

Beautiful and scorching. Brilliant and horrible. It hurt me and I did not let go.

The dying AIs. Thirty-two times, Talis had held their hands. He'd said *look at me* but it had never worked, there was no one who loved them to look at them, there was no circuit breaker for the mind, there was no grace. How could there be no grace?

I loved him, and I looked at him. The room took him apart and I wove him back together.

And it took—oh, it was taking too long. My upload had been twenty-nine minutes. I was trying to slow and gentle these beams, trying to leash them as they ripped and snarled, but still—it was taking too long.

At thirty-one minutes the data was still coming, though in spurts again, sluggish and slow.

I remembered airplanes.

I remembered New York and Amsterdam and Shanghai and Gary the Unpromising and Little Evie in her grey room with no hair and the teddy bear tucked under her arm.

White wings.

An orange quilt.

A first kiss.

A red sea.

A green world.

It was slowing now. It was almost gone. The walls of the grey room were only mesh and I should be able to hear the breathing, but I could not hear the breathing. The screaming had stopped long ago.

Thirty-four minutes. Thirty-five.

Look at me, said Lu-Lien to Michael. Said Francis Xavier to Rachel. I know it hurts. It will be all right. Just look at me. Look at me. Just look.

In the thirty-sixth minute there was nothing.

Nothing.

How could there be no grace?

At thirty-seven minutes fifteen seconds, the beam collimators switched off with a poof of magnetism. The hatch into the room clicked open. I went in at a run.

The new AI was sitting strapped and fastened into the upload chair with her eyes open. Her face was calm. She wasn't breathing.

"You need to breathe," I said.

Her head was bolted down by a halo, a half-circle of surgical steel pierced with screws. I fumbled for the master release. "You need to make your heart beat. Come on. One two three four five, remember? Look at me."

No trace of circulation in the infrared, no heartbeat in the throat, and yet those round, bright eyes were lit like on-buttons, and they swept everything in the room. Everything except me. There was no contact in them. It was like meeting the eyes of a painting.

"Talis," I said. "Rachel. Michael. Look at me." The catch on the halo finally gave. I pulled it away, too roughly and too fast: one bolt scraped a welt across the forehead. The others had left round, dented wounds. "Please," I said. "Please. Look at me."

And suddenly the AI shuddered as if rebooting, and blinked once. Pulled in air, choked on it, and pulled it in again.

"I'm sorry," she said—a stranger's voice, passionless. "It slipped my mind."

Then her eyes closed, and when they opened again, they were—finally—looking right at me. Her voice came softly. "It's very beautiful, isn't it?"

"What?"

"Oh," she said. "Everything."

I started unstrapping the buckles that held her into her chair. I could feel her sensors on me, brilliant and unashamed. She was breathing again. And bleeding a little, now that her heartbeat had resumed.

Oh, I remembered this. I remembered being ripped so far from the human that you could forget to make your heart beat. I remembered the rush of wonder that could take your knees out from under you.

I remembered so many things. I remembered Talis saying what angels always say: "Don't be afraid."

"Don't be frightened," I told her.

"I'm not," she answered.

The last buckle, the one holding her right wrist, finally popped loose. She lifted that hand, balletic, and daubed at the compression wound that was letting blood trickle across her forehead at a slant like a curious eyebrow. "Stings."

"I know."

She dropped her hand, pushed off the chair, and swung to her feet. I put my hands under her arms to steady her. She looked like a child climbing out of bed, like someone awakened from a dream. Lost and little. And yet her voice:

"Nice job, Greta, that's going to be our new procedure if we ever need it. I feel . . ."

But there was no way to end that sentence.

I had walked out of my own grey room like that, awash in wonder and not even sure of my own name. The new AI held my arms, my fingers cupping her elbows, hers tracing mine.

"Do you have your balance?"

"I could dance."

I breathed out the name: "Talis? Is it Talis?"

"No."

I could feel the fine tremblor running through the underside of her arms, the sudden wince in the corner of her eye.

"I'm going to be Talis," she said. "But there is something I need to do first."

"What's that?"

"Find Francis Xavier," she said. "And rescue Sri's horse."

"The orange quilt," I said, and she nodded. Of course she knew it. It had been on her marriage bed. If Sri had been found with that quilt, then she had been found at Refuge 792, Francis and Rachel's station. The horse would be there.

And there, it seemed, this new AI would face the end of the world.

I still had not let go of her arms, and her upturned, amazed, aglow face was close to mine.

"It's a marvelous world," she said, "but I do hate basements. Let's go."

INTERLUDE:
ON ENDGAMES

Talis was standing on a kitchen stool with a wrench in his hand and a multipencil tucked behind his ear, wishing he'd picked a taller Rider for this trip. The other one at the refuge had been big, but this one (her name was Rachel) had had the faster horse, and he really hadn't considered that he might need to reach things.

But—it had turned out to be an odd mission. Not at first. Some idiots from an idiot state called the Cumberland Alliance had taken one of his Preceptures, tried to forestall his actions by using his hostages as hostages.

Yeah, no.

Interfering with his Preceptures was infuriating, obviously—and he was making some quite colorful plans about teaching that Cumberland general a lesson—but handling it had been straightforward enough. Show up, *blow up a city, demand a surrender,* tickety-boo.

And then—

Her name was Greta Stuart, and she was the first person to consent to the upload in a hundred years, despite his system of Preceptures which was meant (among other things: other very important, world-savey sorts of things) to find candidates. After a hundred years, there was going to be a new AI.

Which meant he needed the grey room back online. Right away.

Hence the kitchen stool. The grey room had magnetic collimators embedded all over its walls. They were superconducting, and they'd quenched, then failed entirely—which tended to happen to delicate electronic things when you pointed whopping great illegal EMP weapons at them.

Speaking of. From the doorway came a polite cough.

"Really?" he said, without turning around. "Ambrose, if you're going to insist on going around looking like a pile of Tinkertoys, you don't get to cough."

"I didn't want to startle you," said Ambrose. Ambrose— the Abbot—was the AI in charge of this Precepture, and he had Luddite ideas about not possessing Riders or even pulling information from his datastore. He "cherished his limitations." Talis did not cherish limitations; it was a fight they had been having for 180-odd years.

Ambrose shuffled into the room on his cane and six legs. Talis spun round and hopped down, one smooth motion.

"Forgive me the affectation," said Ambrose. "But you did look precarious."

"Nah. I'm good. Could use a ladder, have you got a ladder? But otherwise good."

"Of course there are ladders. I will have one brought from the orchard." The battered monitor that was the Abbot's head swung from side to side. "How do you bear to work in here, Michael? The grey room . . ."

Talis ran a hand through his hair. This Rider might be short, but she had excellent mess-up-able hair. The grey room—it was not his favorite place to be, sure, but he had the flashbacks under control. "It helps that my room was different than this."

"Mine was this." Ambrose, though in 'bot form, actually shivered.

He was malfunctioning.

Talis could see the cascade failure that was beginning to eat away at his friend's neuronets. It looked bad, maybe even fatal. But fixable. The timing might be tricky, though— he might have to wait until Ambrose was too weak to resist getting fixed.

Because he was not going to lose Ambrose. Not Ambrose. He was the best of them. Saner than Evie or Gambit or Lewy or even Az. Way saner than the ones he kept locked in Matrix Boxes, taking in reality (if they did at all) one carefully screened dribble at a time.

Talis would save him whether he wanted to be saved or not.

"What we are pushing Greta to do," said Ambrose. "It is a terrible thing. And yet I would have her do it. I would have her *do it, because I would not lose her. And I would have her do it because I think you need her."*

"I don't need *anyone.*" Talis rubbed a thumb between his eyebrows (this Rider was subject to small flashes of pain), accidentally smearing himself with graphite. "Did you come in here just to make gnostic pronouncements, or what?"

"I came to see if you were all right. The grey room being . . . what it is."

"I'm fine, Ambrose. Really. I'm peachy."

The Abbot looked around. "All this." He had hands with ceramic phalanges, steel actuator cables, rubber muscling. He gestured grandly with one of them, seeming to take in Talis in his Rider's body, the grey room, the Precepture full of hostages, even the satellites circling overhead. "All this," he said. "Michael—have you ever considered your endgame?"

"This isn't a game."

"No," Ambrose whirred. "But everything ends."

20
THE BORROWED HOURS

Refuge 792, in the heart of lost Saskatchewan. In reach of the ruins of Saskatoon; in reach of Precepture Four. I stood on the gangplank of the spaceship and looked at it. Behind me Elián and Francis Xavier were unbuckling the horses from their gravity harnesses.

Talis had wanted to come, for the horse—and because it was home. The last station of the two Swan Riders known simply as Francis Xavier and Rachel. They had no last names, and no histories but the one they made together. A universal longing, this—anyone would do it. A dog would do it. Slip away to someplace small and familiar. Slip away to die.

It was snowing, because of course it was: the kind of snow that seems to condense from nothing, under a clear, still sky. It built fragile edges of sparkle on the bending blades of the grass, onto the black stems of rush-shaped wind generators, onto the raised grains of the old grey door set in the side of the hill.

"It's your birthday, isn't it?" said Talis, coming out of the hatch to stand beside me.

I blinked. It was: November second. The Feast of All Souls. I was seventeen. And I was as old as the world.

"We'll make a cake," Talis said.

We'd do no such thing. We would walk across that sparkling grass. We would pull open that door, and after that . . . Four of us would walk in, but only three of us would walk out, and we all knew that. We had drugs and bedpans to ease the journey down, but it was still a hard descent, and we knew that, too.

"There's not going to be a cake," said Talis. "But happy birthday."

"Thank you," I said. "When's yours?"

"Fourth of July. There used to be fireworks."

"And . . . ?"

"And. April. The twenty-seventh. Apple blossoms." A pause. "Have you ever seen fireworks?"

"No."

"They're . . ." Talis couldn't find an adjective for fireworks, but in my hand, his hand was sparkling. It put fireworks behind my eyes, of course. "It wasn't all bad, the fallen world."

"No," I said. "It was lovely."

The prettiest thing about fireworks come after the explosion. The cinders falling.

And falling. This version of Talis, who was also Rachel,

was going to die. Most of the Swan Riders took Sri's door, the ravens' door, but Talis was not going to do that. We would monitor the whole process. We would record it, and learn from it. There must be a way to crack the Rider's Palsy, and we were going to find it.

In time, I hoped, to save Francis. And Elián.

Though probably not me.

"Grab the horses, would you," said Talis. She was looking out onto the gathering hoarfrost, the blue sparkle of winter light, the impossibly delicate beauty of the world. I turned to take the horses out of Francis Xavier's capable hands, and he and Talis walked down the ramp together.

"Jesus . . ." Elián stopped at the refuge door.

The last thing that had happened here had obviously been violent.

The feather tick was dragged half onto the floor and a string of onions was torn down and tattered. Three crossbow quarrels were stuck in the wall. There were prints on the rush floor of something—or several somethings—that walked on blades, and scuff marks where someone more human had been dragged.

But there was also, as we had dearly hoped there would be, the horse. Roberta. Talis and Francis went right to her, delighted to have someone, something, that they could actually save. They fussed over her while she whinnied: with pats and cups of water, with handfuls of hay.

But in truth Roberta was fine. Sri had unsaddled her,

made sure she was rubbed down and warmly blanketed. Put her near the water barrel, spread out a dense layer of hay. Had she even reported in, called the Red Mountains so that someone would come for the horse? The control screen beside the upload portal was active. It twittered and blinked. I could have reached for the interface gel. I didn't. I liked the ambiguity. The human ability to rest in wonder.

It had not been long, this strange passage, Talis's journey from AI to human and back; my journey from human to AI and back. You could plot it on a tiny strip of calendar.

And yet.

Sri's saddle was turtled on the floor—she had known she would not use it again. The two beds were as we had left them, pushed apart, each into its own alcove.

I beckoned to Elián, and we pushed the two beds into one. The bed legs scraped against the flagstones that were under the rushes. Talis and Francis Xavier, who had been sweetly fussing over the rescued horse, both looked up.

They both had very open eyes.

Talis's first attack, in that place, was both startling and totally expected. Both shocking and the thing we were waiting for. Talis went to the floor. And Francis Xavier picked her up as if it were effortless, and put her on one half of the bed.

She was fighting herself, fighting the air around her— urgently, dangerously, hopelessly. So Francis Xavier wrapped her in his body and in the indigo quilt we'd brought from their other bed. Wrapped her as if she were Rachel. She made a huge, shuddering effort to still her thrashing hands, and let herself be wrapped. Be held.

It went on until it was over. Francis Xavier lifted his arm gingerly. Rolled away.

"First ground rule," said Talis, flopping onto his back. "No kissing. It would just be fundamentally weird."

"I—" said Francis Xavier. Then stopped and stroked the pad of his thumb against the corner of Talis's mouth. "Whatever you need."

Talis looked away, and somehow ended up catching Elián's eye.

"Don't look at *me*," said Elián.

"You're not tempted?" said Talis. "I'm crushed."

He turned his face and rested his cheek against the smooth skin of Francis's bare stump.

There were things for Elián to do. Not enough of them, but still. Put the horses out to graze; pump them water. Start a pot of beans with onion and rosemary, seasoned with the black pepper that Francis Xavier had brought from somewhere warmer.

There were things for me to do. File the arrival report. Learn about morphalog dosages. Set and calibrate the stick-on sensors that we had brought to make the most of this death—to gather information on the palsy, and thus save the Riders.

I put the sensors on between the first and second attack. It seemed cruel to crown Talis like this, to put sensors where

I had so recently set screws. The compression wounds were still fresh. But I did it, because he wanted me to, stuck on the mesh patches like band-aids to make it better, like diamonds to bind back his hair. They were dark, and they twinkled.

He roused as I did it—I'd drugged him; he was drowsy—and unfolded Rachel's softest smile. "But is it a good look for me?"

"Absolutely," I said—and the seizure shook him to the roots of his teeth. I carded my hand through his hair and murmured *Easy, easy.*

It wasn't easy.

A third attack, and a fourth. Francis Xavier held Talis from behind, wrapped him and whispered things into his hair.

I took the readings. I upped the dosages. Elián brought the horses in.

A fifth attack, and a sixth. A seventh came when we were trying to eat soup, and Talis's aura had become so tangled, so stretched and smudged with the drugs, that I did not see it coming, not even after he set down his spoon with a clink. It knocked him off the stool before any of us could reach him, and when we did, his eyes were desperate, terrified.

Elián and Francis put him back on the bed, got him through it.

"Next rule," he said when it was over. "Don't leave me." His voice was ragged already. "Don't let go of my hand."

The three of us looked at each other.

"We can take it in shifts," FX said. A Swan Rider.

Practical. I knew he could make this death very fast. I knew part of him wanted to.

"Of course we can," I said.

Talis pushed a hand through his hair, showing his twinkling crown of sensors.

We had things to do. Elián washed the dishes. I took the data and upped the dosage on the drugs. And Francis Xavier sat up all that night, holding Talis's hand.

In the middle of the night I woke to yet another seizure, and to Francis telling a long story about the raft cities in the Pacific Gyre. A very young and very foreign Swan Rider, his first time saving the world. The children had been delighted in his false dignity, had made a game of dumping him off every tiny raft he set foot upon. He had saved them, those children who didn't even know they were going down. It was the best thing he had ever done.

It was a story full of dunkings and lullabies. It was full of waves and rocking.

The horses breathing.

We were all half asleep.

"Come here," whispered Elián, lying behind me on the floor. "You're shivering. Come here."

I moved back into his warmth and he wrapped an arm over me.

"My wings went to the bottom," said Francis Xavier. And really it was Talis who was shivering. "It was the best thing I ever did."

✀

I had things to do, but I sat with my hand on Talis's hand. He was asleep. Limp. Innocent. The data showed him weaker.

But the data lied. Invulnerable people cannot be strong, for the same reason fearless people cannot be brave. For the same reason immortal people cannot be human.

Talis slept a mortal sleep, curled up with his back against Francis Xavier's front. The master of the world. The little spoon.

A seventeenth attack, and an eighteenth. I should admit that I had no more things to do. It was ugly and horrifying. It was graceless. I wanted it over.

Elián and I, outside, breathing clean cold frost, walking the horses. I had Gordon and Sri's horse, Roberta the Bruce. Elián had Heigh Ho Uranium and Talis's little firecracker, NORAD. The horses, who really needed more exercise than we'd been giving them, were snorting and misbehaving mildly, stopping short and pulling up mouthfuls of grass. We had stopped, in fact, because Roberta was doing just that.

"I—Greta?"

Though stopped, I froze. There was caution in Elián's voice, something extreme, as if he'd spotted a snake. "What's happening to Talis," he said. "Will it happen to me?"

"Oh," I said. "Oh, Elián. No."

"But—"

"We're collecting the data. We're—" I remembered what Azriel had told me. "The AIs have nearly three hundred exaflops of computational—we have just staggering amounts of problem-solving power, Elián. We can stop it. We can fix it."

"Yeah?"

"Yeah." I was going to save Elián. And Francis Xavier. And all the Swan Riders.

And maybe even myself. Obviously no one had told Elián about my own fate with the palsy. If they had, he would have asked about me first. He always did.

"So we're really going to do this, you and me," said Elián. And he actually saluted me, or at least put his hand over his heart. The tattoo was nearly healed—shining black against his dark olive skin.

Elián would make a good Swan Rider. Not the blind obedience part, obviously (and I wanted to change the rules about that) but the rest of it—the impossibly daunting saving people part. The rescuing raft colonies part. He could do that. He could run vaccines over snowed-in glacial passes like a heroic sled dog. He could dig kids out of rubble. It would be his chance to be a knight-errant, and that would suit him down to the dramatically inclined tips of his new wings.

"As it turns out," I said, "the world is full of problems you can hit."

"And you're going to rule it?" he asked.

I closed my eyes. I tipped up my chin like Queen Agnes Little.

Gordon Lightfoot ambled forward and nuzzled the back of my still-short hair. Around me, the world spread out like a map, like a carpet. I could see it from space, as easily as I could see it from my own eyes. It was beautiful and glittering.

And small.

You cannot see the world small and rule it well.

You cannot see the world small and be human.

"Not rule," I said. "Change."

One last day.

"See?" whispered Talis, over some necessary fuss with a bedpan. "Not ennobling."

I checked his aura carefully and judged him safe for a few minutes, so I left him with Elián and went outside to dump the pan. It was afternoon, but the moon hung in the blue sky. It looked as if someone had split it with an axe. Down the rill I could see Francis Xavier walking the horses. I lifted a hand to him—all well—and he lifted one to me.

I went back in.

Talis was lying there with his chin tipped up, his throat exposed, as if he wanted someone to cut it.

"I'm no good at this," he said hopelessly.

"It's death," Elián said. "You're not supposed to be good at it."

"I don't see why not," said Talis, pure bitterness. "I've had the practice."

The horses needed exercise, and so Francis Xavier was gone some time. I took Elián's place, sitting with my hand on Talis's, both of us speechless. It was quiet. The space was cozy. Warm. Friendly with the smell of the hay and the horses.

It was a refuge and we were refugees. We could stay here only a little while.

"Do you know what to do?" Talis asked finally.

"I know what to do." She would need to be connected to the portal after she died, so that her self could be reintegrated with the master copy of Talis. So that Talis would have been both Michael and Rachel. Lived twice, died twice. Faced the grey room twice. Known me. Known Francis. Loved and been loved.

Been human.

"I know what to do," I said again. I did not want this to be over.

But it was. Almost. I could see it in the pain and damage rising inside her like water rising in a new-struck well. I could see it in the effort it took her to turn her head and look at me. "New AIs rename themselves," she said.

"You don't need to," I said.

"Not . . ." She swallowed, and her hand stirred in mine. "What will you be?"

And I said, "Grace."

"Get Francis," she said.

I went to get Francis.

Francis Xavier had been born on the banks of Lake Tana: dark water starred with white pelicans, the green weir over which spilled the Blue Nile. From him, I had learned what all fishermen should know: what drowning looks like, truly.

Drowning is quiet.

The thing itself, quiet. There is thrashing, shouting, reaching for any solid thing, but that comes first, and it is not part of drowning. Once there is water in you, once the liquid touches the feathery interior of the lungs—once that happens, things are quiet.

Talis sat up as if he could not help it, as if his muscles were all contracting in some tremendous current. But extensor muscles are universally stronger than contractors, and the next moment he was thrown open, resting almost on tiptoes and the crown of his head, caught in my arms and in Francis Xavier's, while Elián took one step backward, then two, then three. There was one last moment of fighting, of shouting, of reaching for any solid thing.

And then it was quiet. For three seconds. For five. Talis took a breath, and it was as if he had finally breathed in the water. He breathed again and each slow breath seemed to fill him a little more. His body got heavier. The sensors of his crown were shining like stars.

"Changed my mind," he said. "About the kissing."

Francis Xavier pressed his lips between one of the eyebrows—those black, startling, quizzical eyebrows—and the sensors. I had Talis's fingers tangled in my fingers. I raised his knuckles to my lips.

Talis sighed. And drowned.

21
FALLING STARS

There was then the matter of the body.

For the mind, for the datastore and the AI-self that was still Talis, I knew what to do. I oversaw the upload. I monitored the integration. Whatever of Rachel that was not her body—whatever could be caught in the net that was the upload—that had survived. But something had ended, too. And for that something, we needed a grave.

Rachel's body spilled out when we opened the upload portal—cooling already; grey as the grey room. Elián caught it. And then Francis Xavier, who I think could lift anything in the world, lifted it and laid it back on the bed.

It did not look as if it were sleeping. Death looks nothing like sleep.

We had, of course, remembered our digging spades: the

Swan Riders are a practical people. Francis Xavier was still not crying when he picked his up.

"Greta," he said. "I would like—"

"I will not let you do this alone."

His face tightened and he looked to the floor. "Don't order me."

"I'm not. But I would never let you do this alone."

His hands seemed so steady, but the blade of the shovel trembled above his boot tops. Elián took it from him. He would need his strength.

The Swan Riders buried their dead in the sky.

In the Red Mountains, they could. All those dry, high places. All those ravens. ("I like them," Talis had said—but I wondered if she still would.) Here we needed a grave, and a different ceremony. We did not know what. All the libraries of the world inside us, but we did not know what.

Francis Xavier had strapped his prosthesis back on: shoveling, like using a crossbow, is hard to do one-handed. We went out of the refuge and down the draw toward the dry creek, out of the wind. There were little curls of snow, like ripples, in the silvery sage bushes. There was a bank of bare sumac, curved black branches with rusty crowns. We found a sheltered spot beneath them. I sat and held the body while FX and Elián dug and dug in the sandy soil. It was easy to cut into; hard to keep open. It didn't make a straight-sided grave. It made a sloped and shallow pit. As if the ground had cupped its hand.

We wrapped the body in Talis's favorite coat and laid

there, curled up, where the sumac would arch over it. It was a pretty spot, as these things go. It was very quiet.

Francis Xavier went back to the refuge and brought a pillow for under the head.

Then Elián drew something from inside his coat. "I thought," he said. He was having trouble looking Francis Xavier in the eye. "Will she need this?" And he held out the tiny, half-finished carving of the horse and rider. "When I was getting the ship, I went back to—I thought she might need this."

Rachel's carving.

Sri's carving had been symmetric and elongated, the faces, horse and human, perfect as blades. Rachel's was . . . plump. Lopsided, because Rachel was no artist. Unfinished, because Talis had never worked on it. And yet it was everything we needed. I could see the way the horse had cocked an ear. I could see that the rider had a splint on her leg, and a smile.

Francis Xavier took the carving, delicately. He stood looking at it, silently. And then he slid down into the pit and bent over the body. He bent there awhile. I could hear that he was saying something, but not what he was saying. Only the rise and fall of his voice, the lullaby hum of it.

Then he stood up, and reached for help. Elián hauled him over the edge of the pit.

The body held the little carving in one loose and stiffening hand.

With our hands, we pushed the sand back into the pit. We let it slide down on top of the body until its outline was softened. Then until it was gone.

"If I had let you go alone," I said, "would you have come back?"

Francis Xavier looked down his elegant nose at me. He was still not crying, but there was shining in his eyes. "Probably not," he said.

He would not stay. I could see it in him. But the moment where he might have walked onto the dry prairie with nothing but a spade—that moment was gone.

"Francis Xavier, do you remember when you promised to protect me?"

"I do."

"I wish someone had promised to protect you."

"I am a Swan Rider," he said.

He turned away then, and walked back to the refuge one more time. When he came back he was holding Rachel's ceremonial wings.

He held the wings up in front of him, as if they were growing from his heart. And then he gave a huge, violent, broken, amazed shout, and wrenched them apart.

Aluminum squealed and leather squeaked, and the two wings separated at their roots, like a wishbone. Francis Xavier handed one to me. And we tore the feathers off one by one, and let each one lift and tumble down into the endless grasses, or up into the glittering sky.

We went back to the refuge. Elián and I went arm in arm, leaning on each other. Francis Xavier was leaning on no one. On an empty space in the air. He went through the door, crossed to the stable, and started packing his saddlebags.

I stood at the half-wall and watched.

"Where will you go?" I asked.

A Swan Rider could not stop being a Swan Rider. They were marked, tattooed, as the hand of Talis. No one would take him in.

And even a Swan Rider needed to be taken in.

Francis Xavier shrugged, which made his pincer click open and closed. "I just can't—"

"I know."

Somewhere in these wide, wild weeks, Elián had picked up the trick of silence. He sat on the doubled bed and let me do the talking. I could feel him watching.

I could feel the room watching.

"Help me saddle NORAD?" asked Francis Xavier.

He didn't need help but was willing to let me give it. I held NORAD's bridle while FX put on her tack. The refuge was warm, dim, alive. FX put saddlebags and a lead on Heigh Ho Uranium as well, and paused to scritch the big horse behind the ear. "Yuri is a better fit for me," he said. "But NORAD would be unhappy as the packhorse."

"Takes after her rider?"

"She—Rachel was an eagle." His eyes were glowing. "I will not say much. But—she was an eagle. A lioness. Such a little thing. But always my lioness. *She* kissed me."

I had seen that. After she fell off her horse. While her leg was broken and her eyes were running with tears and the laughter was tumbling out of her. She'd kissed him.

"You were very surprised."

"Yes."

"She liked that," I said. "She liked surprising you. She liked to make you smile."

And Francis smiled. So rare and so sweet. Like spring coming.

"Leave us Gordon," I said. "And Roberta, for Elián."

"They'll be hard to load on the ship," FX warned. "Without NORAD—"

"We'll manage," I said.

"Open the gate?"

The horses had their own door out of the hill, lower and broader than a human door, double hung. Francis Xavier didn't need help to open it, but was willing—again—to ask for help. To ask, in this oblique way, for my permission.

I opened the doors.

Francis started to get on NORAD.

And the room said: "Wait."

FX froze. "Not yet," he said. "I can't—not yet."

I could feel the sensors around us humming. The voice from the wall said softly: "I would settle for *not yet.*"

That synthesized voice, I knew now, had been Michael's voice, centuries ago. Of course there were not enough rich recordings to mock up Rachel's. But the way Talis used Michael's voice now was . . . altered. Slower. Softer.

"Where are you going?" said the wall. Not a demand. The softness in it said, *Be safe.*

Francis Xavier had no answer. I think, in that moment,

he still didn't know where he was going. But finally—*finally*—he was crying. Tears were dripping off his nose.

"I only wanted to say," said the wall. "I'm not dead. And I might need— Don't leave me, Francis."

Don't push, I thought. *Don't take too much.*

"Come home," said the voice. A hiccup that was pure heartbreak.

What is love but a pain we choose?

"Not yet," said Francis. "But. The long way. I'll bring the horses in."

A slow and listening silence. Then Talis answered him softly: "Then I'll leave on a light for you."

Francis Xavier nodded to the empty air and wiped his face with the tail of his head scarf. And then he led the horses out the door. Elián and I climbed the hill that covered the refuge and watched his plume for an hour as he rode away. South and west, toward the setting sun. Toward the Red Mountains, toward Rachel. The long way around.

Night.

It was strange to lie in the bed where Talis had died. To lie inside Elián's arms as she had lain in Francis Xavier's. To curve my hip into the hollow her body had made.

To lie inside that fate.

Elián was breathing softly on the back of my neck, snoring a little. But I could not sleep. There was something wrong with me, something that made the minutes seem longer, the noises seem louder. Something aching. Something—

I was afraid.

Lying awake, but almost dreaming. Once, in such a state, I had seen the whole world spinning. Once, I had seen the figure of a small and great young god, draped in beads and silk. Outside, in the darkness, little beads of ice that are called graupel fell from the sky and rattled at the door.

Li Da-Xia. She was less than fifty miles away. I could see her now, if I wanted to, under her glass ceiling.

But when I looked—I could not help it, I could see the whole world, I looked—I deployed a keyhole satellite; in another moment I was looking through the glass roof of Precepture Four. And I saw her there, asleep on her bed.

Her hair loose, her body unguarded. Sighing in her sleep, she rolled over.

I threw myself out of the bed and tried to shut off my satellite eyes. You could not be human, if you were using those eyes. Elián whuffled like a horse at the sudden disturbance, then rolled onto his stomach with a sleepy grunt.

The wall said: "Greta?"

And my whole heart said what Francis had said. *Not yet.*

"Can't sleep?" said Talis, from the wall, in her new and softer voice. There was something feline in it, a roundness. A purr. *Lioness.* "I can't either," she said. "Well. You know. Not in a body right now. Literally can't sleep."

"I'm not ready to talk to you. I just helped you die."

"I was there."

"Yes," I said. "But also, no." The distinction was important. "Talis, we just buried you."

"I know."

I crossed closer to the terminal. I wanted Elián to stay asleep. Talis dropped his voice.

"I watched Francis, too," she said. She would have felt my deployment of the keyhole. Knew what I did, what I looked at. Why it got me out of bed. "Used the old global surveyor sat. For a while. But—"

"But it turns out you can't love someone and also monitor them from space?"

Talis laughed—her new sparrow's laugh. "Turns out."

I put my hand into the interface gel and felt it sparkle back at me. A hand in mine.

"I know we can't talk yet," said Talis. A pause. "I know that. I just wanted to say—thank you for helping me."

And I answered so suddenly that my voice cracked. "Will you help me?"

Talis knew what I meant. Always did. The palsy that had killed Rachel would kill me, too. A year. Maybe less. I'd be talking out of a wall, not dead, but first I had to die. I had to die *like that*.

I felt the sensors surge around me. "I will," said Talis. "I promise."

"Greta?" said Elián groggily. "What's wrong?"

Everything. Nothing.

"Go back to bed, Greta . . . ," said Talis.

"Jesus!" Elián jerked upright as if he'd found a tarantula on his face. "That's so creepy! Go away."

"How about if I just stay here, but be quiet."

"Like you could," said Elián.

"Yeah," sighed the terminal. "How about if I just stay here."

And then, miraculously, Talis fell quiet. Present, still: even once back under the blankets I could feel her tapped into the room's sensors, a thing as faint as the breath of someone else in a room.

None of us know what to do in the face of grief, but of this one thing I am sure: the hard work of being there, being quietly there—that is never wrong.

The sensors moved over me like a sigh. I breathed as if matching my breath to Elián's, to the sensors, to the breath of Talis, who was no longer breathing. And thus I was lowered into sleep.

I slept all day, groggily, fitfully, slipping in and out of dreams. I dreamt of Agnes Little, lifting her chin, masked in freckles. I dreamt of Rachel dying, of the little horse carving come alive and squirming its way free of the sandy grave. I dreamt of Francis taking flight. I dreamt of Xie, the princess sleeping in her glass coffin, and the weapons satellite reaching down as if to kiss.

In the dream, I knew what I had to do.

I knew what I had to do.

Two things woke me: the smell of dinner, and a voice from the wall.

"Hi there!" it said.

The voice was male, human, and unfamiliar. The intonation was none of those things.

"Evie?" I said.

"Who's Evie?" said Elián. He was standing at the table, frying something amazing-smelling in an iron skillet.

"One of the other AIs." And not the straightest stripe on the zebra. I made a tell-you-later gesture, and Elián shrugged. He was forming grated potatoes into patties with his hands.

"Is that Evie?" I asked the wall.

"Yes!" said Evie, in the incongruous borrowed voice. I sat up in bed, rubbing my face. It was—my datastore told me—actually late afternoon, winter sunset. But even so, waking to Evie was a little much.

"Talis told me I had to try this."

"This?" I asked.

"This human thing. It's so *weird*."

"I'm sure it is."

Her deep voice dropped to a slumber-party whisper. "*I have a penis.*"

Elián choked so hard that bits of latke came out his nose.

"Do you really?" I ventured.

But there was no answer.

"And she's off," said another voice. Talis. "She is in fact skipping down the hallway; I need you to picture that so that I don't have to live with the image alone."

"Oh, God," said Elián. "Please get that child some help."

"That's the idea," said Talis.

"Was that . . ." Elián flipped a latke into the pan. "What's his name, the big Brazilian guy—Alejandro?"

"Alejandro is Argentine," said Talis. "And he volunteered."

How was the ride, Alejandro had asked Francis.

And Francis had answered: *The ride was hard.*

"Are you two all right out there?" said Talis. A carefully not-loaded question.

"We have horses," I said. "And all the supplies one might want."

"And a spaceship," said Talis.

"Yes," I said. "But for now—we might ride."

Talis was silent, and yet I could trace the path of his thoughts from the lengths of his pauses, the shifts of his attention as it fed through the room sensors.

I answered his unspoken comment. "It's only fifty miles."

Fifty miles to Precepture Four. To my former world. To the girl who knew me better than anyone in the world. Look at me, I would say. I am alive. I am the same but I have changed. Can you see me?

"Nothing like a road trip," Talis said.

Nothing like a full circle.

"And after that," said Talis. "You're coming back?"

"I will."

"Good," said Talis. "Because now that I'm in charge again, I'm going to put you in charge too."

"I don't think authority works like that," said Elián.

"It works like I say it works," said Talis.

"Yeah," said Elián. "That's *why* it doesn't work."

Elián had a reasonable point. "Talis," I said. "Are you saying we're equals?"

"Well," said Talis. "I aspire to that."

"In that case, I would like to propose that peace achieved through terror can never truly be peace."

Talis paused. "Fair point. But I would like to remind you that stories that start with the words 'power vacuum' don't always turn out very well."

Elián had flipped the last of his latkes onto the tea towel. He was watching me. Holding his breath. Knowing the gravity of the moment, if not the content.

"It turns out . . ." I edged out to the idea carefully. "It turns out you can't love someone and hold them in the crosshairs. It turns out you can't love the world, that way. It's not . . ."

"Human," said Talis.

"Just so."

"Grace," said Talis. The name struck inside me as if I were a bell. "Will you help me? I'd like to save the world."

My new name rang through my body. I felt the intricate dance of data and sensing and human soul. All of them were me. I closed my eyes and said: "Let's start."

"Put your coat on, Elián," said Talis. "This, you're going to want to see."

Elián and I wrapped a couple of latkes in waxed cloth and took Roberta and Gordon out into the gathering night. We climbed the hill above the draw to overlook our refuge, and the grave. And there we stopped.

Among the grey-gold grasses, Gordon's coat was the color of the moon. Roberta's dark chestnut almost made her vanish. The two horses breathed out puffs of steam. Elián's hand was warm in mine. Steady. I could feel his newly implanted sensors mesh with my sensors, pulling us closer together. Around us was winter quiet: neither insects nor birds, but the quick sharp wind in the grass. "Look up," I said.

It was almost full dark. The stars were so bright that they came together in clots.

"The ones that are moving are the satellites." I pointed, my hand pale in the darkness. "That one there, the bright one," I said, tracking it with my finger as it swept toward us from the horizon. "That's one of the orbital super-platforms. A city killer. It can fire both projectiles and beams."

"I know," said Elián, and shivered inside his Swan Rider's coat. "Can you—do you already talk to them?"

All the time.

"More than that," I said, and opened my lifted hand.

The star-on-a-string that was the weapons platform suddenly brightened. And then Elián gasped as it turned lightning-bright and blazing, streaking downward and breaking into cinders—a falling star.

"Look up," I said, not to Elián, but to the world. I let Azriel translate it into the three thousand remaining languages. I let it pour from every speaker, every terminal. From each of my ten fingertips. Talis had a point, about power vacuums:

this might not be the beginning of a happy story. But one way or another, it *was* a new beginning.

"My name is Grace," I said, to Elián, to Talis, to Queen Agnes Little, to the listening world. Then I drew with my hand a circle across the whole of the sky, and it filled with streaking, breaking platforms.

Grace, the gift unexpected, unearned.

Grace in a grid of falling stars.